CASSIE EDWARDS
"Sweet Savage Dreams"

"Cassie Edwards writes action-packed, sexy reads! Romance fans will be more than satisfied!"

—*Romantic Times*

SHIRL HENKE
"Billie Jo and the Valentine Crow"

"Shirl Henke mesmerizes readers with the most powerful, sensual and memorable historical romance yet!"

—*Romantic Times*

KATHRYN KRAMER
"Exploration of Love"

"Glamour, intrigue, and excitement...Kathryn Kramer's historical romances are an absolute pleasure to read!"

—*Romantic Times*

EUGENIA RILEY
"Two Hearts in Time"

"Both passionate and dramatic, Eugenia Riley's romances are sumptuous reads!"

—*Romantic Times*

Other *Leisure Holiday Specials:*
A FRONTIER CHRISTMAS
VALENTINE SAMPLER

Cassie Edwards
Shirl Henke
Kathryn Kramer
Eugenia Riley

An
Old-Fashioned
Valentine

LEISURE BOOKS **L** **NEW YORK CITY**

A LEISURE BOOK®

February 1993

Published by

Dorchester Publishing Co., Inc.
276 Fifth Avenue
New York, NY 10001

CASSIE EDWARDS
"Sweet Savage Dreams"

For my family...
My husband Charlie, for 38 years of lovely
valentine wishes;
My sons Charles and Brian, their childhood handmade
valentines pasted on cardboard never forgotten;
And also my daughter-in-law Sheryl and grandson
David;
My parents Virgil and Mary Kathryn Cline;
And my father-in-law Avon Edwards.

Chapter One

Minnesota, February 1888

The fire was burning low, sending a golden, dancing light upon the ceiling and walls of the two-room log cabin. Outside, the wind was just beginning to blow, sending eerie whistles around the corners of the cabin. Even though spring was distant, the inhabitants of the cabin were anticipating the Feast of Saint Valentine.

"I fear a storm is brewing," Susan Felty said, as she cast her eyes toward a window framed by flounces of lace. She rested the valentine she was making on her lap. "The sun is gone and the sky is taking on a leaden sort of appearance. Perhaps I'd best go, Jana. I'd hate to get caught in a blizzard halfway to the fort."

Jana laid her scissors on a table next to her and held up the paper doily from which she was creating a special valentine for her husband, Jed. She adjusted her gold-framed spectacles and peered through them toward the window. "I had hoped this warm spell would last until the Valentine's Day ball," she said, sighing heavily. "If the roads are blocked with drifting snow, Jed and I won't be able to go." She stared at the gray gloom outside a moment longer, then turned back to Susan with a smile. "Don't leave just yet. Surely the clouds will pass over. It's much too warm to snow."

Susan glanced at the window again, her smile much weaker than Jana's as she looked back across the table at her dear friend. "The sound of the howling wind makes me believe the weather has changed. Here in Minnesota one cannot relax about the weather."

She sighed again and picked up her lace doily, admiring the work she had already done. "I can only stay a moment or two longer," she murmured. "I don't want my parents worrying needlessly. And you know how they fuss and fret over my welfare."

Jana picked up her valentine again and began cutting into the paper doily, then paused and gave Susan a studious look. Her friend was an extraordinary beauty with deep dimples on cheeks of alabaster, and cobalt blue eyes that captivated one's attention. And her red hair, so brilliant in its coloring as it fell in waves across her shoulders to her waist, made Susan the envy of all of the women at Fort Louis, as well as the other women who lived on the farms within riding distance of the fort.

A petite woman, whose waist was so small a man could reach his widespread fingers around it, Susan had been courted by all the single men of the area. But she seemed to have her mind on someone else, and most certainly not on Thomas Bradley, a beau who was about to visit from her former home in Michigan.

"Do you truly dread Thomas's arrival?" Jana asked, again adjusting her spectacles on her long, narrow nose. "If so, why didn't you wire him not to come for the dance? Why bother with him at all, Susan?"

Susan picked up a small dish of paste that Jana had made from flour and water and began dabbing it on pieces of the doily that she had cut in the shape of rose petals. For the home artist, these paper doilies were as fine as real lace. She had also purchased sheets of six images to be cut and pasted onto the valentine cards that she and Jana had made from lightweight cardboard.

"I couldn't find it in my heart to tell him not to come," Susan finally said, continuing with her bower of roses which were made of two layers of paper lace. "He was so kind to me when I lived in Michigan. He escorted me to many social functions and never once did he even try to kiss me, much less. . . ."

Her face heated with a blush. But it was her recent dreams more than her words that brought the color to her cheeks. Of late, she had dreamed of red roses and . . . and . . . the young and handsome Chippewa Indian chief, Eagle Hawk. She had always been told by her mother that if a girl dreamed of red roses, the symbol of love, in connection with a particular man, then it was almost certain he would be her husband. In her dreams, she had been thrilled by Eagle Hawk's kisses, and when his hands had molded her breasts, she had felt as though she were floating. Always, she awakened with a jolt . . . and in a strange sort of pleasurable sweat.

Jana leaned forward, squinting with her weak, gray eyes through her spectacles at Susan. "You were saying?" she said, again silently admiring Susan's loveliness. Jana wished that she could be as pretty. Although Jana had found a man to love her, who even promised to give her a future of loving and children, she knew that she was as plain as goat's milk, with a flat chest and slightly bowed legs. But she knew how to love a man at night, and that seemed to have made the difference. Her Jed's eyes never strayed, not even to beautiful Susan.

Susan's mind was brought back to the present. She smiled weakly at Jana. "Oh, I was just telling you what a gentleman Thomas is," she said, holding her cutout roses in place on the cardboard so that the glue would dry. "I just wish I could have some feelings for him, you know, the way you feel about your Jed. Then I would look forward to his arrival. I would be counting the minutes, and the hours, until we danced around the floor at the ball, until I was giddy from the dancing and laughter."

"Didn't you say that he had sent word that he was bringing you a surprise?" Jana asked, now slowly rocking back and forth in her rocker, her fingers busy again making her special valentine for Jed, which she planned to give him on the night of the ball.

All of the women were making valentines for their gentlemen, to present to them at the end of the valentine dance. But while Jana was making hers with much love and affection, she could tell that Susan's heart was not in this project. Susan had complained more than once that she did not desire at all to give Thomas a valentine, fearing that he would misinterpret the meaning of the gift. He already considered Susan his private property. Such a special valentine might give him cause to believe that he could totally claim her as his.

"I wish I had had time to send back a wire asking him not to bring me anything special," Susan said, slowly shaking her head back and forth. "But I couldn't. He sent the wire just as he was leaving for Minnesota. Oh, Jana, I so fear that his gift is a ring, and I shan't ever wear a ring given to me by Thomas."

Susan laid her valentine aside again. "Oh, what am I to do?" she said woefully. "He will be arriving within the week, just in time for the Valentine's Day ball. What if he presents the ring to me in front of everyone at the dance? Oh, Jana, how can I refuse him in front of all those people? I think too much of him to embarrass him in such a way. I've always looked on him as a brother, not a lover."

"Is he all that bad, that you cannot even consider marrying him?" Jana asked, pushing her spectacles farther up her nose with her forefinger. "He seems the sort that would make you feel as special as my Jed treats me. A woman can't find that sort of man but once in a lifetime. If I were you, I'd measure your feelings carefully, and then choose the man you wish to live your life with."

"I already know the man I would choose," Susan blurted out, even before she realized the words were forming on her lips. She gave Jana a quick look, dreading her friend's next question. What man? Susan had not confessed her feelings for the Chippewa warrior to anyone, knowing what her friends' reactions would be. Such an attraction would be considered forbidden. Even speaking of it was taboo among the white community, even if the Indian was from the peace-loving Chippewa tribe. And even if he was a powerful chief, loved and admired by all those knew him.

"You do?" Jana asked, again laying her valentine paraphernalia aside. "You know the man you want to marry?" She cocked an eyebrow as she again leaned over to look into Susan's eyes.

"Land's sake, Susan, you've never mentioned any man to me except for Thomas. Have you met someone new at the fort? Do you want to marry him? What does he look like? Is he handsome?"

Susan laughed nervously. "Please, Jana, no more questions," she said softly. "I'd rather not discuss it." She paused and stared into the fire, again recalling her dreams about the warrior. Perhaps she had had those visions because she had placed a sprig of rosemary under her pillow, a supposed guarantee that her future husband would appear in her dreams. And although she did not see how it would ever be possible for her to marry Eagle Hawk, it had been he who had appeared in her dream once again. Only last night she was lying with him on soft piles of fur beside a softly burning fire in a wigwam, and they were unclothed, discovering the pleasure points of each of their bodies.

She did not know how it could seem so real, for she had never been with any man, nor did she know exactly how it felt to become passionate with them.

Yet it had seemed so natural . . . so real.

Even thinking about it now made her heart pound, and her knees feel weak.

Fidgeting restlessly in her chair, and knowing that the conversation had to be directed elsewhere, Susan tried to put serious thought to making her valentine again, although the person she was supposed to be making it for did not stir any special feelings within her.

She would much prefer giving it to her handsome Chippewa warrior!

"Your valentine is gorgeous," Susan said, as Jana cut gold foil hearts to place on her glittery, lacy valentine. "The angel is so beautiful. I can see every feather in the angel's wing."

"Thank you," Jana said, the compliment making her blush. "Yours is magical in its elegance, Susan. The roses are so pretty. They look so realistic I can almost smell them."

"It was hard for me to choose the theme for my valentine," Susan said, sighing as she gazed down at her piece of artwork. "Each valentine symbol carries its special meaning. A birdcage indicates domestic love; a peacock, vanity; a yellow rose, jealousy; a red rose, purity. Yet red roses also symbolize love. I don't want Thomas to think that this valentine carries a message of love, yet I cannot just throw one together either, and be ashamed for the other women to see it. You know how competitive all the women are. I would simply die if I took an inferior valentine to the ball for everyone to poke fun at."

"Nothing you would ever make would be laughed at," Jana said, stiffening when she thought she heard sleet hitting the panes of her windows. She was worried now about Susan's return to the fort, and Jed's return to the cabin.

Her husband had been gone for several hours now, doing his daily hunting. Jana didn't want to believe that the weather was worsening outside.

Well, Jana decided, if the weather came on them quickly, she would not allow Susan to wander out in it, even though she knew her friend was determined to return to the fort. Susan planned to talk to her parents tonight about her feelings for Thomas, and to try and find a way to make them understand why she could never marry him. Jana wished that *she* knew the true reasons for Susan's decision. Yes, it was a man—but who?

To draw her own attention from the weather, Jana began talking about anything and everything. "Susan, do you know just how and where Valentine's Day originated?" she asked, rising to get the coffee pot from the hot coals of the fireplace. With a pot holder she gripped the coffee pot handle and poured two cups. After returning the coffee pot to the fire, she gave one of the cups to Susan, then sat back down in her rocker and began taking slow sips.

Susan smiled to herself, not surprised by Jana's question, for from her first acquaintance with Jana, she had found her to be a woman with a curiosity about life that outmatched anyone else that Susan had ever known. Susan had finally concluded that this need of knowledge stemmed from Jana having never been given the opportunity to attend school.

"As a lovers' festival, St. Valentine's Day was celebrated as far back as the fourteenth century, but the actual giving of valentines originated in London only a few years ago," Susan explained softly. "In London even now, both men and women send passionate messages to one another. I sometimes wish that I lived in London, where I could be free to show my feelings for the man I have lost my heart to."

There was an awkward pause, during which Jana stared at Susan, and Susan fought back another blush, after realizing that she had again said something that would pique her friend's curiosity.

"Susan," Jana suddenly blurted out. "You *must* tell me the man's name. We are best friends. We must not ever keep secrets from one another." She giggled. "At least when it is about a man. Talking of men is women's favorite topic, don't you know?"

Susan took her final sip of coffee and set the cup aside, then started when she gazed up at the window and saw thick, billowing flakes of snow hitting the window. She paled and jumped to her feet, her fingers trembling as she began gathering up her valentine paraphernalia. "I've stayed too long," she said, gently placing her valentine in her leather satchel. Hurriedly, she grabbed up her hooded, floor-length coat of rabbit fur, then smoothed on butter-soft leather gloves. "If the snow keeps up at this pace, I'm not sure if I can make it back to the fort."

Jana went to Susan and took her hands. "You can't risk it," she murmured. "Stay until the roads are clear. Please stay, Susan. I don't want to be alone. Jed's out there somewhere. What if he doesn't make it home? I'm afraid, Susan. So afraid."

16

Susan eased her hands from Jana's and gave her a reassuring hug. "You don't give me or your husband enough credit for being able to take care of ourselves," she said reassuringly. "I must go, Jana. If not, I might be stranded for days."

She leaned away from Jana. "And Jed will be home shortly," she said, picking up her satchel and moving toward the door. "He hasn't let you down yet, has he? And he's been in far worse storms than this. All of the men in this area have. It's something you have to learn to live with."

Jana hurried to the cabin door with Susan. Her fingers trembled as she lifted the latch. She shivered uncontrollably when a blast of frigid air and wet snow hit her face as she peered outside.

Susan gave Jana another hug, then trudged through ankle-deep snow to her horse and buggy. After securing her satchel on the seat, she climbed up and sat down beside it. She did not hesitate to take the reins, knowing that each minute counted now.

"You really should stay!" Jana shouted, shielding her spectacles from the blowing snow.

"I truly can't," Susan shouted back. She snapped her horse's reins and soon had the buggy circled around and headed back in the direction of the fort. She gave Jana another wave, then sent her horse into a steady trot along what she hoped was the road. The snow was not only impairing her vision, but had erased all signs of the road. All that she had to go by were the trees on all sides of her. As long as she found space between them, she knew that she was on the road.

The wind was blistering cold and the snow blinded her. When her lungs began to ache from having breathed in too much of the stinging air, Susan wondered if she had been too hasty in her decision to leave the safety of Jana's home. The snow was deepening quickly. The wind was drifting it in high piles on all sides of her.

Susan leaned into the wind and snow, her heart pounding, and then everything seemed to turn topsy turvy as the horse lost its footing and jerked the buggy sideways, onto its side. The last thing Susan remembered was a scream that she knew was hers, the painful fall as her head hit a rock that protruded through the snow, and then a strange sort of blackness that engulfed her. . . .

Muffled hoofbeats approached as snow settled on Susan's quiet form. Her horse lay on its side, breathing hard from pain, its leg broken. The sound of hoofbeats stopped. Soon a tall shadow fell over Susan, and dark eyes as black as midnight looked down upon her.

Remembering this woman well, Eagle Hawk knelt down beside Susan and placed a hand over her mouth. As he drew the hand away, he smiled, for although she was momentarily unconscious, she was alive. Her warm breath against his cold hand attested to that.

His hand then went to the blood seeping from a wound on her head. He knew what must be done. And soon!

Susan's horse let out a groan of pain, then whinnied softly. Eagle Hawk knew what must be done for the horse also, although it displeased him that he must take the life of such a magnificent beast.

Going to his horse, he removed his rifle from the gunsling. With careful aim, he fired. The shot sounded like a burst from a cannon in the silence of the forest.

The gunshot jolted Susan awake. She blinked the snow from her eyelashes, leaned up on an elbow, then gasped when she found Eagle Hawk standing there in a thick fur coat, smoke spiraling from his rifle.

He turned his eyes down to her and discovered her awake, and she gazed back at him, but neither spoke. They just looked in wonder at one another, and then Susan once again drifted into the tunnel of darkness as she fell back into unconsciousness.

Chapter Two

Susan awakened with a throbbing headache. She groaned as she lifted her hand and placed gentle fingers on a large lump on the side of her head, then drew them away and placed her fingers before her eyes, wondering about the strange green mixture that was spread across her head wound.

Then her eyes widened and her heartbeat quickened as she gazed upward and discovered that the roof overhead was domed, made of what appeared to be birchbark.

Her eyes moved around her as she slowly rose to a sitting position. The day's events came to her now in a flash of recollections.

The snow.

The spill from her buggy.

The gunfire.

The . . . Indian . . . !

"Eagle Hawk," she whispered to herself, recalling him standing over her after her fall, with kindness in his dark, fathomless eyes.

She looked quickly around her again. "Am I in his wigwam? Did he bring me to his village?"

Her heart pounding so that it made her forget her throbbing head, she gazed from item to item in the wigwam, her eyes stopping when she discovered a magnificent headdress hanging on the wall at the back.

"I am in Chief Eagle Hawk's lodge," she whispered. His obvious power among his people was intriguing to her, yet it made her dreams seem even more impossible. He would surely not allow himself to feel anything for her.

She was white.

He was Indian.

A chief would surely not "soil" his hands with a white woman when there were so many lovely Indian maidens at his disposal.

This disheartened Susan, yet she continued to look at everything in the small room with great curiosity. A firepit dug into the ground in the middle of the dwelling boasted a roaring fire, and Susan was grateful for its warmth. She was sitting on soft bulrush mats, and along the wall were blankets that had been rolled up neatly by someone's caring hands. A large, intricately carved bow hung on one side, a quiver of arrows beside it. There were many buffalo hide canvases upon which had been painted scenes of Indian life.

A noise behind her drew Susan's head quickly around, and when she found Eagle Hawk standing at the entrance, her insides quivered strangely. His fur wrap had been discarded, so she had a full view of his muscled body; a breechcloth and moccasins were the only clothing he wore. He had broad shoulders, thin flanks, narrow hips, and muscular thighs. His was a sinewy, gleaming body, the copper coloring emphasized by the glow of the fire.

"You are better now?" Eagle Hawk said, coming toward her. He lowered himself to bended knee beside her and touched her cheek gently. "You are awake. That is good."

Her heart thundering, Susan could not find her voice quickly. Yet fear did not enter her thoughts, for the Chippewa in these parts were friendly. They had put their antagonism toward the whites behind them long ago, and now enjoyed the profits of trading at the posts and forts.

It was not fear that Susan experienced while in his presence, but something she had never felt before. She was caught up in a spiraling sort of ecstasy, and she knew that she must gain control of those feelings. Never could she allow this handsome Indian to know them.

"I'm going to be just fine," she said, glad when he eased his hand away from her and settled down beside her on the mats.

"Yellow Rose placed a herbal mixture on your wound," Eagle Hawk said, leaning over to lift a log onto the fire. "She will be here soon with food. That will help you regain your strength."

"That's good," Susan murmured, yet she wondered who Yellow Rose was? Surely his wife, she thought despairingly. "I must get back home as soon as I can. My parents will be worrying."

"The weather has halted all travel," Eagle Hawk said matter-of-factly as he laid another log on the fire, then drew his legs to his chest, wrapping his muscled arms around them. "You will stay here until it is safe."

"Do you mean it is still snowing?" Susan gasped, gazing toward the buckskin entrance flap that swayed furiously at the doorway as the wind swept against it. "Oh, what will my parents think? If the weather is so horrible, they won't even be able to send anyone out to look for me."

"*Ay-uh*, that is so," Eagle Hawk confirmed throatily. "And Eagle Hawk cannot return you *en-dah-yen*, home through the snow."

"Please excuse my manners," Susan said, turning to Eagle Hawk. "I haven't yet thanked you for rescuing me. Nor have I told you my name. . . ."

"No thank you's are needed and I already know your *ee-szhee-nee-kah-so-win*," Eagle Hawk said, interrupting Susan, and smiling at her when he saw her expression of surprise at his confession of knowing her.

Deep within his heart, he knew much more than that about her. He had watched her many times, enjoying the way she walked . . . the way she talked . . . the way she laughed.

In his midnight dreams, he had possessed her, her soft, sweet laughter like music in his heart as he had made love to her.

In reality, when he was awake, and dreams were only left there to plague him the long day through, Eagle Hawk had never approached Susan, because he knew the feelings of the white people. It was forbidden for a white woman to become infatuated with a man with red skin.

But this was different. She was here, as though *Wenebojo*, the Great Spirit, had guided her to him. He would make her love him before she left his village. Then no matter what the white men said or did, she, herself, would declare that she wished to stay with her Chippewa chieftain warrior forever.

Let any of them try to force her to leave him then!

There had not been warring between the Chippewa and the white pony soldiers for many moons, but there could be now—because of his desire for this woman.

Susan blushed. "You . . . know . . . my name?" she murmured, thrilled at the thought that he had sought out someone to ask her name. Those times at the fort, when their eyes had met and held, something *had* been exchanged between them, and it made her heart pound to think that, just perhaps, he was as attracted to her as she was to him.

Nervously she brushed her fingers through her tangled red hair, realizing that he looked at it often as he spoke to her. She had even noticed how he had gazed into her eyes, as though mesmerized by their color.

It was strange to her, that her unusual coloring could make any difference to anyone. To her the color of her hair was ugly, and she had always hungered for green eyes rather than blue.

But the fact that he was attracted to her for any reason made her feel as though she were melting inside.

"*Ay-uh*, your name is known to me," Eagle Hawk said, nodding. "As mine is to you. You do know my name, do you not? You have asked my name after seeing me at the white man's fort? Your intrigue has matched my own?"

Her pulse racing at the thought that what she had always dreamed of just might be coming true, yet somewhat fearing it, Susan could only give him a slow nod . . . and smile.

Then her smile faded when the entrance flap was shoved aside and the loveliest Indian maiden that Susan had ever seen entered. Susan's heart seemed to sink as she realized that Eagle Hawk had surely seen the magnificence of this woman, so much that, surely, he had married her. To have allowed herself to forget his mention of Yellow Rose was more than foolish. It was heartbreaking.

She watched as Eagle Hawk rose and went to the woman, treating her with a gentle ease that tore at Susan's heart. She scarcely breathed as Eagle Hawk took the heavy pot of steaming food from the woman's hand and hung it from a tripod over the fire.

Susan watched the woman slip off her white rabbit fur coat, revealing even more reasons why Eagle Hawk gazed at her with such appreciation as she stood opposite the fire from Susan, staring back at her with the darkest of eyes. Her long, black braids, oiled with bear's grease, lay across her shoulders, settling onto well-developed breasts that pressed against her buckskin blouse, so that any man's eyes could not help but take a second glance. Her tiny waist was evident, and her beautifully beaded moccasins revealed the smallness of her feet. She walked with such grace and ease that Susan could not help but again feel the pangs of jealousy stabbing at her heart.

"As promised, Yellow Rose has brought you nourishment," Eagle Hawk said, settling down beside Susan again. He nodded to Yellow Rose, who obediently bent to one knee and began ladling the rich rabbit soup into a wooden bowl and handed it to Susan.

"Thank you," Susan managed to utter. She half-heartedly accepted a wooden spoon, yet sank it into the soup and sipped from it, knowing that this was expected of her since both sets of eyes were watching her, waiting for her to eat.

Each sip was harder, the liquid warmth almost lodging in her throat the more she thought about how much Eagle Hawk must love this gentle, lovely woman. What man could not? She was much prettier than herself, Susan silently despaired.

Susan tried to focus her full attention on the soup, her eyes glued to the bowl as she continued eating. This man of her secret infatuation, and the one she really had wanted to make her valentine for, was not even available now to receive it. She had to force herself to forget him, yet how could one stop one's dreams? They had overtaken her nights ever since she had first set eyes on the handsome Chippewa chieftain.

Unaware that Eagle Hawk had moved from beside her, Susan was surprised when he was suddenly there again, holding something up for her to see.

"My satchel!" she gasped, having forgotten about it and what was inside it: the valentine that she had wished to give to Eagle Hawk. She would have thought that only her life would have been saved from the storm. She knew that the gunshot she had heard had been fired to relieve her horse from its misery of a broken leg. That Eagle Hawk had thought to save her satchel was a surprise.

"When I found you, your fingers were clutched to the traveling bag," Eagle Hawk said, offering it to her. "This showed that it was important to you. Take it. It is yours again to keep. The value of the belongings inside is not lessened. The wet of the snow did not seep through the leather."

"My fingers were clutching the bag?" Susan said, her eyes widening. "I . . . I don't recall grabbing it as I fell. I guess it fell beside me and I . . . I just happened to reach over and it was there."

Eagle Hawk knelt down on one side of her, Yellow Rose on the other, their eyes locked on the satchel. "It is of much value?" Yellow Rose asked, her voice tiny and sweet. "Can we see?"

Susan clutched to the handle of the satchel, looking slowly from Yellow Rose to Eagle Hawk. "What is inside is of some value to me," she murmured, her face growing hot with a blush as her eyes lingered longer on Eagle Hawk. "It is something that I was making. Thus far, it has taken me many hours to make it especially beautiful."

"Especially?" Yellow Rose said, furrowing an eyebrow as she spoke the word slowly and quizzically. "What word is that? What does it mean?"

Susan had to laugh as Yellow Rose's curiosity reminded her of her dear friend Jana's constant onslaught of questions. This made Susan feel closer to the lovely maiden, somewhat lessening her feelings of jealousy.

" 'Especially' means 'special' in the English tongue, also 'particularly favored,' " Susan explained, knowing that the Chippewa knew the

English language well from having dealt with white traders for many years. But she understood that some words still seemed foreign to the Chippewa, as all of the Chippewa words were strange to Susan. She was glad that Eagle Hawk and Yellow Rose only used a Chippewa word here and there. She had no trouble following their conversation.

Yellow Rose smiled and nodded. Her eyes were on the satchel again, her hands clasped in her lap as she waited for Susan to reveal her 'especial' belongings to her. She had always liked viewing anything that belonged to white women. She had gained possession of combs, ribbons, even ways of coloring her lips other than the paints she made from the earth and flowers, by showing interest in the women's belongings. She had found that most white women had gentle, generous hearts.

Eagle Hawk's heart soared as he saw Susan's happiness at regaining her prized belonging. He eyed Yellow Rose, having decided to allow her to stay awhile longer, and then he would send her to her own dwelling.

He wanted time alone with Susan, to talk—to touch—hopefully, even to kiss. . . .

Susan opened her satchel and pulled her valentine from it. She felt Eagle Hawk and Yellow Rose's eyes on her and the beautiful valentine, and realized they had no idea what it was.

And why should they? She had only been aware of Valentine's Day for a short time herself.

"This is a valentine," she slowly began to explain. She told them the meaning of it, and how it was used to celebrate Valentine's Day.

"It is beautiful," Yellow Rose murmured, reaching out to touch the roses that had been glued to the cardboard cut in the shape of a heart.

"Hold it if you wish," Susan said, handing the valentine to Yellow Rose. She smiled to herself as the young maiden carefully took the valentine and closely studied it, as though she were a child instead of a woman of Susan's age.

Susan proceeded to explain why she was making the valentine, her heart bleeding to know that she would be giving it to Thomas after all.

"There is to be a dance at the fort on Valentine's Day," Susan said softly as Yellow Rose still scrutinized the valentine, delicately touching it with the tips of her fingers. "All of the women who will attend the dance are making valentines for the man who will escort them. This valentine is being made for a man who is escorting *me*. He is coming from far away, just to make sure that I have an escort."

Susan was surprised to see a frown cross Eagle Hawk's face as he heard this declaration and a strange hurt entered his eyes. She could not understand why it should matter to him that she had spoken of another man, when Eagle Hawk himself was married.

Yet she knew that she was foolish to presume that his frown had anything to do with her, and tried to cast the thought aside when she heard Yellow Rose asking her something.

"Could you show me how to make a valentine for my special, *ee-nee-nee*, man?" Yellow Rose was asking as she handed the valentine back to Susan.

Susan looked slowly at Eagle Hawk, jealousy hurting her heart to think that she would teach Yellow Rose how to make a valentine to give to Eagle Hawk, the very man to whom Susan had wanted to present her own valentine.

"Yes, I shall show you," Susan said quietly, thinking that surely the Indian word that Yellow Rose had spoken had meant 'husband.'

"Oh, thank you," Yellow Rose said, beaming. "Thank you."

Having forgotten her head wound, Susan began pulling all of her valentine paraphernalia from her satchel. Out of the corner of her eye she watched Eagle Hawk move to the rear of the wigwam, where he began painting designs on one of his stretched hides, used as a canvas. She had heard that he was quite a skilled artist who was paid well both by white men and other Indians in beads and paints. She tried to see what he was painting now, but the stretched hide was turned so that she could not view it.

Feeling as though she had been forgotten by Eagle Hawk, Susan half-heartedly began telling Yellow Rose how to make valentines from the delicate lace paper doilies, her heart elsewhere—where it did not belong!

Chapter Three

Susan handed Yellow Rose a plain sheet of cardboard. "From this you will create your valentine for your special man," she said, giving Eagle Hawk a sad, secret glance. She was glad that he was too occupied in his painting to notice her sadness in knowing that he belonged to another. For so long, she had fantasized about nothing but him. And the way he had looked at her earlier, she had thought that perhaps his dreams might have been filled with her.

Yet how foolish she was to think this. They had only seen one another at the fort, and not even spoken a word of welcome to the other. She now had to cast such foolishness from her mind and concentrate on returning home as soon as possible. There she would meet Thomas with a smile and try to make a future with him. He *was* one of the kindest men she had ever met.

Perhaps in time he could stir passions within her that would make her dreams be filled only with him. . . .

Yellow Rose was sorting through the beautiful paper doilies and the die-cut flowers, hearts, and cupids that would be glued on the doilies to make the valentines. Sighing, she picked up a bower of gold foil roses. It reminded Yellow Rose of her name. Her special man would enjoy receiving a valentine with this decoration on it, for it was he, many years ago, who had suggested the change in her name after she reached the age when one could change one's name, if they wished. From that point on, she had known who her husband would be—the man who had chosen her special adult name!

"Do you like that one?" Susan asked, turning back to the task at hand. "If so, we can paste it on the doily after pasting the doily on the cardboard. Then we'll paste other glittery things on the valentine to make it extra special for your . . . for your man."

"*Ay—uh*, yes, my husband will enjoy such a valentine as this," Yellow Rose said, her eyes dancing. "I can hardly wait to give it to him." She looked at Susan seriously. "Tell me again the meaning of . . . what did you call it? Valentine's . . . Day? I like to hear the story. I will repeat it to my children when I am blessed with little ones."

Yellow Rose's mention of her husband, and of having children, made Susan's heart take on a heavy, sinking feeling again, and she hated that she could not let go of her feelings for this handsome Chippewa chieftain. Sitting here with Yellow Rose, trying to pretend that nothing was wrong, was the hardest thing she had ever done. She prayed to herself that the snows would soon end and the sun would shine brightly in the sky, quickly melting the snow.

If only she could flee this place now. But she was there, not really as a captive, yet feeling as if she were one.

Susan once more explained the meaning of Valentine's Day and the giving of valentines to loved ones, all the while busying herself in cutting out various shapes to place on the lovely maiden's valentine. "You see, Yellow Rose," she continued, "the magical way of making lacy valentines requires a great nicety of touch so as not to tear to tatters what might have been a gorgeous messenger of love."

"I shall be most careful," Yellow Rose said in her broken English. She started to say something else but suddenly looked at Eagle Hawk.

Susan followed her gaze to Eagle Hawk just in time to see him give Yellow Rose a nod, and Yellow Rose quickly rose to her feet and left the dwelling without so much as another word to Susan.

Susan was stunned by Yellow Rose's quick escape, and by Eagle Hawk's steady gaze on herself, which began to unnerve her.

Then she finally found the words that had seemed lodged in her throat, Eagle Hawk's mesmerizing eyes having stolen all thought and logic from her mind. She remembered that she had no hold on him whatsoever, and that he surely loved only Yellow Rose.

"Did you give her an order to leave?" Susan asked, her voice weak.

"*Ay-uh*," Eagle Hawk said, setting his stretched hide canvas aside, its back to Susan so that she still could not see what he was painting on it. He rose to his dignified height of six feet and went and settled himself down beside Susan.

Her heart throbbing, his manly smell and his nearness driving her to distraction, Susan scooted away from him and began picking up her supplies and placing them in her satchel.

"Why . . . did . . . you send Yellow Rose away?" she dared to ask, setting the satchel aside. She settled down beside the fire and cleared her throat nervously. "Isn't this her dwelling, also? Where did you intend for her to go? It is surely growing dusk now. She should not be outside in the cold."

"My *gee-shee-may*," he began, then corrected himself: "My sister has returned to her husband for the night to warm his blankets," Eagle Hawk said matter-of-factly. Susan gasped aloud and blushed at the stunning surprise.

"You react strangely to knowing my sister sleeps with her husband," he said, forking an eyebrow. "Is that why you look at me with such a strangeness in your eyes? Does the thought of Yellow Rose sharing blankets with her husband embarrass you? They are married. And even before they were married, I knew that my sister secretly slept with her intended. I was not embarrassed or angered over it. It is good to measure the truth of one's heart before giving it away to another."

So thrilled to know that she had misinterpreted the relationship between Yellow Rose and Eagle Hawk, Susan was momentarily at a loss for words. Her dreams and fantasies flashed before her eyes, as she realized now that perhaps they *could* come true.

Oh, how she loved this handsome Chippewa chieftain. . . .

But then her heart seemed to stand still at the remembrance that he was a powerful chief. Again she reminded herself how impossible it would be for him to ever be free to love her, a white woman.

Feeling the loss, as though she had truly had his love for a while and then lost it, Susan cast her eyes downward, an emptiness at the pit of her stomach assailing her. "None of those things you mentioned are the cause of my strange behavior," she finally said. "Please excuse how I behave. I . . . I . . . guess it is because I feel that I am intruding. If I had listened to my parents, I would never have gone to Jana's house today, and then get caught in the blizzard." She still could not look into his wondrously dark eyes, afraid that her feelings for him would overwhelm her. "I truly apologize for having become such a bother to you."

Her heart leapt into her throat when she felt a sudden hand cup her chin. She closed her eyes, fighting the ecstasy of the touch of his flesh against hers.

But she could not keep her eyes closed for long. She could feel his eyes on her, hot and demanding, as he turned her face upward to be directly in front of his.

When she opened her eyes, it was not his eyes that she saw. It was his lips!

They were moving toward hers, as though he might kiss her!

She did not move away to deny him the kiss. When she had thought that he was married, she had came so close to never having it. She melted when his lips touched hers. She sighed with pleasure when she felt his arms wrap around her and drew her close as his kiss deepened.

In her dreams it had been wonderful.

In real life it was rapturous!

Because of Susan's deep love for him, she had no more will of her own. Her arms twined around his neck as though bidden by some unseen force. She snuggled close to his powerful, bare chest, pressing her breasts against it. When he emitted a low groan, she was not sure why, yet she did know that it was filled with pleasure, which matched her own as he moved one hand between them and slowly cupped her breast through her dress.

Pleasure spread through Susan's body as Eagle Hawk began to stroke her breast. Her senses were reeling. When she had dreamed of his caresses, none had compared with the way it truly felt.

Wanting more, she leaned into his hand.

She clung to him and drew a ragged breath as he still kissed her with a fierce, fevered passion.

With quick eagerness, his fingers were in her hair. When he touched the lump on her head, causing pain to shoot through it like fire, Susan winced and drew quickly away from him, moaning. She reached a hand to the lump and rubbed it lightly as tears swelled in her eyes.

Eagle Hawk touched her cheek gently. "Did I hurt you?" he asked, his voice drawn, yet husky. He was trying to will his heartbeat to slow down, and to ignore the ache in his loins that being with Susan had caused. It had been too long since he had felt such a hungry need for a woman. It was hard to stop what had started between them.

But he knew that he must.

For a moment he had forgotten why she was there.

He had even forgotten that she had been wounded in her fall from the buggy. It was not honorable to take advantage of her, no matter how much he wanted her—and no matter how clearly she had shown how much she wanted him.

This confused him.

She had spoken of another man, one to whom she would be giving her special piece of pretty paper called a valentine. Yet she had returned Eagle Hawk's kiss with much ardor, with a hungry need that matched his own.

"The pain was only slight," she murmured. "Please don't think one more minute about it."

Torn between feelings of sudden shame over having behaved so wantonly, and feelings which ate at her heart with want of him, Susan lowered her eyes as she flicked tears from their corners.

She wanted to grab his hand back when he eased it from her cheek, yet knew that she had already behaved foolishly, which was quite unusual for her. She had the reputation of being level-headed, one who thought before she acted. She had never allowed a man to touch her breast . . . even if Eagle Hawk had not actually touched her bare flesh.

That she had allowed many things to transpire tonight made her wonder how she could bear staying with Eagle Hawk until the snows melted. It seemed that she had no control of her heart while she was with this handsome Chippewa, and a part of her did not care. She just wanted to be in his arms again and to feel the pleasure of his kiss and hands.

So afraid that her feelings might carry her off again, Susan looked up at Eagle Hawk. "Perhaps there is someone of your village who might take me in for the night?" she asked, then regretted it the minute the words had crossed her lips.

She saw a sudden hurt leap into his eyes, as if her suggestion had insulted him. Susan realized now that he had meant for her to stay in his lodge.

She wondered if he had planned to seduce her at that very moment when he had decided to rescue her and bring her back to his lodge.

"You will stay here," Eagle Hawk said solemnly. He went to the blankets that were rolled tightly along the wall of his wigwam. "You will stay in Eagle Hawk's lodge, not elsewhere. You are Eagle Hawk's guest, not someone else's."

Susan's heart pounded as she watched how many blankets Eagle Hawk chose to bring back to the fire with him, his cold, determined voice having sent spirals of fear through her heart, that perhaps he was planning to force himself upon her. Although she wanted desperately to be held by him, she did not want it ever to be by force.

She breathed with relief as she watched him take many blankets. That surely meant that he did not expect her to sleep with him, which might lead them into doing something she now felt would be wrong, at least until they knew each other better.

She wanted never to have to look back and regret her first moments of love with the man she adored.

Eagle Hawk came back to the fire, bent a knee, and spread first one blanket and then another atop it, making Susan's heart skip a beat. It seemed that although he had gathered many blankets, most would be used to sleep upon, as one pallet. So he did plan for her to warm his blankets after all! Even though he knew that her head was paining her, he expected more than mere companionship from her tonight.

He would finish what had started between them.

A part of her deeply wanted this to happen, and another part cried out not to allow it.

Yet how could she say no to a man of such power . . . a man of such charisma? In his presence, she was lost to him, totally lost, no matter how hard she fought her feelings.

Then Susan's heart seemed to sink when Eagle Hawk began to spread another blanket away from the first pile and to pile more blankets on it, spreading them with great care. Two pallets meant that he was not going to ask her to sleep with him. He had even placed the pallets far apart, so that if she unconsciously reached out for him during the night, he would not be there for her.

Looking over at Eagle Hawk, Susan studied his expression, wondering if she had wounded him too deeply and if he would ever kiss and hold her again. When he turned his eyes suddenly to her, and she saw in them no more hurt, nor anger, her whole body seemed to relax and she felt that she might hope again for this wonderful warrior's love.

"Come," Eagle Hawk said, gesturing toward the pallet that was closer to the fire. "You will sleep, and tomorrow your head will pain you less. The herbs applied on your wound will have time to do their magic. Lay yourself down. Close your eyes. Tomorrow is another day. We shall explore then our feelings for one another again."

With a racing pulse, his words touching her heart like a song, Susan crawled to the blankets and stretched out atop them. Her eyes widened and her breath caught when Eagle Hawk leaned over and gently removed one of her shoes and then the other, then placed them beside the fire so they would be warm in the morning.

She felt loved when he gently covered her with a blanket, bringing it up to just below her chin. She waited with bated breath as he gazed down at her with his midnight dark eyes, thinking that surely he was going to kiss her. She knew that all she had to do was reach her hands out for him and he would be there.

But she held back, too afraid of the strange blaze of urgency that was flooding her insides. She sensed that once they kissed again, there would be no stopping the flood of emotions. She would learn things with him that could never be a part of her dreams, for never had she been with a man sexually, and had no way to know exactly how it felt to become a true woman. . . .

Susan sighed with relief when Eagle Hawk turned from her and went to place several logs on the fire. She watched him as he went to his blankets and sat down to remove his moccasins, then stretched out on the blankets on his back, his feet toward the fire.

She waited for him to cover himself with a blanket, but to her surprise he never did. She could not help but move her gaze over him, silently admiring his beautiful copper skin and bulging muscles.

When he turned on his side to face her and the fabric of his breechclout dropped loosely to one side, more of him was revealed to her eyes than she had expected.

Blushing, she flipped over on her side, quickly placing her back to him. Her eyes were wide with wonder, yet there was a soft smile of anticipation on her face. . . .

Chapter Four

The day had been gruelingly long for Susan after she had slept restlessly the night through. Having been awakened to true passion in Eagle Hawk's embrace, her dreams had not come to her this night. The memories of the real thing had kept her eyes open throughout most of the night.

Even now as she was again helping Yellow Rose make her special valentine, Susan's heart would soar at the thought of Eagle Hawk's hand on her breast. The feelings it had caused within her had been deliciously sweet, sweeter than any honeys or jams that her mother had made when Susan was a small child.

She was afraid to look directly into Yellow Rose's eyes, fearing that the lovely maiden would see the difference in her today, feeling as though she were moving on a cloud, in love for the first time in her life.

Using Yellow Rose's concoction of paste, Susan attached another glittery gold foil rose onto Yellow Rose's valentine, dreading finishing it. Once the valentine was finished, her fingers would be idle and her thoughts would stray even more to how much she loved Eagle Hawk. Slowly she pasted first one pretty object on the valentine and then another. She was afraid that it might be becoming too gaudy, but every time she added another rose or a piece of cut doily, Yellow Rose would sigh and say how much she liked it "even better now."

The one thing troubling Susan was the absence of Eagle Hawk. When she had awakened, she had found him gone, and he had not yet returned. She had shared her morning and noon meal with Yellow Rose, the young maiden chattering more than eating. Susan had not yet asked about Eagle Hawk's whereabouts, afraid that her questioning might reveal too much of her feelings for him.

"Where has Eagle Hawk been all day?" she finally blurted, unable to hold her curiosity any longer. And she was aware of the sun lowering in the sky. That, and the growling of her stomach, attested to the time of day— that soon it would be dark, and time to eat again.

Her heart thrilled when she thought about how soon she would be going to bed again amidst the blankets that Eagle Hawk had lent her. Would he be gone even then, she wondered, hoping not.

She wanted to look at him.

She wanted to touch him.

She wanted to run her fingers through his raven-black hair and tell him how much she loved him, yet knew that she could never be as bold as that. Her actions last night had shocked her. Surely she would be more guarded next time and behave more like a lady.

Yet she doubted she could keep her feelings to herself.

He already knew that she loved him.

How . . . could . . . he not . . . ?

"My brother has been in council with his warriors today," Yellow Rose said matter-of-factly. She wiped paste from her fingers after helping Susan paste another pretty rose onto the valentine. "They speak of spring hunts and of many things only men speak of in the absence of women." She giggled. "One day I hid in the council house and listened to the men," she softly confessed. "They not only spoke of men's feelings toward the hunt, but also about women. After putting seriousness behind them, they shared smokes from their long pipes, and talked of women. My face grew hot and my body tingled strangely all over while I listened to them brag of their prowess with women. You see, Susan, I was only a mere child then. I had never been with a man." She blushed and lowered her eyes. "You know what I am speaking of I am sure."

Susan's face grew hot with a blush too. She said nothing in return about the subject.

"When you came to Eagle Hawk's lodge this morning, could you sense how the weather might be by tomorrow?" Susan asked quickly. "My parents must think I'm lost, or perhaps even dead. I hate to worry them. They are getting up in the years. Both are forty winters of age."

"That *is* old," Yellow Rose said seriously, nodding. "But my parents were even older than that when they died."

"Oh, I'm sorry to hear that they are no longer among the living," Susan murmured, dreading having to experience the death of her parents.

"They were on the river many moons ago and it seemed that some animal reached up from the depths of the water and tipped their canoe," Yellow Rose said, her eyes sad. "The animal even held them under the water. I know that it must have. My father and mother both were excellent swimmers."

Susan's eyes widened. She paused from her valentine making to stare at Yellow Rose. "Lord, how horrible," she gasped. "This animal you are speaking of. Did you see it? Was it grotesque? Is it still in the river even now, waiting to tip over another canoe?"

Yellow Rose shrugged. "It was never seen, then or now," she said, taking the valentine from Susan's lap and holding it out to admire it. "But I know it was there. My chieftain father's skills with canoeing were many. Nothing less than an animal could cause his canoe to tip. And it had to be a large animal, for had it been small, like an otter, my father would have hit it over the head with a paddle."

Susan's lips parted as she stared at Yellow Rose, now realizing that the maiden had concocted this tale in order to save face for her father in her mind.

In truth, there was no animal. In truth, Yellow Rose's father had not had full control of his canoe the day it had capsized. She just did not want to think that her father could be at fault. And the story was innocent enough. If it made Yellow Rose accept her parents' deaths better, so be it!

"The weather today?" Yellow Rose then said, smiling at Susan as she placed the valentine back on Susan's lap. "You will be here even tomorrow. The clouds are still heavy with snow. It may be days before you can leave." She reached a hand to Susan's cheek. "And I am glad. When you leave, I will never see you again. It has been much fun making beautiful papers with you."

"Thank you," Susan murmured. "I've enjoyed it, too."

"You say that Valentine's Day is celebrated once a year, at the same time in the month of *O-nah-bun-ee-gee-zis*, hard crust moon?" Yellow Rose asked, her eyes wide. She eased her hand

48

away and twined her fingers and rested them on her lap.

"I did not understand what you said," Susan said, squinting over at Yellow Rose. "You were describing the month of February? Is that what you were doing?"

"*Ay-uh*," Yellow Rose said, nodding. "*O-nah-bun-ee-gee-zis*, hard crust moon means February."

Susan laughed softly and resumed making the fabulously decorated valentine. "Yes, this time next year you will want another valentine to give to your special man," she murmured.

"But you will not be here to help me," Yellow Rose said, her lower lip curving into a pout. "And I will not have the beautiful papers for which to make a valentine. What shall I do then, Susan? I want to make valentines every February from this time forth for my husband."

Susan paused from her work, her mind's eye seeing herself this time next year sitting with Yellow Rose, but not as a visitor forced there by a blizzard. She could see herself in soft buckskin clothes, with intricately beaded moccasins on her feet, and her hair drawn back and braided. She could see herself anxiously awaiting the arrival of her husband, realizing that he had been in council much too long. When Eagle Hawk would return from the council, he would sweep her into his arms and carry her to the blankets. There they would make endless love. . . .

"Susan?" Yellow Rose said, bringing her back to the present. "You were thinking of what? Within your eyes there was such happiness . . . such wonder."

Susan blushed. "I don't know what got into me," she said softly. "My mind wandered. That's all."

"Susan, how will I make a valentine for my husband next year without you here to help me?" Yellow Rose asked again, but her words faded and her eyes were drawn around when a cold breeze washed over her, and she knew that her brother had opened the entrance flap, letting in much wind and blowing snow.

Susan's gaze moved quickly to Eagle Hawk as he stepped into the wigwam. She was overwhelmed by a desire that she could not fight off. When he slipped off his heavy fur coat and came into the light, and his eyes locked with hers, a shiver of pleasure swam through her that she could not deny. When he moved toward her in his brief breechclout, his muscles flexing with each step, her heart began to race and she had to look away from him so he could not read her thoughts and see her passion.

"It is time to return to duties of your husband, little sister," Eagle Hawk said softly. "But first, tend to your chieftain brother's needs. Bring one of your dresses for Susan to wear and water for bathing, and then later bring the pot of food that you have prepared for us beside your own pot of food over your lodge fire. Then you will not return to my dwelling until tomorrow."

A bath? Susan thought, embarrassed at the thought of him even thinking she needed one, yet knowing that she truly did. And a dress? A buckskin dress that she had envisioned herself wearing?

And did he expect her to take a bath in front of him? Although he had familiarized himself with one of her breasts, he had not actually touched it, or seen it.

She looked guardedly around her, not seeing any way she might have privacy while taking a bath.

She then looked up at Eagle Hawk, her heart thundering at the thought of him taking a bath in front of her. . . .

But surely none of this was expected of her, unless it was normal for Chippewa men and women not to feel uncomfortable while unclothed in each other's presence.

But she was not Chippewa! Why did he not realize that her customs and his differed?

Yellow Rose scurried from the wigwam.

To keep from looking up at Eagle Hawk again, Susan busied herself in gathering up all of the valentine materials. She hated it when her fingers visibly trembled. She dreaded that he might even hear the pounding of her heart!

Oh, why couldn't she gain more control of her feelings? Why must his mere presence disturb her so much?

If she were made to feel that she must bathe in his dwelling, with his eyes on her all the time, she feared more than a pounding heart and trembling fingers. She knew that she might lose her inhibitions and float into his arms, ready to give her all to him—as she had done so often in her sweet, savage dreams.

Suddenly Eagle Hawk's hand covered Susan's, stilling them from picking up any more of the glittery foil roses or lacy paper doilies. Susan was being swallowed whole with such wondrous feelings, the fear of what might happen lessening. Slowly she looked up into his eyes, his hand still firm on hers.

"Why are you doing that?" she asked, her voice foreign to her in its strange huskiness. "Why are you stopping me from picking up my valentine materials? I . . . I . . . must put them in my satchel for later."

He moved his hand away and nodded toward what remained on the bulrush mats. "Finish, and then we must talk," he said thickly. He sat down beside her and watched as she nervously finished placing her equipment in her satchel.

Susan set her satchel aside and turned wavering eyes at Eagle Hawk, wondering what he wanted to say that was so serious, for never had he cracked a smile since he had returned to his lodge. All that she could gather from this was that he was still hurt and angry for her having suggested she stay elsewhere, away from his wigwam. If he had not ordered his sister to bring bathwater and food, she would even believe that perhaps he was going to send her out into the snow to find her way home, alone.

"What is it that you wish to say to me?" she asked, the suspense killing her.

"My wife has been dead now for four winters," Eagle Hawk began in a drawn, solemn tone. He looked away from her and stared into the dancing flames.

Susan gasped and paled. "You were once married?" she murmured. "Your wife? She died?"

"*Ay-uh*, she died of some strange fever," Eagle Hawk said, slowly turning his eyes back to Susan. "Since the day of her burial rites, Eagle Hawk was not drawn to another woman until one winter ago. It was then that he knew that he could love again. But he never approached the woman, fearing she might laugh or turn her back to him. But now Eagle Hawk thinks she will do neither and even believes she might allow him to kiss her. Should Eagle Hawk approach her with a kiss?"

Again jealousy assailed Susan, fearing there was another woman after all! And his asking her advice was insulting, to say the least, after he had shown such affection for her.

She lowered her eyes and swallowed a lump that was fast rising in her throat as she gave him her answer. "If you truly love the woman and want her, yes, you should kiss her," she murmured. She slowly lifted her eyes to his again. "If she will allow it."

Eagle Hawk reached a hand to her cheek and leaned closer to her. "Would you allow it?" he said thickly. "Would you allow me to kiss you again?"

Susan's heart skipped a beat. "What did you say?" she asked thinly, her widened eyes filled with question and hope.

"Eagle Hawk asks if you will allow the kiss," he said, his lips now only a breath away from hers. "You are that woman of one winter ago. You are the woman of my midnight dreams. Before, when we kissed and embraced, I knew your feelings for me, but you were afraid of them. Am I wrong? Do you feel deeply for Eagle Hawk? Will you allow a kiss? Will you allow an embrace? Tonight is forever, while with you."

Her insides melting, Susan twined her arms around his neck and gave him his answer by kissing him passionately. When he lay her down on the bulrush mats and reached a hand up inside her dress, everything within her tingled with pleasure, and she hated it when Yellow Rose was suddenly there in the wigwam.

"My brother, I have brought you bathwater," Yellow Rose said, looking sheepishly from her brother to Susan as they moved quickly to their feet. "I have brought you a dress, Susan."

As Yellow Rose handed Susan the dress, and Susan saw its lovely beaded design and felt its softness, she was at a loss for words. She hugged it to her and looked slowly up at Yellow Rose. "Thank you," she murmured. "I will wear it proudly. It's so beautiful."

Eagle Hawk took the large wooden basin of water and thanked his sister. Yellow Rose made a quick escape, leaving Susan standing there with a thudding heart, Eagle Hawk looking down at her with eyes hazed over with a need that she knew she would soon fulfill. There was nothing that would keep her from fully experiencing the wonders of Eagle Hawk's arms now. She did not object when he set the basin aside, gently took the buckskin dress from her and laid it aside, and slowly disrobed her, leaving her absolutely nude before his feasting eyes.

When he took a wet doeskin cloth from the water and began washing her face, ever so softly, she allowed it.

When he led her down again on the bulrush mats onto her back and began washing her breasts, she sucked in a wild breath and allowed it.

She closed her eyes in ecstasy when the cloth trailed across her quavering stomach and then to her private place at the juncture of her thighs.

She trembled as Eagle Hawk began caressing her swollen bud with the cloth.

Then when she felt something else there, she opened her eyes in panic, having never felt a man's fingers on that part of her that had been denied all men.

As his fingers caressed her throbbing center, she closed her eyes and tossed her head back and forth in pleasure she had never imagined. And then she felt something new there, something warm and wet, which made her feel that she might faint with the pleasure. She opened her eyes and saw that it was his tongue that was giving her such intense delight.

"Lord," she whispered as he loved her with his mouth and tongue. She shuddered with ecstasy as she felt something rising within her, as if a warm candle were passing its glow throughout her. She bit her lower lip to keep from crying out when the intensity overwhelmed her, not understanding it at all when her whole body trembled with the pleasure of the moment.

When this subsided, she opened her eyes and stared in wonder up at Eagle Hawk lying on top of her. She was not even shocked that he was now unclothed and moving his body atop her. He smelled clean and fresh, like the snow and wind, and she realized that he had bathed away from her somewhere so as not to embarrass her.

When he nudged her legs apart and she felt his swollen member probe where she still throbbed from pleasure, her blood quickened and she did not deny him anything. She framed his face between her hands and drew his lips to hers. She kissed him softly, then cried out against his lips when she felt a stabbing pain as he filled her with his hardness.

Eagle Hawk kissed her more passionately, causing her to forget the pain and soon realize that it was replaced by something wonderful. As though having done it a thousand times, she wrapped her legs around his waist and met his thrusts with abandon. She moved with him, pulling him deeper and deeper. His hands soon found her breasts and kneaded them.

The spinning sensation flooded Susan's body, and Eagle Hawk could not hold back any longer himself. He plunged into Susan more energetically, and when the explosion of rapture seemed to spread to every cell of his body, he smiled when she responded in kind, her climax as strong as his.

Afterwards, Eagle Hawk rolled away from Susan, yet could not keep his hands from touching her, afraid that if he closed his eyes, she would not be there. He had wanted her for so long. It scarcely seemed real that he had finally shared such wonders with her. Now he had to convince her that she must stay with him and be his princess!

Susan, unashamed over what had transpired between herself and the man of her midnight dreams, turned to fit her body next to his. She closed her eyes in happiness, loving the feel of his warm, sleek, copper skin next to hers. She reached a hand around and cupped his shrunken manhood, then did something she would have never thought herself capable of. She moved to her knees, bent over him, and kissed that part of him that had given her such bliss. When his shaft trembled at the touch of her lips, she circled her fingers around him and began to move them, watching, amazed, as the shaft grew to a length that seemed impossible.

Smiling mischievously, she looked up at Eagle Hawk. When he smiled back and placed his hands on her waist and lifted her atop him, she sucked in a wild breath as he thrust his renewed hardness inside her.

As he bucked up into her, beginning his rhythmic thrusts again, half lifting her from him, Susan held her head back so that her hair tumbled down to almost touch his muscled thighs, and welcomed again the joys of being in truth with the man of her heart, instead of just in her sweet, savage dreams. Never again would her dreams be the same, for now they would take her farther than before, to heaven and back again with ecstasy.

Chapter Five

The wigwam smelled of many varieties of pots of food sitting in the coals around the fire pit. Susan smiled from one Indian woman to the next as they sat wide-eyed, watching her every movement as she began making valentines for each of them. In payment for her sharing this talent with the women, they each had brought an offering of food for Susan.

She and Eagle Hawk had just dressed when Yellow Rose had lifted the entrance flap and stuck her head in, announcing that she had brought many friends with her on this cold early morning to see the lovely papers that Susan had made.

When Eagle Hawk had nodded his approval,

the wigwam had quickly become filled with giggling women and tantalizing aromas from the pots of food they carried.

A leisurely breakfast had been shared among them all, and then Eagle Hawk had retired to the back of the wigwam to paint on his buckskin canvas. Every once in a while Susan could feel his eyes on her, making her insides hot with memories of what they had shared almost the entire night.

Even now, while her mind was attentive to the women, her heart felt like soaring, as an eagle might feel in flight high in the heavens, weightless and happy.

"It is good that you show us how to make the pretty papers now, but as I was asking yesterday . . ." Yellow Rose paused to give her brother a slight frown for having disrupted her conversation the day before, then continued. "Next February you will not be here. Can Yellow Rose and friends come to the fort? Will you trade with us? Will you take pretty beaded necklaces for pretty valentine papers?"

Next year? Next February? Susan pondered to herself, looking slowly over her shoulder at Eagle Hawk.

She blushed and swallowed hard when she found his eyes on her. He had heard the question and was surely waiting to hear her answer.

Their feelings were so strong for one another, how could she ever leave him? This time next year she would so want to be living here among these lovely people, as Eagle Hawk's wife.

Although she was wearing an Indian dress, and her hair was braided long down her back like the women in his village, Eagle Hawk had not made any mention of the possibility of her staying with him as his wife.

She hoped with every beat of her heart that he was not using her to warm his bed in winter, just to send her away and never be thought of again once the snows melted.

She now realized that she could never be happy with anyone else, or anywhere else.

To her own astonishment, Susan already felt as though she were a part of the Chippewa.

Wrenching her eyes away from Eagle Hawk, not wanting to think about ever having to leave him, Susan looked at Yellow Rose. "It would please me very much to trade the fancy papers with you next February for your lovely beadwork," she said softly. "But, Yellow Rose, even if you don't have the papers to make the valentines, there are other ways to do it that are just as lovely. Would you like to know how?"

"*Ay-uh*, yes, tell us," Yellow Rose said, the others anxiously nodding as Yellow Rose smiled at each of them. "Please tell us how, Susan."

"Bouquets of flowers can be gathered in the fall of the year and pressed into a heart picture to save for Valentine's Day," Susan explained. "Flowers and herbs are enduring expressions of love, fidelity, and caring."

When Susan saw how intently the women were listening, she laid her valentine paraphernalia aside and continued. "The pansy at first was pure white, but became a rich purple when it was pierced by Cupid's arrow. The pansies' sweet little faces suggest the visages of loved ones—it is the flower that can make a lover think of you. Long ago, the Celts brewed a love potion from the pansy's heart-shaped leaves, which were also thought to cure a broken heart."

"Tell us more," Yellow Rose said, scooting closer to Susan. "It is all so beautiful a tale."

Susan smiled warmly, gave Eagle Hawk a glance, finding his eyes approvingly on her, then continued. "On Valentine's Day, anyone who places a bay leaf under the pillow and dreams of love will be married within a year if she remembers to chant this little couplet first: 'Saint Valentine, be kind to me, in my dreams, let me true love see.'"

Susan was stopped when she noticed bright rays of sunshine smiling down upon her from the opening in the domed ceiling of the wigwam. Her heartbeat quickened as she realized the meaning of the sun.

The snows would begin melting.

She would be returning home.

She was torn with feelings. She was anxious to let her parents know that she was all right. But she hated saying goodbye to Eagle Hawk.

She did not want him just to be a part of her dreams again. She wanted to be able to touch and hold him.

She was afraid that if she returned home, this wonderful bliss that she had found in the arms of the man she loved would be lost to her forever. He had told her that he had loved her for one full year, and yet he had not come forth to tell her so. She was afraid that if she left, he would become shy again and would turn his back on her because of their different cultures and beliefs. Surely, only while she had been with him, stranded, had he been able to forget all the things that should keep them apart.

Susan was aware of movement behind her. Her mouth parted in surprise when the women quickly rose and left the wigwam. She turned and saw the reason. Eagle Hawk had come up behind her and had surely given the quiet nod which they knew the meaning of—that he wanted to be alone with his woman.

When he offered Susan a hand, she took it and rose to her feet before him, so taken again by his dark, fathomless eyes and handsome, sculpted features. He placed his arms around her and drew her close, his lips moving toward hers.

Closing her eyes, Susan became awash with ecstasy as Eagle Hawk kissed her, his hands gently disrobing her. When she felt the soft buckskin of her dress slink down the full length of her body and settle around her ankles, she became breathless with desire. She twined her arms around Eagle Hawk's neck and clung to him as he lowered her to the bulrush mats.

"My *gee-wee-oo*, my woman," he whispered huskily as he eased his lips from hers. He gazed into her eyes as his hands slid over her trembling body. "You are *neen-nee-dah-ee-een*. Stay with me, *ah-pah-nay*, forever. Be my wife."

Susan had not understood all that he had said, but had certainly understood his question, and now realized that his love for her was as strong and as deep as hers was for him. She swooned at the thought of marrying him, of waking up every morning in his arms, and of going to bed with him each night with the promise of making love.

"I want nothing more than to marry you," she said softly, brushing his lips with a kiss. "But, darling, have you thought it all out? Would your people accept me at your side—a woman with white skin and red hair? You are their chief. Would they not expect you to choose a woman of your own skin color? A woman who would give you children that would be in your image, instead of . . . instead of . . . possibly with white skin and red hair? Would such a child born of me be scorned in the eyes of your people, instead of accepted?"

He touched her hair almost reverently, making sure to avoid the lump on her scalp that was now all but healed. "Your hair the color of the sun is beautiful," he said. "Who could not admire it? As well as your skin that is as white as the fairest clouds of spring."

He leaned his lips to her eyes, kissing them closed. "Your eyes are beautiful as the skies," he whispered. "My people will accept all these differences in you and any child born of you, because they see the beauty of these things about you, as well as your kindness toward them. A child born of you will be adored by all. So do not fret, my love. You worry about things that make no sense. Say that you will be mine. Let me show you then the truth of my words."

Susan had listened raptly, her heart pounding as his hands wandered from breast to breast, then across her trembling stomach, to cup the throbbing center of her desire. When he slowly thrust a finger inside her, she sighed and laid her head against his chest.

The rhythm of his heartbeat matched her own pounding, erratic beats. She clung to him and moved her hips in unison with his slowly thrusting finger, lifting her somewhere separate from herself in a slowly spiraling ecstasy.

There was no way that she could say no to him.

She could never deny him anything.

She knew how to say "yes" in Chippewa and used it now, for the first time, when it would be most important to him.

"*Ay-uh*, I will marry you," she whispered. "Oh, darling, I want nothing more in life than to be your wife."

He moved his fingers away from her passion's center and with both arms pulled her to him so tightly that her breath was robbed from her.

His lips came down upon hers with such an explosion of passion that Susan was stunned, then returned his kiss in kind. They clung to one another, and then he eased his lips away and loosened his grip on her.

Instead of saying anything, Eagle Hawk responded to her agreement to marry him by loving her with his lips and tongue in maddening ways. She gripped his shoulders and cried out when the ecstasy began to overwhelm her.

He then rose above her and parted her thighs with a knee. With eyes dark with passion and a heart pounding as though many drums were beating inside his chest, he thrust his throbbing manhood deep within her and began his rhythmic strokes.

She twined her fingers through his hair and drew his lips back to hers. Their tongues met as they kissed. Their bodies strained together hungrily, sucking at each other, flesh against flesh, as he pressed endlessly deeper.

Eagle Hawk's hands went to her buttocks, finding them smooth and soft as she strained into him. His spiraling need spread through him like wildfire. He kissed her more intensely, his mouth urgent and eager. His hands moved to the soft swells of her breasts, and then his lips were there, fastening over a soft, pink nub, sucking it hard.

Susan cried out with pleasure. Her body arched to his, and soon both of them clung fiercely to one another as that most wondrous, joyful bliss overcame them.

Afterwards, Eagle Hawk was hesitant about letting her part from him. He knelt above her, his hands framing her face. *"Gee-zah-gi-ee-nah?"* he asked softly.

Susan gazed rapturously up at him, knowing that what he had asked her meant much to him, for it showed in his eyes and in his voice. She covered his hand with hers. "Darling, I don't understand you when you speak to me in Chippewa," she murmured. "Please ask me again."

"I asked if you loved me," he said, placing a soft kiss on her lips as he took her hand. "*Ah-szhee-gway*, which says, 'Let me hear you say it.' Tell me that you love me."

Susan sighed, her whole being floating on clouds. "You know that I do," she said, twining her fingers through his hair, again drawing his lips close to hers.

"*Ah-szhee-gwah*," he persisted, his breath hot on her lips.

"I love you," she whispered, delicious shivers melting through her when his lips came to hers hot and demanding.

Enfolding her within his arms, Eagle Hawk once again entered her with his swollen, throbbing shaft. His groans of pleasure fired her passion. Her breasts tingled with aliveness when he cupped and began kneading them, his tongue soon there, tasting and licking them to taut, pink peaks.

As the feelings built within her, Susan placed her hands at his cheeks and drew his mouth back to hers, seeking his lips with wild desperation. As he took her mouth by storm, he worshiped her body with his hands. His fingers pressed urgently into her flesh and then with fierceness he held her close.

He drove into the yielding silk of her, over and over and over again, feeling the climax drawing near. He stiffened, then plunged into her more deeply.

Together they shuddered, the climax intense, almost violent.

When it was over, Susan lay panting beneath Eagle Hawk worn out by the repeated love-making. As he rained kisses on her eyelids and hair, tears splashed from her eyes.

Startled, Eagle Hawk leaned away from her. "Why do you cry?" he asked.

"Because I am so happy," she murmured, drawing him back down over her as though she needed his protection. She dreaded leaving him for any amount of time. She dreaded having to *tell* him that she must leave, but she must. She had to set things straight in her other world, which included a mother and father—and a man who was perhaps planning to give her a ring on the night of the Valentine's Day dance.

"Hold me," she murmured, clinging to him. "Please hold me."

Eagle Hawk drew her into his embrace and cuddled her next to him. "Your voice does not sound happy," he said, stroking her satiny back. "What is it? Tell me what burdens your heart. It should be soaring like a dove because we have proven our love for one another. You have said that you will marry me. Have you changed your mind? Do you not wish to be my Chippewa princess?"

"Princess?" Susan said, leaning away from him and looking into his dark eyes. "I will be a princess?"

Eagle Hawk shrugged nonchalantly. "I am chief, you will be princess," he said. "Does that not please you?"

"A princess," Susan said, sighing. She lay back down and cuddled close to him again. "*Ay-uh*, I want nothing more than to be your princess. But . . ."

She paused and she could hear his breath quicken. He leaned away from her and stared down at her. "Finish what you have to say," he said, his voice drawn.

She sat up and drew a blanket around her bare shoulders. "Darling, I will marry you, but I must first go and tell my parents about it," she said guardedly. She saw the immediate hurt that appeared in his eyes. Perhaps even a lack of trust. "It would not be fair to them if I didn't explain my feelings about you to them. And then, darling, I shall return and marry you. Nothing or no one will stop me."

Eagle Hawk rose quickly to his feet. He drew on his breechclout in angry jerks. "If you return to your people, they will not allow you to come back to me," he said. "If you leave, I go with you. I will stay in the forest, just beyond the fort walls, and wait for you."

Susan felt as though she were getting deeper and deeper into what might seem to him a lie, yet she knew what was proper, and she had no choice but to do it.

"Darling," she said, going to him. She placed her hands on his cheeks and directed his eyes down to her. "If I promise you that I will come to you, I will. But I must be allowed to do it in my own way. I need time with my parents to make them understand. You know . . . how forbidden it is for white women to marry Indians. I must make them know and love you by telling them over and over again about you. By the time I return to you, I hope my parents will love you and respect you the same as I."

Eagle Hawk placed his fingers on her shoulders, causing the blanket to slip away from her to the floor. His dark eyes roamed slowly over her, then he looked into her eyes again. "This man you were making the valentine for," he said in a low growl. "You will see him? You will give him the valentine, as planned?"

Susan wanted to forget her promise to Thomas that she would attend the dance with him. But after he had traveled so far for this reason, she did not see it as fair to deny him this one last time with her.

But how was she to make Eagle Hawk understand without making him jealous, and oh, so deeply hurt?

"All that I can say about this man, Eagle Hawk, is that I have never loved him," she murmured. "I have given you my heart, my darling. The piece of paper I made for Thomas is nothing in comparison. So please don't fret so over him, or the valentine that I only half-heartedly made."

"You will still give it to him?" he growled. "You will still attend the dance?"

"Darling, this is one thing I cannot back

away from without causing many hurts and embarrassments," she murmured. "Please try to understand."

His eyes gleaming with anger, the vein throbbing at the base of his throat, Eagle Hawk turned his back to her and doubled his hands into tight fists at his sides. . . .

Chapter Six

Water was dripping from the trees all around Susan and Eagle Hawk as they made their way through the forest on horseback toward Fort Louis. They had begun their slow trek through the melting snow early in the morning, and scarcely a word had been spoken between them. When Susan had put on the dress she had worn on the day of her accident and handed Eagle Hawk the buckskin dress, that had seemed to be the last insult, fueling the fires of his anger.

She had tried to explain that returning the dress did not mean she would not return to him, but he had not listened to reason, and she had half-heartedly followed him to the horses and mounted the one assigned to her for the trip back to her parents. He simply did not trust her, it seemed. He truly did not believe that she would return to his arms.

He believed that her parents would stop her at all costs.

"Eagle Hawk, please say something," Susan pleaded, gazing at him, flinching when he gave her another silent, angry stare.

Quickly she turned her eyes away and reached to draw the hood of her fur coat more securely around her face, needing to do something to busy her trembling fingers. She felt that she had lost Eagle Hawk, perhaps forever.

Yet she had no choice but to be fair to her parents by sharing her plans with them. She knew they would be disturbed by the news, but would come to accept what she was so determined to do.

Now, she had only Eagle Hawk to convince, and had run out of words that could make him believe that nothing would stop her from coming back to him.

It seemed that their different customs and beliefs might be what was causing his anger. Perhaps in his culture, a daughter always did what her parents told her.

Susan had been an obedient daughter, yet when she felt strongly about something, and knew that it was right for her, her parents had not interfered, except to offer advice, which she had always welcomed.

"All right then, be stubborn," Susan blurted out, giving Eagle Hawk a heated glare. "Don't say anything. Don't believe me when I say I will come back to you. I shall prove it by doing it. I shall be back in your arms soon. Just you wait and see."

Eagle Hawk still said nothing, only gave her a frown, then stared straight ahead to keep from seeing the frustration in her eyes. He wanted to believe her. But it was hard for him to understand why she did not stay *now*, and send word to her parents that she had chosen to stay with him.

To him, that would be the better road to take, rather than risk it never happening at all. *Ay-uh*, he had known of other white women marrying Chippewa braves, but only after many trials and tribulations to make their marriages accepted by the white community. Chief Yellow Feather had married a white woman named Lorinda many moons ago. They'd had a son named Gray Wolf who now lived among the St. Croix band of Chippewa with his white wife not far from Eagle Hawk's own village of Chippewa.

Ay-uh, their marriages had worked out well, but for himself, for Chief Eagle Hawk, he did not want to trust anything to fate. Since Susan had already been in his village, and had partaken of food and held hands with him, which was all that was required to bring two hearts together in marriage in the Chippewa manner, it did not seem right that she should leave.

He had not told her that in the eyes of *Wenebojo*, the Great Spirit of the Chippewa, she was already his wife. Since she was determined to return to her parents, he was just as determined not to share this secret with her. She was his wife, but for now the secret was locked within his heart. In case she did not return to him, he was not going to be humiliated by her knowing that she was turning her back on her *husband*.

"It is not far now," Eagle Hawk finally said, tightening his fingers around the horse's reins, the leather biting into his cold flesh. His heart throbbed as he looked over at her. "It is not too late to turn around and return to my village."

Susan's sad eyes when she looked his way was Eagle Hawk's answer, and tore at his heart. He glowered and nudged his horse with his knees and rode away in a faster trot, wanting to get to the fort swiftly and get it over with.

Susan snapped her reins and hurried her horse after Eagle Hawk. When she came to his side again, she looked at him, ready to apologize, but her eyes were drawn away by a movement in a break in the trees a short distance away.

Susan placed a hand over her eyes to shield them against the sun and stared at the horsemen quickly approaching across an open meadow. Her heartbeat quickened, and she gasped when she recognized the man in the lead.

"Thomas!" she whispered, paling. Then she saw her father riding beside Thomas, leading many soldiers behind him.

Eagle Hawk spied the approaching band also. He drew a tight rein and stopped his horse. His pulse racing, he gazed at Susan, then at the horsemen again. "Your father," he mumbled.

"*Ay-uh*, my father," Susan murmured.

Her use of the Chippewa word seemed an insult at this moment. Frowning deeply, he leaned his face into hers. "You have chosen the white man's road, so do not speak in Chippewa," he snapped. "It sounds like a forked tongue!"

Stunned numb by his reaction, Susan's lips parted and her eyes widened. "Darling, I . . ." she began, but his hand covering her mouth sent chills of despair through her, for she felt for certain now that she had lost his love.

"The word *darling* should be used for the white man you made your valentine for," he said, then yanked his hand away. He wheeled his horse around and rode away in the opposite direction of the horsemen.

Susan turned and watched him, tears streaming from her eyes. "Eagle Hawk," she whispered to herself. "Why . . . ?"

Her thoughts were quickly interrupted and she was catapulted back into the life she had known before she had met Eagle Hawk. She wiped tears from her eyes and smiled as her father and Thomas drew rein on each side of her. She looked from one to the other, waiting for the onslaught of questions, knowing that they had seen Eagle Hawk there with her, and perhaps had detected his anger.

"God does answer prayers," her father said, leaning to wrap a thick arm around her. "You're all right. Your mother and I both thought . . . the worst. The storm. We thought you might have perished in the snow."

"No, I'm quite well, Father," she said. She looked over his shoulder at Thomas, feeling nothing but affection for him, feelings that a sister had for a brother. Her father hugged her so hard, she almost toppled from her horse.

Then her father drew away from her and stared past her at Eagle Hawk who was still in view through the trees. "Wasn't that Chief Eagle Hawk?" he asked, his bulkiness making him look squatty and strange in his saddle.

"Yes, that was Eagle Hawk," Susan murmured, hoping that the sudden warmth of her face would not be detected by either her father or Thomas. But neither of them were looking at her, both too engrossed in watching Eagle Hawk.

Although her father was a colonel in the Army, he never wore fancy uniforms. In charge of an outpost far from any superiors who might demand that they go by set rules, he made his own rules and wore what was comfortable— fringed buckskins, coonskin hats, knee-high leather boots, and heavy fur coats to ward off the cold.

As for Thomas, he sat straight in the saddle, tall and slim. He always wore the most expensive clothes, and a heavy wool cape instead of a coat.

To Susan, he was handsome, yet his chin was too pointed and his nose too long. His eyes were golden brown and always seemed to be dancing, his personality pleasant.

To change the subject from Eagle Hawk, Susan edged her horse closer to Thomas's. She reached out a gloved hand toward him. "Thomas, I see that you made the journey to Minnesota without mishap," she said, glad when he turned his eyes from Eagle Hawk's departure. "It's good to see you again."

"Knowing that you were waiting for me, I did not even notice the hardships of the journey," Thomas said, politely kissing her gloved hand. Then he gave her a worried look. "When your father told me you were missing, I had to join the search for you. It was terrible to have to wait for the snow to melt. I wanted to leave the moment I heard that you were out there somewhere, perhaps freezing, or perhaps . . . even . . . already dead."

"Your concern touches me deeply," Susan murmured, glancing down at the satchel secured to the side of her saddle, dreading having to give him the valentine.

And, just perhaps, she might not have to. It all depended on whether she had a chance to talk to her mother and father in private.

The only problem was that this was the night of the dance. She would not have much time, if any, to take her mother and father aside to tell them her plans.

Yes, she would attend the dance with him, because it was the right thing to do, but that would be the last time she would be escorted to anything by him.

Unless Eagle Hawk turned his back on her totally. Then she might give Thomas a second chance, if only to have a means by which to forget Eagle Hawk.

"You were with Eagle Hawk?" her father asked, reaching a hand to her chin, moving her eyes to his. "You were with his people all this time? Did one of his warriors find you and take you there?"

Susan swallowed hard, wanting to blurt out everything to her father now, but with Thomas and all of the soldiers watching and listening, she could not.

"My horse stumbled in the snowdrifts and threw me," she said. She reached a hand to her head, where the lump was no longer in evidence. "I was knocked unconscious. Chief Eagle Hawk came along and rescued me. He took me to his village. His sister treated my head wound and gave me food. I was treated quite well until the snow began melting. Then Eagle Hawk himself escorted me this far. When he saw you approaching, he left for his village."

"That's strange," her father said, kneading his chin thoughtfully. "That man deserved my thanks. Why didn't he stay to receive it?"

Susan's heart skipped a beat and she swallowed hard, not knowing how to answer him without revealing her feelings about Eagle Hawk. And she had never been skilled at telling lies. Yet he was waiting, his deep blue eyes on her, seemingly looking inside her heart for the answers she was denying him.

"Why?" she said softly. "I'm not quite sure."

"I've always had a good relationship with Chief Eagle Hawk," her father said, shrugging. "Perhaps he'll tell me why he avoided me the next time I see him at the fort."

"Yes, perhaps he will," Susan said quietly, then was glad when her father wheeled his horse around and gave the command to his soldiers to head back toward the fort.

Thomas edged his horse around so that his was right beside Susan's. He gave her a wide grin as they began riding across the meadow, where the snow was now only a thin layer of white. "It's good to be with you again, Susan," Thomas said thickly. "I'm glad to have the opportunity to escort you to the dance. I hope we get back to the fort in time."

Susan smiled weakly at him. The talk she wanted to have with her parents was much more important to her than a mere dance.

Chapter Seven

A string quartet had journeyed from St. Paul and their music wafted through the throng of people waltzing in a large room that was bare of carpet and furniture. Susan's long, wavy red hair bounced on her shoulders as she danced with Thomas, her floor-length silk dress swirling around her ankles as they continued circling the floor in time with the heavenly music.

Susan smiled weakly up at Thomas, even though he was perhaps the most handsome man in the room with his expensive suit and diamond stickpin in the cravat at his throat. His blond hair, worn to the top of his stiff, white collar, was combed to perfection, and his cheeks shone from a fresh scrubbing and shave. The aftershave he wore had the fragrance of something brought from France, it was so divine.

Yet Susan could not loosen up and enjoy herself. Having to be there at all made her stiff and anxious. She had not arrived home soon enough to talk to her mother and father about Eagle Hawk. Her mother had swept her up into her bedroom and had begun fussing over her clothes and her hair, telling her about the many couples who had already arrived for the Valentine's Day ball from near and afar.

When Susan had fussed back, saying that she had something of great importance to tell her mother and father, her mother had told her to go ahead and tell *her*. She would then discuss it with her father while Susan danced the night away with handsome Thomas.

Not wanting to rush into telling just one of them her secret, Susan had clammed up and decided that after the dance would have to be soon enough. When she had stared back at herself in the mirror, she did not see herself in the soft silk dress with its low-cut bodice displaying the gentle upper swells of her breasts, and a waistline that most women would kill for. She instead envisioned herself in the intricately beaded doeskin dress that had clung to her figure, and knee-high moccasins that matched the dress. When her hands had gone to her hair to lift its thickness from her shoulders, she had so wanted to braid it and place a headband around her brow, to go into the ballroom and announce that this was the way she would look from this day forth, and she was proud of it!

Her mother's voice had broken through her reverie, bringing her back to the present. Downhearted, she had gone with her mother down the steep stairs, stopping with a start when she found Thomas waiting at the foot, his hand extended toward her, his smile bright.

It had been hard to force herself to go on down the stairs and accept his hand. It had been even harder to go into the parlor where everyone stopped and stared at her and her escort. She had always been told how lovely she was. This night, by the way everyone had stared, she had almost believed it, except that she knew that there was much lacking in her smile, which she hoped no one would notice.

Now, dancing with Thomas, she gazed at her father's desk that had been shoved against a far wall. She had placed the valentine that she had made for Thomas there, along with all of the others that the women had brought tonight. Soon the valentines would be distributed. That was the moment she dreaded. The gesture might be all that was needed for Thomas to believe that he had a chance with her. And if he had brought a ring with him from Michigan, that might be when he would present it to her.

She desperately hoped not. She had gone far out of her way tonight, by going to the dance with him, to make sure that he would not be embarrassed. She could not go as far as accepting his ring.

The music ceased. By her elbow, Thomas led Susan from the dance floor. "Are you ready for some refreshment?" he asked as he ushered her to the sidelines, where they stopped and stood among the others who were waiting for the music to begin again.

Susan smiled up at Thomas. "*Ay—*," she began, but stopped herself before saying the Chippewa word. She quickly said instead, "Yes, I would like that very much, thank you. I'm quite thirsty."

Thomas nodded and walked away from her. Susan began fidgeting with her skirt, shifting her feet nervously, her eyes scanning the crowd for her mother and father. When she caught sight of them on the far side of the room, dressed elegantly and talking with several people, she frowned. It seemed that everyone else but her could get their undivided attention. She wanted to stomp over to them and take their hands and lead them away from the crowd to speak her mind to them, yet she had to spare *them* embarrassment tonight, too.

As the minutes ticked away, she was growing tired of pleasing everyone but herself. She was not sure how much longer she could stand this charade. Her heart throbbed at the idea of just up and running away and being done with worrying about what her parents might say over her pronouncement of loving Eagle Hawk.

What would it gain her, anyhow? she despaired. They would just give her a lecture, which she would get no matter what she did at this point if it had anything to do with Eagle Hawk.

They wouldn't understand.

No one would understand.

In truth, it was the world against her and the man she loved.

Just when she thought she would flee and be done with it, someone stepped to her side.

"Susan, oh, I'm so glad to see you," Jana said, flinging herself into Susan's arms. "I didn't know about your mishap until only moments ago. All of the time you were in the Indian village, I thought you were home, safe. Was it horrible, Susan, to have to live like a savage those days you were stranded?"

Susan hugged Jana, then eased from her arms, thinking to herself, *You, too, Jana? Even you look upon the Indians as savages? Won't even you understand when I announce my feelings for Eagle Hawk?*

Knowing the answers without asking, and disappointed in Jana for having such callous feelings, Susan tried to force a smile.

"No, it was not horrible at all," she said. "The Chippewa were very kind to me." She cleared her throat nervously and felt a blush heat her cheeks. "Even more than that, Jana. They treated me as though I were . . . a princess."

"A princess? Really?" Jana asked, shoving her spectacles farther back on the bridge of her nose, her eyes wide. "They . . . they . . . did not threaten you in any way?"

"Not at all," Susan said stiffly. "In fact, I became close friends with one of the women. Yellow Rose is one of the sweetest women I've ever known."

Susan wished she had not been so direct in her description of feelings for Yellow Rose, for she saw an instant hurt in Jana's weak, gray eyes.

But then, the hurt was perhaps deserved. Jana had spoken unknowingly of the Chippewa. Susan's declaration of friendship toward a Chippewa woman should be proof enough of the gentleness of those people, for they would have to have treated Susan kindly for her to feel as close to them as she confessed.

Jed came to Jana and took her hand, his dark eyes gleaming into Susan's. Susan was embarrassed that she had not asked Jana about his welfare, now remembering how frightened Jana had been when he had been somewhere out in the blizzard the same day that Susan was.

But no questions were needed now. There he was, all muscle and brawn and ruggedly handsome in his dark suit and highly polished boots, his golden-red hair hanging down to his shoulders. He did not seem the sort to ever have any trouble, with man *or* nature.

"My, but aren't you beautiful tonight," Jed said in his warm way of speaking, his dark eyes moving approvingly over Susan.

Then just as quickly he placed an arm around his wife's waist and drew her close to his side. "Sweetheart, have you told Susan the good news?" he asked, adoration shining in his eyes as he gazed down at his wife. "You said that after me, she was going to be the first to know about our little surprise."

Susan's eyes widened. "Surprise?" she asked, looking from one to the other. Her eyes locked with Jana's, seeing a radiance in their depths. "Tell me, Jana. We're not supposed to keep secrets from one another. We promised. Remember?" Then she felt the deceit of her own secret, which no one yet knew, now especially Jana since Susan knew her friend's feelings toward the Chippewa.

Jana took Susan's hands and squeezed them. "Susan, since I last saw you, I became certain that I am pregnant," she murmured. "I suspected it earlier but I didn't say anything, fearing being disappointed and not wanting to disappoint you, also, if it were not true. The doctor came as soon as the snow began melting. He examined me. Oh, Susan, Jed and I are going to be parents."

The news brought tears to Susan's eyes. She drew Jana away from Jed and hugged her. "I'm so happy for you," she whispered. "Oh, Lord, I am so very, very happy for you."

Deeply within her heart, she so envied Jana. In her dreams she would be pregnant with Eagle Hawk's child. That would be the most wondrous of all of her sweet, savage dreams!

Susan's mother's voice was suddenly heard addressing the crowd from the center of the dance floor. With a skip of her heartbeat, Susan realized that it was time for the women to go and get their valentines and give them to their special men.

When Thomas returned with two glasses of punch, just as Susan's mother told the women to get their surprises from the desk, Susan felt trapped, knowing for certain now that she could not give Thomas the valentine, no matter how much embarrassment he would have to endure.

She had been wrong to carry this charade this far. She could not, would not, go any farther with it.

Lifting the skirt of her dress, Susan began pushing her way through the crowd. She could hear Thomas shouting her name, and Jana's voice speaking her name questioning.

Ignoring them both, Susan rushed to the desk and slid the front open. With trembling, shaking fingers, she sorted through the valentines until she found hers, then held it to her breast and ran from the room. She had decided that if anyone were to have this special valentine, it would be Eagle Hawk! Only he was her special man. She would be lying if she gave it to Thomas.

And even if Eagle Hawk turned his back on her forever, she now knew that Thomas, or any other man, could never be a substitute for the man she loved.

If Eagle Hawk did not want her, then she would grow old alone!

Her parents' frantic voices came to her above the shocked whispers of the crowd as everyone watched Susan, frantically fleeing away from them all. Since the staircase leading to her bedroom was blocked by people, the only escape was the outdoors.

Grabbing her shawl, she ran outside into the cold February night and did not stop until she came to a cluster of pine trees, to hide behind. She wanted to get her breath and summon her courage to face her parents with their humiliated looks and pounding questions. And so be it. If this was the only way she could get them alone, for her to tell them of her feelings for Eagle Hawk, well then, that was the way it had to be!

At least it would be done and over with and she could return to Eagle Hawk and begin life anew with him, a life of learning and loving among the beloved Chippewa.

Her only fear, still, was that perhaps he would no longer want her. But she brushed those fears aside. She must, to keep her sanity, she thought sadly.

Clutching her valentine to her heart, she started to step out into the open in full view so that her parents would not be forced to search frantically for her, but stopped when someone else was there, blocking her way.

"Eagle Hawk," she gasped, gazing up into his midnight dark eyes. Her gaze shifted to something rolled up in his hand, which she quickly recognized as one of his hide canvases. She gazed into his eyes again.

"You did not wait for me to come to you?" she murmured. "You came for me, instead?"

"*Ay-uh*, that is so," Eagle Hawk said, his eyes shifting, stopping at the valentine she held between her hands. Then he looked slowly up at her with a look that she could not define in the dark cloak of night.

"You did not give your pretty paper to the white man?" he said thickly, his heart racing at the thought she might have changed her mind.

"*Gah-ween*," she murmured, glad she had remembered how to say "no" in Chippewa. "I didn't. It was made for my special man. Thomas is not special to me in any way." She quickly held it out for him. "Please take it, Eagle Hawk. It truly should be yours, for you are the only man special to me, now and forevermore."

A smile fluttered on Eagle Hawk's sculpted lips. He took the valentine, then thrust the rolled-up canvas into her hand. "You are my special woman," he said softly. "This is my valentine for you."

A thrill grabbed Susan's insides as she held the rolled canvas in her hands. "Mine?" she said, her voice breaking as she gazed up at him. "You've made a valentine for me?"

She was glad that the moon had slipped from behind the clouds so that she could see his handsomeness and the pleasure that her gift had given him. His look was one of complete peace and radiance with the knowing that she was his, for all eternity.

"*Ay-uh*, it was made for you with much feeling," Eagle Hawk said, clutching his valentine, planning to always cherish it among his most beloved belongings of a chief. He nodded toward the rolled canvas. "Open it. See how I give you my heart in paints."

Hearing voices drawing closer, knowing that her parents had taken the time to dress warmly on this February night before searching for her, Susan knew that time was running out. When she heard Thomas's voice, Susan did not want to have to offer lengthy explanations. She wanted to go to Eagle Hawk's horse and flee. She would do as he had suggested earlier. She would send her parents a message with the news of her marriage to this powerful, handsome chief.

"Can I wait until we get to your village before unrolling the canvas?" she asked anxiously. "Eagle Hawk, take me away now. Quickly. My parents and Thomas are almost here. Let's not place ourselves in the position of having to give them explanations they will not want to hear. Please, Eagle Hawk. Take me to your horse. Let's escape into the night."

Eagle Hawk placed a hand to her cheek, adoring her, then grabbed her free hand and led her to his horse tethered a few footsteps away. As though she were no heavier than a feather he lifted her onto his saddle, then mounted behind her.

Hurriedly he slipped his valentine and his gift to her into his buckskin bag that hung from the side of the saddle, then plucked the horse's reins from a low-hanging limb. Before he had a chance to ride away, Susan's mother and father were there, shouting for Susan, desperation in their voices. Thomas was also there, pale and drawn and with keen wonder in his eyes.

"Susan, what do you think you're doing?" her mother asked, looking small and frail against the backdrop of night.

Susan, torn with feelings, did not know quite how to begin her explanations. She looked guardedly from her mother to her father, and then to Thomas, her gaze shifting quickly from him and back to her father as he took a step closer.

"Eagle Hawk! Susan! What is the meaning of this?" he demanded, his eyes never leaving Eagle Hawk. "Susan, get off that horse this minute," he quickly added without giving Susan or Eagle Hawk a chance to explain.

"Father, Mother, I tried to explain earlier that I had something to tell you," Susan said, holding her chin proudly high, not giving an inch in her determination to leave with Eagle Hawk tonight. "You didn't allow it. All you could think about was the valentine's ball. So I'm sorry that I was forced to go ahead and do as I pleased without sharing it with you."

"What on earth are you talking about?" her mother asked, her voice drawn. "Was it about this Indian? Was he what you wanted to tell us about? If so, daughter, what on earth could you have to say that has anything to do with him?" She lowered her eyes, then lifted them slowly up again. "You are behaving shamefully, Susan. Get off the horse. Return to the house with me."

Susan and Eagle Hawk were suddenly aware of soldiers pressing in on all sides of them.

Susan gave Eagle Hawk a look of warning.

He nodded, understanding her meaning.

He snapped his horse's reins, wheeled his horse around, and rode like lightning toward the open gate as he clung to Susan in front of him.

"Susan, don't!" Thomas cried.

"Susan! Oh, Lord, Susan, please don't!" her mother cried.

Susan turned her gaze over her shoulder. "I must, mother," she shouted in return. "I love Eagle Hawk. I'm going to become his wife!"

It tore at Susan's heart to see her mother collapse in a dead faint. A part of her wanted to go back to tell her mother that it was going to be all right, that what she had chosen to do with her life was right. But deep within her, where her wants and needs were formed, she knew that she could never turn back. She was where she belonged, and her parents would have to learn to accept it.

When a soldier raised a gun and shot at her and Eagle Hawk, Susan screamed and cast her father a look of bewilderment. Then she relaxed inside when she heard her father shouting to the soldiers not to fire. She then heard him shouting orders for everyone to return to their posts.

She knew that he was not going to send anyone after her.

Eagle Hawk kept his horse at a fast gallop. Looking back, Susan could barely see her father stooping and picking up her mother. And it was obvious that her mother had regained consciousness, Her sobs and wails sending the message to Susan's heart that perhaps her mother would never accept her daughter into her life again.

"We do not have to ride far," Eagle Hawk said as he pulled Susan closer to him. Her hair was lifting in the wind, the perfumed smell of it almost driving Eagle Hawk wild as it caressed his face. "I knew that you would come with me. I prepared a fire in a cave not far away. I have a change of clothes for you. My woman, I have much news to share with you that will make your heart sing."

"News?" she asked, giving him a glance over her shoulder.

"Soon I will share it with you," Eagle Hawk said, smiling down at her.

Susan returned his smile, her contentment building as she was able to brush the troubling thoughts of her parents from her mind. As the breeze picked up the hem of her silk dress and whipped it wildly around her ankles, she felt the chill wind waft upward, chilling her.

Yet she smiled to herself that Eagle Hawk had been thoughtful enough to bring her a change of clothes and to prepare a warm fire for her. She was glad that he had felt so confident that she would choose him over Thomas after all. He had surely pondered this long and hard in his mind and had concluded that never could she love anyone else.

And he had been oh, so right, she laughed softly to herself.

They rode only a short distance and then Eagle Hawk led his horse into the wide entrance of a cave. Once inside, Eagle Hawk tethered his horse and lifted Susan from the saddle.

After taking the buckskin satchel from the horse, Eagle Hawk draped an arm around Susan's waist and led her farther into the cave until they reached the fire, where many animal pelts were spread luxuriously soft and warm-looking around the fire.

Eagle Hawk lay his satchel aside, then turned to Susan. Removing her shawl, he tossed it aside, then reverentially began disrobing her. She felt the warmth of the fire as she stood nude beside it, her fingers now working at disrobing Eagle Hawk. First his floor-length fur coat, then his breechclout, and then his moccasins, until he, too, stood sleekly nude beside the fire, his sinewy, gleaming body setting Susan's heart to throbbing.

"My wife, I will show you my gift to you, and then let us concentrate on making a child for us to cherish until we walk hand in hand on the long road of the hereafter," Eagle Hawk said thickly.

"You called me your wife," Susan said as Eagle Hawk stooped and picked up the satchel.

Eagle Hawk gave her a dancing smile. "You have been my wife since you partook of that first meal with me and locked your hand to mine," he said as he slowly unrolled the hide canvas.

When she did not answer, but just stood staring at him with wide eyes and parted lips, he leaned closer to her face, their lips only a heartbeat away. "Does that not please you?" he asked as he brushed a soft kiss across her lips. "That you are already my wife in the eyes of *Wenebojo*, the Chippewa's Great Spirit?"

Susan was at first stunned by the news, then found it wonderful to know. It made everything so perfect, that she was already his wife. "*Ay-uh*, it pleases me," she said, leaning her lips up to his to give him a soft kiss. "And I won't ask you why you didn't share this with me earlier. I believe I know."

"*Ay-uh*, you do," Eagle Hawk said. Then finally he unrolled the last roll in the canvas and turned it so that she could see the painting.

Susan stood with her lips parted as she viewed the painting in the soft light of the fire. It was a painting of herself dressed in a white doeskin dress, and at her bosom, nursing, was a baby, its skin copper, with a full head of hair as black as a raven.

And standing behind her and the child was Eagle Hawk dressed in his full chieftain regalia, looking handsome and proud.

"Why, it's a family portrait of what it might be in a year," Susan said, deeply touched by the painting, and amazed at the likeness of herself and Eagle Hawk. Not only was he a wonderful man, a marvelous lover, and leader of his people, he was a greatly talented artist.

"Oh, thank you, darling," she murmured, holding the painting to her heart. "I do love it so."

She gazed up into his eyes ever so seriously. "This does portend the future, doesn't it?" she murmured. "This is the way it will be?"

"*Ay-uh*, that is the way it will be," he said, gently taking the painting from her.

He lay it aside, then eased her down on her back on the animal pelts. His eyes burned with passion as he gazed down at her and then kissed her.

A delicious languor stole over Susan as his kiss deepened. She twined her arms around his neck, arched her hips, and opened herself to him as he plunged inside her. She clung to him as he moved rhythmically within her, his groans of pleasure firing her passion. His each stroke promised more, assuring everything that she had ever wished for in her sweet, savage dreams.

For a moment he became still. He leaned a fraction away from her and framed her face between his hands. "*Mee-goo-ga-yay-ay-naynda-man*," he whispered, gazing with a loving devotion into her eyes.

"I don't know what you said in Chippewa, darling," Susan whispered, splaying her fingers onto his buttocks, urging him to begin his thrusts within her again.

As his body rhythmically moved, he touched her tongue with his, then lay his cheek against hers. "My darling, in Chippewa I said you are my happiness," he whispered. "Now, *ah-szhee-gwah*, let me hear you say it to me."

Susan shivered with rapture as she felt the warmth spreading through her as his thrusts moved more quickly and deeply. "*Mee-goo-ga-yay-ay-nayn-da-man*, my darling husband," she whispered back.

He smiled down at her, then gathered her into his arms and held her tight as their bodies quaked and rocked together sensually, having once again found the wonders of total bliss together.

Afterwards, as Susan lay snuggled in Eagle Hawk's arms, she smiled to herself, knowing that she no longer had the need for her sweet, savage dreams. She had the real thing, forever and ever.

SHIRL HENKE

"Billie Jo and the Valentine Crow"

For my own Southern valentine, Jim Henke, who prefers women to ladies—thank goodness!

Chapter One

July 1885, A westbound train, Dakota Territory

It was a hell of a note when a body didn't even know what her husband looked like. Maybe he was plug ugly as an Ozark polecat. Or fat as a five-hundred-pound hog. Billie Jo Mingo stared disconsolately out the sooty window of the speeding train. The landscape blurred in monotonous flatness. She was grateful for nightfall, which at least brought some surcease from the merciless heat.

"How in Johnny Blue Blazes did I get myself into this pickle?" she muttered beneath her breath, twisting the thin gold band round and round on her finger. A low throaty croak came from the canvas-covered box at her feet. "Easy there, Pecker, easy," she soothed, glancing surreptitiously around her. The old drummer in the seat behind her let out a sharp burst of snoring, then subsided. Everyone slept.

When the rustling noises emanating from the box ceased, she breathed a sigh of relief and again stared morosely out the window. Billie Jo could see the dim reflection of a small heart-shaped face in the dirty glass. Did she look as pale now as she had the previous week when she had stood in the Dade County Courthouse and recited marriage vows before that stern judge? Willis had stood as proxy for her groom, so far away in the wilds of Montana Territory. She shivered in spite of the heat, while the enormity of events in her twenty-year-old life caught up with her.

"Wanted: A wife for an established stockman and widower. Young woman from good family, of high moral character and utmost gentility, accomplished in all the domestic arts, to raise his young daughter. References essential. Write to Jason Lee Emory, Miles City, Montana Territory." That was what the Joplin newspaper had said. "Accomplished in all the domestic arts" indeed! Well, Billie Jo opined she *could* bake a mean peach pie and beat biscuits fluffy as summer clouds, but gentility? Good family?

It was her shiftless, good-for-nothing brother who had railroaded her into this nightmare in the first place. Gloomily she recalled the night Willis had approached her with that want ad for a mail-order bride. For once in her headstrong life she could solve all his problems, he'd said, if only she would see reason. He wanted to marry May Bell MacDougall.

"What you really want is to get your hands on her daddy's general store," she had snapped at him.

His thin, ruddy face had suffused with heat as he huffed that he truly loved May Bell, but she had made her feelings crystal clear. Before she would wed him, his crude, troublemaking spinster sister must go. Since sister and brother shared a small cabin on the outskirts of town, that presented a considerable problem.

"You should be married by now," he had whined. "Would've been, too, if'n it warn't for Pa spoilin' you rotten, treatin' you like you was a boy."

"If I'm so terrible, how do you think you could get that fancy Jason Lee Emory to take me?" she had shrilled, but the implication was clear. When their ma had died six years ago, their pa had turned to drink, spending his few sober hours in the woods, hunting and fishing, always a jug of his home-brewed corn likker at his belt. Billie Jo had sought to comfort him, spending her days skinning squirrels and rabbits, gutting deer and catfish. Dressed in boys' britches, she had learned to shoot and cuss and spit. For a while life seemed to be fun again, before the likker got a real strong hold on Pa.

Willis had smiled nastily at her question. "Oh, I know this Emory feller will take you. Aunt

Pearline'll write me a letter 'n' I'll send a picture of Cousin Wanda Lou in your place. Now, she looks like a real lady."

"I ain't going to Montana Territory to marry some stranger!"

"Are too," Willis had said with a hard, crafty glint in his eyes. "Pa's up in the hills, drunk at that still. Sheriff's been lookin for it nigh onto six months. Election comin' up real soon. If I was to . . ." Willis had been ready to betray his only sister and his father, all for May Bell MacDougall's miserable general store.

Everything had happened in a blur after that. Letters were exchanged, references sent from the most respectable folks in southern Missouri, even one from Aunt Pearline's cousin Joshua who was a federal judge—all attesting that Billie Jo Mingo was a paragon of ladylike virtue. She snorted in derision. Well, she had played along with them, knowing she could never bear the look in Pa's eyes if the sheriff arrested him and told him Willis had turned him in. But she had concocted her own plan. She had married Jason Lee Emory by proxy and boarded this train to Montana Territory, but when she arrived, she would not be a demure corseted little wisp of femininity. No sirec.

Billie Jo had brought along her old hunting clothes, a skinning knife, and a Colt revolver. She planned to get off the train dressed in her grubbiest shirt and britches, armed to the teeth, spitting and swearing, until the stodgy, proper old Mr. Emory had an apoplectic seizure. She would then offer him her bargain—an annulment in return for enough cash money to give her and Pecker a grubstake to the silver diggings down in Colorado.

Smuggling Pecker onto the train had been a mite tricky, but Willis had said he was well rid of the thievin' crippled wretch. Pecker was the only friend she had left, and she was counting on him to help her scare the gallopin' galoshes off Jason Lee Emory!

Billie Jo had found the baby crow in a meadow with a badly broken wing two years ago. Pecker never did learn to fly; he could only flap his wings and crash into whatever or whoever was luckless enough to be nearby when the notion to try seized him. Raised on a diet of milk-soaked cornbread and wild game, he had grown into a veritable monster, standing nearly two feet tall with a wingspan of over a yard and a beak large enough "to drive nails in a horseshoe," as the town blacksmith said. His keen black eyes were alight with intelligence— and he was the best thief in three counties.

Staring out the window of the speeding train, she replayed every detail of her plan in her mind. She could pull this off. She *had* to— or stay saddled with a fat old cowman and his snooty daughter for the rest of her life. Timing was everything. She had to pretend to be a respectable lady until the train drew near Miles City. If they put her off, Lord only knew what might happen. Thinking of the endless stretch of arid wasteland, peopled only by wild animals and red Indians, she shivered. "I never knew there could be so much of nothing."

No, she must wait until the last stop before her destination, then use the awful cramped "convenience" in the caboose to change her clothes, arm herself, and free Pecker from his prison. Rubbing sweaty palms on the itchy calico of her skirts, she leaned back and tried to sleep.

The train stopped with an abrupt lurch after its gradual slowdown at the water stop, jarring Billie Jo awake. People were rising and wiping sleep from their eyes. Some shuffled off the train to purchase food from the vendors crowding the depot platform. Most of the fare offered was greasy or stale and always expensive. Billie Jo had brought along her own food, but she was not hungry just now.

Instead, she watched with fascination as the fancy-looking woman from the private sleeping car breezed past her to alight on the platform. Several other older, respectable matrons whispered behind their hands as they sniffed at her perfume. Billie Jo had heard their clacking tongues say she was a "scarlet poppy," a dance hall entertainer en route back to her place of disreputable business in Miles City. If so, the business must furnish her a handsome living. Billie Jo wondered what gawdawful amount of money it cost to rent one's own private sleeping car, with its very own convenience, no less!

The woman was a tall brunette with a bold, handsome face, carmined lips, and kohled eyes. Her dress was made of yellow silk, cut low enough to reveal a lot more of her ample bosom than was seemly.

The fleeting thought about the convenience led Billie Jo to consider that this was a good time to use it, while most folks were off the train. She looked down at Pecker's box and decided no one would be fool enough to try and steal him, then rose and went to answer the call of nature.

Once finished with her essential business, Billie Jo approached the open railing of the caboose and looked out on the raucous scene about her. Children chased dogs, who begged food from vendors. Mothers wiped spilled milk and fried chicken from the faces and clothes of their offspring. Here and there a nearly naked red Indian lounged, gazing impassively on the spectacle. Billie Jo watched the kaleidoscope of color and movement, her own troubles momentarily forgotten.

A shriek from inside the train quickly reminded her of it. When the scream was followed by a loud, belligerent cawing, Billie Jo flew through the cars toward her seat. Bellowing shrieks and high-pitched caws grew louder as she reached the general passenger section.

"Eek! Get away from that, you thievin' beast! You ain't goin' ta git the last o' my ham sandwiches." A fat woman dressed in floral-printed calico wielded a parasol with uncommon skill, thrusting its sharp point toward Pecker, who was flapping from side to side, trapped between two of the passenger seats. Beneath him was a large open hamper of food. The napkin wrapping its contents was partially uncovered and caught on the big crow's talons.

Pecker snapped at the parasol and raised his wings, although his movement was greatly impeded by the narrow confinement of the horsehair seats.

"Ouch! The rabid vulture bit me! It bit me! I know I'll die of poisoning! Take that! And that! You—"

"Leave him be! He's only hungry," Billie Jo cried as she wrested the parasol from the red-faced, perspiring female, who then backed away and plopped onto a seat cushion, which whooshed out all its air with a loud groan.

Holding her hand where several small punctures were oozing blood, Calico Dress began to sob. "It's done poisoned me. I'll get the rabies."

"No, you won't—at least not from Pecker. He's my pet," Billie Jo replied as she reached out one hand for the big bird.

Pecker looked down consideringly at the sandwiches in the basket, then eyed her, cocking his head quizzically as if saying, "Well, what do *you* have to offer me?"

"You damnblasted rascal," Billie Jo muttered beneath her breath as she realized the screeching encounter had drawn a crowd, including the conductor, who was scowling at her with narrowed eyes. She quickly darted across the aisle and grabbed a hunk of cheese from her carpetbag, then laid it on the seat beside Pecker. As soon as he had seized his prize, she freed the linen from his foot. When she placed her fist on the basket, he perched on it and she lifted him, depositing him neatly in her seat across the aisle.

"What is that critter?" one man asked in a voice filled with awe.

"Looks like a black bear with a beak and skinny paws," another replied.

"There are no critters allowed on this train except in the baggage car, young lady," the conductor said gravely.

"It bit me! I'm poisoned." Calico Dress held her meaty fist up for the conductor's inspection.

"I can't put Pecker in the baggage car. He'll just unlock the cage and come looking for me. Besides, he might get hurt all alone in there." Billie Jo faced the conductor bravely, standing protectively in front of her crow, who was unconcernedly devouring the cheese.

"Humph, more like he'd wreck the rest of the baggage. I think you had better leave the train, miss—that, or get rid of this . . . crow." The conductor eyed the big bird with distaste.

"No! I can't leave him—and you can't put me off the train. I'm on my way to Miles City. My husband, Mr. Jason Lee Emory, is expecting me. I'll keep Pecker in his cage. He only got out because I went off and left him." Her heart sank to her toes as his slate eyes hardened and he shook his head.

The fat old sow in the flowered dress continued to babble on about having her hand amputated and dying of lockjaw, when suddenly a low, musical voice interrupted.

"I'd be happy to offer Mrs. Emory the use of my car for the duration of the journey."

Everyone turned amazed eyes to the infamous madam, Adele Wheaton, who stood beside the conductor with a secret smile curving her beautiful lips.

"Beggin' yer pardon, Miss Adele, but I don't think—"

"Why, Emett, surely you don't believe that poor crow will eat me, do you? I can assure you I've dealt with a lot more dangerous two-legged critters in my day."

"Well . . ." The conductor looked dubiously from Miss Adele back to Mrs. Emory.

"You say you're married to Jason Emory?" he asked dubiously.

"Yes. By proxy back in Missouri. He'll be powerful mad if I don't arrive on time," Billie Jo added with bravado, delighted with the scandalized expressions of the potato-faced women in the crowd.

"Well then, it's all settled," Adele said. "Mrs. Emory, please gather up your crow and follow me. Emett, please fetch the rest of her things, won't you?" With that, Adele Wheaton turned imperiously. Billie Jo followed her. Pecker gave Calico Dress a baleful glare as they left the car.

The crowd cleared with great alacrity to let them pass.

"Glory be! If this ain't the beaten'st thing— kinda like the palaces Sir Walter Scott wrote about," Billie Jo said with wonder as she ran her hand over the quilted satin coverlet on the bed and gazed at the silk curtains covering the windows.

Adele chuckled. "Not quite so grand as all that, but it'll do. Why don't you put your things in the bottom drawer of that armoire while I send for some refreshment?" She watched the crow for a moment as it waddled about the room and then perched on a footstool. "Er . . . he won't . . ."

"Aw, no. He's housebroken," Billie Jo replied cheerfully. "He'll go in his cage to do his duty. I change the papers every night. I'm much obliged to you, ma'am, but if you don't mind my askin', why did you offer to help us?"

Adele smiled at Billie Jo. "Perhaps I found the idea of a girl with a trained crow to be amusing. Lord knows it's a boring enough ride from St. Paul to Miles City." She paused, then shook her head and said, "Truthfully, it was more what you said to Emett that piqued my curiosity. You've married Jason Emory—by proxy?"

A guarded look came into Billie Jo's eyes. "You a friend of his?"

"Let's just say I'm acquainted with him. Everyone in eastern Montana is. He's one of the richest cattlemen in the territory." She eyed the small, slim girl in the dusty brown dress who stood nervously twisting the gold band on the third finger of her left hand. Jason's wife was a bedraggled waif, soot covered and wrinkled from her days on the train.

"Well, I'm right glad to hear he told the truth about his ranch 'n' all in that newspaper ad."

"So, he did advertise back East for a wife." Adele was certain this pale little hill girl with her pet crow was not what Jason Emory had in mind, but she was not sure how to break the news to the child. Chuckling, she envisioned Jason's face when he found his new wife ensconced in *her* car! "What's your first name? I'm Adele. We needn't be formal."

"I'm Billie Jo Mingo—er, Emory."

"The name may take some getting used to," Adele replied, patting Billie Jo's hand.

"Not so much the name as the feller it's attached to," the girl replied glumly.

A sharp rap sounded and the steward entered with a tray. Uncovering the silver dishes, he set out a feast of cold roast pheasant, potato salad, and crisp pickles, all the while assiduously avoiding the big bird hovering in the corner. He scurried from the room as soon as he'd poured the white wine. The two women sat down and began to eat as Pecker watched restively.

"I'll be real honest with you, Adele," Billie Jo said as she tossed a piece of French bread to the crow, "I didn't want to marry a stranger. Hell, I didn't want to marry anyone. Shoot, he's probably as old as my pa and fat to boot."

Adele choked on the bite of pheasant she was swallowing and quickly washed it down with some wine. "What makes you think Mr. Emory is old—or fat?" She dabbed at her lips with a napkin to conceal her amusement.

"Well, any man who has to advertise to get himself a wife can't be a bargain."

"I think you may be in for a surprise, Billie Jo," Adele replied. *So will Jason*.

On the last night before they reached Miles City, Billie Jo confided in Adele about her plan to get Jason Emory to give her an annulment and a grubstake. "So, you see, I gotta put on my britches 'n' carry my guns 'n' pig sticker. He'll take one look at me and run the other direction."

"Are you so certain that's what you want?"

"Now, don't go tellin' me about how fine-looking and rich he is again. I never aimed to get hitched, especially to the likes of some cattleman too uppity to even bother lookin' for his own wife."

"With a big ranch to run and a small daughter to care for, Jason couldn't just pack up and go East to court you, Billie Jo." Adele considered the mulish expression on the spunky girl's face. Billie Jo Mingo was full of surprises. For all her crude speech, she was amazingly well educated, having read everything from Homer and Cicero to the latest popular novels. When Adele had offered her the luxury of her bathtub, she had observed that Billie Jo's figure was certainly well formed and her ratty red hair fell to her hips in lush waves.

"So you plan to scare him off, do you? What if it doesn't work? Jason and his father settled this land, fought rustlers and Indians to carve out an empire. He doesn't frighten easily."

"I can do it—and Pecker can help."

A slow smile infused Adele's face as she envisioned the encounter. It might just be fun to see Jace taken down a notch or two.

Chapter Two

Jason Lee Emory stared at the small picture in his hand, trying to see beyond the banal expression on the vapidly pretty face of Wilma Joanne Mingo. She looked proper enough, he supposed, tightly laced up, her back ramrod straight and her hair neatly piled in a smooth pompadour atop her head. He wondered what color it was, then cursed his own stupidity. "I'm acting like some lovesick schoolboy," he muttered as he slid the dog-eared photo into the vest pocket of his suit. He'd dressed like a fool swain, too—in a brand new suit with a fresh haircut and shave.

Damned if he didn't know better. He had courted Callista in the traditional manner, but he'd been a green boy then. Leaving his pa to run the ranch, he had dallied in Virginia, convincing the beautiful belle of Richmond to abandon her home and family to become a cattleman's wife. He had won her.

But now he was a seasoned loner. Pa had died a year after he'd married, around the same time Charity was born. A little over a year later came little Seth, who only lived a scant six months. Callista grieved so, blaming the harsh Montana winter for the baby's croup. Within another year she, too, was gone. He was a widower with a small daughter to raise.

Charity was a beautiful child who desperately needed a mother. She could not be allowed to run wild, and Jason didn't want her growing up lacking the womanly graces that were her heritage. Neither could he bear to part with her and send her to Richmond for education.

No, he would keep Charity with him, provide her with a mother to teach her, and provide the Circle E with an heir who could one day run the big spread—a son to make up for the tragic loss of little Seth. This marriage would be a good thing, both for Charity and for him. At least he prayed it would.

Jason checked the gold watch on its chain, then replaced it in his pocket. The train was late. Again he was assailed by doubts. His lawyer back in Joplin had assured him everything was quite proper. He had checked into the girl's family with Judge Joshua Whitherspoon, who said they were fine upstanding folks. And, after all, a young lady all alone could hardly journey over a thousand miles unescorted unless she had the protection of his name.

He wondered why she had never married by the rather substantial age of twenty years, then dismissed the idea. He wanted no simpering child bride, but a woman of common sense and strong propriety to guide his daughter. He could hardly have that unless she was a bit on the shelf. Just then a whistle echoed in the distance and a thin gray plume of smoke appeared on the horizon.

He waited anxiously as the train pulled into the station. All the passengers filed off in a steady trickle, but he saw no lone female bearing a resemblance to his new wife. Never a patient man, Jason stalked over to the conductor. "Emett, there was supposed to be a young lady aboard." He fished in his pocket and showed the photograph.

"So you did go and get hitched. Be damned. Don't look much like her, though. She's—." Suddenly realizing where the new Mrs. Emory was, Emett blanched and froze.

"What the devil's the matter with you, Emett? Is my wife aboard or not?"

"Well . . . yes. We got us this here private sleeping car. She's stayin' in it."

"I didn't know there were any Pullmans on this run or I'd have booked it for Mrs. Emory. How did she get the use of it? Was it vacant?"

"Nope, no sir, not exactly vacant . . ."

Emory looked at the conductor in exasperation. "Make sense, man. Oh hell, never mind, I'll find her myself," he said and climbed aboard the train.

Jason quickly made his way to the fancy new sleeping car and raised his hand to knock on the door. A familiar voice from the other side caused him to freeze.

"I don't really think the weapons are necessary, Billie Jo." Adele's voice held a hint of a chuckle. "Pecker is quite sufficient."

Without further ado, Jason flung open the door and entered. "By all that's holy, Adele Wheaton, what is going on?" His eyes swept from the beautiful owner of the Paradise Saloon to the slight figure standing beside her—dressed in a plaid shirt and britches! His eyes narrowed and his expression turned to granite as he took in her appearance. She looked like one of those Irish immigrant waifs he'd seen on the streets of Chicago, all big green eyes and freckles. Her hair was bound in a ratty plait that hung over one slim shoulder. The shirt and pants were so baggy he could tell nothing about her build except that she was barely over five feet tall.

Billie Jo stood rooted to the ground, staring at the incredible-looking man. He was not old. He was not fat. But oh, Adele had not done justice to exactly what he was! Perhaps no one could. She had never seen a man in Missouri who was so tall and broad-shouldered, yet lean, with thick wavy black hair and steel blue eyes. His face was burned dark by the sun, the features chiseled in perfect proportion, hawkish and harsh yet virilely beautiful. For a fleeting moment Billie Jo reconsidered her plan, but his arrogant stance and forbidding scowl quickly made her realize that such a foolish fantasy would never serve.

"Jason, may I present your wife, Billie Jo," Adele said with a theatrical flourish.

"My wife's name is Wilma Joanne, not Billie Jo," he said tightly.

"That there's just a name Willis and Aunt Pearline thought up. My pa named me after himself—William Joseph Mingo, only with me bein' a girl, Ma convinced him to call me Billie Jo." She stood, legs spread apart, hands on her hips, daring him to dispute her name.

Pecker let out a loud caw, chorusing his agreement.

"What the devil is *that*?" Jason turned to the huge bird and nearly dropped the photograph he'd fished from his pocket.

"That's my crow. Name's Pecker. He goes with me. Everywhere," she dared him.

"Well, you're going nowhere until you change those disgraceful men's clothes." He looked at her photo and studied her face again. "You don't much resemble your picture."

"That's cause it ain't me. Willis sent that picture of my cousin Wanda Lou. She likes to gussie up in stiff corsets and all that folderol. I don't." She dared him again.

"No wife of mine will walk off the train in britches."

"Try 'n' stop me," Billie Jo said coolly, pulling a wicked-looking knife from her belt.

Jason swore in amazement. What in God's name had he gotten himself into? Better to have married sour old Essie Parker, even spoiled Emmaline Pruett! But no, he wanted a lady from back East! Cursing himself for seven kinds of a fool, he pulled a small .40 caliber Pepperbox from his coat pocket and leveled it at the belligerent-looking crow. Then his steel blue eyes fixed on her and he said, "Now, either you get behind that screen and dress like a proper female or I'll shoot your fat feathered friend and cook him for dinner."

"You wouldn't dare!" She clenched the knife in her hands until her knuckles whitened on the hilt. This wasn't going at all the way she had planned.

"One or the other of us is going to eat crow, Mrs. Emory. You decide who."

Billie Jo stared at that implacable, beautiful face. Were all cattlemen this crazy? No wonder they had so many range wars! Suddenly her scheme to stampede Jason Emory into annulling this marriage seemed rather unrealistic. "Damn Willis and Aunt Pearline to blue blazin' hell!"

She threw down the knife and stomped toward the dressing screen, while her mind whirled frantically, looking for a way out of this tangle. Then she saw the glint of her old

Sharps carbine leaning against the wall near the dressing screen.

"Damnblast it, Adele, get me a dress out of my trunk, would you please? It don't matter which." She walked behind the screen, making a big production of shucking her boots and unbuttoning her shirt.

Jason slid the gun into his pocket and scowled at Adele as she crossed the room to the trunk. Before he could say anything, Billie Jo leaped from behind the screen and seized her rifle. He crossed the space between them in a split second, shoving Adele out of the way and seizing the rifle by its barrel. He flung it onto the floor and tried to subdue the scratching, gouging hellcat. She swore some remarkable oaths, shrieking at the top of her lungs. Jason seized both her small wrists, pinning her flailing legs between his, and held her head immobilized by a fierce grip on her braid.

Pecker, who had observed the tense confrontation erupt into such a violent melee, decided it was time to intervene. He flapped his wings, rising a foot or so off the ground in a poorly aimed lunge that landed him behind Jason's booted feet. Not wasting his time on hard leather, he reached up and sunk his beak into the much more tempting target of his adversary's backside.

A stab of agony in his right buttock caused Jason to loose Billie Jo and whirl in amazement before the cawing, dancing bird.

"Don't you dare hurt him!" Billie Jo shrieked,

hurling herself onto his back and boxing his ears. The crow now flapped up again, that long, sharp beak drawing blood from Jason's fist as he attempted to punch the creature out of his way.

Adele stood flattened against the wall, choking with laughter as the three embattled protagonists made a shambles of her elegant car. Finally Jason managed to get the girl between him and the lunging beak of the crow, who subsided to wait for an opening.

"Call him off or so help me I will kill him—in self-defense." He held her in one arm with a breath-squeezing grip around her waist while he waved his other bleeding fist in front of her face.

Totally disarmed, bruised, and humiliated, Billie Jo saw stars before her eyes as he tightened his grip around her ribcage. "All right, all right. Let me breathe so's I can talk." When he loosened his hold, she said, "Pecker, back."

The crow cocked his head quizzically for an instant, then backed off into a corner. Jason shoved her toward the dressing screen and bent over to pick up her rifle. A searing pain in his buttock made him grimace. That damn bird had sunk in his beak clean to the bone! Warily he watched the beast as he gathered up her weapons. Then he turned slitted eyes on Adele. "I suppose you're enjoying this?"

Wiping her eyes, Adele subdued her laughter. "It did get a little dangerous for a minute, but frankly, Jace, I wouldn't have missed seeing this show for all the silver in Comstock." She handed a dress over the screen to Billie Jo.

Jason searched the room, found the ancient Colt, and added it to his arsenal. He limped with as much dignity as he could to the door. Leaning against it, he inspected his bloody hand and swore. "Get me some water and bandage this," he commanded Adele in a deadly tone.

While Adele did as she was bidden, he looked toward the screen at the opposite end of the car.

"I'll give you exactly five minutes to dress decently or I'm coming in after you—and this time I'll take care of the crow first. Do I make myself clear?"

"As Ozark spring water," Billie Jo replied. In an act of defiance, she refused to wear the corset.

On the way to the hotel, Jason debated about how to broach the subject of his wife—he cringed at the word—associating with Adele Wheaton. "I realize Miss Wheaton did you a kindness when she shared her private car with you," he began hesitantly.

"Saved Pecker 'n' me from bein' put off the train."

"I shall be forever grateful to her," he said grimly, then persevered. "You do realize she's not the sort you should socialize with, don't you?"

She looked up at him measuringly. "You mean because she's a whore?"

"Lower your voice!" He realized he was shouting. "That's a rather bald way of saying it, but far be it from you to sugar the medicine. A girl from

123

a good family—one with the Emory name," he amended, "shouldn't even know women in her line of work."

"But you know her, don't you, 'Jace'?" She smirked with a cynical grin that belied her years. "In the biblical sense, I'd just bet." She was rewarded when his face reddened beneath its tan, but it was a hollow victory. She felt suddenly betrayed, even though she knew all men were alike. Hell, before drink got him, even her pa used to visit old Lizzie LaRue's place.

"What I do has nothing to do with your behavior. You are supposed to be a lady."

"Oh," she said, appearing to consider, " 'n' ladies are supposed to be hypocrites who turn their backs on folks who've done them a kindness."

"You know that is not what I mean." He ground his teeth.

"Ain't it, now?"

They walked in silence to the big white-washed building that proclaimed itself the Excelsior Hotel.

As he signed the registration at the desk, Jason thanked whatever luck he had left that he had reserved two rooms for their first night in town. He had done it out of respect for what he believed would be the maidenly modesty of his bride, deciding to wait until they were settled at the ranch before claiming his husbandly rights.

He spilled a puddle of ink on the hotel registry, shuddering at the thought of sharing a bed with that foul-mouthed, knife-wielding beastmistress. She'd probably slit his throat in his sleep! Feeling her eyes boring into his back, sharp as the crow's beak, he considered how to rid himself of her with a minimum of scandal. Sending her packing on the morning train to Bismarck held great appeal. But no, there was the matter of a very legal marriage to be surmounted. If she simply vanished, he could spend years getting free. Then, what decent woman would consider marrying a divorced man? He cursed again. Perhaps if he handled it carefully, he could talk her into a quiet annulment, but first he had to get her out of town before any more mischief occurred.

Billie Jo watched him sign their names, Mr. & Mrs. Jason Lee Emory. Perversely, she liked the sound of it. On the walk over he had chivalrously carried Pecker's cage, after making quite certain it was securely locked. She didn't tell him the bird could pick any lock faster than a teamster could spit.

Billie Jo was in a quandary, infuriated with his priggish high-handedness, yet forced to admit she had deliberately set out to antagonize him. And he could have shot Pecker. If the crow had ever attacked Willis or Pa as it had her new husband, she knew they would not have hesitated.

When he turned toward her and picked up her carpetbag and Pecker's cage, she was again struck by his handsomeness and the effect his nearness seemed to have on her. Awkwardly she followed him upstairs.

"This is your room. I'll be just across the hall. After such a taxing day, I imagine you'll want to retire early. I'll have a tray sent up with dinner for you."

He turned to leave, but her words stopped him. "You're ashamed of me, aren't you?" Why in blue blazing hell had she asked that?

Jason paused and considered the impertinent urchin standing so bravely in front of him. "Let's just say I don't want any repetition of that fiasco in the rail car."

"You arrogant bastard, do you always get your way?"

One black eyebrow raised at the epithet. "You prove your own assertion, Mrs. Emory," he said, his voice dripping with sarcasm. "How on earth did you manage to furnish all those letters of testimony to your gentility and erudition?"

"Willis did it."

"I should have known," he replied drily. "The clever fellow who sent your cousin's photograph."

"Well, it wasn't my idea to marry you, that's for sure. I was blackmailed into it, all because my brother wanted to get rid of me."

Jason rolled his eyes heavenward. "I can't possibly imagine why." He yanked open the door and left, slamming it with a sharp crack.

Billie Jo Emory stood in the middle of the big room, never having felt so alone and confused in her life. Pecker opened his cage with a few adroit maneuvers of his beak and stepped out, ruffling his feathers and looking at her.

"Caw." He regarded her with interest, hoping for another treat.

"Oh, shut up," she said crossly, kicking the chair in front of her as she began to pace.

Jason spent a restless night mulling over whether or not to take Wilma—no, Billie Jo—to the ranch. Billie Jo. Even her name was crude. He punched his pillow and willed his problems to go away. All he saw when he closed his eyes was the small, wistful face of his daughter, who had such high hopes for her "new mommy." He swore again and started to turn over when a hysterical female shriek nearly caused him to snap his spine as he jerked upright in bed.

Rolling from beneath the thin sheet, completely naked, Jason seized a pair of denims from his satchel and jumped into them. The shrieking continued. He grabbed a Colt from the satchel and checked it, then flung open the door and stepped into the hall. The sight that greeted his eyes elicited a groan of pure misery.

Billie Jo was attempting to placate the screaming woman who had apparently gotten up early to visit the ladies' convenience at the end of the hall. "It's only my pet crow. He brings these mice in all the time. I reckon I didn't feed him enough last night."

The thin old woman with the incredible lung power was not reassured. Her eyes bugged out of their sockets and she continued to yell, moving away with her back flattened against the wall.

"Damnblast," Billie Jo muttered. By this time all the doors up and down the hall were opening with heads peering out. Ignoring them, the girl, barefooted and clad in a tattered robe, stalked to the rear stairs where the culprit causing the commotion stood. Pecker had a very large mouse firmly clenched in that long beak of his. It hung limply, obviously quite dead.

"He steals them from traps," Billie Jo said with a nervous smile at an elderly man she passed en route to the crow. "He won't eat them, just brings them to me to sort of make a point. So's I'll give him somethin' he really wants, like a cookie or a hunk of buttered cornbread." She reached down and grabbed the crow's head with one hand, then yanked the dead mouse by its tail to free it.

Jason watched in fuming fury while she calmly carried the corpse to an open window and flung it nonchalantly into the back alley. Briskly rubbing her hands, she turned to Pecker and knelt, extending her fist. He hopped onto it and she started to rise, then froze as she saw the bare feet striding purposefully toward her.

Her eyes traveled up the long legs, past narrow hips, slim waist, to a splendid bare chest generously furred with curling black hair. Lordy, he looked tall as a sycamore tree. She rose unsteadily as Pecker fluttered his wings. Jason's face was a stormcloud. Wordlessly he shoved the revolver into his waistband and seized hold of her by her free arm, practically dragging her back to her room.

"Be ready to ride to the ranch within the hour. You do ride, don't you? Or is that something else created in the ever inventive mind of Willis?"

She jerked her arm free, trying to get away from his muscular chest before she made an idiot out of herself by touching the wonderful patterns of black hair on it. "Yes, I ride. I also cuss, spit, and I'm a dead shot."

"You may end up just plain dead if you utter another word of profanity—or spit—or fire a gun. Is that understood?" His voice was low and hoarse.

She shooed the crow into the room, then stood in the doorway to face him. "You don't want to be married to me and I don't want—"

"Frankly, Billie Jo, I don't at the moment care what you want, only that you behave quietly." His icy gaze swept the hallway, and heads vanished behind closed doors faster than a twister could touch down. "We'll discuss this matter once we're at my ranch. I'm certain it can be resolved to our mutual satisfaction."

She gave him a suspicious look, then nodded and closed her door in his face. When she heard his door slam, she leaned against the wall and closed her eyes. For some utterly inexplicable reason, she felt the urge to cry.

Chapter Three

"Be quiet. Be demure. Be a lady. Well, Mr. Jason Lee Emory, you picked yourself the wrong female and that's the truth!" Billie Jo fumed and muttered as she changed into her riding clothes—another baggy shirt, leather vest, and a pair of denims.

"And you, you mangy critter, you stay in that cage. I don't fancy havin' to chase you from here to Canada if you take the notion. Just might leave you for some big fat eagle to swoop down and eat," she added with a petulant glare at Pecker, who merely studied her with keen black eyes.

"Caw." It was neither an argument nor an agreement.

Since her trunk had already been collected by a bellman, Billie Jo stuffed her robe and nightrail into the carpetbag, then picked it up in one hand, Pecker's cage in the other, and headed for the door. He didn't consider her fine-born enough. Damned if she'd wait for *him* to act the gentleman and carry her belongings!

She arrived at the livery just in time to see Jason leading two horses from inside. One was a big rangy-looking buckskin with powerful lines, doubtless Jason's horse. The other was a dappled gray filly, the most beautiful horse Billie Jo had ever seen—a gift for his lady wife, rigged up with a sidesaddle! She set down the birdcage and bag so she could pat the filly's velvety muzzle. Then she looked at Jason with fierce green eyes. "I know you don't much like me, but breakin' my neck with that damn fool sidesaddle ain't fightin' fair."

Jason's eyes swept from her pugnacious expression down her body and back up again. "I told you, no more men's clothes."

"How in hell do you expect me to ride?"

"I also told you no more cussing."

"Then don't provoke me by being so consarn dumb." She reached for the cinch strap.

His hand shot out and seized her wrist, enveloping the slender bones in a crushing grip. "No way do I ride out of town with you in that get-up astride a horse. Now either you put on a riding habit or I'll do it for you, and paddle your backside in the process." His eyes turned from blue to pewter, filled with ice cold anger.

"I don't own a riding habit—and just you try and paddle me." She rubbed her wrist when he flung it back at her. "I'll change into a skirt," she said sullenly and stalked off with her bag.

Jason looked at her retreating figure and swore. One quelling look from his cold eyes sent the crowd of curious onlookers scurrying about their appointed chores. He had manhandled her, something he would never have dreamed he could do to any female, but this small chit of a girl drove him to distraction. He rubbed his aching posterior and cussed some more. "Riding is going to be pure hell, thanks to you," he said to the caged crow.

Back at the hotel, Billie Jo opened the carpetbag and searched for one particular dress—not that she had much of a wardrobe from which to choose. "That's it," she murmured, intent on showing Jason how idiotic his outmoded propriety was.

In a trice she had changed and headed back to the livery. By this time the city streets were bustling with people. Miles City had become a booming cattle town and railhead since the Northern Pacific had arrived. She spied her little filly tied to the corral post by the stable. Jason's buckskin was nowhere in sight. Billie Jo marched resolutely to her mount and swung up into the sidesaddle. Just as she had known it would, the straight cut of the blue gingham skirt rode up, revealing an indecent amount of slim sun-browned leg; even her white cotton pantalet showed up to the knee of the leg caught on the sidesaddle's pommel. She watched as several stablehands leered and two prissy-looking women froze in scandalized horror, staring at her from across the street.

Billie Jo was just gathering the reins when Jason pulled up in a fancy leather-upholstered rig. He took one look at her and vaulted from the carriage. In a couple of swift strides he was hauling her off the filly as she kicked and cursed.

He set her roughly on the ground. "Never in my life have I seen such a display of women's unmentionables in public!"

"I bet you seen lots of women's unmentionables in private, specially Adele Wheaton's," she replied nastily.

"Adele Wheaton is not my wife."

"Lucky for her."

He pointed to the carriage. "Get in. I just rented it. I thought it would be more comfortable—"

She burst out laughing. "I just bet you did! Your backside hurt much when you tried to mount up on that big buckskin?"

Jason knew his face was redder than a coal fire and he couldn't help the slight limp in his gait. "Just climb in and don't say another word or I'll paddle *your* backside until you can't even sit on a padded cushion!" He glared at the onlookers and was rewarded to see most of them nodding their assent, but it was small consolation for his humiliation.

She climbed into the rig without further protest.

They left Miles City with the buckskin and the filly tied to the rear of the rig. Pecker rode in his cage at her feet, and her trunk and carpetbag were in the boot of the carriage. At first Billie Jo said nothing because she was so furious, but as they rode further north toward the Circle E, her silence stemmed from fascination. The countryside was awe-inspiring. The horizon seemed to stretch endlessly in every direction. Rippling waves of thick emerald grass met the vast cloudless vault of azure sky. Here and there a slow, clear creek meandered with fat cattle grazing along the banks. Jagged outcroppings of rock sheltered scrub pines that gave the air a pungent clean perfume.

Watching her rapt face as she drank in the big sky country that he had grown to love, Jace felt constrained to make some conversation. "It is something, isn't it? Montana."

It's the most beautiful place I ever saw," she said quietly. Then realizing that he might construe that as an admission that she wanted to stay, she changed the subject. "Were you born here? You don't talk like it."

"No. My family's from Virginia. My father lost everything in the war. When it was over, he pulled up stakes and moved here. I was eight years old. We went home to Richmond from time to time. Still have lots of kin there."

"You were rebels," she accused. "I knew that buttery accent sounded Secesh."

He looked at her scornfully. "Your family's from southern Missouri."

"That don't make us Secesh. Nobody in three counties around us owned slaves,'n' we weren't dumb enough to fight for them that did."

He gave the team a swat of the reins to speed them up, his mouth thinning as he replied, "Well, ma'am, you won't find any slaves at the Circle E either. Everyone there works to earn his keep."

They rode in strained silence for another long stretch. Billie Jo studied the countryside, and when he wasn't looking, she covertly studied her husband's striking profile. His face was burned copper dark by sun and wind, his eyes, with crinkle lines in the corners from squinting against the brilliance of the sky, were startlingly blue. He stared straight ahead, refusing to look at her. She observed his hands, with their long, tapered fingers, brown and sinuous with fine black hairs on the backs. Remembering how he had looked that morning clad only in a tight pair of denims, her mind conjured up the cunning pattern of hair on that hard, muscular chest and she wondered how it would feel to run her fingers over it. She licked her lips nervously and tried to think of something else.

"How old is your little girl?"

"Charity will be seven this fall." He did not smile, thinking of how disappointed his daughter would be. "She's been anxious to see her new mama," he said with a bitter twist of his lips. Then he sighed. "Look, Billie Jo, you obviously regret this marriage as much as I."

She did not reply, but a sudden lump formed in her throat. Did she?

Taking her silence for assent, Jace continued. "I'll talk to Abe Garner as soon as he gets back from the capital. He's a lawyer and has influence with the territorial government. It won't be easy to get an annulment, but it can be done. It's not as much stigma as if it were a divorce."

"Since I don't plan to repeat the mistake, it doesn't signify to me." She, too, stared straight ahead as they rode on.

When the ranch came into sight, Billie Jo could not hide her amazement. A long sweep of cottonwood trees sheltered the two-storied frame house. The building was freshly painted and gleamed blinding white in the late afternoon sun. A verandah ran along three sides of both stories. Corrals filled with livestock, barns, bunkhouses, and other outbuildings made the place resemble a small kingdom.

"The house looks like an antebellum Greek Revival mansion."

He cocked an eyebrow at her in surprise. "How do you know architecture?"

"You ain't the only one who ever read a book," she replied with a huff.

"From the ungrammatical way you speak, not to mention your vocabulary, I assumed you were illiterate."

"Just some poor white trash hill gal. Well, for your information, Mr. High and Mighty Confederate Cavalier, I got reading. My ma was a schoolmarm before she married Pa. She died when I wasn't much older than Charity."

Charity. Jason was relieved that he'd sent a rider ahead last night to arrange for his daughter to spend a few days with the Kincaid family until he could untangle this coil with Billie Jo. Strange. Every time he thought he understood her, she surprised him with some new facet of her personality.

"Papa, Papa!" A small girl with shiny ebony curls and deep blue eyes came bounding down the front steps and ran to greet them. "Oh, you brought her, truly you did!"

Jace alighted from the rig and scooped her up in his arms, giving her a big hug and kiss. "What are you doing here? I thought you were to spend a few days with Estelle Kincaid."

"Her brother Randolph has the measles. They couldn't take me, but I'm glad! I wanted to be here when she arrived." Charity turned shyly in her father's arms and looked at the small, dusty woman sitting so quietly in the rig. "Hello. Are you my new mama?"

Billie Jo saw hope and vulnerability in those clear blue eyes. What an enchantingly lovely child she was, but so pale, surrounded by all these sun-drenched ranch people. She cleared her throat and smiled. "Well, pumpkin, I don't know about bein' your mama, but for now I'd be proud to be your friend." As she climbed down from the rig with the help of one of the hired men, she could sense Jason's rigid disapproval. He'd tried to keep his daughter from being contaminated by her!

Charity hugged her adored father again and asked excitedly, "Please, can you let me down? I should make my curtsy." She spread the tiered pink cotton skirt as grandly as a ball gown and curtsied to Billie Jo.

Billie Jo returned the favor gravely, feeling awkward under Jason's scrutiny. "You're a lot better at that than I am. Maybe you could teach me."

"Me teach you?" the child piped in surprise.

"Grown-ups can learn all sorts of things from children, if they're not too stuck-up to try." She couldn't resist a glance at Jace as she reached into the carriage for Pecker's cage.

"What's that?"

"My pet crow. His name's Pecker and he's real smart."

Charity looked dubious. "I never heard of a pet crow before. I have a dog. His name's Reddy. He's out with the hands right now. Can I pet Pecker? Will he fly away if you let him out of that cage?"

"He won't fly away. He can't because he has a busted wing, but you can pet him. Here, I'll show you how." She sat the cage down and said to the bird, "All right, Pecker. You can come out now."

"I'll be damn—durned," one ranch hand said, flushing hotly as he watched the bird deftly pick the lock, shove the cage door open, and hop out.

He strolled around, fluttering his wings and preening under all the attention. Billie Jo knelt and stroked his glossy feathers, then urged Charity to do likewise. When she squatted in the dust and petted the bird, Jason said softly, "Be careful of your dress, Charity. Ladies don't get dirty."

At once the child stood up and brushed off the pretty ruffled skirt, then looked at the bird again and said, "I'm pleased to meet you, Pecker. I hope you like Reddy."

Irritated by Jason's chiding of the girl, Billie Jo said, "I'm sure he will, but we'll have to introduce them very carefully. For now he'll need a place for his cage." She looked at Jason with a dare in her eyes.

"Hank can take him to the kitchen—if you can convince him to stay in that cage long enough."

Billie Jo decided it was the best she could ask and quickly coaxed the crow back into his shelter.

Jason introduced her to a multitude of people who worked on the big ranch. Red-faced cowboys with cowlicks mumbled nervous howdies and tipped their hats politely. On the porch stood a tall, thick-set woman with thinning gray hair pulled into a tight bun. Her face was weathered and creased into a broad homely smile.

"Howdy, Miz Emory. I'm right pleased to meet you."

"This is Garnet McCrey. She's our cook and housekeeper," Jason said.

" 'Bout time this young rascal was hitched again." She eyed Billie Jo's dusty traveling dress and bare head. *Why, she's as sun-browned as I am! None of them fancy parasols to shade her face.* "You come with me and I'll show you to yer room. Yew might like to freshen up a bit. Won't be long till supper. The little one here's been drivin' me crazy waitin' for her pa to get here with you."

Billie Jo warmed to the big woman at once, feeling she now had two allies against her formidable husband. "I'm so pleased to meet you, Mrs. McCrey, but please, call me Billie Jo."

"Then yew gotta call me Garnet."

With that settled, the three females entered the house. Jason instructed two of the hands to return the rig to town the next day. They led the horses off for rubdowns at the big horse barn. He hurried into the house, realizing that he had to explain a very awkward situation to Garnet, especially regarding the night's sleeping arrangements.

Billie Jo stood in awe at the door to the front parlor. It was the stuff of dreams, filled with brocade upholstered oak furniture and thick Turkey carpets, even a handsome grandfather clock.

"Most of the furniture has been in my family for several generations. I've added a few pieces over the years. Why don't you let Charity show you the rest of the downstairs while I talk to Garnet about stowing your belongings," he said with a meaningful glance at her.

I can't sleep in the same room with him! Her cheeks flamed in embarrassment as she nodded and turned to the little girl. "Your house is ever so grand. Please show me the rest of it."

Charity was delighted as they wended their way through the big parlor toward an elegant dining room. On one marble-topped table sat a photograph of a strikingly beautiful woman with pale hair.

Catching Billie Jo looking at it, Charity said wistfully, "She was my mama. She died when I was two or so. I don't remember her much."

"She was very beautiful," Billie Jo said softly. "A real lady."

"Papa wants me to be a lady, too, but I don't always behave as well as I should." She sighed. "He needs you to make another boy baby for him. My brother Seth died when he was real little. Papa has to have a son to run Circle E. Girls can't do that."

"Who says so? I've read about girls who run ranches. Some grow up to be lawyers and doctors, all sorts of things—if they want to," Billie Jo replied, remembering some of the dreams from her childhood when her mother was still alive and Pa didn't drink. She refused to think about the prospect of "making a baby" with Jason Emory!

Charity's eyes grew round. "Really?" Then her face fell. "I don't think my papa would like for me to be a doctor or any of those things."

"And you set a lot of store by what your pa likes, don't you?" She already knew the answer.

*   *   *

Dinner was a strained affair. The three of them sat at the big formal oak table with more linen, silver, crystal, and china than Billie Jo had ever seen in her life. Although the china was Haviland and the crystal Heisey, the food was plain terrible. Obviously the first Mrs. Emory had decorated the house and furnished it with the finest. A pity, Billie Jo thought, that there was no cook to do justice to the setting.

Stabbing a lumpy grayish mass of mashed potatoes, she asked, "Has Garnet cooked since your first wife passed on?"

"She always did the cooking. She and her husband Asa came west with my father. Callista didn't cook."

He said it as if it were a task relegated to slaves. Billie Jo bristled. "Well, I do. And I'd love to help out in the kitchen—well, for now." She had almost blurted out *until I leave*.

"You can talk to her about it in the morning," Jace said noncommittally. Then he turned to Charity with a smile. "As for you, young lady, it's time for your bath and then to bed with you."

"Will you read me a story?"

"If you hurry along. Garnet's drawing your bath right now.

"Can I see Pecker first?"

He shrugged stiffly. "If it's all right with Garnet, then off to that bath."

When she had scampered from the room after polite good nights to the adults, Billie

Jo said, "She's a delightful little girl with lovely manners."

Her soft, serious expression took him by surprise. "Thank you. I've tried, but it's difficult without a mother's touch."

"I'm sorry about your little boy." Her face heated as she recalled Charity's rather blunt declaration earlier.

Jace felt something warming deep inside of him as he looked at her. Was it just a trick of the candlelight or did her small heart-shaped face with its luminous green eyes seem beautiful? Her hair was still done in its ratty plait and her dress was ill-fitting and wrinkled. "Yes, well, Seth's death was devastating to my wife and to me. She never recovered."

Have you recovered from her death?

Garnet nervously showed Billie Jo to her room, rather conspicuously down the hall from Jason's. If the shrewd old woman thought this arrangement odd, she kept it to herself.

"You'll be wantin' a bath. We got us a tub up here." She walked over to one corner of the spacious room and pulled a curtain to reveal an elegant claw-footed porcelain hip bath. "I can have Hank and Festus start hauling water—"

"There's a bathroom off the kitchen. If everyone else uses it, I see no reason for the hands to haul all that water upstairs just for me."

"Miz Callista never used the common bath. Said it made her skin break out, like I didn't keep the tub clean enough for her," Garnet volunteered, nodding her approval at Billie Jo.

After the old housekeeper left to prepare the bath downstairs, Billie Jo pondered the mystery of the delicate and apparently spoiled Callista. If this was her tub, why did it sit in a room so far from Jason's? Did she not at least have a room adjacent to his? Or had he had it hidden here because the memory of her in her bath was so painful?

Once she sank into the big copper tub downstairs, Billie Jo tried to relax in the tepid water. She washed her hair and toweled it partially dry, then let it hang over the back of the enormous tub. Obviously it had been built to accommodate a big man. Visions of Jace naked in this small Spartan bathing room made her flesh heat. She squelched the thought. In a few minutes, she dozed.

Pecker, given the run of the kitchen after the food was put away, lifted the door latch with a soft click and entered the room, his black eyes curiously taking in his mistress. Once assured she was resting, he began to explore.

Jason had read Charity to sleep and then discussed some stock purchases with his foreman down at the bunkhouse. He was bone weary and desperately in need of a good soak and a soft bed. Visions of his little hellcat wife sharing the bed with him flashed into his mind as he passed the crow's cage in the kitchen.

He swore beneath his breath. The damned bird had picked the lock again! Just then he heard a ruffling of feathers coming from the bathroom. "If that bear disguised in feathers is in my clean bathwater, I'll wring his neck," he muttered and stormed through the partially open door. He froze directly in front of the big tub at the sight that greeted him.

Billie Jo was awakened by a muffled oath. Jace stood towering over her. She looked around the small room, desperate for a towel to cover her nakedness.

Jace's eyes drank in her small, perfectly formed body, and he instantly reevaluated his opinion about her being a thin little waif. Pert, well-rounded breasts bobbed gently in the water as she sat up with a splash. Her legs were slim, with flared calves and delicate ankles. As she leaped from the tub and seized a towel, he caught a glimpse of a pale firm pair of buttocks, just the right size to fit his palms when he lifted her—*Stop it!*

He commanded his mind to obey, but his wayward eyes continued to feast as she swaddled herself in a towel and glared at him. Unconsciously he took a step toward her and reached for a tendril of fire red hair. "I never imagined there was so much of it," he whispered, feeling the silky spring of a curl. The hair cloaked her from crown to hips in flaming splendor.

"What are you doing in here?" She finally managed to gather her scattered wits enough to speak. She knew she ought to turn and run, at least give him a good cussing for barging in on her bath, but her body refused to obey her commands. Instead, she stood rooted to the floor, mesmerized by the naked desire she felt sizzling between them. He wanted her. She could see it in his face, read it in those smoldering steel blue eyes, now silvery with passion. Hesitantly she took a step forward.

So did Jace. His blood hammered in his veins and he could feel the painful pressure of his sex, straining against tight denims. Her body, so soft and warm from the bath, gave off the delicate perfume of lilacs, the same scent Callista had used, but on Billie Jo it was subtly different, mixed with her own essence.

"Jace," she whispered, half afraid of him, half hungry for what he might do, she who had never thought to marry. But that was when all the men she'd known were loutish hill boys with dirty fingernails and missing teeth. Never in her wildest dreams had she imagined a man like this one. *And he is my husband*. She placed one hand lightly on his chest and felt the pounding of his heart.

Her touch was like a brand of fire as she stepped into his arms and whispered his name so softly. He felt himself drawn to those generous lips and lowered his head to kiss her. A sudden rustling noise broke the spell, followed immediately by a loud "Caw"!

Pecker fluttered up, his wings brushing against Jason's leg. Jace moved away quickly, and felt a stab of pain from the wound the bird had inflicted the previous day. Cursing, he glared down at the crow. "Damn your feathered hide, but this once I should thank you," he said hoarsely as he turned and stalked out of the room, pausing only long enough to rasp out, "From now on keep this door closed while you're using the bath!"

Chapter Four

Morning dawned with a brilliant sunrise. Jason, usually an early riser, had slept well beyond it after tossing and turning fitfully most of the night. His new wife was costing him a lot of sleep. He shuddered, thinking how near he had come to being permanently bound to her last night. "I just need a woman. As soon as I get things arranged with the lawyers, I'll visit Adele . . ." He dismissed Billie Jo's innocent allure, certain that the madam could assuage his hunger. She had always done so before.

Jace ambled downstairs and was greeted by the heavenly aroma of biscuits baking and bacon frying. Only when he traveled had Jason Emory smelled such mouth-watering foods.

Garnet's kitchen always smelled of stale grease and burned bread. When he walked through the door of the dining room, Garnet was setting the table for three. He heard Charity's laughter from the kitchen.

The old housekeeper looked up at him, fairly beaming.

"Your cooking smells divine, Garnet."

"Ain't mine. Miz Billie Jo and I made us a deal. I'll set table 'n' wash dishes if'n she cooks. I never was much good at it."

Not wishing to comment on that remark, he made his way into the kitchen. Billie Jo was leaning over the oven, removing a tray of fluffy golden biscuits. Her fiery hair was again confined to a fat plait, but now it was neatly fashioned and gleaming clean. She wore a plain brown checked dress that seemed to swallow up her diminutive curves, but now Jace knew they were there, every forbidden inch.

Hearing him enter the room, she turned toward him, knowing her face must be flaming with embarrassment. *How can I meet his eyes after what happened last night?* "Good morning, Jace," she said quietly, then began to busy herself by shoving the biscuits from the tin sheet into a basket. Pecker watched the bread with avid interest from his vantage point across the kitchen.

Billie Jo had a smudge of flour on her nose and Jace fought the urge to walk over and kiss it off. "I understand you and Garnet have divided up household chores." That sounded altogether

149

too permanent an arrangement to him. "You don't have to cook, Billie Jo."

"I know. But I enjoy it." She handed him the biscuits, then reached for a big platter piled with thin slices of perfectly cooked bacon and a mound of fluffy scrambled eggs. "There's fresh-churned butter on the table. Garnet says we're out of honey, but Charity knows where the bee tree is, so we'll gather some later today."

"I don't want Charity doing that. She could get stung." He looked past her to the open back door where Charity was playing with Reddy.

"I'll be careful with her, Jace. She only has to show me the tree." She called to the girl, who scampered in for breakfast.

Jace was forced to compliment Billie Jo on the meal, the best he had ever eaten beneath his own roof. Finishing it, he quickly excused himself and headed to the corral after admonishing Charity to read her lessons. The fact that he kissed his daughter goodbye and not his bride was lost on neither female. Billie Jo quickly rose and began to clean dishes.

"May I help?" Charity asked hesitantly.

Billie Jo smiled. "Of course. Why ever not?"

"Well, these are my mama's dishes, all the way from Virginia. I've never been allowed to touch them before."

"Well, you're a big girl now and I don't see any reason why you can't begin helping. And don't fret if you should happen to drop a dish. I've broken more than my share, and I'm sure Garnet has too." She fumed silently. *Even the*

damn dishes have to have a Virginia pedigree.
What a smothered childhood Charity had! As
they made their way into the kitchen where
Garnet was filling a dish pan with soapy water,
Billie Jo had an inspiration.

"Is there a fishing hole anywhere near
here?"

"Fishing?" Charity asked dubiously.

"You know, the creek or pond where you
swim."

"I don't know how. Papa says ladies don't
swim."

"Right. They drown. I think your papa is . . ."
Billie Jo stopped in mid sentence as she saw
the crestfallen look on the child's face. Jason
Lee Emory was obviously his daughter's hero.
"Let's just say he keeps too tight a rein on you
at times because he doesn't know that you're
growing up," she amended.

"Is that what you're going to do? Teach me
how to grow up?"

Billie Jo blinked back tears and hugged the
small, dark-haired child. "I hope so, pumpkin.
I hope so."

They cleared the dining room table, and Garnet shooed them from the kitchen when the
last of the dishes were safely on the work table.
Charity watched Pecker, fascinated by the big
bird as he strutted around the kitchen.

"Do you think we could take Pecker outside
to meet Reddy? Or don't crows like dogs?"

Billie Jo smiled. "This one was raised with my
pa's hounds. He likes dogs well enough. We can

take them both with us to that fishing hole, but first we have to change our duds."

Charity looked puzzled. "This is just an every-day gown. Do I have to dress up to go fishing?"

"Nope." Billie Jo abandoned the ideas of honey gathering and fishing. This was much more important. "You're gonna undress to go swimming—but I think we have to find something that's old enough to get dirty in 'n' not worry about it."

Charity's blue eyes darkened in amazement, reminding Billie Jo of Jason's. "Get dirty? And . . . and take off my dress to swim?"

"Can't swim with a long skirt on, can you? Come on, let's see what we can find." As they climbed the steps to the second floor, Billie Jo was certain she heard Garnet chuckling to herself.

They spent the better part of an hour sorting through Charity's wardrobe, filled with frilly dresses and dainty undergarments, until Billie Jo found a dress that was rather the worse for wear and a much mended chemise and panta-lets. She had debated teaching the girl to swim mother naked the way she had learned, but decided that was likely to shock Charity and certain to infuriate Jason. He'd be mad enough about the swimming anyway.

"Here, put these on while I—"

A loud commotion from the yard in back of the house interrupted Billie Jo.

"That's Pecker cawing—and Reddy barking!" Charity said in alarm.

"And I hear Garnet cussing some, too." Billie Jo raced downstairs with her young charge following close behind.

"Give me thet, yew thievin' varmint, afore thet hound does fer yew!" Garnet, armed with a broom, was poking the bristles at Pecker, trying to knock the large piece of steak from his beak and at the same time keep the dog at bay.

Reddy, a large, shaggy, cinnamon-colored mutt, was enjoying the new game almost as much as the crow. He barked and lunged around the broom, trying to wrest the prize from Pecker, who had stolen the juicy hunk of meat from the kitchen table when Garnet's back was turned. Every time he snapped at the steak, Pecker fluttered up, narrowly evading him.

Realizing the meat was beyond redemption, Garnet stood back with a fierce scowl on her weathered face to watch the contest. The dog made another run at the crow, who beat his wings loudly and levitated about three feet off the ground. Whether intentional or not she could not tell, but the bird landed atop the startled dog's back.

Barking furiously, Reddy raced in a circle to dislodge his unwelcome rider. The crow, using the momentum of his unseating, again took to flight, this time soaring higher than he could have done unaided. He landed atop a clothesline stretched between two poles in the backyard. In the struggle to gain purchase on the hemp rope, Pecker lost his prize. The heavy piece of steak fell to the dusty ground, where the dog quickly snatched it up and ran a tight figure eight around the clothes poles.

As if cheering on the one who had helped him rise to such lofty heights, Pecker let out a loud "Caw, caw."

Reddy cut another close turn, dropped the meat between his front feet, and barked up at the crow.

"Oh, look, Billie Jo, he's going to fall!" Charity cried out.

Billie Jo restrained her with a chuckle. "No, he isn't. Watch."

"Why thet durn critter's turnin' hand-springs—er claw swings—er somethin'," Garnet said in amazement.

The crow, holding onto the clothesline with both taloned feet, fell forward until he was hanging upside down, then rocked back and forth until he built up enough momentum to swing upright and regain his balance. Charity shrieked with laughter, and Pecker responded by repeating the trick.

"Just like the acrobats in the circus," the child cried gleefully. Reddy, the prize of mud-coated meat forgotten, quickly realized the crow had become the center of attention. He barked and ran over to Charity, jumping up on the little girl. His big dusty paws landed on her shoulders, knocking her backward into the grass, but Charity held onto his neck, pulling him down beside her.

As they wrestled and laughed, Pecker let out another loud "Caw". When all eyes were rightfully turned to him, he repeated his rope trick.

Charity sat in the dust, arms wrapped around Reddy, giggling as the dog barked and Billie Jo chuckled. Even Garnet was smiling in spite of the stolen steak.

"What on earth is going on here?" Jason had run from the corral when the squawking bird and barking mutt had scared his best stud bull into a frenzy. He looked down at his filthy daughter, sprawled in the dirt, wrestling with the dog, but before he could reprimand her, a loud "Caw!" caused him to raise his eyes to the clothesline, where that damnable crow was hanging upside down!

Everyone around him erupted into gales of laughter. Surely the stupid bird hadn't hung himself somehow. He took a step toward the crow and felt his boot slide on something squishy—a mud-caked hunk of meat! He arched one eyebrow at Billie Jo, knowing that she and her crow had created this mess. "Is this some new way to make chicken fried steak?"

"Nope. Pecker stole the steak," she replied, wanting to divert his attention from Charity. She had seen the way he looked at the girl's dirty clothes and unladylike pose. "But maybe I could try dirt instead of flour on your piece."

Garnet couldn't suppress a snicker. "Shucks, it'd still taste better'n what I cook."

Charity laughed and said, "Look at Pecker, Papa! He can swing himself round and round on the clothesline—and he and Reddy are going to be friends."

Jason scraped the smashed meat off his boot heel, cursing silently, then turned to his daughter. Reaching down to pull her gently from the ground, he said, "This is no way to act, Charity. Girls shouldn't roll in the dust with their dogs and get their dresses dirty."

"Why not?" Billie Jo asked.

He turned to her with a hard glint in his eyes. "Because ladies don't behave this way."

"She's just a little girl havin' some fun; she don't have to be a lady yet."

"With you for an example, she never will."

Pecker chose that moment to flutter to the ground and waddle up to Jason's boot, where he tried to peck at the remains of the steak.

"Get that mayhem-inciting beast back in his cage before one of my hands shoots him for rustling Circle E beef."

"One little bitty piece of steak," Billie Jo scoffed as Jason stepped clear of the curious crow. "Real reason you'd shoot him's because he bit you."

"Why would Pecker bite you, Papa? You wouldn't shoot him, would you?" Charity asked incredulously, moving between her father and the crow.

Sighing, Jason replied, "I won't shoot him, Charity, but you must do as I say. And I distinctly remember telling you at breakfast to read your lessons."

"Oh, but Billie Jo promised to—"

"I promised to help you with your lessons—first thing," Billie Jo interrupted before Jason flatly forbade any swimming, unclothed or clothed.

He looked at her skeptically, remembering her surprising bursts of erudition. Still, he did not want Charity growing any more attached to Billie Jo than she already was. "I think it would be best if my daughter read her lessons unaided." He turned to Charity with a smile. "You finish reading Miss Alcott's book and we'll discuss it tonight, but first, wash up and change your dress."

"All right, Papa," the girl replied, disappointed and confused by the interplay between her father and Billie Jo. She turned and walked into the house.

"*Little Women*." Billie Jo scoffed.

"And what's wrong with *Little Women*? I think its eminently suitable—and Charity reads well in advance of her age."

"I think it's puerile, and a bright girl deserves better."

He looked at her with narrowed eyes. "Do you now? What, dare I ask, would you have her read? Those pulp dime novels by Ned Buntline?"

"That's made up as play actin'," she scoffed. "If you want her to read lady authors, why not Mrs. Stowe's famous book?"

Jason clenched his hands into fists to keep from strangling her. "*Uncle Tom's Cabin* is a piece of vile, distorted propaganda."

Shrugging indifferently, she said, "There's always things like Franklin's autobiography or President Lincoln's speeches."

This time he refused to rise to the bait. "My daughter will read what I select, with no help from you." Gesturing to the meat smeared across the ground, he ordered, "Cage that creature and clean up this mess." Reddy was busily chewing up a big hunk of it while Pecker watched balefully. Jason stormed off.

"Reddy can finish up here, and as for you—" she turned her angry glare from Jason's retreating back to the unrepentant crow "—you acrobat, no more stealing, or I'll sell you to a traveling circus!"

That afternoon, when Charity had finished her reading, she and Billie Jo walked to the small pond hidden by a copse of pines about a half mile from the ranch house. The child's swimming lessons began. Within three days she was paddling short distances without any support from her teacher. The two of them kept it a secret from Jason. Billie Jo explained carefully to Charity that first she should learn to swim really well. Then she could surprise her father with her new skill. If, as was most likely, he forbade her ever to do such an unladylike thing again, at least the girl would no longer be in danger of drowning!

In spite of his arrogance and overprotectiveness, Jason did love his daughter. That night at the dinner table, Billie Jo watched the way his eyes lit up when he looked at Charity. When he laughed or smiled, she found herself wishing to be within the charmed circle of his love. But it had been clear from the moment they met that such was never to be.

Charity had described her parents' fairy tale courtship, a magical story she had had her father retell her often over the years since Callista's death. How sad that such a lovely, bright child had to grow up motherless. Billie Jo tried to think only of Charity, but the child's father intruded in her dreams far more than she wanted to admit. Especially after her private conversation with Charity during their afternoon swimming lesson yesterday.

"How come you and Papa don't sleep in the same bed?" she had asked guilelessly as they sat letting the sun dry their undergarments.

Billie Jo felt the heat steal into her cheeks and it was not from the sun. "What makes you ask that?" she hedged.

Charity shrugged, a careless gesture she had quickly picked up from her new mentor. "I don't know. It just felt easier asking you than Papa. Estelle Kincaid's parents do. I've spent lots of nights at their house 'n' they only have three bedrooms. Her brother has one and she has one and her mama and papa have one. Is it because we have such a big house?"

"Well, there are lots of bedrooms at Circle E." How could she tell the child that this wasn't a real marriage? That it was not going to last? One day all too soon she would leave. Jace would find another wife, a true lady who would share his bed and his life.

"Billie Jo, do you have to sleep in Papa's bed to get me a new little brother?"

Billie Jo nearly swallowed her tongue. "That is a question better left until you're just a tad older, pumpkin. I think we're dry enough to dress and get back. I have chicken to fry for tonight's dinner."

Jason casually informed her at breakfast the next morning, "Abe Garner's back in Miles City."

He waited for a reaction. Did she pale ever so slightly as she placed a platter of golden griddle cakes on the table? Jason, too, had spent the past days in an agony of confusion, watching the growing bond develop between Billie Jo and Charity, powerless to stop it without seeming mean-spirited and cruel to his daughter. What could he say to her when Billie Jo disappeared from their lives? Did he want her to leave?

Of course I do! He gave himself a mental shake as he watched her small inelegant figure, clad in another of those shapeless ugly cotton dresses she seemed to favor. Her hair was pinned into a tight unattractive bun, serviceable he imagined, considering the heat. A light film of perspiration gleamed on her forehead as she cleared the table after breakfast. Jace tried to remember if Callista had ever perspired—no, "glowed" was the word Southern ladies used.

160

"Only men and horses perspire," she had remonstrated. Billie Jo would have said everyone sweated, he was certain. Callista had never even glowed, to his recollection. Of course, she had not worked around the house as his new wife did. Was he actually making a comparison favorable to Billie Jo? Jason was caught short, bemused by the course of his thoughts as Charity's childish laughter echoed from the kitchen.

She finished her new chores, helping clear the table, then went off to her morning lesson. Billie Jo, too, excused herself and vanished out the kitchen door. He took a final swallow of coffee and handed Garnet the cup. Unwilling to admit to Garnet that he was curious about where his wife was going, he casually bid the housekeeper good morning and headed out the back door.

Jason watched Billie Jo walk resolutely toward the horse barn, where she hailed Hank Allen and engaged him in a brief conversation. Then they both disappeared into the stable. Jason ambled in that general direction, wondering what she was up to now. A few moments later she emerged, awkwardly clinging for dear life to a sidesaddle as the gray filly he had brought her trotted daintily across the yard. The full cotton skirt at least decently covered her legs. He remembered their furious argument in town about riding astride. She had said she did not own a riding habit. Then he remembered something else she had said—she did not know how to ride sidesaddle.

Cursing, he quickly strode into the barn, saddled up Rawhide, and headed out after her. By the time he had rounded the first turn on the rutted old pasture path she was taking, Jason could see that Billie Jo was riding faster than the rough terrain would safely accommodate.

Billie Jo was too preoccupied to pay much attention to the beautiful day or to the increasing speed of her spirited little filly, who was nervous with such a clumsy rider aboard. As she clung like a leech to the stupid contraption her husband insisted she use, Billie Jo kept hearing his words, "Abe Garner's back in Miles City," over and over again.

"He's probably riding hell bent for leather right now to start that annulment." She swore and tried to shift her weight on the uncomfortable saddle. After several tries that only succeeded in making her and the horse more miserable, she gave up, deciding to rein in to a slower pace. But before she could do so, a rhythmic click of rattles sounded just ahead of her, in a patch of thick bear grass. When the terrified filly reared up, nearly dumping her, all Billie Jo could do was grab onto the horse's mane and hold tight. The gray bolted as if fired from a cannon, and Billie Jo lost the reins.

Jason saw the horse rear and gallop off with his wife hanging on desperately. He spurred Rawhide after them, cutting across a brushy swale to gain time before Billie Jo was thrown onto the hard stony ground.

"Little fool," he muttered to himself as the big, rangy buckskin overtook the small gray. "Kick free of the stirrup," he yelled, reaching out and yanking her from the filly's back. He tossed her on the saddle in front of him, then reached over and seized the filly's reins, pulling both horses to a stop.

The gray was still rolling her eyes and dancing with fright as Jason firmly held both reins and let Billie Jo slide slowly to the ground, where she crumpled in a heap.

Slapping the gray's reins around Rawhide's pommel, he leaped off his horse and seized her, dragging her into his embrace. Her hair had come unpinned and flew around them in the morning breeze. Its thick, silky strands wrapped about his face, caressing his cheek as he held her roughly, feeling their hearts slam furiously against each other's chests.

"What kind of a fool stunt was that? You're no kind of rider to go off alone and let your horse be spooked by a rattler. You couldn't control her." As he yelled at her, his eyes swept her body and his hands traveled from her shoulders to the slender curve of her waist and hips. Was she injured in any way?

Billie Jo's eyes blazed with a fury that overrode her fear as she tried to wrench free of his touch. "I could too have controlled her, if I wasn't riding on that dangerous damnfool torture rack!"

"You were riding too fast for a tenderfoot, sidesaddle be damned! You could've broken your neck!"

"Then why the hell did you rescue me? You could've been rid of me. You don't want me!"

"I don't want you dead!"

"You don't want me any which way!"

"The hell I don't!" he said savagely as he pulled her against his body. Before either of them realized what he intended, Jace lowered his mouth to hers and kissed her.

Caught by surprise, Billie Jo's mouth was open and she felt his tongue plunder inside, hot and seeking. His breathing was ragged and his hold on her fierce and possessive. Startled by his rough invasion, she pushed and twisted in his embrace, but he held her head in one hand, his fingers tangled in her hair, massaging her scalp as he immobilized her.

His lips pressed and glided over hers. Then her fury turned to a molten, liquid heat, as different from anger as water is from whiskey. Billie Jo felt her arms stop pushing against his chest and creep up to encircle his neck. She rose on tiptoe, leaning into the kiss as his mouth slanted over hers, brushing her lips, molding them to do his bidding.

When he felt her tongue touch his, delicately, experimentally, Jace was lost. He could feel her soft little body, feel every sweet curve of breast and hip as his hands explored and caressed. He pressed her more tightly against his body, which was rigid, clamoring for release. Visions

164

of her naked and wet, rising from that bathtub, flashed in his mind and he groaned, grinding his hips against her belly. His lips left her mouth, trailing small licks and bites downward to the sweet curve of her neck, that beautiful slender neck that could have been broken so easily. "I want you, Billie Jo. God, how I need you," he breathed as he nuzzled her neck and felt her arch into the embrace.

"You have the right, Jace . . . I am your wife," she whispered breathlessly.

I am your wife. The words hammered at his lust-fogged brain, finally penetrating. He broke off their embrace and held her at arm's length. Still breathing as if he'd run for miles, he turned from her and laid his head against the buckskin's neck. "Get on your horse, Billie Jo," he gasped.

She stood with her fingers raised to her kiss-swollen, tender lips. Billie Jo was as confused by his sudden withdrawal as she had been by his passionate onslaught. She slowly walked around to where her gray stood, now patient and calm after the brush with the rattler. She struggled to mount the cumbersome sidesaddle.

"Here, let me help you," Jace said in a hoarse voice.

When his hands circled her waist and lifted her as effortlessly as chaff on the wind, she again felt the electric thrill of his touch, but when she looked down into his eyes, they were darkened with anguish.

He quickly tore his gaze from her and mounted Rawhide, then handed her the filly's reins. "I'll escort you back to the ranch."

They rode in silence for a few moments. She studied his profile, memorizing every beautiful contour of his striking face, his hard, lean body. *Those lips kissed me, those hands touched my breasts.* Why had he stopped so suddenly? She knew they could not have made love here on the open road, but why was he so forbidding, so tense and angry? A slow smile spread across her face as she thought of stud bulls and stallions when they were kept from cows or mares in season. Sometimes being a Southern gentleman must be a real pain in the nether regions she reckoned.

If he desired her as a woman, perhaps there was some hope. Until now, Billie Jo had tried not to think about this marriage as real. But maybe . . . just maybe . . .

166

Chapter
Five

"Billie Jo Emory, what the hell are you doing here?" Adele Wheaton belted her satin wrapper about her slim waist and wiped the sleep from her incredulous eyes. "If Jace finds out, he'll be furious."

"I know. He'll skin me like a polecat and stretch my hide on the bunkhouse wall. But I have to talk to you about something real important," Billie Jo said earnestly.

"Did anyone see you come in that door?" Adele motioned to the rear stairs, which some of the town's leading citizens used during "calling hours."

"Nope. I came to town with Garnet. She's at Cummins' Emporium buying supplies. I told her I had a few errands to run." Billie Jo eyed the plush red velvet love seat and canopied bed draped with red silk hangings. Adele's private apartments were as expensively decorated as Jason's home, but in a totally different way. The tasteful understatement of muted colors and solid dark furniture at the Circle E spoke of generations of wealth and breeding. The bright hues and ornately carved pieces in this room spoke of opulence without regard to sensibility.

For all her beauty of face and body, was Adele the one to help her? Having no one else, Billie Jo plunged ahead. "I have a favor to ask, Adele."

Adele rang for coffee and invited Billie Jo to sit down at an elaborate gilded table near a curtained window. "Now, what sort of favor?" She could tell the girl was nervous.

Billie Jo fidgeted with the scratchy fabric of her calico skirt. "I want to dress like a lady—to look like one."

"And you came to me?" Adele could not keep a hint of amusement from her voice. "Billie Jo, you know what I am," she remonstrated gently.

"Yep. You're the only female I know in Montana Territory who smells good." She hesitated when Adele chuckled, then added, "And you're my friend. Your dresses fit you 'n' men look at you . . ."

"The way you want Jason to look at you?"

Billie Jo sighed miserably. "I don't think he'll ever . . . that I'll ever . . . oh, blue blazin' hellfire, maybe this whole thing's a mistake." She jumped up, as if to leave. "Just because he kissed me—" She stopped short, cheeks blazing now.

Adele smiled. "So, the aloof Mr. Emory isn't immune after all." She circled around the table and began to inspect Billie Jo critically, pulling on the shapeless calico dress. "Is everything you own this big?"

"I hate dresses, 'n' if I had to wear one, I just sorta left enough room to breathe in 'em."

Smothering a laugh, Adele nodded. "Well, if we're to take advantage of your figure—and you do seem to have one beneath all this drapery— you'll have to learn to take smaller breaths."

Thinking of the way Jason's kisses made her breathless and panting, Billie Jo doubted this was going to work, but was too embarrassed to say more. Adele unpinned her hair and had her strip down to her chemise and pantalets, then summoned one of her girls, a petite blonde named Priscilla.

"Most of Priss's new clothes aren't exactly what a lady would wear, but she comes from a tony Eastern family. You have any of those things left, Priss?"

Priss studied Billie Jo, taking in her coloring as well as her size. "I have one good gown. It was always too dark a color for me. Might work on her."

"Bring it in—and whatever else you think would look good. I'll send for Hazel to do the alterations." She turned back to Billie Jo and said, "We can outfit you, but there's more to keeping a man than dressing like a picture from *Godey's Ladies Book.*"

"I can cook well enough,'n' as for the other, well, I guess I'll just let nature take its course."

Adele's bright laughter reddened Billie Jo's cheeks. "Maybe it will at that. *God knows, you have more spirit and passion than Callista ever did.* "Now, let's see what we can do with the hair, hmmm."

Billie Jo left that afternoon with a box full of new clothes, including one item of which she was certain Jason would not approve. When she had told Adele about her brush with death on the sidesaddle, Adele had Hazel cut down one of her own split riding skirts. Although Billie Jo had seen several Montana women wearing them, she instinctively knew that none of them was the paragon her husband wanted his wife to be. That was why he had sent East for a "Southern lady." She vowed to keep the riding skirt hidden, at least for the present.

When he came in for dinner that evening, Jace noticed at once that Billie Jo's appearance had changed dramatically. She wore a simple muslin dress, but it fit, following every delicate curve of breast and waist. It was a dark clear green that made her skin glow and accented her eyes. Her hair was piled in a soft, elegant chignon with a full pompadour in front and wispy tendrils curling around her face.

A sudden stab of desire pierced him, sending heat coursing through his body as he watched her fuss, arranging a big bouquet of fresh wildflowers in an antique crystal vase. Then he noticed that the table had only two places set with Callista's finest china and sterling. The house was oddly quiet. "Evening, Billie Jo. Where is everyone?"

Surprised by his silent appearance, she turned with a small "Oh" on her soft pink lips, clutching a golden daisy in one hand. Her cheeks flushed as she looked at his tall, rangy body leaning casually against the door frame. "I thought you and I needed to . . . to talk, Jace. I gave Garnet the night off. She took Charity with her. They went to visit the Kincaids. Their son is over the measles." She was babbling.

"What do we need to talk about?" His voice sounded harsh even to his own ears.

"Have you gone to see Abe Garner?" she asked, holding her breath.

Jason needed a drink. Hell, he needed a whole bottle full of tangle leg. "I've been too busy," he answered curtly, then walked over to the sideboard and poured some sherry from Callista's cut crystal decanter. It was not nearly strong enough.

"I thought fall roundup was the busy time, not summer," she said with a secret smile welling inside her.

He tossed off two ridiculously small crystal thimblefuls of the sherry, then gave up. A quart of it wouldn't help. "I'm going to take a bath. How long until dinner?"

"The roast is done and the vegetables are almost tender. I have to put the rolls in to bake and make gravy. That should give you enough time to get cleaned up." She inspected his tall figure, from the top of his sweaty hat band to the toes of his dusty boots.

With a noncommittal grunt, he walked past her and headed for the tub. She noticed how careful he was not to touch her, but she knew he smelled her lilac bath perfume. She sure as blazes smelled his pungent essence, a blend of male sweat, horse, and tobacco. She licked her lips and went to finish the dinner.

As Billie Jo carefully placed a steaming bowl of gravy on the pristine ivory linen tablecloth, she heard a commotion from the back yard. Loud caws were interspersed with sharp barks. Quickly surveying her masterpiece on the table, she dashed through the kitchen and opened the back door. Pecker, his beak firmly embedded in a large corn dodger, flapped past her. Before she could stop him, Reddy almost knocked her to the floor as he sped in hot pursuit of the crow and his loot, doubtless stolen from the bunkhouse cook's cooling rack.

"Git, you blue blazin' pests!" She seized a broom from the corner and raced down the long hall after the two culprits, praying she could shoo them out the front door. But Pecker unexpectedly veered to the right and into the parlor before she could reach him. Thinking of all the delicate knicknacks and gilt-edged photographs cluttering the beautiful room, her heart stopped beating for a moment, then pounded.

A shattering, sour crash of notes sounded from Callista's piano as the crow flapped up onto its keyboard. She tried to grab him, but the jumping, barking dog ruined her aim and all she came away with was the damned corn dodger, which crumbled all over the silk bench cushion.

"Oh, Pecker, no! Reddy, stop!"

"What the hell is—" Jason, clad only in a pair of hastily pulled on denims, stood in the kitchen door as the catastrophe unfolded with the speed and destructiveness of a tornado. Pecker bounded two hops across the floor between the parlor and the dining room, then with a Herculean flapping of his wings aimed for the sanctuary of the dining room table. His talons caught in the delicate embroidery of the tablecloth as he fluttered and flopped, causing gravy to slosh in a rich brown puddle around its bowl and roast potatoes to roll from their platter onto the carpet.

The dog jumped at the table, barking loudly. Pecker whirled and spread his wings in preparation for flight, but his talons were still held fast by the tablecloth. When he lurched to the ground, the embroidered cloth came with him. So did all the silver, crystal, china, and the heaping bowls and platters of Billie Jo's feast.

Everything shattered in an avalanche of flying glass and gooey gravy. Callista's fragile moss rose plates were reduced to shards of pink and gold floating on a river of gravy and mashed vegetables. Slices of pot roast dripped their juices into the pale carpet. Reddy, ever eager to please, began to lick up edible parts of the mess, while Pecker continued to hop around the table, shredding the linen tablecloth in a vain attempt to free himself.

Billie Jo saw her whole life flash before her eyes as the table's contents fell to the carpet. Frozen in shock, she watched the dog and crow milling in the debris until Jason's voice cut into her consciousness. His voice was low, quiet, deadly. "This was my wife's wedding set, shipped all the way from Richmond without breaking a piece." Kneeling to pick up a fragment near the kitchen door, he examined it in the light. "A thing of grace and beauty. I expect it's just as well destroyed, like everything else from my heritage."

Billie Jo trembled as she seized Pecker and freed his foot from the shredded, stained linen. With the bird tucked beneath one arm, she grabbed Reddy's ear and hauled both culprits toward the kitchen door.

Jason stood up to let her pass without saying anything. After shoving them out the back door, she turned. "Jace, I'm sorry." The words stuck in her throat as she surveyed the empty room. She could hear his footfalls on the stairs.

He dressed in a faded blue shirt and pulled on his boots, then headed down to the bunkhouse, where he knew Hank and Clem always kept a stash of tangle leg. He planned to get drunk tonight.

Billie Jo began cleaning up the mess, using the destroyed tablecloth to sop up the gravy. Then she wrapped the roast and vegetables in it and disposed of it. When she returned, the ruined carpet was still littered with broken glass—as shattered as her dreams . . . foolish dreams. Jace was furious over the loss of Callista's treasures. Her misery choking her, Billie Jo realized that Charity would be heart-broken about her mother's dishes. "I've gone and messed everything up, even the pretty dress Adele gave me." Throwing down the broom, she fled upstairs to her lonely room, blinded by tears.

It was late. Hell, it was the middle of the night. Somewhere in the distance several coyotes howled. Jason walked in a gently weaving path toward the house, wondering idly if coyotes ate crows. Maybe, if he was really lucky, he could get that mutt to run off with the pack. But that still left Billie Jo . . . his wife. Drunk as he was, he could not erase the memory of her standing there with a flower clutched in her hands, dressed in green. He had almost crossed the room and placed a kiss on those soft, parted lips. The whiskey hadn't helped. He still wanted to do the same thing.

"Then I'd be stuck with her. And that damn crow!" He swore, thinking of the gawdawful mess in the dining room. Funny that he'd always hated the delicate little cups and crystal stemmed glasses that were too dainty to fit a

175

man's hands comfortably. But they were a tangible reminder of home, roots, tradition. "All gone now, my man," he muttered as he weaved his way through the kitchen. "Have to be quiet. Mustn't wake my hard-working wife."

He sat with a lurch on one of the sturdy kitchen chairs and pulled off his boots and socks, folding them with the meticulous care only a drunk can bestow, then stood up and looked around the dark room for the door to the hall.

Billie Jo heard a horrendous thump, followed by strident male cursing coming from the kitchen. She combed her tangled hair from her eyes as she scrambled off the bed and headed downstairs in a bolt. Jason was leaning against the kitchen sink, extracting a piece of glittering crystal from the heel of his right foot.

"Are you hurt? Let me light a lamp," she said, noting the slight ooze of blood on his foot. She almost tripped over the chair that he had overturned when his foot slipped on the broken glass.

"I don't need any doctoring," he said crossly as he stood up, then grimaced when the foot twinged.

"You're bleeding all over the floor."

"Considering the rest of the mess, what difference can it make? There isn't that much blood in me."

She crossed the kitchen and reached out for him as he limped toward the hall. When she took his arm and wrapped it about her shoulders to help support his weight, he realized she wore only a nightrail.

"Jesus! You're practically naked!" He looked down at a pair of small, perfectly upthrust young breasts revealed through the thin batiste. The bright moonlight shining in the window made her skin glow like pearls. He stopped, growing quickly more sober . . . and more aroused. His hand cupped her breast.

She gasped. "Jace, you're drunk."

"That's the only reason I can think why I'm doing this," he said, continuing his sensuous assault. He slid his hand along the curve of her waist, then lower to where her hip swelled. "Sweet, so slender and sweet," he whispered, bending over her and drawing her into his arms.

Billie Jo stood immobilized, smelling the whiskey on his breath, telling herself that it was drink that had loosened his inhibitions. *But what about the other day on the trail? Or that night in the bath?* As she argued with the taunting voice that offered her dearest wish, Jace scooped her into his arms and began to walk with surprising steadiness from the kitchen. When he stopped at the foot of the stairs and kissed her, she wrapped her arms tightly about his neck and returned the kiss with abandon.

Growling low in his throat, he climbed the steps and carried her into his room. Billie Jo could see that it was larger than hers with heavy dark furniture, dominated by a large bed against the far wall. He crossed the carpet in three long strides and placed her on the bed. She lay trembling as he stood over her and yanked off his shirt. When he unbuttoned his fly and began to kick off his jeans, she sat up on the bed.

"Jace—"

He cut off her half-hearted protest by pulling her into a kneeling position at the edge of the bed and kissing her soundly. They tumbled back onto the rumpled covers and rolled onto their sides. He held a fistful of her hair in one hand, pulling her closer, wrapping it around his shoulders. Then his fingertips grazed her breast. Her nipple pebbled to a hard, aching point and she moaned.

"I want to see all of you, touch all of you," he whispered as he pulled the nightrail up over her legs and hips. His hand moved down then, gliding along a silky thigh, over the flare of calf to take one delicate ankle and envelop it. "You're so small yet so perfectly formed," he said with wonder in his voice. "Sit up," he commanded as he released her leg.

Billie Jo obliged, letting him pull her nightrail over her head and toss it to the floor. Then he laid her on top of his long body, raising her like a doll so her breasts hung suspended like pearl drops, waiting for his eager mouth.

When he suckled one, teasing the nipple with his tongue, she cried out his name and dug her nails into his biceps. He felt her arch into the caress, then switched his attention to the other breast. What a passionate little creature she was, writing against him, driving him wild with desire. He slid her down his chest, letting her breasts rub against the hair-roughened surface until he could again claim her mouth.

Their tongues dueled. That part of making love was no longer new to her. Billie Jo remembered their first shattering kiss and met the savage onslaught of his mouth with her own. As they kissed, he ran his fingers up and down the curve of her spine, cupping her buttocks and moving her hips in a lazy circular motion against his lower body.

She could feel that hard male part of him pressing between her legs although she had not looked at it in her earlier nervousness. It felt huge! When his hand reached between them and touched her soft nether lips, she forgot to be afraid. A stab of liquid flame shot through her. When he withdrew those clever, caressing fingers, she moaned, aching for him to continue.

Jace felt the creamy moisture of her sheath and knew she was ready. Her hips caught the rhythm he had guided her through and continued undulating on their own. He rolled her beneath him and slid his knee between her thighs, raising his body over her in a haze of lust.

Billie Jo spread her legs and arched up to meet his thrust of penetration. The sudden pressure, delicious in itself, was momentarily joined by a small sharp pain that quickly settled into a burning ache when he penetrated deeply within her. Not knowing anything else to do, she simply held still and clasped him tightly, her legs pressed around his narrow hips.

Never, never, his liquor-fogged brain told him, had he experienced anything like this. She was so small, so tight and slick. The pleasure of feeling her envelop him robbed him of the desire to move. She clung to him tightly. There was none of Callista's frozen dutiful resignation. Billie Jo wanted him inside her. After a few moments, that old overpowering urge to move overrode the peculiar sense of peace. He arched his back and began to thrust. Quickly she caught his rhythm and followed him.

Jason had taken only one virgin before this, and Billie Jo's reactions were so different from Callista's, so wonderfully responsive, that he could only react, not reason. He rained feverish kisses over her face and throat as he tangled his hands in her hair, all the while his staff moved with long, slow strokes that gradually increased in intensity until finally he was blind, riding a seemingly endless crest.

Billie Jo did not understand that liquor slowed Jason's sexual performance, but she did experience the benefits of his overindulgence. Her body, so eager yet so untutored, had time to get past the brief twinge of unexpected pain on the sundering of her maidenhead, time to assimilate every new, glorious sensation, until she, like her husband, was blind and mindless in passion, hungry for completion. She arched, bucked, clawed at his back, and rode the crest with him into a series of glorious, blinding explosions.

Finally she was aware of his body, collapsed on top of hers, burying her in the big soft mattress. His breath, hot and swift, tickled her throat. She could feel their sweat-slicked skin, his hairy and rough, hers smooth and soft, perfectly complementing each other. Dreamily, she ran her hands over his shoulders and down his broad, muscular back to the slight curve of his buttocks. *He's mine now. We're really married*, she thought as he rolled off her and proceeded to fall instantly asleep. She snuggled at his side and dreamed of the future.

Chapter
Six

Jace woke when something brushed across his face. He reached up and felt hair. His eyes flew open. Long, bright red hair! As he tried to sit up, he instantly became aware of two things—his head nearly flew off his shoulders when he raised it from the pillow, and his right arm lay beneath Billie Jo's neck. He fell back against the mattress and stared at the spinning ceiling, cursing silently.

What have I done? He knew, of course. Jason Lee Emory seldom got drunk, but when he did, he always remembered every detail of his debauchery with excruciating clarity in the morning. That was why he seldom got drunk. But this had been the ultimate madness! The whole passionate encounter replayed itself in his aching head as he carefully slid his arm from beneath his wife's neck and rolled off the bed.

My wife. Well, she sure is now. He cursed some more. There would be no annulment. As he fished his hastily discarded pants off the floor and slid into them, Billie Jo awakened. He turned to face her, thinking of what to say. The impish smile on her face as she sat there, all bright-eyed and energetic, infuriated him. What right did she have to look so damn happy?

"Good morning, Jace," she said uncertainly, her smile evaporating beneath his baleful scrutiny. She clutched the sheet to her chest like a shield.

"I reckon it's good for you." He savagely jammed his arm into the sleeve of a shirt he yanked from his bureau. "You certainly enjoyed last night enough."

"I reckon I was under a mistaken impression. I sure as blue blazin' hell thought you enjoyed it, too!"

His face flushed with embarrassment. "Men are supposed to."

"And women aren't?"

"Ladies don't."

"I never pretended to be a lady, Jace. I didn't come after you. You came after me last night," she said, trying to build a simmering anger to displace the pain.

"Oh? You didn't, huh?" He quirked one black eyebrow. "What was that fancy new dress and hairdo all about—and the elegant little dinner for two? You were trying to seduce me."

"You arrogant bastard! I was trying to see if our marriage had a chance. You've been the one slaverin' like a hound dog after me—ever since that night in the bathroom!"

"Our marriage," he repeated sarcastically. "Well, one thing we do agree on—we're damn sure married now."

"Fine! Get a divorce instead of an annulment. I don't care which. Just get it done," she gritted out, wrapping the sheet protectively around her naked body.

He looked down at her with a scowl that cattlemen usually reserved for sheep. "There is one small matter you might want to consider. I imagine it'll take at least a month before I can talk to Abe about a divorce."

She stared at him blankly. Her lips trembled but she held her spine rigidly stiff.

He cursed. "Are you really that naïve?" He knew the answer. She had certainly been a virgin, albeit a passionate one. "What if you're pregnant?" He was rewarded as she blanched and clutched the sheet even tighter. "If you're carrying my child, I can't abandon you—or an innocent baby. You'll have to stay at Circle E until we know, but stay out of my way." He seized a pair of clean socks from the bureau and stalked toward the door.

"I may have been naïve last night, but I'm from Missouri, remember? Once you show me a polecat, I know to avoid him the next time." She seized a walnut-handled hairbrush from the bedside table by his shaving mirror and hurled it at him as he stepped through the bedroom door.

He caught it and sketched a mock bow. "Thanks. I needed that."

Charity's eyes grew round as saucers when Billie Jo strode into the kitchen late that morning. "Glory be, Billie Jo, where did you get that riding skirt? Are you going to ride astride like Mrs. Hutchinson does?"

"And just let that pole—your father try to stop me," Billie Jo snapped. Then she realized her anger was for Jason, not his daughter. "I'm sorry, pumpkin, I'm not mad at you. You're the one who should be mad at me about your mama's dishes."

"That's all right. When we came home this morning, Papa told us how Pecker and Reddy broke them. Garnet has everything cleaned up now. Can I ride with you?"

Billie Jo smiled and hugged Charity. *God, how I'll miss her!* "I think you'd better finish your studies this morning. I need to ride off some steam, and that takes bein' alone. Then we can take another practice swim this afternoon."

"You and Papa had a fight, didn't you? He was sure crabby this morning, too. He stomped on down to the stable like his tail was on fire!"

Garnet, overhearing the girl's vulgarity, suppressed a chuckle as she debated correcting Charity. She decided against it. It was Billie Jo's place to do that—especially since last night. The shrewd old housekeeper always made the beds and knew where Billie Jo Emory had spent the night. And about time, too!

Without confirming or denying Charity's remarks, Billie Jo headed for the stable. Charity watched her stalk out, awed by her riding skirt, but even more awed by her willingness to defy Jason Lee Emory. When the girl went up to study, she overheard her father's and Billie Jo's angry voices all the way from the corral. They were really arguing! When Billie Jo swung up on her gray filly and rode off, Jason slapped his hand against his thigh and swore.

Suddenly Charity was frightened. What if Billie Jo never came back? In the past weeks she had had such fun with her father's laughing, unconventional young wife. Billie Jo wasn't like any of the ladies in Miles City, or any of the ranchers' wives either. Charity didn't want to lose her.

"But what can I do?" she asked Pecker when she saw him approaching the back porch steps after lunch. She had taken to sharing pieces of cornbread and scraps of meat with the greedy crow, who would perform all sorts of tricks for a snippet of food. Reddy went out with Hank to search for stock every day, and the crow had become her boon companion. He was always stealing brightly colored objects—hair ribbons, polished belt buckles, even jewelry—and bringing them to her. Billie Jo had explained that he only did this to show affection and didn't really mean to steal, but it was up to her to return the "gifts" to their proper owners.

"What have you got now, Peck?"

The crow approached the melancholy child with a new gift—a shiny stone flecked with iron pyrite. Occasionally he did bring something she could keep. "Thank you, Pecker." She petted the crow, then examined her present. "Look, Garnet," she called out to the old woman hanging clothes in the yard. "Pecker's brought me a piece of fool's gold—and it's shaped like a heart . . . well, sort of." She turned the small glittering stone this way and that.

"Yep, it is sorta heart-shaped, ain't it? Just like one of them valentines yer daddy give to Miz Callista," Garnet said as she passed with her empty wash basket.

Dinner that night was a dismal affair with little conversation, most of it between Charity and Billie Jo. Jason ate in virtual silence and excused himself early.

Charity didn't like this strain between the two people she loved. Even when she had swum all the way across the pond by herself this afternoon, she had received less than enthusiastic praise from Billie Jo.

The child wondered about how her father and Billie Jo really felt. Had he loved her mama so much that he was sorry for having remarried? Charity could remember nothing about the beautiful Callista and knew only what her father, Garnet, and other adults told her. She desperately wanted Billie Jo to stay and be her new mama, but she also wanted her papa to be happy. What if no one but her mama could make him happy?

Confused, she wandered upstairs and entered the small room at the end of the hall. Behind its door were all her mother's personal things. Her father never came in here, except when she asked him. From time to time as she grew up, Charity had sifted through Callista's trunks and boxes, examining silk shawls, lace fans, gold jewelry, everything that might give her some clue about her mother.

Once, her father had shown her the special box filled with valentines that he had sent his wife. Charity had thought it the most romantic thing she had ever seen. Remembering Garnet's comment about Pecker's gift, the girl decided to look at the valentines. Of all her mother's things, they were the most special to her. She shoved a trunk aside and pulled open the box.

The valentines were still beautiful, big red velvet hearts trimmed with inch-wide ivory lace on the outside. She opened one, which was tied with bright red satin ribbons. The inside page was made of thick vellum paper, slightly yellowed with age, and the ink was faded but legible. She followed the familiar lines of Robert Burns's poem "My Love Is Like a Red, Red Rose" and ran her fingers across her father's bold, clean penmanship. "To Callista, my beloved wife, as ever, Jason."

"Too bad it isn't Valentine's Day. Maybe if Papa gave Billie Jo one of these they could make up and not be mad at each other anymore." She laid the old valentine in the box atop the others. Just as she was closing the lid, she heard her father's voice calling her for her bedtime story. Somehow she didn't think he would want to see these reminders of Mama right now. She jumped up and dashed from the room, pulling the door shut hastily.

"That's enough stories for tonight, Charity," Jace remonstrated, closing the book and bending down to kiss his daughter good night.

"Couldn't we read just one more?"

"You can read as well as I, you little minx. Read another story in the morning," he replied with a chuckle as he gave her silky black curls a pat.

"But there's one I want you to hear, too—it's about Mr. Lincoln." Seeing the warning look that often came into her father's eyes when anything connected with the War Between the States was mentioned, she hastened to add, "It's about his growing up. You see, when he was a boy his mama died—'n' his papa remarried a really nice lady named Nancy Hanks and—"

"I know the story, Charity," he said, pain squeezing his heart. *Damn her!* "Did Billie Jo pick out this story for you, by any chance?"

"No. She told me I could choose any of her books and read them. I just like stories about other children who didn't have mamas—at least

189

for a while. Some of them grew up to be real important people."

"Do you worry much about not having a mama?" His voice was thick.

"Sometimes I used to . . . until Billie Jo came to live with us. I really like her, Papa."

"She's done some things with you, given you attention that I can't, I know, Charity." His voice faded. How could he tell her that in a few weeks her companion might be gone? "Is she that important to you, Charity?"

The child studied his face. "I thought she was important to you, too. You need her if you're going to get another boy baby."

His face heated. How close to the truth that might be the child could not know!

"Billie Jo says girls can grow up to do most anything boys can—especially out West, but if you want a boy, I reckon it's all right with me."

"You're my firstborn child, Charity and I'll always love you. Don't ever forget that."

"But don't you love Billie Jo, too?" There was a wistful sound in her voice, as if she feared his answer.

Jace sighed. "She's not anything like what I bargained for, Charity. I wanted a lady to teach you as your mother would have, if she'd lived."

"Then you'll always be in love with Mama. No one else can take her place." It was not a question.

He rubbed his head as a thousand fragmented images spun around in it. "It's not that no one can take her place, Charity. But the woman I wanted for a wife should be . . . well . . . should be someone who doesn't wear pants and doesn't have a pet crow who steals things and wrecks the house." It sounded petty even as he said it. The look in his daughter's eyes confirmed his fears.

"I like Pecker," she said bravely. "He didn't mean to break those old dishes. You never liked them anyway. I heard you say so to Garnet."

The conversation was definitely not going the way he wanted, and there was no answer he could give her about Billie Jo—at least not until the issue of her possible pregnancy was settled. Sighing, he kissed Charity's nose affectionately. "I'm sorry I was angry about Pecker. You get a good night's sleep and I'll see you in the morning."

As he lay staring at the ceiling in his big lonely room later that night, Jason knew he was destined not to get a good night's sleep as long as Billie Jo was down the hall from him. *Do you want her here with you? In your bed?*

She broke every rule about what a wife and mother should be. She was foul-mouthed and outrageously outspoken, blatantly disobedient of his wishes, and for a woman who professed not to want marriage, she responded in an altogether shocking manner in bed. *But she was a virgin, and you did carry her upstairs in a fit of drunken lust.*

He tossed and punched the pillow. What the hell did he want? His house reduced to shambles and his authority over his daughter

completely undermined? Billie Jo's sweet, lilac-
scented little body clinging to him every night?
Jason swore and rolled over. *I just need time to
sort this all out.* He swore some more, stared at
the ceiling, and started to count cattle.

In the wee hours of the morning Pecker, who
had been deprived of his run of the house after
the dining room debacle, untied the rope Jace
had used to secure his cage door. It took a lot
more doing than picking a simple lock, but the
bird was dextrous and patient. Once free of
the cage, he wandered through the downstairs,
searching for Billie Jo. Climbing the steps, he
proceeded to check the second floor. All the
doors were securely closed but one. His keen
eyes saw it standing ajar at the end of the hall,
with a narrow shaft of moonlight streaming out
the door.

The room was piled high with things to
explore. Bright colors peeped from trunks and
boxes. As was his wont, he began to search for
a "gift" for his unhappy mistress. Yesterday he
had given Charity one. Now he would find one
for Billie Jo.

When he could not pull a royal blue satin gown from beneath the heavy trunk lid
imprisoning it, a scarlet ribbon gleaming in
the moonlight caught his eye. He fluttered over
to it and shoved the lid of the box open. The
brilliant colors and crinkling lace trims made
his black eyes dance. He shoved the bright tro-
phies around, then pulled on the scarlet ribbon

until he had freed one large valentine.

Billie Jo heard Pecker's low croak echoing down the hall. "Durn fool crow. It's not even dawn!" She scooted from her bed and rushed to open the door before he awakened Jace. "Maybe he oughta shoot you 'n' cook you," she muttered.

Pecker waddled in with the prize dangling from his beak by a red ribbon. Billie Jo took it from him and walked over to the window. In the dim light she could see it was a valentine. "It's so beautiful . . ." She opened the lace-covered velvet with trembling hands. By now she knew Jason's bold scrawl well. " 'Beloved wife,' something for sure I'll never be," she said softly as she patted the crow and fought back her tears. "We have to return this, Pecker. Where did you—" She stopped short in dawning horror. Surely he hadn't stolen it from Jace's room!

Pulling on a robe, she tiptoed to the hall and looked down it. With a sigh of relief, she collapsed against the door frame when she saw that his door was closed. But where had Pecker obtained his gift? She began methodically checking each door. The one at the end of the hall, always securely closed before, was open now.

She walked to it with the crow patiently shadowing her. As soon as she stepped inside, she knew it was where the crow had found the valentine. A big box of them lay scattered across the floor. "A fine mess you've made," she said, trying to sound cross, not heartbroken. She knelt and began to pick up the big, lacy valentines. Expensive, beautiful tokens of Jason's love for his lady.

"Even if I'd been a proper female, he'd never have loved me. He's still in love with her." She swallowed hard but could not keep the acid tears from spilling down her cheeks. Dashing them away, she gathered up the sonnets and rhymes, protestations of chivalric love—a love that Billie Jo Mingo would never know. Carefully closing the box, she tiptoed from the room.

"Come on, Pecker. We have to pack."

Billie Jo labored over the letter to Jason, throwing away several drafts in frustration. "If a body didn't blubber so damn fool much, maybe she could see to write," she muttered to herself and stared at the third sheet of blank paper. She heard Jace arise and walk downstairs for breakfast and wondered fleetingly if he'd miss her biscuits. For sure more than he'd miss *her*!

Finally she composed a terse note, telling Jace how Pecker had brought her one of Callista's valentines and that she understood why he had kept the collection over the years. No one, least of all her, would ever take his first wife's place. It was too painful for her to remain, and a great cruelty to Charity, as well. He could contact her through Adele when he'd arranged the divorce.

Of course, she couldn't impose on her friend for more than a few days, but she'd have to have that much time to figure out what to do. "Maybe she'll stake me to a train ticket south.

I hear they're looking for women to do laundry and cook in the Colorado gold camps."

When she heard Jace ride out for the day, Billie Jo knew she must face her most difficult task—saying goodbye to Charity. Quietly she brought down her battered old carpetbag and set it on the porch next to Pecker's cage. She would have Hank haul down her trunk and send it to town this evening.

Garnet took one look at the bag and knew what was happening. Her faded brown eyes filled with tears, and she hugged the younger woman. "Thet fool man don't know what he's missin', but mebbe after yer gone, he will. It'll fair break Charity's heart."

Billie Jo let out a strangled sob. "Where is she, Garnet?"

"Down at the coral watchin' the men break them new horses."

"But I don't want you to go!" Charity cried out and ran into Billie Jo's arms.

They were alone at the pond, where she had taken the child to explain her decision. It was not any easier than she had imagined.

"I don't want to leave you either, pumpkin, but sometimes things just don't work out. You knew your papa and I had never met before we were married. Well, when I got here . . . I wasn't the kind of wife he expected."

"You mean you weren't a fancy lady putting on airs like Emmaline Pruett?" the girl said with disdain in her voice.

"A fancy lady like your mama is what your papa wants, Charity," Billie Jo said gently.

"Then he's stump stupid!" the child pronounced vehemently.

"There, you see? You're even startin' to talk unladylike and say cussed things like me. You know that's not what your papa wants."

"I don't think Papa knows what he wants," Charity said, tears again threatening.

"Well, until he makes up his mind, I have to go. If he decides . . . to divorce me, staying here would only hurt you both more. Sometimes the best thing you can do when you love a body is to just walk away and leave 'em be."

"You do love me, don't you, Billie Jo?" She buried her head against Billie Jo's chest and sobbed.

Stroking the shiny black hair, Billie Jo replied, "Yes, Charity, I do love you just as if you were my own, but I have to go. I've left a letter for your papa at the house. Come on now and walk back with me. You'll want to say goodbye to Pecker, and I know he'll want to say goodbye to you."

They walked arm in arm along the dusty trail to the ranch house, saying little, pondering much. Pecker waddled out to meet them. Charity knelt down and hugged the crow, who fluttered his wings and made low croaking sounds. Billie Jo went into the stable and saddled up the beautiful little filly she had named Quicksilver. When Hank brought the trunk, he could return her to Circle E. She tied the carpetbag to her saddle, then brought the cage from the porch and called Pecker.

The crow cocked his head and looked at her, then looked at Charity. Scratching the dusty ground, he acted for all the world like a schoolboy unable to decide which girl to ask for a dance.

"He doesn't want to go," Charity said.

Billie Jo fought the tears welling up and replied, "Well then, I reckon he can stay here for now. I expect when Hank brings my trunk, Pecker'll change his mind and come along." She could not stay a moment longer without breaking down in front of the girl. "You take care of your papa." She swung up into the saddle and waved at Charity and Garnet, then rode off, afraid to look back.

Chapter Seven

When Billie Jo had vanished down the road, Charity turned and trudged into the house, numb with grief and disappointment. "How could Papa not see how perfect Billie Jo is for him, Pecker?"

The crow cocked his head and observed the girl with his piercing black eyes. "Caw . . ." He subsided into several croaks, then ruffled his feathers as if shrugging over the stupidity of humans.

"He's got to go after her and bring her back. He just has to. I'm going to ride out and find him and tell him so."

Knowing that Garnet would not allow her to ride alone, Charity did not change into her riding habit but kept on her ruffled petticoats and frilly dress. She had heard her father say at breakfast that he was riding over to the Kincaids' spread to bring back a number of Circle E cattle that had strayed onto K-Bar land during calving season. It was a long ride and meant crossing Sandy Creek, swollen from summer rains, but she had to do it. Their whole future as a family was at stake.

She saw the letter that Billie Jo had written her father, sitting on the dining room table, neatly folded in an envelope, addressed simply to "Jason." She debated taking it, but decided it best if her father read it in private. With her chin set in stubborn determination, she slipped from the house after Garnet started shelling peas.

The ride was a long one, made more difficult by her full skirts that caught and twisted miserably around the sidesaddle, but Charity had never learned to ride astride. "Maybe Billie Jo can teach me—and Papa will let me have one of those split skirts . . . if only he brings Billie Jo home." Renewing her determination, she kicked her pony into a full gallop.

Within another hour she had reached the ford at the Sandy. She could hear the bawling of cattle from across the river. Gripping the saddle pommel with one hand, Charity urged her pony into the swiftly flowing water.

Jason chased a maverick through a low rolling stretch of scrub pines near the river bank, then lost the cussed beast. Just as he cleared the trees, he saw his daughter start to cross. He also saw the calf plunge headlong into the current, where it quickly began to flail.

"Charity, go back!" he yelled at the top of his lungs as he urged Rawhide toward the creek. The calf floundered, and his daughter turned her pony toward it midstream to help the fool critter. His cry came too late, for he had no more than reached the bank several hundred yards upstream when she grabbed for the calf and was pulled from her precarious perch on the sidesaddle, into the swirling water. She would drown!

In a red haze of terror, Jason raced along the bank, frantically calling for Charity to hold on. He saw her head bob beneath the water, then she kicked clear of the churning hooves of the pony and began to move with clean, strong strokes for shore. By the time he reined in his buckskin and catapulted from the saddle, she was on the bank, urging the pony, with the idiotic calf following it, to swim to her. He raced to her and grabbed her in a fierce hug, going down on his knees, too weak with relief and fear to speak. He held her silently for several moments before her voice registered.

"Papa, you're squishing me. I'm all right. Pretty Girl saved the calf, too. Let me breathe, won't you?"

He released his hold on her and looked into her face, brushing back sopping strands of inky hair. He could never have reached her in time.

If she hadn't swum to the bank so quickly, the current would have carried her to her death. "Where did you learn to swim—you were swimming, weren't you?" His voice was still hoarse with fear.

"Yes, Papa. Billie Jo taught me. We practiced every afternoon at the pond while you were out working. It was supposed to be a surprise for you."

"It certainly was! I ought to tan you good for riding out here all alone. Whatever possessed you? Why weren't Garnet or Billie Jo watching out for you?"

She hung her head like a drooping little flower with its petals soaked after a rainstorm. "Billie Jo's gone. I sneaked off on Garnet." Tears mixed with the rivulets running down from her soaked hair. "That's what I came to tell you. I just couldn't wait until tonight. She loves us, but she said that sometimes the only thing a body can do for someone they love is to just walk away and leave them be."

Jason knelt on the muddy river bank, dumbfounded, unable to reply to that bit of wisdom. He knew that the attachment between Billie Jo and Charity had grown steadily, but . . . *She loves me?* A child's wishful thinking.

Charity plunged on, "She thinks that just because she's not a lady like Mama, she's not good enough for us, but she's wrong!"

Jason could see she'd been crying for some

time—probably since parting with Billie Jo that morning. "Charity, it's more complicated than—"

"But, Papa, I don't need a fancy lady. I need a real woman to be my mama. I need Billie Jo!"

Jason Lee Emory looked away from his daughter's tear-streaked, pleading face into the swirling water of the Sandy, whose turbulence reflected his own inner turmoil.

Gathering courage from her father's silence and the strange, faraway look of uncertainty on his face, Charity pressed her suit. "I think *you* need Billie Jo, too."

Did he? He remembered all their arguments about propriety and how to raise Charity. If Billie Jo had been the kind of wife he thought he wanted, his only child would be dead now. He considered the cruel words he had flung at her the morning after he had taken her to his bed. She had awakened with an expression of such soft bemusement on her face—until he'd ruined it with his selfish accusations. She'd been right about that night, too—he had desired her and seduced her, then blamed her for what was his fault.

"Charity," he began tentatively as he stood up and took her hand, "what made Billie Jo leave this morning? Did she say anything else to you?" The least she could've done was wait until they knew if she was carrying his child!

"She left a note for you. It's on the dining room table."

"Then we'd better get you home and into some

dry clothes while I read that note." *And do a lot of thinking*, he added to himself.

Jason swore as he crumpled the note and threw it across the stained dining room carpet. He ran his fingers through his hair as he paced distractedly. The irony of it! Those damn valentines. Of all the fool things to set her off. He glared accusingly at the crow who stood silently in the kitchen door. "Of all the things you could've stolen to give her, you worthless sack of feathers and claws."

"Caw," Pecker accused, observing Jason's guilty agitation.

Jace was damned if the bird wasn't smirking at him! Pecker's head was cocked and his eyes intent as always when he was studying humans, but did that beak seem to tilt just a bit? Suddenly Jason had an idea—an insane, wild idea that just might work.

On the ride home, holding Charity's small body safe in his arms, he had realized that she was right. He needed his wife just as much as his daughter did. "And you, my fine feathered friend, are going to help me win her back."

Getting the crow into the cage was not easy, but Charity finally achieved the feat by luring the greedy scavenger with a pork chop. Jace tied the cage door securely with rope, now aware of Pecker's considerable skills in picking locks. "We'll be back . . . tomorrow," he promised Charity and Garnet, praying he was right about the "we" part. He would allow time for a second and more suitable honeymoon night in town.

Of course, there was the matter of Billie Jo choosing a most unsuitable place to stay—Adele's fancy house! He could see the sly smile on the beautiful madam's face when he came, hat in hand, to fetch his wife. He wondered uncomfortably why it never seemed to bother Billie Jo that he had been one of Adele's customers. But he supposed it squared with his wife's unvarnished sense of honesty. He had obviously never been in love with Adele. Billie Jo believed he was still in love with Callista.

When he arrived in Miles City, Jason stopped first at the livery stable and put up Rawhide for the night, then headed to Cummins' Emporium. Old Cy would probably charge him triple the price to dig through his crowded back room for such an out-of-season item. Then there was the matter of getting the crow to deliver it, but somehow he had a hunch the canny critter would, this once, do what he wished. He looked down at the crow in the cage as he approached the big mercantile. "There's another pork chop in this for you, you molting old rascal, if you do your part."

After he transacted his business with Cy Cummins, Jace and Pecker checked into the Excelsior, where the dusty rider ordered a bath. As he soaked away the day's grime, he reread the big lace valentine and decided he'd made a judicious choice. It was ironic that he'd never read the verses on any of them before. He had a great deal to say to Billie Jo—if he could only get her to listen.

"In Adele's cathouse," he groused as he dressed with nervous care. Again he wore his best summer suit. This time he *was* going courting. He hoped Billie Jo had left her guns and skinning knife in the trunk along with her britches!

"Well, I'll be damned," Adele breathed as she watched Jason Lee Emory stride into the bar. "I figured you'd come after her, but I didn't expect you so soon—dressed like you were going to the governor's ball," she said, descending the stairs. Her eyes glowed with a combination of amusement and amazement. He was some kind of a man! She'd miss having him for a customer.

"Where is she, Adele?" Jason set the crow's cage on the bar, then began to untie the rope fastening, ignoring her smug expression.

"Upstairs. In my apartment. Not at all a proper place for the wife of a leading cattleman. You hurt her, Jace. She wouldn't say how, but I know it was bad."

"That's between me and my wife, Adele." He could see the customers scattered around the big half-empty room prick up their ears, trying to eavesdrop on their quiet conversation.

Adele looked at Pecker as he climbed from the cage onto the polished bar. "Why did you bring him—as a go-between?"

Jason grinned darkly. "In a manner of speaking."

"I wouldn't bet she'll be willing to see you, Jace."

"She'll do more than see me. She'll leave here with me, but first I do need your help." He took her by the arm and they walked to the rear of the room and sat down at the private table where Adele dealt poker when the mood struck her.

After a brief conversation, she rose and took the fancy lace valentine from Jace, then walked back to the bar and spoke to the crow. "Come on, Pecker. Let's go find Billie Jo." At the mention of his mistress's name, the bird fluttered to the floor of the bar and began to follow Adele.

"I heered 'bout thet critter," one big cowboy said, backing away.

"Damned if'n it ain't bigger than an eagle!" another said with awe in his voice.

Pecker followed Adele while Jace sat at the rear of the room, waiting. The audience below grew silent in anticipation. Word had spread like wildfire that Jason Lee Emory's mail order bride had left him and come to stay with Adele and her scarlet poppies. And now here was Jace, dressed up for a Fourth of July dance, fixing to collect her—and her crow following Adele Wheaton like a well-trained stock dog! Within minutes after Jace's arrival, the slim afternoon crowd swelled rapidly. Everyone's eyes were glued to the top of the stairs where the crow had disappeared. What were Jace and Adele up to with that bird?

"All right, Pecker. Now it's up to you." Adele waved the brightly colored valentine, and Pecker's eyes followed it with avid curiosity. Quickly he seized it from her, then stood, uncertain of what to do with his prize.

"Billie Jo, someone's here to see you," Adele said. "Are you decent?"

"Who is it? Oh, Hank with my trunk. Have him put it in the back room downstairs."

Her voice was flat and low, but the crow immediately recognized it. He dropped the valentine and rapped loudly on the door, demanding admittance as Adele vanished down the hall.

The persistent pecking noise quickly brought Billie Jo to the door. "So there you are, you fickle sack of feathers." She jerked open the heavy door and the crow waddled in, once again bearing the gift.

Billie Jo took one look at the exquisite red satin creation and felt her throat close off. "Blue blazin' hell. I will not cry one more tear! Why did you have to bring me more of *her* treasures? I don't need to have my nose rubbed in the dirt again."

She snatched the valentine from Pecker and raced to the open window across the room. Hurling it onto the front porch roof, she turned to the bird and glared. "There, that's what I think of—ooh, my great blue blazin' gawdalmighty! You couldn't have flown to town with that valentine—and Jace wouldn't have let you bring it with Hank . . . Jace . . ."

She whirled around and leaped out the window onto the steep porch roof. The skirt of her yellow gown caught and ripped on the rough shingles as she careened forward toward the gutter, all the while clawing for the frothy lace valentine. The breeze kept it just out of her reach, fluttering down the length of the roof until it reached the edge. Screeching at the top of her lungs, she seized her prize . . . and pitched headlong off the roof, landing with a loud splash in the horse trough directly below.

The crow, who had followed her out the window, now stood at the edge of the roof until she hit the water. Then with a raucous series of caws, he flapped ungracefully to the muddy ground and hopped up on the edge of the trough. Cocking his head at her, he stared impassively, as if to say, "What a fool thing to do."

Several horses tied in front of the trough broke free from the post. In all the commotion, they skittered off, whinnying loudly while a stray dog barked at Pecker.

The instant Jace heard Billie Jo's strident oaths, he was out of his chair and up the stairs. By the time she screamed, he was racing through the door toward the open window. He heard Pecker's clumsy descent as he climbed out and walked to the edge of the porch roof. By then a crowd had assembled below.

There lay Billie Jo in the center of the horse trough. Her slim legs were shockingly revealed as she splashed the encircling crowd and crow with water. Her hair was plastered to her head and dripping in her eyes as she spit strands away from her mouth while coughing and choking. The only part of her anatomy that remained dry was her right arm, which was held high in triumph. In her hand she clutched the valentine. The lace trim remained pristine and crisp. Nothing about Billie Jo was either crisp or pristine.

She felt Jace's eyes on her and looked up to the edge of the roof, where he was scowling down at her. Blue blazin' hellfire, he was taller than ever from this angle! "Jace, I saved the valentine," she called up to him as she waved it in her fist. When just a hint of a smile curved his lips, she sighed in relief.

He vaulted from the low roof and landed, graceful as a cougar, on the muddy ground next to Pecker, who observed everything with unflappable calm. The crowd parted in gape-jawed amazement, then watched as Jason Lee Emory reached down and hauled Billie Jo from the water, soaking his fancy duds as he picked her up. She wrapped her arms around his neck, still clutching the valentine.

The crow remained perched on the trough as Jace carried Billie Jo across the street, heading toward the hotel. Adele Wheaton stood at the door of her saloon, watching with a broad smile on her face. "Come on, Pecker. Looks like I'm stuck with you for tonight. And don't you go getting in my whiskey and raising another ruckus, either. Billie Jo says you can be one mean drunk!"

Chapter Eight

The sallow-faced clerk behind the hotel desk watched Jace carry his drenched wife across the lobby, dripping puddles of water onto the pale gray carpet. Adam's apple bobbing and eyes bugging from their sockets, he raised his hand to remonstrate, but then remembered Jason Emory's famous temper and decided to search for a mop instead.

Jace called out to him as he cowered behind the counter. "Send up warm bath water, lots of it—fast!"

When he reached the door to his room, he let Billie Jo slide down his body and fished for the key as he held her close with one arm around her waist.

"I've ruined your beautiful suit," she said in dismay, suddenly aware of the distinct odor of wet wool.

He grinned at her. "Not to mention that fetching yellow dress . . . but I do rather like the way it fits you soaking wet." His eyes raked the nearly translucent muslin clinging to every curve of her body. He turned the lock and scooped her up again, carrying her over the threshold.

"Jace, not on the bed! I'll ruin it."

He set her down and wrinkled his nose. "We do both smell like spunk water, don't we?"

"But I saved my valentine." She waved it, then carefully began to open the lace covering.

"How the hell did you lose it in the first place?"

Her face reddened. "Well . . . when Pecker came in with it, I thought he'd stolen it from . . ."

"From the boxful I sent Callista?"

She nodded in misery. "I grabbed it and threw it out the window—"

"And then realized your mistake." Jace felt a smile tugging at the corners of his mouth again. "I can imagine the rest."

Billie Jo nodded. "I guess I'm sorta like Pecker—accident prone, I mean."

"That's an understatement, but I don't mind. In fact, I've sort of gotten used to it. Read the valentine, Billie Jo. I had old Cy Cummins dig through half his storeroom to find valentines in August."

* * *

Shyly she lowered her eyes and read the verse:

Come live with me and be my love;
And we will all the pleasures prove
That hills and valleys, dales and fields,
Woods or steepy mountain yields.
If love's delights thy mind may move,
Then live with me and be my love.

"It's a rough abridgement from old Kit Marlowe, if I recall my school days," he said with a catch in his voice. "I read dozens of those maudlin things, Billie Jo . . . trying to find one that said what I wanted it to. Then I added some to it."

She read his bold, sweeping scrawl across the bottom of the page. It said, "Would you do me the very great honor of being my wife? I love you, Billie Jo." It was signed, "Jace."

"I know we're already married by proxy, but I think Charity would like it if we said the words in church. I'd like that, too," he added quietly, waiting for her response.

Billie Jo thought her heart would burst as she clutched his beautiful declaration of love in her trembling fingers. "Oh, yes, Jace, nothing would make me happier," she whispered. She wrapped her arms about his neck as he held her tightly, stroking her long wet hair. "Oh, Jace, when I saw all her things, the clothes and jewelry, especially the valentines, I thought you'd always love her. Are you sure—"

"I'm sure. I've never been so certain about anything in my life. It's ironic that you found those valentines, Billie Jo—or rather Pecker found them for you. I only kept Callista's things for Charity's sake. If it had been just me, I'd have burned everything, especially the damn valentines."

Her eyes grew enormous and she touched his cheek. "Maybe you ought to tell me about it," she said gently.

"I married Callista after a long, ardent courtship back in Richmond. I was barely twenty, still a boy, filled with childish ideals about cavaliers and Southern belles—ladies to put on pedestals. Well, Billie Jo, I found out how hard it is to live with a woman when she is up on a pedestal." The anguish in his eyes was eloquent.

Oh, Jace. Billie Jo wanted to reach out to him as he paced, combing his fingers through his hair, but she knew he had to get it all out, now that he had begun.

"Callista never liked making love. I believed her when she said only harlots did. Everything I'd been taught as a boy upheld the notion. But I was faithful to her until Seth died. She blamed me for his death because I insisted on living here. She hated Montana and wanted to go back to Virginia. After that—" he shrugged helplessly "—she told me I would have to satisfy my carnal instincts elsewhere."

"So you turned to Adele." So much made sense now.

"Yes, I broke my marriage vows, but for Charity's sake I had to keep up pretenses with Callista. She was a perfect wife in every

213

way that her society dictated she be—tasteful, elegant, soft-spoken, a gracious hostess and doting mother to her children. She presided over Circle E like a queen bee. In return, I was supposed to be the perfect husband—squire her to all her social events in town, shower her with expensive gifts—"

"And send her valentines," Billie Jo added.

"I never read the inside of one . . . until today. I was a fool to want another woman like her to raise Charity, but I was afraid. I never wanted to fall in love again—or be fooled into thinking I had. I knew what to expect from the kind of lady I'd arranged to marry. And she would've known what I expected in return, an instructor for Charity and . . ."

A small smile wobbled on her lips. "Charity told me you wanted a wife to make a boy baby who could run Circle E. Then I turned up and ruined everything."

"You turned up and saved me from my own folly. You also saved my daughter's life. She fell in Sandy Creek this morning and swam to shore, thanks to your teaching. If I hadn't insisted on that fool sidesaddle, she probably wouldn't even have been pulled from her pony."

"Is she all right?" Billie Jo jumped up and grabbed his arm.

"Yes, thanks to you."

She beamed at him then, and asked with a saucy turn of her head, "Does that mean we can both ride astride now?"

He returned the grin. "As if I could stop

you—or wanted to." He pulled her close and lowered his head to kiss her. "About that baby business . . ."

A loud rapping on the door interrupted the kiss. Jace released her, sighing. "That's probably our bath water."

A few moments later the big round tub in the corner was filled to the brim. Jace tipped the bellboys and closed the door, then began to peel off his damp clothes. "Well, what are you waiting for? Last one in has to scrub the other's back."

Billie Jo felt a burble of laughter escape her lips as she began to tug off her sodden gown and underwear, but Jace beat her into the tub. Standing splendidly naked in the knee-deep water, he reached out one hand, palm up.

"I'll help you. Turn around." She did as he asked, raising her wet, tangled mane while he untied the knotted laces of her undergarments. "Fancy silk," he murmured, wondering again about her new wardrobe.

"This belonged to Priss."

"Priss from the fancy house?" His voice choked. Then he burst into laughter, saying, "I should've known. Adele's the only friend you made in town."

"And I mean to keep her as a friend, which means you better not be making any more trips to see her . . . alone . . . at night."

"I don't believe that'll ever be necessary again," he said as he peeled the last wisp of wet silk from her legs and tossed it on the pile of wet clothes soaking into the varnished oak floor. "Come here."

She complied as he knelt in the tub and helped her step into it. "Let's wash the smell of horses away," he whispered as he raised a dripping cloth and pulled her down between his knees. When he began to massage her breasts in a silky circular motion, she gasped and arched forward. "I think I'll scrub your back, even though you owe me," he said with a wicked low chuckle.

Billie Jo ran her hands down his chest, watching droplets of water bead on the springy black hair. She could feel his heartbeat accelerate. "I'll scrub your backside, too," she said in a breathy voice, ripe with promise.

They soaped each other with languorous caresses, laughing and kissing as they experimented with this new way of making love. Finally, when Jace had sudsed her masses of hair, he reached for one of the big rinse pots and dumped cool water over her head while she squeezed her eyes tightly closed against the soap.

"You devil! I'll get you for that!" She pounded on his chest between coughs, then shook her head, spraying water across the floor.

Jace reached for a towel and wrapped her head in a big turban. "Hold that and stand up," he commanded. When she complied, he used another towel to rub her dry, marveling at the delicate beauty of her small, perfect woman's body.

Billie Jo toweled her hair roughly to wring as much moisture out of it as she could while Jace finished drying a slim ankle.

"Now it's my turn," she said playfully, seizing a towel and beginning at his shoulders. By the time she reached his belly, he was breathing very irregularly. She surveyed the hard, pulsing evidence of his desire, then moved swiftly past it to kneel and dry his legs.

When she dropped the towel and stroked his rigid staff, still water-slicked, he felt as if lightning had struck him. "Don't do that or I'll be finished before we even get started!"

She released him with a smile as he pulled her into his arms. As he kissed her he whispered into her open mouth, "Wrap your legs around me . . . like that." He lifted her up against him and she held on tightly with her legs. In a few swift steps they fell onto the bed and rolled across it until he had her lying beneath him, with her hair spread like a scarf of flame across the pillows.

Looking down into her eyes, huge pools of green, darkened by passion, he whispered, "I love you, Billie Jo, and I always will."

"Even if I'm a shameless hussy?"

"Especially because of it—don't ever change. I want you just the way you are."

"I might get a lot fatter if we go on with this baby thing," she said, running her hands down his chest, then lower.

"Yes," he gasped. "Well, I'll love you round as a pear, too—just wait and see." He lowered himself between her thighs and felt her open to him. "Like coming home," he murmured as he entered her. "This time I won't hurt you, love. I'll never hurt you again."

"Shh, Jace, I love you. Love me," she whispered, urging him on as he began to move slowly, savoring every thrust, feeling her arch and fall back in perfect sync with him.

They moved slowly, gazing into each other's eyes, their naked emotions revealed now, nothing held back in their silent, glorious communion. Gradually he increased the pace. She responded, clutching him tightly, drawing his head down to hers for a deep, probing kiss. Their tongues moved in liquid strokes that perfectly matched the rhythm of their lower bodies.

Jace waited for her, feeling her body begin to ascend to completion, sensitive to every nuance as she dug her nails into his shoulders and began to tremble. He kissed the frantic pulse in her throat, then raised himself up to watch the pale skin across her breasts pinken as she gave in to her release, crying out his name.

Billie Jo felt the first rippling contractions of ecstasy pulling her toward culmination. It was what she craved, yet it was so good, she never wanted it to end. Then she felt Jason swell inside her body and begin to shudder as he spilled his seed deep within her. And it was right.

He collapsed onto her, feeling her arms and legs cocooning him, his wife, his small, perfect wife. Gently, still breathing with great difficulty, he rolled over with her, pulling her atop him. Her damp, fragrant hair curtained his face and spilled in flaming glory all about them.

Finally, when she could speak, Billie Jo nuzzled his ear and said, "Well, I guess that settles it. Don't say I never warned you."

"About what?" he asked, stroking her back.

"I just knew I was going to like what we did. I'll never be a lady," she added with a sigh. She felt the rumble of laughter well up in his chest.

He took her chin in his hand and raised her head till their eyes met. "Just keep responding like you did—forget about that lady business. Like the valentine said, 'Live with me and be my love.' That's all I'll ever ask."

She kissed him softly. "Then Pecker will never have to deliver another valentine for you, Jace. From now on, every day will be Valentine's Day."

KATHRYN KRAMER
"Exploration of Love"

To Bob Nicholson,
my special valentine.

"The loving are the daring..."
—Bayard Taylor (1825-1878),
American writer

Chapter One

It wasn't possible to fall in love at first sight; at least that was what Brittany Whitindale had always thought. That was, however, before she glanced up and saw *him* striding across the ballroom floor like a wayward god come to earth.

She could not take her eyes from him. For longer than proper etiquette allowed, she stared. He was a big man, tall and muscular. The breadth of his shoulders threatened to tear asunder the seams of his buff-colored frockcoat. His skin was tanned. Swarthy, a writer would have called it. His thick and vibrant dark brown hair held a hint of curl and was just long enough to brush the back of his collar.

There was no denying that he had a commanding manner or that he was devilishly handsome. His facial features were chiseled, yet there were a couple of imperfections that emphasized his masculinity—a scar from temple to cheekbone and an almost imperceptible bump on the bridge of his nose where it had been broken. His was an interesting face.

"It's the explorer. That's Adam Kingsley!" she heard several young women twitter behind their fans, her younger sister Bessie among them. With sighs and giggles they ooohed and aaahed.

Brittany knew very well who he was. She had seen his picture and read his writings. He was really not a stranger, though she had never been in his presence before. Brittany had been introduced to him and other African explorers through the books in her father's library. Burton, Du Chaillu, Reade, Brazza, and Kingsley. Brave wanderers in the impenetrable reaches of the Dark Continent. She admired each and every one of them, and right from the first Adam Kingsley had drawn her heart as well as her mind.

Brittany had pored over his prose, savoring every detail, reliving every moment of his experiences. Adam Kingsley was a scholar, author, and swordsman who had spent ten years in a half-mad quest for the exotic. A brilliant romantic adventurer whose superb travel books had whetted her appetite for more information about the mysterious foreign continents. As she read his words she had felt at once that they were kindred spirits. Brittany knew that if she had been born a man she would have gone where Adam Kingsley traveled, would have carried out the same bold searches and deeds.

"He hardly looks civilized, I dare say," Bessie prattled in her ear. "Oh, but who cares. He is so handsome. A man guaranteed to turn any girl's head."

And capture her heart as well, Brittany thought. How surprising that a man who looked as hard, strong, and fierce as he did could also have the soul of a poet. He had put the tale of his travels down on paper in a language that was manly yet emotional. The bold and vivid accounts of his journeys to China, India, Africa, and Ceylon had a certain charming sensitivity too.

Now he sought to penetrate the continent of Africa via the waterways. His upcoming quest was to follow the rivers' courses all the way from where their mouths emptied into the salt sea to their source. He would be traveling through unexplored territory on a daring and dangerous venture, the boldness of which was not surprising to Brittany. Were she able, she would have wanted to do the same thing.

From her reading she felt she knew him nearly as well as he knew himself. He was a brave and capable man willing to take risks. His experiences had hardened his features, and she knew in looking at him that he would be a man whom only a fool would cross lightly. Yet Adam Kingsley had a gentle and caring side, exhibited in his outspoken defense of the natives in the lands he had traveled. They were not to be scorned as "deficient Europeans" or "undeveloped white men," he swore, but should be seen as people of great dignity who should be admired for the intricacies and differences of their cultures.

What thoughts were going through his head right now? she wondered. Certainly he didn't seem to be in any hurry to join the throng of revelers. He just stood there for a long time watching the party-goers as if with a secret amusement. Comparing them to the natives he had seen along his pathways? If so, then his expression seemed to say that he found the men gathered here dull and uninspiring. What did he think of the women?

Suddenly he turned his gaze on her, watching her from across the long distance between them. Putting her hand to her throat, Brittany wondered how he viewed *her*. Tall, yes. Slender, most certainly. Graceful, most people said.

She was clothed in a fragile mint green silk gown that swirled around her ankles when she moved. The bell-shaped skirt was tiered and flounced, embroidered with emerald green swirls and pink flowers. The bodice was high-necked, framing her face with a frill of lace and fastened at the throat with a large ivory brooch. The sleeves fit tightly at the armhole but were full at the wrist where they were gathered into a narrow band. A jacket, with embroidery matching that of the skirt, was cut in a V in front and had elbow-length bell-shaped sleeves. Three emerald green ribbons tied in bows held it together.

Adam Kingsley's eyes touched on what Brittany was wearing, then traveled to her hair—thick and long, fashioned atop her head in a bun. The severity was softened with temple and forehead curls. Some called the color strawberry blonde. His gaze, however, moved quickly to her face. He studied her intently. Her skin, while flawless and smooth, was noticeably sun-darkened from walking, riding horseback, or working in the garden. Brittany's face had high cheekbones and a well-molded nose. It was her eyes, however, that most people remembered. They were green, the color of summer grass, rimmed by lashes that were long and thick. Wide eyes that sparkled when she smiled, as she did now.

Adam Kingsley returned the friendly smile with one of his own. He was drawn to the slim, graceful woman with red-gold hair whose features were as classic and tranquilly beautiful as a cameo's. Something about her seemed to offer a sense of peace and tranquillity to one such as he. She was a vision, a mirage, set apart from everyone else in the room by a certain inner glow. A warmth that drew him.

Unlike the other women in the room, she did not make a display of her bosom. She looked pristine and perfect. Nor was she fluttering around him like an agitated butterfly. Instead she seemed calm. Aloof. A woman with a great deal of pride. Adam found himself wanting to get to know her.

"Who is she, William?" he asked the man at his side.

Looking through his monocle, William Fensworth, the host of the gathering, rasped gruffly, "Who is who?"

Realizing that there must be at least fifty women in the room, Adam laughed. "The tall woman in light green who is looking this way."

Squinting for a moment, William announced, "Brittany Anne Whitindale. Tristan Whitindale's daughter."

"Tristan Whitindale . . ." Something about the name rang a bell in Adam's brain.

"The Oxford professor. Historian, biologist, and popularizer of science." William Fensworth cleared his throat, then added, "The one who always sided with Darwin on his theory."

Now Adam remembered. "Of course!" There had been quite a debate on the subject at Oxford. Tristan Whitindale was a man he had greatly respected and whose death he had mourned. Now he was doubly interested in meeting the woman with the red-gold hair. As the small orchestra struck up a waltz, he headed in her direction.

"Ohhh! He's coming this way!" a young woman near Brittany gasped excitedly to an accompaniment of fluttered fans. There was an intake of breath as all the women standing there eagerly awaited the famous explorer.

A quiver danced up and down Brittany's spine. Her senses were a jumble as he made his way toward her. The conquering hero! For so long she had dreamed of meeting Adam Kingsley; now the moment was here.

The music was vibrant and melodic, but the moment he looked into her eyes she hardly heard it. His eyes were even more compelling at close range than she had imagined they would be. Dark brown eyes that seemed to delve into one's soul. The colors in the room were bright, yet it was as if the whole world suddenly blurred as he reached out.

"May I have this dance, Miss Whitindale?" Her hand was captured by long, strong, supple fingers.

Nodding mutely, flattered that he knew who she was, she allowed him to lead her to the middle of the floor.

"I'm Adam Kingsley," he said in a husky rumble, as if he as guest of honor needed any introduction. Pulling her into his embrace, he whirled her into a waltz with a grace that belied his strength. As he moved her across the dance floor with ease, it seemed that her feet barely touched the ground.

It's as if I were flying, she thought. And she was. Or at least her heart was soaring. Out of all the women in the room he had chosen her. The envious eyes of Bessie and the others seemed to burn Brittany as Adam Kingsley guided her by them.

Brittany felt the firm flesh of his fingers on her lower back as he exerted a gentle pressure that pulled her closer to him. Her breasts brushed against his hard chest, and the heat from his body enveloped her. She could feel the strength of his legs brushing against hers with every step. Usually graceful, she felt herself falter and forced herself to concentrate lest she trample on his toes.

"For one so tall you are as light as a feather in my arms," he was complimenting as he led her into an intricate pattern of turns, dips, and swirls.

"Thank you." Oh yes, she was tall, but he was taller. Brittany liked the sensation of feeling fragile and feminine. Lifting her head, she was nearly dazed as she found herself looking directly at the chiseled strength of his lips. Before she could push the thought away she found herself wondering if his mouth would be firm or soft.

"I hope you are enjoying this dance as much as I am." His full lips curved up, and for a moment she feared he had read her thoughts.

"Oh, I am . . ." Her voice was choked. She whose gift of eloquence often commended her as an excellent lecturer now found her voice nearly feeble. Her hand trembled in his. She stiffened, trying to regain her poise. Being so close to him sent her senses spinning.

"Then if you are, please relax." His reputation had proceeded him, he thought wryly. No doubt she misunderstood what she had heard and thought him to be a womanizer. A rogue. A man barely civilized. A "semisavage" as some called him. He squeezed her fingers and whispered in her ear, "Despite what you might have heard about me, I don't bite. At least unless I'm very, very hungry."

Brittany's icy reserve and nervousness thawed. "Then I hope you are not," she said with amusement.

His brown eyes twinkled as he looked deeply into her eyes. "I wasn't when I came in here." Adam was experienced enough about life to know that at certain times there was an instant attraction between a man and a woman, a primitive kind of allure that clutched at him now. "Now I'm not so sure."

Before Brittany could second-guess his intentions, his head lowered and his mouth, warm and hard, touched the soft flesh of her throat just beneath her ear. It was an intimate action that caused more than a few eyes to stare, yet a deeply stirring gesture that gave her no offense. From her reading she knew that Adam Kingsley was the kind of man who gave in to emotions of the moment and did just as he pleased. She would have been lying to herself not to admit that what he had just done had pleased her. For a moment they were both immersed in a world of their own, giving in to the spell of their mutual attraction. But they had forgotten about the rigidness of Victorian society.

Heads turned, eyes stared. Shock froze the features of the onlookers' faces. A stunned, hostile silence spread over the room in reaction to Adam Kingsley's breech of etiquette, a contagious chill that passed quickly from one person to another until it infected the entire room. Even the musicians hurried the ending of their waltz so that they could scrutinize this scandal in the making.

Adam damned himself a hundred times for his impetuosity. "I'm sorry," he murmured, thrusting his dancing partner from his grip and striding away. He had been away from civilization too long, had allowed himself to live by his own laws and rules. Now not only he but an innocent victim of society's pettiness would pay. The sharp tongues of the gossips would be far more dangerous than any swords or spears.

Brittany watched helplessly as the magic of the moment was shattered. She tried to go to Adam Kingsley's side to try to salvage the moment, but the other guests blocked her way.

"Well, sister dear. You certainly made a spectacle of yourself, though I can't say that I wouldn't have done the same." Bessie swooped down upon Brittany like a smiling cherub.

Brittany had taken care of Bessie since the child was ten years old, though at seventeen she herself had been little more than a child. It had been nine years. Years when most young women were in the midst of courting. Instead Brittany had assumed the role of guardian to her little sister, trying to replace the mother and father that had been lost. A thankless job that had all too soon rendered her a spinster. As

Bessie often said, Brittany was way past the age most men referred to as "marriageable".

Brittany took a deep breath, trying to regain her composure. "He really is an amazing man . . ."

"Mmm, but you haven't captured him yet," Bessie cut in peevishly. "Be forewarned that I intend to give you some competition."

"I have no doubt that you will," Brittany answered, looking her sister in the eye.

If Brittany was pretty, Bessie was beautiful. The perfect Victorian idea of what a woman should be. Her eyes were blue, her hair flaxen. Her mouth was pink and full, showing white pearl teeth when she smiled. She was petite as was the fashion, with voluptuously rounded curves that made all men susceptible.

"All is fair in love and war." Any man Bessie went after succumbed to her charms, including those who had first been Brittany's beaus.

But not this time, Brittany thought, clenching her jaw in determination. Adam Kingsley was not just *any* man. Brittany knew in her heart that he was the man for her, the answer to her prayers. A man she intended to fight for in her own subtle way.

Chapter Two

Grimacing and grinning masks, handwoven baskets, and various amulets decorated the east wall of the room, visual reminders of faraway journeys. A hide-covered shield and two criss-crossed spears stood in a corner, honored prizes bestowed as gifts. A large four-foot-high bronze statue stood guard near the doorway, staring as if to see beyond the walls and into the darkness.

It was well past midnight. Adam Kingsley was still up, sequestered in the stuffy, overheated room. A wobbling pool of lamplight illuminated the page he was working on, as well as the various maps, notes, and other scribblings that littered the desk top. Valiantly he was trying to put his thoughts down on paper, but he was not inspired. Since returning to the damp, chill climate of England from the warmth of the East, he'd found himself unable to put his experiences into words.

"BiGod!" Crumpling up the page he had just finished, he tossed it into the wastebasket with a moan of frustration. "Useless, meaningless drivel!"

Trying to blot out the chill and approximate the climate of the foreign lands he loved so well, he had turned up the heat, yet even so he was having a difficult time readjusting to living in his own country. It was not just the weather. He felt alone in London, despite the adulation he was receiving. No one understood him. No one knew much about him. Not really. He was an oddity here, albeit an idolized one.

Oh, he knew he had a following. Readers bought his books by the hundreds and crowded into lecture halls to hear him. He was in demand as a celebrity at parties, a hollow honor bestowed upon him by vain and foolish people. He was a hero for all the wrong reasons. He wasn't a traveler just for adventure's sake or to prove that he was a man. There was a reason for his explorations. Adam Kingsley wanted to make the world a better place.

"They just don't understand."

Nor perhaps did he. Because of what he had seen in his travels, he was a misfit among his own kind. It was difficult for him to be interested in the petty problems of high society when he had seen so much suffering, not only on his travels but here at home in London. Hunger. Disease. Homelessness. People without hope. Adam wanted to do more than just write or talk about it, he wanted to do something, but no one seemed to want to listen to his ideas. They were too concerned with themselves.

Once in his youth he too had been just as shallow as most of society's "gentlemen," encouraged to do as close to nothing as possible. He had raised fighting cocks, drinking and gambling and bedding his share of wanton women. He had hated himself and his way of life. His first journey to Ceylon had started as a kind of suicidal journey, a self-punishment. But if his trip had begun in depression and self-loathing, it had evolved into a quest, an inner search.

"How do I make them see? How can I make them feel what I feel?" It seemed an impossible task.

He was having trouble preparing for his lecture tomorrow morning at the Royal Geographical society, but then he shouldn't be surprised. He had always abhorred standing in front of audiences.

As to the subject matter of his lecture he was more than a bit put out. His audience didn't want to learn about the dignity and beauty of the people he had seen, their codes of honor, the uniqueness of their beliefs, the fairness of their tribal laws. Oh, no. The topic of his lecture was to be "sexual and mating customs among the natives," a titillating subject.

"I should have declined," he said between clenched teeth.

He would have if it weren't for his need of money. He intended to use the funds he would earn for the betterment of the proud, noble people who were even now being threatened by his own countrymen, men who were determined to "civilize and Christianize them." Fools. There was so much they could learn from those they haughtily dubbed "savages." If only they would open their minds. But they wouldn't. All they could think about was mating customs!

And if the men were infuriating, the women were just as bad, viewing him like some prize stud. Adam Kingsley's lips curled up as he thought about the parade of young women who had passed by his room at the club. He would have had to be a fool not to realize what these ladies wanted with him. Marriage!

Some were more brazen than others. Bessie Whitindale, for example. Having found out Adam Kingsley's address and familiarizing herself with his habits and routine, she had made it a point to "bump" into him any chance she could. Forming her mouth into a tempting pout, batting her eyelashes, she had issued several invitations that had little to do with having a cup of tea. Mating customs indeed.

"Fools that we are, we think ourselves so superior. So civilized." He laughed sarcastically. At least among the "primitives" there were certain courting rules.

Dipping his pen in the inkwell, Adam was inspired. Furiously he scrawled across the page. He knew just what focus his lecture would take now. A comparison between his own country's way of finding suitable marriage partners and those of the natives.

"I guarantee that no one in the audience will yawn tomorrow!"

He had witnessed the mating rituals of several different cultures and tribes, but damned if his own countrywoman's didn't beat all of them for daring. And he had no intention of being the prize at the end of some woman's hunt.

Marriage? It was not for him. He squinted as he looked at the lamp's flickering flame. It wasn't that he didn't like women, he did. It was just that he didn't want to be tied to one permanently. No woman could possibly comprehend or share what was in his heart and mind. Adam was happiest when he could be alone with his thoughts and memories. At the back of his mind he was already planning his next excursion. He didn't need a woman and yet . . .

"Brittany Whitindale." Her name invaded his mind despite his attempt to concentrate on other things.

There wasn't an unmarried woman in all of London who hadn't made it a point to pursue him, except *her*. She was conspicuously absent, a fact which was strangely disappointing to Adam. She appealed to him, perhaps because he had caught a tantalizing glimpse of an interesting, passionate woman when he had looked into those fascinating green eyes of hers. Eyes that had sparked with an inner fire that seemed to match his own. Then why wasn't she making herself available?

It couldn't possibly be because she wasn't interested in him. He had seen the way she had looked at him when she hadn't known he was watching her. He had felt the tremor in her fingers when he had taken her hand. Why had she been avoiding him, then? Because he had been so bold as to give her a kiss?

Adam tapped his pen against the desk, trying to tell himself that whether or not she sought him out didn't matter, but the truth was it did. A week had passed and yet she was still on his mind. What was she like? Not as shallow as the others, or so he perceived. What thoughts ruled Miss Brittany Whitindale?

He had asked William Fensworth for various details about her, hoping to quench his curiosity. What he had learned was impressive. The death of the patriarch of the family toppled most families and brought them to financial ruin, but Brittany Whitindale had flourished.

The price of educating sons was so prohibitive that few bothered to educate women. To circumvent this, Brittany Whitindale had educated herself, then had challenged the authorities at Oxford to test her on what she had learned. Defying prejudice, she had passed each test with flying colors. Quite an accomplishment for one of the "fairer sex."

She was a woman of knowledge, esteemed and highly respected. Of all things, Adam valued intelligence the most. Fensworth told him that Brittany was now competing with expensively educated professional men in the "gentlemanly" professions. She was employed as a solicitors' clerk, all the while working her way toward becoming a lawyer. Adam smiled as he thought how that accomplishment would set London on its ear. Undoubtedly she was also one of those women staunchly in favor of the movement afoot to admit women into Britain's learned societies.

"BiGod!" He hoped that whatever she intended, she would be successful. From all Fensworth had told him, she was a woman of spunk, as out of the ordinary perhaps as he. Was it any wonder then that despite all the women who were clamoring for his attentions, he wanted to be in her company again? The only question was how to manage it.

Chapter Three

Standing in front of the hallway mirror, Brittany adjusted her bonnet, taking an inordinate amount of time to complete such a simple task. Perhaps that was because she kept letting her thoughts wander.

An uneventful week had passed despite her hopes to the contrary. After her meeting with Adam Kingsley and their dance, she had been filled with optimistic daydreams, hoping against hope that he might pay a call or that somehow she might see him again. Instead the days had passed by in a monotony of routine. She imagined that today would be much the same.

"Don't tell me that you are going to wear that

hat again." Bessie was quick to give her opinion of the small ribbon-and-feather-trimmed brown felt hat as she came upon the scene.

Brittany was defensive. "What's wrong with it?" It was suitable for a woman who intended to look businesslike.

"Wrong?" Bessie wrinkled her nose. "Oh, Brit! It looks like an old maid's bonnet."

As always the words "old maid" stung, but Brittany refused to let it show. "To the contrary, this hat clearly states that I am a lady who takes her work seriously." Brittany tugged at the brim, tipping the hat from the left of her forehead to the right. "Lace and flowers are for carriage rides, dances, and teas. For what I am doing and what I hope to accomplish, this is proper attire."

"Proper attire," Bessie mimicked, throwing up her hands in frustration.

Brittany's expression showed her displeasure. "We're living in a man's world, Bessie, playing by men's rules. I don't want to call undue attention to myself."

With a toss of her blonde curls Bessie was flippant. "That's where you're wrong. A smart woman uses what charms she has to get what she wants."

Brittany knew exactly what her sister meant. "Well, I won't! I don't connive or flirt to get my way." She abhorred her sister's manipulative way of using her good looks to further her desires. "I want to be appreciated for my intelligence, not for my talent at batting my eyelashes."

"Sister dear, you are such a priss. If you don't stop being so damned proper all the time you will never find a husband." Stepping in front of her sister, Bessie hogged the mirror as she ran her fingers over the velvet expanse of skin that showed above her low-cut bodice. From her smile it was obvious that she was pleased with herself.

"And if you don't stop flaunting your bosom all over London you will never become a wife," Brittany scolded. "A mistress, yes, but not a married woman!"

Brittany shook her head, wondering how she could have failed so completely in her attempts at mothering her younger sister. Had she been too permissive? Perhaps. Wanting to make up for the fact that Bessie had barely known her mother or father, Brittany had bent over backwards to give her nearly everything she wanted, even if it had meant sacrificing her own social life. First she had had to study, then to work such long, tiring hours. Somewhere along the way Bessie had become selfish, spoiled, and self-centered. Any pretense of closeness between them had long since been shattered.

Bessie puckered her mouth into a pout. "Oh, what do you know about it? What could you ever understand of . . . of those feelings? I wouldn't be at all surprised to find that ice water flows in your veins." Reaching up, Bessie plucked at one of her golden curls. "You'll be eating your words when I capture Adam Kingsley."

"Capture?" It sounded so cold, so heartless.

"Yes, capture!" Laughing softly, Bessie recounted all her "chance" meetings with the handsome adventurer.

Brittany was quick to take note of her sister's plan of action, a pursuit that was anything but discreet. But though she yearned for Adam Kingsley herself, it wasn't in her nature to stoop to her sister's tactics. Brittany had far too much pride to offer herself up on a silver platter. It was her plan to try a more honest approach.

"And with Valentine's Day quickly approaching, I think I know just the way to lure him into my golden cage," Bessie was saying.

"Lure him . . . ?"

The chime of the hall clock striking eight silenced Brittany's caustic inquiry as to Bessie's strategy. She was late. Pulling her woolen coat from the coat rack, she struggled into it as she hurried out the door. As she walked briskly down the street she fumbled in her coat pocket, clutching the two coins she would need to take the horse-drawn omnibus.

"Any room?" she called out as the omnibus rumbled up the street.

"Plenty o' room, miss," the conductor replied. He opened the door and gave her a hand up. Once Brittany was inside, his falsehood was revealed. There was hardly enough room to stand, much less sit. She doubted that anyone had ever ascertained precisely how many passengers an omnibus could contain. She elbowed her way through the chattering crowd as the man slammed the door.

Brittany looked out the window at the phaetons, dogcarts, carts, landaus, pedestrians, and carriages. The congestion in the streets slowed the omnibus down, that and all the stops to let people on and off. It always amused her that the people already in the omnibus always looked at newcomers as if they had no business coming aboard. She was reminded of what Adam Kingsley had once written concerning a man's fight to preserve his territorial rights, whether that territory was vast or little more than a place to stand.

Adam Kingsley. The very thought of him conjured up a pleasant memory. Even Bessie with all her contriving couldn't take that away. Touching her neck, Brittany closed her eyes, remembering the feel of his lips. The way he had looked at her and touched her had made her feel special.

"Bedford Row!" called out a voice.

Brittany's eyes flew open. She had reached her destination. Once again she used her elbows to maneuver herself through the throng of passengers, but she paused just before she got to the door. A handbill was pasted on the wall of the omnibus with words that leaped out at her. Adam Kingsley was giving a lecture for the Royal Geographical Society. This afternoon . . . Did she dare? The Royal Geographical Society was closed to women. And yet if she were to sit in the very back row . . .

Chapter Four

The area between St. James's Park and Piccadilly, known as St. James, was undeniably the haven and preserve of the male sex. Now the area virtually brimmed over with gentlemen anxious for a chance to hear Adam Kingsley. Like a colony of well-dressed ants they filed into the Athenaeum.

Founded in 1823 for "scientific and literary men," the Athenaeum on Pall Mall Street was spacious and splendidly furnished with thick Turkish carpets and plush puce-colored velvet sofas and armchairs. Mirrors, paintings of country scenes, and portraits of stoic dignitaries covered the walls.

There were several rooms at the disposal of

club members, including two libraries, two writing rooms, three reading rooms, baths, and dressing rooms. To accommodate all those interested in the day's featured lecturer, the double door between one of the libraries and a reading room had been opened, forming one huge room. Wooden-backed chairs and upholstered sofas were crammed tightly together, leaving little room to walk about. As the "gentlemen" filed in there was a great deal of pushing, shoving, and stumbling.

Adam Kingsley looked up from the podium, watching as the audience took shape. There were young men and old, tall and short, lean and plump, those who were clean-shaven, a few with beards, and many who were mustached. Some wore spectacles, a few had monocles. All quickly doffed their hats, several revealing bald pates, others heads of blonde, brown, black, or gray hair. Most wore expressions that said to Adam that they expected their lust for amusement to be satisfied.

Look at them, so smug in believing themselves to be superior, Adam thought. Undoubtedly they expected him to give a long talk pointing out the inferiority of the natives he had met on his long trek. They were prepared to feel pity, to laugh condescendingly, and to acknowledge their supremacy over God's other two-legged creatures. Adam had something far different in mind.

"Gentlemen . . ."

There was a hush of expectancy as a short,

stout, black-bearded man stepped in front of Adam at the podium.

"It is my honor and pleasure to introduce to you Adam Kingsley, who has recklessly courted danger and death in his travels, all in the pursuit of scientific knowledge. Now he has come back and has brought us a vibrant portrait of those individuals whom civilization has not yet touched. The topic of his lecture today is 'The Mating and Marriage Customs of Lesser Man.' "

The applause was deafening. Adam shuffled his notes, bowed his head deferentially, then reclaimed his position at the podium.

"First of all, let me say that my motive for traveling was to study other peoples, to satisfy my curiosity regarding the other societies of the world, to expand my horizon past Dover's white-chalk cliffs."

As always when he talked about his adventures, Adam felt impassioned. "I was not satisfied with the voluminous reports of missionaries, for these good people wrote reports not to tell of how the country really was but how it should be, unfortunately from *their* perspective. Little wonder, then, that I too thought I would find barbarous human beings, unfortunate creatures all. Instead I found these whom you term 'lesser' to be in some ways far more civilized than I. Or you." Adam smiled at the general intake of breath.

"The custom of polygamy, for example," he said quickly, "while viewed by us as scandalous, makes a great deal of sense in some societies." There was a buzz of whispering. "Polygamy is widespread in Africa. Mothers nurse their babies until they are over two years old and refuse to have sexual relations with their husbands at this time, thus making polygamy essentially a necessity."

Taking note of the condescending smiles on a few faces, he added, "Women among many of the countries I visited need not know the isolation of our English spinsterhood with all its pathetic braveries and hidden sorrows. These African women are never alone. No woman is forced into a life of seclusion. They have a husband, a family, and a home to which they belong and contribute. No woman lacks a male provider. No woman is forced into prostitution to feed and clothe herself, or is cast out onto the streets." Realizing that his tone had taken on a semblance of preaching, Adam cleared his throat, then said, "But I'm getting ahead of myself. Let me begin at the beginning."

Quickly Adam gave a brief description of his latest journey. "I traveled as a trader, exchanging such goods as glass beads, wire, fishhooks, cloth, and tobacco." He smiled as he explained that it did little good to push oneself in among strangers, asking rude questions about their religious and private affairs. Being a trader gave a man respectability among those he met.

"When you appear from out of nowhere to mingle among people who have never seen anything like you, they naturally regard you as a devil. Those with white skin seem to them to be an oddity, staggeringly different from their darker complexions. If, however, you want to buy, sell, or trade with them, they recognize that there is something human about you." Adam looked up, his train of thought disrupted as he saw a tall, slender figure toward the back.

"BiGod!" he breathed. It was a woman. There was no mistaking that. Squinting his eyes, he appraised the intruder and smiled as the strawberry blonde hair gave away the lady's identity. Brittany Whitindale. "Well, well, well . . ." The lady had fortitude and courage to challenge the authority of the Royal Geographical Society. Though the others bristled, Adam was delighted. Her presence in the audience would enliven an otherwise dull assignment.

"As I was saying," he continued, quickly regaining his composure, "Strangers are viewed with far more tolerance if they are providing something that is necessary."

Adam looked down at his notes, but he didn't have to see Brittany to know that she was staring at him. He could feel the heat of her gaze. Why had she come here? Was she showing her dissatisfaction with the male-imposed rules in London town? Thumbing her nose at the "all-boys" club? Satisfying her curiosity about his travels? Or could it possibly be that she had come just to see him? Had their brief moment together haunted her as much as it had him? From time to time those questions intruded into his thoughts as he talked on.

"I was asked to come here today to talk about . . . let us say love . . . among the peoples I have visited. Hardly 'lesser' human beings as Dr. Adams called them, despite the fact that some of their customs are different from ours. I found their manner of doing things far less restrictive than ours."

Glancing up, Adam thought that the starched, stiff collars worn by the men in his audience typified everything about them, the way they talked, walked and made love to their women.

"To begin with, they are more open in their sexuality," he said bluntly. "More honest. If a man wants a woman he shows her without any attempt at pretense. In courting they get right to the point. A man claims a woman by touching her on the shoulder for all to see. Likewise, a woman lets her feelings be known without game-playing. The word 'coy" is not in their language." Adam made it a point to look toward Brittany Whitindale as he said this, and was surprised that instead of looking hastily away she steadily met his eyes. The potency of their mutual gaze stirred him so deeply that he reached up to loosen his own collar.

Oh, Miss Whitindale, he thought, *if only you knew how very much I wish we were alone. Just you and I. Would you blush if you knew how tempted I am to claim you this very moment?*

What would she do if he ever put his desires into actions? What would she think if he placed his hand on her shoulder to lay his claim? What if he gave in to his feelings and did exactly what he wanted to do and carried her away?

"Many of the people I saw on my journey believe in aphrodisiacs or love philtres, and use them often," Adam said, forcing himself to look away. "They use herbs or exotic items like powdered rhinoceros horn that are supposed to increase sexual desire and provoke deep passions—"he heard some of the men chuckle so he added, "just as oysters, watercress, and curry are said to do in *our* society."

Aphrodisiac, Adam thought. Certainly that was something he had little need of. His appetite for lovemaking had always been strong. Even so, he had yet to find the right mate even among all the women he had met on his travels. But then, perhaps he wanted too much.

"In some areas I visited, the groom has to pay the 'bride price,' money, goods, or services to the bride's family in recognition that her services are valuable and that the family's loss of her requires compensation." The scowls on the gentlemen's faces clearly showed disapproval. "You frown, and yet in some areas of our own country the bride has to bring a dowry. A throwback to our past." There was a murmur of assent. Strange that while they objected to a man paying for his wife, they accepted a woman paying for her husband.

"In other countries, marriages are arranged by the couple's parents, due in great part to the respect that the elders are held in. Unlike our women who are searching for romantic love, such a thing is of negligible importance to the peoples of China, India, Ceylon, and Africa. Sometimes a man and wife have not even met before their wedding night. The bonds are those of blood, between parent and child, sister and brother, rather than husband and wife."

Adam could see several yawns and decided to omit some pages. "My research into initiation rites has made me familiar with both male and female circumcision." Brittany Whitindale's presence in the audience caused Adam to lower his voice as he said, "Various forms of female circumcision diminish or even destroy a woman's capacity for sexual pleasure." Such a pity, he thought, for there was nothing more beautiful than a man's knowing he was bringing a woman the ultimate pleasure. "This practice takes the place of the chastity belt that our own ancestors elected to use to make certain their wives were faithful." And yet a woman who is given a man's full love and devotion has little need to turn elsewhere, he thought.

Adam touched on several additional subjects: omens, superstitions, ancient rituals, traditions. As he talked he emphasized how the English too were still governed by the beliefs of their ancestors, though they might be unaware of the significance of some of their traditions.

"The unbroken circle of the ring has influenced spells, rituals, and legends since the days of the pharaohs. The ring has no beginning and no end and symbolizes perfect unity for lovers," he said, looking directly at Brittany once again. "Unwillingness to marry is indicated by putting a ring on the little finger of the left hand, while wearing one on the index finger shows that one is searching for a partner." He smiled as he thought he must be certain to take a look at her hand. "The third finger of a woman's left hand has always been reserved for an engagement or wedding ring because of the erroneous belief that an artery runs directly to this finger from the heart."

Once again Adam's gaze centered on Brittany Whitindale, only this time he couldn't look away. Strange, but he hardly knew what he said next or how he concluded his speech. It was as if he were moving in a dream. He heard the gentlemen applaud, then the next thing he knew he was standing beside her. She was poised to leave, but Adam was having none of that. There might not be another chance to be with her.

"Please . . . Miss Whitindale . . ." Without knowing that he did so, Adam reached out and touched her shoulder.

"Why, Mr. Kingsley. Are you staking a claim on me?" she asked, looking him right in the eye.

Remembering that he had talked about that custom in his lecture, Adam smiled. "Perhaps. Do you have any objections?" He looked at her long and hard.

"Objections?" Brittany felt strangely calm for someone who might well be playing with fire. "No . . ." To the contrary, she felt the excitement of standing at the edge of a precipice.

Chapter Five

A half-moon lay over the Thames like a prop on a stage set. There was just enough moonlight gently stealing down to dust the pavement with silver as Brittany and Adam strolled along. London was magical at night, a half-real maze of gray spires and dark stones. A faint mist gave the gas-lamps an eerie glow as the lamplighter set them afire.

"Such heart-catching beauty has this London of ours," Adam said, lost in the spell of the moment. "I'd nearly forgotten just how mysterious the city looks when it grows dark." After having "laid his claim" on Brittany by touching her arm, he was walking her home.

"To me London is a dark puzzle, a place of

secrets," Brittany said softly, looking at the Tower in the distance. "Haunted by the past."

London Bridge was deserted, little more than twin rows of lamps over the dark river. The Tower of London lifted its gray walls and bastions in the night. Only one small window was lit, a tiny square of gold high up in a turret.

"And its ghosts," Adam whispered. He shivered as he remembered all the stories he had heard as a child. Sir Thomas More, Anne Boleyn, the nephews of Richard III, and so many others had met their bloody deaths in the Tower. And the English called others uncivilized.

It was eight o'clock; the baked-potato man had departed, the kidney pie man had just walked away with his warehouse on his arm. The cheese monger had drawn in his blind. The little chandler's shop with the cracked bell behind the door was shutting up. The small brilliantly lighted shops that stayed open were all the more splendid because of the contrast they presented to the darkness around them.

"Roman London must have been deadly dull after dark," he said, imagining himself back in that time.

"Without these marvelous street lamps." Brittany gestured toward the arc lights burning over the streets.

"Uh huh. But probably not as dangerous." He paused to look behind him, keeping his eye on a man who clung to the shadows. Adam led Brittany across the street. "Did you know that the law of the Middle Ages assumed that any man who walked the streets at night was bent on evil?"

"Certainly *that* one looked as if he were up to no good," she answered, hurrying along.

Everyone knew that there were day people and night people in London. Thieves, pickpockets, and all sorts of rogues walked the night. Brittany felt grateful that Adam was with her.

For a moment his expression was clouded. "Sometimes London reminds me of a jungle."

"A jungle?"

"Ancient and primitive things come out at night. Beasts of prey." Strange, Adam thought, but in some ways he actually felt safer moving through unexplored territory than walking the streets of his own country. Who knew what cutthroat might jump out to separate a man from his purse or a woman from her virtue? He put his arm around Brittany protectively as they walked through the shadier areas of London.

A big gray and white striped tomcat of great girth and dignity strutted out from behind two large crates. Brittany dubbed him Henry VIII when she noted that he was preening for his feline harem, six in all. She and Adam paused to watch as the tom wooed one favorite female friend with savage sonnets.

"He's a thief of another sort," Adam whispered in her ear, his breath stirring her hair.

"Out to steal their hearts." *Just as you have stolen mine*, she thought, pausing to listen to the tomcat's serenade. It was the only sound that broke the melancholy stillness of the night as they walked along.

It feels so right being with him, Brittany thought. *As if it were meant for us to be together like this*. She wanted to tell him how she felt but said only, "I haven't told you how much I enjoyed your lecture."

"Nor have I told you how surprised I was to see you among those stiff-necked gentlemen." He looked over at her and smiled as he asked, "Are you always so bold?"

"Always!" Brittany answered, trying to keep up with his long stride. "When there is something important to me."

"Such as challenging the authorities at Oxford?"

She was surprised that he knew. "That among other things." Remembering that he had expressed annoyance at women who played coy, she made her confession. "I also wanted to see you again."

So her being there was no accident, Adam thought. He was pleased and flattered. "I'm glad. I wanted to see you again too, Brittany. Very, very much."

Several men and women moved slowly through the streets. Parties returning from the different theaters congregated at occasional corners. Hackney coaches, carriages, and theater omnibuses rolled swiftly by. They had reached a congested but safer area of the city.

Brittany despaired as she saw the familiar outline of her home looming up ahead. "Mine is the third house on the left." She pointed toward a small but elegant two-storied brick house which had been built in the previous century.

He's going to see me to the door and say his goodbye, and perhaps I'll never see him again, she thought wistfully. She didn't want that. There were so many things she wanted to tell him. They had only begun.

"We're here already?" Adam couldn't hide his disappointment. Had he known they would reach their destination so quickly he would have walked more slowly.

"I don't live that far from the Athenaeum." Brittany took a long time in searching through her reticule to find her key.

"Not far at all." And now he would be expected to politely take his leave. "Brittany . . ." Oh how he wished they were in Cabinda, following the natives' rules. They thought nothing of a man staying with a woman as long as he pleased.

"Oh, here it is." She produced the key, moving slowly as she unlocked the door. Her eyes were huge as she looked up at him. "Thank you, Mr. Kingsley, for walking me home." She held out her hand and felt her heart stir when he took it in his. His hands were large and warm. Even through her gloves she could tell that.

"You are most welcome, Miss Whitindale." He leaned against the door frame, his eyes glittering as he looked at her. *No, BiGod, he wasn't going to tip his hat and end the evening so quickly*. At least he had to try. "Aren't you going to ask me in?"

It was late and propriety stated she should say no, but Brittany didn't care. "All right." Stepping aside, she motioned him into the house, hoping he wouldn't hear the thumping of her heart. Taking off her hat, she carefully put it on the hat rack, then removed her gloves. "Would you like some tea?"

His grin was lopsided. "How about something a little stronger? Whiskey perhaps?" He needed something to relax him.

"The only thing I have is brandy." She had a small glass of it occasionally to help her get to sleep, but she said quickly, "for medicinal purposes."

"Of course." He winked at her, then followed as she went into the study.

Though she didn't look at him, Brittany knew he was examining her home, as if by doing so he could know her better. "This is where I live. I redecorated it after my parents died to suit my tastes. And of course my sister's."

The rooms were large and airy with several windows. The natural wood floors were polished to a high shine with colorful throw rugs here and there. The chintz draperies gave it a homey touch. A fire glowed in the stone fireplace. There was a large blue velvet settee, a desk, and several high-backed wooden chairs. A profusion of plants made it appear as if she too had journeyed to faraway jungles.

"Very warm and comfortable." He watched as she took two glasses from the cabinet, then poured the dark golden liquid into each.

"We can toast your successful lecture," she said, handing him a glass.

Walking to the bookshelves, Brittany ran her finger across the spines of the books, pausing when she reached those on Adam's travelings. "I've read every one."

"I'm flattered." He didn't believe her. It was what people told him to be polite. "And which one was your favorite?"

"The one on your journey with the Bantu peoples," Brittany answered right away. "It was interesting to me that their language has characteristics that are not common to any other language. I remember your theory that their original homeland in Africa seems to have been Cameroon Mountain and the surrounding area and that they displaced or absorbed the Bushmen." Brittany paraphrased the highlights of his journey in which Adam had attempted to retrace the pathway the original Bantu had taken. "But perhaps what fascinated me most was their belief in a supreme god."

"Nzambi."

"The creator." He took a gulp of his brandy, welcoming the warmth it brought to his blood. "Undoubtedly Christian influence played its part. Nzambi has driven out the ancient deities. They have been reduced to the rank of demiurges, enemies of the supreme god. Spirits."

"You wrote of the importance of family ancestors to the Bantu tribes, that they are intermediaries between mortals and Nzambi.

261

Sometimes I wish our ancestors could or would intercede . . ." Her voice trailed off.

Adam was impressed. He was certain now that this woman *had* read his latest journal. "Enough." He took another sip of brandy as he appraised her. Now he knew what caused that sparkle in her eyes. Intellect. He sensed that there was passion there too.

"I'm what you would call an armchair explorer, Mr. Kingsley. You travel physically, I do it vicariously." Brittany's housekeeper had left one lamp burning. Now Brittany lit another. The light cast their silhouettes on the wall.

Adam looked at his surroundings, taking in the many books, the half-finished needlepoint, the writing paper and pen on the small corner desk. "Are you a writer too?" he asked.

"I dabble in it. Poetry mostly. Soulful scribblings." She curled up in her favorite position in a corner of the settee, but he remained standing.

"A poet. I am too . . ." His eyes moved slowly over her. "But I will shamelessly borrow a verse from Lord Byron in describing you. *She walks in beauty, like the night, of cloudless climes and starry skies . . .*"

She was under the dizzying spell of his sensuality. Her heartbeat was erratic, her breathing quick and shallow. She shouldn't be doing this. It was late, and the very fact of his being here might well start a scandal. But how could she tell him to leave?

"You look lovely in the lamplight," he whispered. "Your hair picks up the vibrancy of the fire's flame." Walking over to her he reached forward, taking out one of her hairpins. "Let it down. Please."

The way he made the request was provocative. Brittany's common sense told her to refuse, to tell him that it was time he went on his way, but her emotions, not her intellect, were in control. Slowly she reached up, taking the pins one by one from her upswept curls. Like a red-gold waterfall they tumbled down. She shook her head, sending her hair swirling in a soft, fragrant cloud around her face.

For a moment his eyes were unreadable, but then his fingers stroked the cool silk strands. He got down on his knees, leaning forward so that his eyes were on a level with hers. What was it about this woman that drew him so? He wanted to embrace her, wrap her up in a protective silken cocoon, yet at the same time his blood surged with yearnings of a more carnal nature.

"What do you know of me?" he asked, taking a deep breath to regain his composure as he stood up. She was obviously well-bred. A lady. A Victorian-raised woman who would think just as her society did. She would be shocked if she knew that he had his own set of rules.

"I know you have raised your voice on behalf of the African peoples, that you have in your writings tried to show others how important it is to understand them and respect their cultures. I know you have been involved in trying to fight the injustice that we English, as well as the French, Belgians, and Germans, are wreaking upon them."

He pulled away from her. Going to the bookshelf, he picked up one of his books, then flung it aside. "But what do you really know? Not about the author, but about the man?"

Her voice was impassioned. "I know that you are a man of deep emotions, a caring man. A man with a yen for adventure."

Slowly he walked back toward her. "It's said that I am a connoisseur of women. Do you believe this?" If she was afraid of him, now was the time to end this moment before it went any farther.

Her powerful attraction to him made her uneasy. Her voice faltered a bit as she said, "I believe you are a man who appreciates beauty in all things. I admire you for that."

Adam looked at her long and hard, trying to fathom what was going on in her mind. Would she understand the potency of what he felt for her, or would she be like most women and desire a long, sterile courting? Something he did not have the time to pursue. Could she comprehend how it felt to walk with danger at your back, to know that you had to reach out for happiness while it was in your grasp or lose the moment forever? Did he have the right to make love to her and then ask her to wait for him while he was off in distant lands?

"Perhaps I should go," Adam said sharply, thinking to protect her.

"No. Don't." Looking up at him, seeing the emotions in his eyes, she was caught up in an enchantment. With him she felt herself to be everything she had always wanted to be. The kind of woman a man like Adam Kingsley could desire. He made her feel beautiful, and she loved him all the more for it.

"Did you know that I like to make love by candlelight?" He was candid.

"Yes." She didn't even blink. This was what she had wanted since she had first set eyes on him, perhaps even before that when she had read his books. She was so lonely, so incomplete, so needing of his love. "I remember reading that you like to examine your lovers slowly, using a candle as your guide."

"You read that in my poetry." He thought at that moment how he would like to write a poem about her, about how she made him feel at this moment.

"Once a small drop of hot wax branded one of your mistresses on . . . on her . . . derriere," she said, using the French word.

He was amazed. "How did you know that?"

"From a letter you wrote to Roger Blackstone," she said softly. "Needless to say, his wife Agatha made it the talk of the town." She couldn't help but smile.

"Is that so?" Going to the nearest lamp, the one by the settee, he blew it out. "Well, I promise to be more careful with you."

The thought of him viewing her by candlelight brought a warm tingle up and down her spine. "I often wondered if that was a native ritual."

"To the contrary. A Kingsley tradition," Adam

said matter-of-factly. Oh, she was calm and controlled now all right, but what would she look like in the throes of passion? Slowly his eyes moved from the hem of her skirt to her face.

Bending down, he gently touched her arm, turning her to face him as he sat down beside her. Time seemed to stop as they looked into each other's eyes, then without a word he pulled her close against him. Wrapping his left arm around her waist, anchoring her to him, he cupped her chin in his hand. His mouth traveled to her ear, his teeth nibbling on the lobe.

Brittany caught her breath, gasping as she felt his warm lips slide down the column of her throat. His fingers unfastened the top three buttons of her blouse and he nuzzled the tender hollow just below her collarbone.

A tingling warmth coursed through her body, spreading like wildfire as his tongue tasted her flesh. "Mr. Kingsley . . ." Considering the intimacy they were sharing, such formality seemed ridiculous. "Adam . . ."

Her fingers tangled in his thick, dark hair. She clung to him with all her strength. She had never realized the depth of her own need until now. Her body was innocent of sensuality, but it came vibrantly alive. Her thoughts scattered into chaos. Her body was a maelstrom of need.

"I knew it." His voice was husky. "I knew you would be a passionate woman." Slowly he lowered his head, keeping his gaze on her soft mouth, then his firm lips claimed hers. Their breaths mingled.

Brittany had been kissed before, twice in her life. Even so, she was not prepared for the jolt of liquid fire that swept through her veins as Adam Kingsley's lips pressed against hers. She could only stare at him mutely, then closed her eyes. Shyly at first, then with increasing boldness, her mouth and tongue moved to meet his.

For Adam the reaction to her nearness, the soft yielding of her mouth, unleashed a strong surge of desire. He knew an intoxicating yearning that had nothing to do with brandy. He was stunned and shaken to the core by the depth of his response to this woman. His fingers fastened in her hair as he kissed her deeply.

Again and again he kissed her, his tongue dancing and dueling with hers. Brittany strained against him. He was so hard, warm, and strong that all she wanted in the world was to be near him like this, to spend the rest of her life locked in his arms. She was so entranced that she didn't hear the front door slam, didn't know they were being watched until her sister's voice broke the spell.

"Well, Brit, it looks as if you have cornered the famous Adam Kingsley. Tell me, just what kind of exploration is he doing?"

As if she had been stung, Brittany pushed away from Adam's arms and bolted to her feet. Raising her hands to her hair, she frantically tried to smooth it into some semblance of order. "We . . . we were discussing his books," she murmured, embarrassed at having been caught and wishing Bessie would just vanish.

For all her scolding of her sister's habits, it appeared she herself was every bit as wanton.

"Of course. I can see that for myself," Bessie scoffed, looking pointedly in Adam's direction. "And giving him something to write about as well? The mating habits of English women perhaps."

Adam's gentlemanly instincts quickly arose. "Now see here, Miss Whitindale," he said stepping forward. "I merely walked your sister home from one of my lectures. We were discussing the courting rituals of one of the Congo tribes and I was demonstrating."

"In great detail," Bessie said with forced sweetness.

"Yes . . . well . . ." Adam was uncomfortable. He knew that it wasn't because of propriety that Brittany's sister was acting as she was. It was jealousy pure and simple. Well, he didn't need to be prodded toward the door. Jumping up from the settee, he strode to the door, pausing only to say, "Good night."

Chapter Six

It was just three days to Valentine's Day, and though it was a holiday that Brittany usually ignored, Adam Kingsley's presence in London and the kiss they had shared gave her a different outlook this year. She wanted to do something special, something that would let him know how she felt. Sitting at her desk surrounded by a world map, colored paper, scissors, lace scraps, glue, pens, paint, and ink, she was fashioning a valentine. Not an ordinary valentine or one that was foolishly sentimental, but one that would have special significance for him.

"Really, Brit, that is the strangest-shaped heart I've ever seen," Bessie said, coming closer to examine it.

"That's the way I want it," Brittany retorted, her tone sharpened by the fact that she was still peeved with her sister for her rudeness the other evening. Since that time, Brittany had not heard a word from Adam Kingsley.

Bessie looked again, crinkling her eyes. "It's lopsided."

Brittany cocked her head. "So it is." She wanted it to be that way. Little did Bessie know that it wasn't a heart at all but the shape of Africa, sometimes called the heart-shaped land. Adam's beloved Dark Continent.

"I can fix it for you." Bessie held out her hand as if to snatch it away.

It was the straw that broke the camel's back. "Don't touch it!" Clutching it to her breast, Brittany was adamant. Bessie wasn't going to spoil this the way she had that magic moment with Adam.

Throwing up her hands, Bessie shook her head. "All right. All right." She tossed her blonde curls and looked as if she might storm off, but she hesitated, her temper cooling. "If you are still angry with me for ruining your little tête-à-tête, I said I was sorry."

Brittany's voice was stern. "Your manners were appalling! Mr. Kingsley was a guest in this house and as such should have been made to feel welcome."

A high-pitched giggle filled the room. "Welcome? You were making him more than welcome, sister dear."

A blush stained Brittany's cheeks. She had to

admit to herself that she had been found in a compromising situation. "That, Bessie Lynne, is none of your concern." And yet she knew that it was. Her conscience stabbed at her. She had most certainly not set a good example despite all her preaching of Victorian morality. Had Bessie been found in a man's arms, in the semidark, unchaperoned, Brittany would have reprimanded her severely.

"Have it as you may." Bessie shrugged her shoulders as if to say what difference did it make, then took a step closer, peering down at Brittany's "heart." "You've always said that Valentine's Day is silly. Why did you change your mind?" she asked, changing the subject.

Brittany answered in one word. "Adam."

"Ohhh . . ." Bessie drew her clenched fists to her bosom. "Cupid strikes at last. Tell me, did you place a bay leaf under your pillow before you went to bed last night so that you could dream of him?"

Brittany ignored her and concentrated on making the valentine a masterpiece. First she bordered it with lace through which she threaded a thin red ribbon. Carefully with pen and blue ink she drew waterways on her small replica of Africa, according to the way Adam had said he imagined them to be. Next she glued leaves and flowers in the areas known to have jungles. On the back she wrote a poem.

Like an island waiting to be explored, my heart awaited you.

Kathryn Kramer

*Keeping a dream close to my heart, I
   longed to be fulfilled.
Then one moonlit night you came and
   taught me wishes do come true.
Now with wings on my heart I wait for
   what fate has willed.*

Critically Brittany reread her verse. She
wasn't exactly Elizabeth Barrett Browning,
but she thought she got the message across.
But was she plunging headlong into heartache?
Would she love only to lose Adam Kingsley? He
was a man who had had many women in his life
and his bed. Did that matter to her?

Closing her eyes, Brittany felt a chill flash
down her spine as she remembered the way he
had kissed her. She couldn't get the taste of his
mouth from her lips or forget how right she had
felt in his arms. She cared deeply about him,
and that caring had a need to be fulfilled, just
as her verse had said.

*The chance for love sometimes comes but once
in a lifetime*, she thought. Wasn't it said that
it was better to have loved and lost than
never to have loved at all? Remembering one
of Shakespeare's sonnets in which he had
written about a young woman taking her
virtue to the grave, she felt assured of her
decision.

"Are you finished?" Sitting at a small table a
few feet away, Bessie was working on her own
valentines, making bright red hearts trimmed
with ribbons and lace in triplicate. Instead of

272

making up her own poems, she was copying out of a book of verses.

Brittany carefully appraised her own handiwork, reading and rereading her poetry. "Yes, I'm finished." With a large scrawl she wrote, "Love, Brittany." Fumbling in the drawer, she found a large white envelope. Carefully she slipped the valentine inside.

"Aren't you going to let me see?" Craning her neck, Bessie didn't try to hide her interest.

"And have you criticize my masterpiece?" Brittany shook her head, saying crisply, "No!"

Walking to the window, she peered out at what had been a cloudy day. As if giving her a sign, the clouds had lifted and now it was a beautiful sunny afternoon. A perfect day for a walk. So thinking, she wrote Adam's name on the envelope and headed for the door.

Chapter Seven

There was a chill in the air that Adam felt to the very bone as he rode in the open carriage. The humidity made it worse, he supposed, buttoning up his outer coat. "Valentine's Day be damned!" Should he turn back? Was he on a fool's errand? His head told him yes, but his heart whispered no.

I always considered myself to be a more than reasonable fellow, yet here I go, off to get a Valentine's Day gift like some love-besotted puppy! he thought, clenching his jaw. But despite all his musing, he seemingly couldn't help himself. He who had always considered this lovers' day a nuisance, who had never before given in to the spell of the day, was intent on getting something for his lady.

"Valentine's Day," he said again, "as pagan a ritual as ever I've seen." A tradition that he had traced back to the Roman days and the Lupercalia, a festival of youth. A time when young people chose their sweethearts by lottery. Young girls deposited love letters in a large urn and the letters were drawn out by young Roman men who in the following year courted the girls whose names they had drawn. It was not unlike several native customs wherein a woman wrote a favored symbol on a stone and dropped it in an earthen jar. The man who drew out her "sign" was thought to be selected by the gods to be her lover.

"BiGod, the next thing you know she'll have me eating out of her hand. I'll be searching for a love potion." He gripped the sides of the carriage. "I'll be thinking about marriage." The very idea made him panic. Tying himself down with a wife was the last thing a reasonable, adventurous man would do. It would be like clipping one's own wings.

"Driver! Driver!" It was better to turn the carriage around and head back to his room at the club.

"Wot yer be wantin', sir?" Craning his neck, the carriage driver stared down from his perch.

Adam shook his head. "Nothing. Nothing at all, my good man. Just carry on." His destination was a jeweler's shop in the fashionable West End.

The carriage passed several shops, the apprentices and shopmen busily engaged in cleaning and decking the windows for the day. Signs and emblems announced a bakery, a haberdashery, and a tailor. Large red, green, and yellow bottles in the window, sparkling like rare jewels, gave evidence of an apothecary.

"Here we are, sir." Well-shaped gilt letters shone above the jeweler's door.

Alighting from the carriage, Adam stood before the jeweler's window, scanning the array of watches, rings, bracelets, pins, and necklaces, wondering which to choose.

Perhaps a ring. Something simple. No. Rings signified betrothal. Brittany Whitindale might misunderstand. A bracelet? He decided against each one as being too gaudy. Brittany had reserved and elegant taste.

"Would you like to look at my array of necklaces?" Poking his head around the corner, the jeweler beckoned Adam in. "I've several that I'm certain will be just what you are looking for."

The jeweler held up a black velvet cushion draped with strings of pearls that looked like gleaming white teeth. Adam waved it away.

"Would you be interested in diamonds, sir?"

"No!" Adam had seen firsthand the sweat, pain, and toil of the natives who worked the diamond mines. "Something in gold."

"Something for Valentine's Day?" The balding man smiled. "In the shape of a heart?"

It seemed appropriate. "Yes."

Reaching beneath the counter, the jeweler pulled out a black velvet box and opened it. There, surrounded by lockets in every shape and size, was the ideal one. The gift Adam had been looking for. A locket formed like a heart. Sparkling in the light, it seemed to Adam that it had been fashioned just for Brittany's delicate, swanlike neck.

He had it inscribed, "To Brittany, that I may know the secrets of your heart, Adam." Reaching in his money pouch, he paid the jeweler, selected a small red velvet box for his purchase, and left the jeweler's store.

Adam climbed back into the carriage feeling lighter of heart than he had in a long time. Was it possible that the poets were right? Was there really such a thing as love? Up until today he had dismissed such a notion as romantic nonsense; now he wasn't so sure.

The carriage bumped and jolted as it careened through the midday traffic, but Adam didn't complain. Damned if he didn't even find himself humming a tune, a melodic ditty he had heard aboard ship. Reaching his club, he took the steps to the second floor two at a time.

As a younger son of a well-respected family whose income was limited to four hundred pounds a year, Adam had not felt the need for a house or a retinue of servants. The club was his home when he was in London, and it had served him well. Even so, he would have been lying to himself not to admit that there were times when it was devastatingly lonely to open the door to his room and not have anyone there to greet him. It was a thought he put far from his head as he turned the brass knob.

"What the . . . ?" Two envelopes fluttered to the floor as he opened the door, a large one and small one. Adam opened the big one first, smiling as he pulled it out. Immediately he knew who it was from. What she had done warmed him. His heart was in Africa. She knew. "Brittany." A clever valentine. Definitely not the usual.

"Like an island waiting to be explored, my heart awaited you.
Keeping a dream close to my heart, I longed to be fulfilled.
Then one moonlit night you came and taught me wishes do come true.
Now with wings on my heart I wait for what fate has willed."

He read it aloud. Her poem touched him. Like a flower waiting to blossom she was opening up her heart to him.

"Fate . . ." So she too felt that their being together was destiny. He thought about the other night, how fragrant her hair was, how wide her eyes, how soft her lips and wanted to see her.

Adam hung Brittany's valentine on his wall, along with his other mementos. Then remembering that there had been another missive, he opened that envelope. His feelings were in tur-

278

moil as he read it. It was from Sir Winthrop Baker, a member of the British Association for the Advancement of Science. The good news was that he had received backing for his latest venture, a goodly sum. The bad news was that the ship was leaving for Africa the next week.

Chapter Eight

The setting sun was a huge orange disk hovering like a ball in the sky. It was an unseasonably warm night for February, without rain, wind, or fog as if London had been kissed by Cupid's warm breath just to make a special Valentine's evening. The night could not have been more suitable if he had planned it, Adam thought as he helped Brittany descend from the carriage.

"It's a lovely night, I am with a beautiful woman, and there is magic in the air," he whispered in her ear, leading her in the direction of Covent Garden and the Haymarket.

Brittany had taken special care to look fashionably radiant. She wore a full-skirted white wool dress trimmed in black piping with pagoda sleeves that gave it an Oriental flair. Her hat, a far cry from the plain one she had worn to Adam's lecture, was richly trimmed with black braid and peacock feathers. For his part, Adam looked dashing in a brown and black plaid frock-coat that emphasized the breadth of his shoulders, and black trousers.

"We dine in style tonight," he said as they approached one of the more elegant dining houses.

Stepping inside, Brittany was dazzled by the Edwardian decor, done in plush red and gold. There were ten chandeliers, each flickering with six candles illuminating the paintings of night scenes that hung on the walls. Several tall sculptures added to the artistic ambience. Folding screens afforded privacy to each dining party, and a warm fire gave the room a special glow.

Helping her off with her coat, Adam hung it beside his own on the coat rack, then motioned to a waiter to show them to a table in the corner where they would have the utmost privacy. "I'll order red wine in honor of the occasion, unless you would prefer something else."

"Wine would be perfect." Like everything else, Brittany thought. How glad she was that she had given him that valentine if that was what had spurred him into inviting her out this evening. Certainly he had told her again and again how clever it was, how unusual.

Adam watched as the waiter poured the wine, then lifted his glass. "To Saint Valentine, even if

he didn't really have much to do with this lovers' day."

"To Saint Valentine," Brittany replied, gently
clicking her glass against his. Her eyes caressed
him. She felt vibrantly alive with Adam, like a
butterfly finally trying its wings. It was as if she
had been sleeping in a cocoon waiting all this
time for him to free her.

Oh, Brittany, Adam thought, staring into his
glass. *I'd conjured up such wonderful ways to
seduce you, to consummate what we began the
other night. But the way you look at me, as if I
were some kind of hero and not a heel, makes me
think twice.* The fact that his stay at home was
going to be cut so short put his potent feelings
for Brittany Whitindale in a new perspective. A
passionate love affair that lasted a month, or
two, or three was one thing; one that lasted less
than a week was another.

"You're not drinking your wine," Brittany said
and took two long gulps of hers, letting it warm
her.

"Yes, of course. The wine." She looked especially pretty tonight. Her dress had a yoke that
dipped in a V, exposing a teasing view of her
breasts. Her hair was also different than he had
seen it before. It was drawn atop her head as
usual, but instead of being pulled back severely,
she had styled it in a soft upsweep. She looked
much younger than usual. Vulnerable.

*How am I going to tell her that I must leave
in a few days? How can I give her my valentine
gift and then blithely say goodbye?* Always before

with lovers Adam had felt free to do just that, but everything he sensed about this woman told him she wasn't the kind who took love lightly.

"I'm starved, how about you?" he asked, trying to act as if nothing were troubling him.

The waiter gave Adam a long recitation of all the tasty things that were "just ready" as well as a written bill-of-fare. There was roast beef, boiled beef, roast haunch of mutton, boiled pork, roast veal and ham, salmon with shrimp sauce, pigeon pie, and rump-steak pudding. Brittany decided on the salmon with shrimp sauce, Adam on the mutton. The order was quickly attended to. The dishes were quickly brought hot and steaming from the kitchen, along with a large pewter plate of green beans and mushrooms.

The food was delicious, and as they ate, they talked. But even though he was hungry, Adam picked at his food. His travels had been his life, had given him purpose; now for the first time his plans for a journey were jumbling his emotions. And yet he hardly knew this woman. Or did he?

Strangely enough, he had felt from the first moment that he did know her. Was it because she was a composite of all the things he was searching for? Or did his reaction run deeper? Some of the natives believed that souls mated in the pre-life and that a man must locate that one woman who had been predestined for him. Adam had shrugged such ideology off, but now he wasn't so sure.

"Was there something wrong with the mutton, sir?" Taking away the plates, the waiter looked as if he feared he might have to deal with a complaint.

"It was fine." The waiter gave a sigh of relief and asked whether pastry or cheese was wanted. Adam ordered a cherry tart for himself and one for Brittany.

"I have something for you," he said as soon as the waiter was gone. Reaching in his pocket he brought forth the red velvet box.

"Oh, Adam." She would have lied if she'd said she wasn't pleased. Her fingers trembled as she opened it.

"It's a locket. All women treasure them, or so I've heard."

The chandeliers' flickering flames made the golden heart sparkle. "It's lovely." Brittany's eyes misted as she read the inscription. It was confirmation that he did care. "Help me put it on." Rising from her chair, she came to his side and bent down.

Adam's fingers gently caressed her shoulders, lingering on the velvet of her skin as they slid upward. For a moment his hands were suspended at her throat. She had such soft skin. He wanted to touch her like this forever, wanted to run his hands over her naked flesh.

"The clasp is stuck," he fibbed. In truth it was because he was so caught up in the moment that he couldn't seem to fasten it.

"Here, let me." Brittany's fingers quickly found a way to maneuver the fastening, but she didn't return to her seat right away. Lowering her head, she kissed him on the mouth, gently but with feeling. It was her way of thanking him. "Oh, Adam, it feels so right, our being together."

It did. So very right, but he had to spoil it. "Brittany, I thought I was going to be here in London for some time, but I must leave on my next exploration in five days."

She was mortified. "So soon?" She wanted to reach out to him, to draw him into her arms, but all the years of society's teachings held her back. "How long will you be gone?" She sounded so composed, so calm, but the bitter truth was that she couldn't have felt more pain if he had kicked her. Her legs trembled as she moved back to her seat and sat down.

"A year. Or more."

It sounded like forever. "Oh . . ." He was going on a man's journey, a place where women never ventured.

"Brittany." He took her hand. "There is so little time for me to go about a formal courting. All I know is that from the moment I saw you I felt something in here." Adam touched his chest.

"Me too." Only it had begun much earlier for her.

He wanted to ask her to wait for him but knew that wouldn't be fair. Where he was going, danger lurked behind every bush. He might not come back. "Brittany . . ."

The waiter interrupted Adam's train of thought as he set down the cherry tarts.

"Cream?" Adam and Brittany shook their heads.

Looking down at her plate, Brittany was certain she would choke. "So this locket is your way of saying goodbye." She had thought the locket was to be a beginning, but instead it was an end. Now more than ever she regretted Bessie's intrusion of the other night. At least she would have had one night of love to remember.

"It seems so." Goodbye. How he hated that word. There was such finality to it.

She knew she had no right to make complaint, yet her disappointment goaded her. "Then at this moment I hate being a woman! A fragile creature that is always left behind to wither on the vine. Your life is complete, my life is empty!" Her voice was impassioned. "Adam, I've seen Africa in my heart and in my mind. Please, take me with you."

Her request startled him, but though the idea was tempting, he couldn't think of it. The journey itself would be bad enough—seasickness, the chance of the ship being caught in a storm and sunk. Even if they reached Africa, there were diseases, animals of prey, cannibals, and untold dangers in the deserts and jungles. "No."

Although it wasn't in her nature to beg, she said one more time, "Please. . . ."

"It's out of the question." Adam turned his head, annoyed that the waiter had intruded again. Quickly he reached in his pocket for money to pay the bill. When he looked up, Brittany was gone. Glittering in the candlelight was the locket she had left behind.

Chapter Nine

The streets were swarming with hackney coaches, carriages, and silk-lined leather sedan chairs transporting splendidly dressed men and women to theaters, taverns, cozily lighted inns, or perhaps to more intimate rendezvous. It wasn't difficult for Adam to find transportation.

The tall, lanky carriage driver jumped down, opening the door. "Where yer be goin', gov'ner?"

Adam didn't know. "I've no special destination. Just drive me around for a while."

I hurt her. I didn't want to but I did. How could he forget the look in her eyes when he told her he was leaving? That the locket was his way of saying goodbye? Her expression had mirrored the devastation he had felt. And yet that wasn't half as bad as telling her he couldn't take her with him. She had told him her life was empty in such a mournful tone of voice that for an instant he had been tempted to change his mind.

"Which would have been the ultimate selfishness," he said to himself.

Taking her with him would have been a dream come true. Her softness would have been the perfect haven for escape when the world showed its cruelty. But what kind of toll would Africa exact upon someone like Brittany? Oh, she was an amazing woman, but she was a *woman* after all. Far better for her to do her traveling via books.

Listen to me! I'm not much better than those pompous gentlemen from the Geographical Society who look upon women as their inferiors.

In her anger Brittany had lashed out about the freedom of men who could go where they pleased. Now that he thought of it, it was true. Moreover, there was a pattern to male dominance in African exploration, a pattern of masculine penetration and conquest. A need to deify manhood by proving its bravery. But couldn't women show such bravery too?

No, get the very idea out of your mind. There are areas you'll be going through that are much too dangerous. He intended to trade his way through Africa, subsisting on local food and taking shelter in mud and thatch village houses, or sleeping under the stars. He didn't intend to assemble a long caravan of porters to carry tinned food, camp beds, or tents. Nor would he be traveling in swaying hammocks with an African bearer at each end. His was to be a long trek, hacking through thick foliage, wading through snake-infested water and mud. Not the kind of life for a properly brought up woman.

Adam wouldn't allow himself to remember that there were women who accompanied their men on various journeys. Women with the English ideal of being useful partners. Samuel Baker's mistress, for one, who was accompanying him down the Nile. Or Katherine Petherick who was journeying with her husband so that they could co-author a book. Or the long-suffering Mary Moffat Livingstone, wife of the famous doctor. He remained steadfast in his determination that despite the heartache Brittany Whitindale was suffering now, he had done what was best for her in the long run.

"Driver, take me to the docks." Adam hoped that taking a look at the ship waiting to take him to Africa would be just the antidote he needed. The ship was named the *Timbuktu* and was a cargo boat, not built for passengers. One more reason to leave Brittany Whitindale behind.

"Be there in two shakes of a horse's tail, we will."

It was decidedly more than that, yet soon the docks came into sight. There were ships everywhere, gliding about like swans on a lake. The further his eyes traveled down the river, the more closely packed the vessels were on either side, a visible sign of how quickly London was growing.

It was noisy on the waterfront, a cacophony of voices and sounds. There was the seemingly ever-present warbling of the peddlers, the drunken singing of sailors, mixed with the chattering of people strolling about.

"Would you like me to wait, sir?" The carriage driver cocked his brows.

"No, I don't know how long I'll be. I just want to wander about a bit." The truth was he didn't want to go back to his room at the club. Perhaps he'd confiscate a bottle of whiskey, drink himself into oblivion, and sleep aboard ship.

"Clean yer boots, sir? Shoeblack, yer honor! Black yer shoes, sir!" A young lad stepped out from the crowds carrying his three-legged stool and a pot of blacking.

"No!" Sensing he had been overly gruff, Adam said, "Well, a hurried shine might do."

Diligently the lad set himself to the task, wiping his hands on his pants to get them clean. "There ye be, sir. Made yer boots look as good as new, I did."

"So you did. Here, take this shilling in token of my gratitude." Adam pressed the coin into the boy's hand. It was enough for ten shoeshines or more.

"Blimey! Thank ye, sir!" Biting the coin to ascertain that it was real, the bootblack beamed his gratitude, then hurried off down the quay.

On the Thames barges and ships could be seen laden with goods from faraway places.

Gazing out to sea, Adam remembered his own adventures. Whenever he smelled the salt in a breeze or caught sight of the billowing white sails, he was touched by his boyhood dreams. Dreams that had been fulfilled.

My dreams, yes, but Brittany's . . . She had been right about hers withering on the vine, he thought. Taking the locket from his pocket, he stared at it for a long time. What does the future hold in store for her? Marriage? Or would she continue as she was now, living with that irritating man-hungry sister of hers?

When I come back in a year from now, is it possible you will still be free? He didn't even want to hope. No, if he truly cared about Brittany, and he did, he would want her happiness above all.

Trying to put her out of his mind, Adam returned the locket to the safety of his coat and gazed out at the forest of masts that loomed on the horizon. A flag fluttered in the breeze, a sailor hung on the spars of a ship, another sailor, agile as a monkey, skylarked on the topmost cross-trees of a vessel anchored at port. Sailors strolled the docks, making their way to the tavern.

"That's where I want to go." The Thames was at high tide, the waters lapping loudly against the quay as he followed the sailors.

"Ev'nin', luv," a woman crooned. "Nice ev'nin', ain't it. 'Ows 'bout you and me 'avin' a bit o' fun?" Her breasts lightly brushed against his chest as she tried her best to seduce him.

But she had more than fun on her mind. Adam caught her trying to steal his money pouch, and she did succeed in lifting the gold locket gently from his coat pocket.

"Give that back!" He had a particular loathing for women who used their charms to lure men on, only to steal from them and send them to their deaths in the Thames. "Thief!" Snatching the locket out of her fingers, he held it tightly with his right hand while he held her with his left.

The woman's eyes darted around for a way to escape. Adam was so busy watching her that he didn't see the two men stealing up behind him, but he felt the clubs they wielded. Like exploding thunder. With a groan he slumped to the ground.

Chapter Ten

The streets were dark except for an occasional street lamp that flickered and sparked. Clad in a pale blue nightgown, her hair loose about her shoulders, Brittany sat huddled in a chair by the window, her eyes fixed on the pane as she listened to the monotonous ticking of the grandfather clock in the hall. How long she sat staring she didn't know. Minutes? Hours?

He is leaving. He'll be gone for a year or more. The agony of the truth echoed through her over and over. He was going and taking her happiness with him.

Trembling, she glanced toward her turned-down bed, but her mind had been too active, too troubled to permit sleep. Leaning her head

293

back, she tried to fight against the sorrow the memory of Adam evoked, but the moment her eyes closed she was tormented, yearning for what might have been.

Perhaps it would have been better if I had never met him. No, she couldn't believe that. Though the moments they had spent together had been brief, they were moments she would treasure. Even last night had been memorable, despite the circumstances and the way she had left. If only . . .

She had felt betrayed, yes, but Adam had no more control than she over what had happened. Neither of them could have foreseen that circumstances would dictate his leaving so soon. He was an adventurer. An explorer. A man who seldom stayed in one place. She knew that. And yet like a spoiled, disappointed child she had run away.

Picking up a brown leather-bound book, she lit the lamp and turned the pages listlessly. Always before, she could escape all boundaries of time and space by reading the printed pages, but not tonight. The words were a blur.

Why didn't he ask me to wait? Didn't he know that I would? I'd have waited till the end of time for him. Why? Because Adam was a man who valued his freedom. How could she have forgotten that even for a moment? A man with no ties.

"No promises, no commitments." And yet she had read a special tenderness in his eyes when he had looked at her. A protective look. A longing. Remembering that look now, Brittany felt sure that he had truly cared. That he, like she, had recognized a soul mate.

There is so little time for me to go about a formal courting. All I know is that from the moment I first saw you I felt something in here, he had said. But it was over now. Over before it had begun.

Seeking the safe haven of her bed, she pulled the covers up to her chin to bring warmth to her chilled body, but she couldn't push Adam Kingsley from her mind no matter how hard she tried. Desire was too primitive and powerful a feeling. Her mind, her heart, the very core of her being, longed for him. Her body, lying warm and yearning for the touch of his lips, rebelled against her common sense.

I want him so. But it is better this way. Adam knew that. He didn't want to make love to me and then sail away. He didn't want to cause me pain. And yet he had. The most devastating kind of ache that consumed her whole being.

Tossing and turning on her feather mattress, she could not keep her thoughts from him, picturing every detail of the evening they had spent together. Immersed in a cocoon of blankets where everything was soft and safe, Brittany stared up at the ceiling of her bedroom. She couldn't sleep. How could she after what had happened tonight?

Beams of moonlight danced through the windows, casting figured shadows on the roof overhead. Two entwined silhouettes conjured up memories of the embraces they had shared. She lay awake for several long, tormented hours, but when at last her indomitable will won out over her fevered body, she closed her eyes. Wrapping her arms around her knees, she curled up in a ball, envisioning again the face of the man who haunted her.

From outside the window Brittany thought she could hear Adam Kingsley demanding that she come down and hear him out. "Damn it, listen to me. I love you. I do. You must understand. What I did, I did for you. Anna . . . !" Alas, it was somebody else calling to his lover, not Adam.

Fitfully Brittany dozed off, awakened, slipped back into sleep, then opened her eyes. The first light of the sunrise painted the room with a rosy glow. Morning already! She sat up so quickly it made her head spin. Oh, how she hated to see another dawn. It meant there was one less day before Adam's ship sailed.

I should have kept the locket. It would have been something tangible to remember him by. Why hadn't she? Because it had been a symbol of their parting and of the happiest and yet saddest Valentine's Day she had ever known. But she wouldn't allow her heart to be broken. She was a survivor. Somehow she'd get through this. Some way.

Shivering, she slipped on a robe. Already the house was stirring. She could hear the thin tinkling of the watchman's bell in the distance and his loud voice calling out, "All is well."

"For him perhaps but not for me," she whispered forlornly.

She wanted to run away with Adam, to follow him to the ends of the earth if necessary. She thought of stowing away, packing up her belongings, and hiding where Adam Kingsley would not find her until they were out to sea. And yet she could not perpetrate such a scheme. It wasn't right—she knew that with a frightening clarity. She would lose his trust with such a scheme. But just what *was* she going to do?

Hurriedly putting on a russet-colored dress, she rushed down the stairs to join her sister at the breakfast table. Bessie was just finishing her pork and kidney pie. As if to emphasize that Brittany was thirty minutes late, Bessie looked at the tall case clock which stood outside the door.

"How unusual. Miss early riser isn't very punctual this morning."

"Good morning." Brittany ignored the barb as she slipped into her place across from her sister.

Bessie picked at her breakfast with a fork. "I would assume by your tardiness that you had a pleasant time last night."

Nodding to the housekeeper, Brittany turned over her cup. "A half cup of tea and an omelette, please." The woman hurried into the kitchen and soon returned with a fluffy yellow concoction. The savory aroma of onions and peppers filled the air.

"And Adam? How was he? Did you enjoy his company? Is he going to call on you again? Are the two of you going to be the gossip of

London?" Bessie's asked sarcastically.

"I don't want to talk about it!" Brittany's tone was emphatic, but as the silence lengthened, she confided, "He's going away, Bessie. Back to Africa. In five days!" It took all her self-control not to break down and cry, but somehow she kept her poise. She had never cried in front of her sister and she wouldn't start now.

"Oh, Brit. I'm sorry. Really I am." For once Bessie sounded sincere. Briskly she touched her mouth with the corners of her napkin. "But that's a man for you. They're heartbreakers every one."

"Not him. Not really." Some men might have made love to a woman, then told her he was going away, but Adam had been truthful. Brittany forced herself to eat a bite of the omelette. Adam hadn't meant to break her heart. To the contrary, he had by his actions tried to avoid it. "Adam Kingsley is one of a kind." A man she would always remember, not just because he was handsome or because they had shared a few kisses but because of what he was. Honest, brave, gentle, and caring.

Rising from the table, Brittany walked toward the door. Although going to work was the last thing in the world she wanted to do, it had to be done. Besides, keeping her mind occupied with other matters might help her through the day.

"You're going to the law offices?" Bessie was astonished. "And so, it's over just like that," Bessie said with a snap of her fingers. "But does my stone-faced sister break down like any other woman would do? Oh, no. Does she cry herself into a tizzy, throw things, demonstrate her anger? No. She handles the moment with her usual perfection and calm." She shook her head. "Sometimes I wonder if you are even human, Brit."

"Oh, I'm human, all right!" This time Brittany couldn't keep her eyes from misting. "All too human." She squeezed her eyes shut, trying to keep her tears from rolling down her cheeks. "But I've had to be strong and hide my feelings. I've had to be for your sake, Bessie, as well as my own. Can't you see that?" Oh, what was the use in explaining? she thought, opening the door.

Bessie blocked her way. "Brit, for the love of God, for once in your life don't keep your emotions tucked inside. Don't let your pride get in the way of your feelings."

Pride. Wasn't that the real reason she had run away from Adam last night? But what good was her pride, when all was said and done? Did it keep her warm at night? Comfort her sorrows? There were too many things left unsaid for their relationship to have ended like that. She had to see him again. Had to set things right. Even if it meant swallowing her insufferable pride, she had to tell him how she felt, had to promise him that she would wait. Forever, if need be.

Chapter Eleven

The hospital ward was dimly lit with just enough lamp light to illuminate the forty cots carefully laid out in rows. A fire burned in the corner but did not give off enough heat to warm the room. It was raining outside, and the dampness seeped through the walls and dribbled from holes in the ceiling. The drip, drip, drip of rain as it pattered into pewter pots merged with the cries and groans of the poor unfortunates laid out on the sodden mattresses.

The bespectacled doctor scowled as he patrolled the patients. "How many new ones, Willy?" Holding a thick pad of paper, he was making notes on each patient.

A bent and stooped elderly man answered in a squeaky and harsh voice, "Five." As they slowly walked by the beds, he pointed them out. "This one was in a carriage accident. Run over by the wheels. Two broken legs and profuse bleeding."

"Have the bones been set?"

"Dr. Johnson did that an hour ago and gave him some laudanum for the pain."

They moved on.

"Looks to be multiple knife wounds on this one," the doctor said, prodding at the patient. "I can see that he's been sewn." He looked annoyed when some of the blood from an oozing cut got on his hands. With a grumble he wiped them on his already dirty brown frock coat. "He's the fifteenth one in two days. Bloody hell. Something needs to be done."

"He won't be the last one. London's being overrun with thugs and thieves." With a nod of his head the man led the doctor in the opposite direction to where the diseased were sequestered. He motioned toward a dark-haired woman and a little girl, both with pale faces and staring eyes. "Those two look as if they won't make it through the night."

"Cholera!" Careful not to touch the mother and daughter, the doctor shuddered. "Take them out of here. Downstairs."

"To the morgue?" Taking another look, Willy cocked his head. "God love a cockroach, they're already dead!" As the doctor watched, he pulled them from the bed, then called to two women with unkempt hair and gave the bodies into their keeping. " 'Tis a pity."

For a moment the doctor's cold reserve seemed to be softening, but he quickly stiffened, saying only, "That will give us two more beds." He made a notation on his papers. "And the last?"

"Clubbed into unconsciousness at the docks. Robbed and left for dead." He led the doctor up one row and down another, pausing at a bed in the middle of the room. "Can't rightly say who he is. They picked him clean. Don't know who we should notify to get payment of his bill."

Leaning forward, the doctor took a close look at him. "Hmm. Strange, but for some reason he seems familiar."

"Hard to tell with all that swelling and those bruises. Poor bloke was in the wrong place at the wrong time." Seeing that the naked dark-haired man had kicked off his covers, Willy reached down and pulled them up, a rare show of kindness. "Can tell he's a fine-looking one, though, despite it all. Looks to be a gentleman."

"A gentleman, you say. In this hell hole?" The doctor scribbled something, then asked, "How was he dressed?"

"Dressed, you ask?" Willy snickered behind his hand. "Almost naked as the day he was born. Except for his pants and boots."

"They stripped him clean? That seems to say that whatever he was wearing it was worthy of being stolen." Once again the doctor scrutinized the man lying on the bed. "By jove, it seems I know this man but I can't quite remember . . ."

"Just have to wait until he wakes up. If he does." He shook his head. "If he doesn't 'twill be another pauper's grave."

"One of many in the city." Seeming to take special interest in this patient, he carefully examined him, appraising the wounds on his shoulders, neck, and head. "Well, at least his heart is beating." Just to reaffirm that statement he felt for a pulse. "What's this?"

Willy looked down at the gold object with a twinge of guilt in his eyes. "Necklace of some kind. Made out of gold."

The doctor's expression was accusing. "I'm surprised it's still in his possession, Willy, knowing you."

"Well . . ." Willy's face turned red as he made his confession. "I'd be lyin' if I didn't admit I've had my eye on that since the minute he was brought in here. Whoever attacked him seems to have missed it when they were stealing everything else. Trouble is I couldn't get it loose. He's holding it as tightly as a ticket to heaven."

"Let me see." After several tries the doctor had to admit defeat too. "It must be something very precious to him. A locket in the shape of a heart it seems to be. Maybe it belonged to his mother."

"Maybe." That thought seemed to touch Willy. "Poor blighter." But he was not so sentimental that he didn't wait until the doctor's back was turned to try to get the locket away once again.

"No!" The man's moan startled Willy and he jumped back.

"Lord love a duck, I think he's coming to."

Images teased Adam's eyes as he slowly emerged from darkness. From somewhere far away he thought he heard the sound of men's voices. Willing himself to wake up, he passed in and out of consciousness.

"Brittany . . ." Closing his eyes, he reached out. He tried to move, but it only made his head hurt. With a groan he reached up to touch his head. There was a pounding there, a dull, throbbing ache. "Brittany . . ."

His brain was befuddled. He was cold but didn't know why. He seemed to remember being half-carried somewhere, but in his confused state he couldn't decide whether that was part of a dream or something real.

What was going on? Where was he? He forced himself to become calm. It was all right. Perhaps if he lay on his side the pain would recede. With that thought foremost in his mind he struggled to roll over. This time he was successful in opening his eyes all the way.

"Where . . ." He saw two men staring down at him and looked from one to the other in shocked disbelief. "Who . . . ?" He tried to make out the conversation but it was only a low mumble. Were they talking about him?

Where was he and how had he gotten here? Why was he sleeping in a strange bed? Painfully he tried to remember who he had been with, where he had been, but his brain was a like a dish of figgy pudding.

BiGod, my head hurts!

Relax. He would be all right if he could just keep his head. He'd be fine. Easy. Easy. Just try to sort things out carefully. Concentrate. Think. Remember.

He felt helpless. It was as if he'd suddenly become two people, one lying in bed, the other looking down at him and urging him to get up. What made his situation even worse was that he was at the mercy of someone whose voice he didn't recognize.

I have to get away! He tried but somehow didn't have the strength. *Darkness closing in on me . . .*

"He's out like a light again." Willy clucked his tongue. " 'Tis a pity."

"He was calling out for someone. Brittany. Oh, well." The doctor shrugged his shoulders. "There is every possibility he'll come to again. All that can be done is to wait and see."

Chapter Twelve

The cold rain which had been drizzling all day was beginning to pour down in earnest. As Brittany stepped out the door of the Bowman, Winston and Fudd law offices, she was bombarded with raindrops. They tapped out a rhythm on her brown felt hat as she merged with the throng on St. James Street.

"What I wouldn't give for an umbrella." All the people who were at home on such a dreadful day, snug and comfortable by their firesides, didn't know how lucky they were. Even so, she refused to seek comfort and shelter. She was on her way to see Adam, and nothing could sway her. "Not even Noah himself sailing by on the ark."

It had been a tediously long morning of meetings, consultations, and note taking. Brittany's thoughts had faltered more than once as she sat beside Matthew Winston, helping him prepare three cases for the barristers. Over and over again her musings had turned to what she would say when Adam answered his door.

I won't let you leave me behind! All my life I've wanted to go beyond England's white cliffs and see the world through my own eyes. With or without you I intend to do just that, Adam Kingsley. I will traverse Africa from side to side even if I have to book passage on the West African steamer. I'll go alone if I have to. Brave words. *But I'd much rather go there with you.*

"Think of how pleasurable it would be if we were to travel there together," she whispered to herself. From Adam's writings she could tell that Africa was unusually beautiful. Exotic. Unlike anywhere else on earth.

How romantic it would be to view the sunset over the Nile together, to listen to the symphony of the birds when night fell. Adam had described Africa's landscape, the variety of birds, the unique animals, and the people in such colorful language that she nearly felt as if she had witnessed it all herself. Now she would.

Adam of course would tell her how dangerous it was to traipse along the jungle pathways, but Brittany wasn't going to listen to his list of the three "d"s, the dangers, the diseases, and the disagreeables of Africa, which some men referred to as the deadliest spot on earth.

London has its dangers too, as you have said yourself. Fate doesn't give anyone a guarantee of longevity.

She remembered Oliver Layton, who had made it his business to sail around the world. He had touched on the shores of India, New Zealand, Egypt, and Siam. An expert traveler, he had braved storms, illness, coral reefs, sharks, and cannibals, only to fall victim to a tragic accident when he returned to London. The poor man had shot himself while cleaning his gun.

I could stay behind in England and be miserable while Adam is gone, only to die in my bed. Or worse yet in a hospital somewhere. Thinking about the squalid conditions of the "doctors' abodes," Brittany shuddered. Many of those who went in never came out again. And Adam thought Africa was dangerous.

The clicking of pattens on the slippery and uneven pavement, and the rustling of umbrellas as the wind blew against the shop windows, bore testimony to the severity of the storm. Brittany was getting soaked yet she pushed on, perhaps because she was anxious to prove her mettle. Despite her femininity she was strong, as Adam Kingsley would soon see.

Yes, she was going to Africa. It was a decision she had made today as she was sequestered with Misters Winston and Fudd. Moreover, her determination was unswervable. The time had come in her life when she wanted to do something daring, something she had only dreamed about doing before. Perhaps some of Adam's adventuresome spirit had rubbed off on her.

"Adam, you must understand . . ."

Brittany passed by a policeman whose oilskin cape flapped open as he held his hat on his head. Turning around to avoid a gust of wind and rain, he nearly trampled her. "Excuse me, miss."

The storm was turning frightful, as violent as the tropical gales Adam had written about. Brittany was thankful when she saw the outline of the Carlton looming up ahead. Two floors high with nine windows along the frontage and eight on the sides, it dwarfed the buildings around it. In addition to feeling relief that the interior would offer her comfort from the storm, Brittany also felt a twinge of resentment.

The Carlton men's club was one of those impregnable fortresses that played such an important part in the lives of its members, who belonged to the highest circles of the industrial and financial worlds. The club was a symbol of their masculinity, their aristocracy, their superiority over women, just as being an explorer was. To make certain that their precious sanctity wasn't invaded, a porter sat at a desk in the lobby to guard against intruders imposing on its portals.

"May I help you, miss?"

"I want to see Adam Kingsley. I believe his room is on the second floor." Brittany started to walk past the porter but he blocked her way.

"I'm sorry, but women are not allowed past this point. Rules, you know."

"The rules." Brittany frowned at the little man. How could she have forgotten how difficult it was to impregnate these "British monasteries"? Most English matrons, and unmarried women as well, detested the clubs. "Then if you please, send him a message that Brittany Whitindale is here to see him." Taking off her hat and coat, she wearily plopped down in the chair beside him.

"Whitinwhale?"

"Whitindale!"

Motioning to a lad dressed all in green, the porter gave him the message. The newly appointed messenger hurried away.

While she waited, Brittany looked around her at the colonnades supporting a large gallery, the Roman mosaic floor, the dome lights, the mirrors, the marble stairways. It was little wonder that so many men came here to this opulent hideaway to hide from their wives or that bachelors who nested here were so reluctant to wed. The clubs offered a man everything he could desire in life with the exception of one thing: the softness and caring of a woman.

"Miss!"

Brittany looked up to see that the messenger had returned, but Adam Kingsley wasn't with him. "Is he out?" The thought of not being able to talk with him while she had her courage was extremely disappointing.

"Out, yes."

"I see." She contemplated what to do for only a moment. "When will he return?"

The boy shrugged. "Hard to say. From what I understand from the household staff, he didn't come back last night." The smug smile on the lad's face showed that he thought Adam Kingsley had been carousing.

"He didn't come back?" All sorts of thoughts rushed through Brittany's head, but she brushed them away. Now was no time to be jealous. "May I leave him a note?"

"As you will." The porter politely handed her a pencil and a small piece of paper.

It was far more difficult to express her feelings in written words than spoken, but she tried her best. She wrote that she wanted to see him, that she had made an important decision, and ended by telling him that although they had known each other a very short time she cared deeply about him. She was just signing her name when the silence exploded in a hubbub of voices.

"Attacked on the docks, you say? How dastardly."

"Yes. Robbed and beaten, to put it quite simply."

"You don't say. To think that after traveling all over the East with hardly an injury, he should meet such a foul fate in London."

"Gads, but I'm not at all surprised. The London underworld is becoming much too cheeky."

"I say, old boy, if that isn't all too true."

"But do tell the rest of the story, Farley."

Brittany paused in the act of crossing the "t's" in her name to listen.

"Seems they stole nearly every thing the poor chap owned. That's why they took him to the paupers' ward at the hospital. Didn't have a clue as to who he was and all. But the doctor at last recognized him. Saw his lecture at the Geographical Society, you know. Put the puzzle pieces together."

"You don't say . . ."

Brittany paled. Her heart skipped a beat. Anxiously she pushed in among the gentlemen. "Who?"

Being a woman, she was ignored. "But say, my dear man, how on earth is he faring?" A monocled man turned toward the man who had broken the news.

"The same as you might if confined in such a dastardly place . . ."

"Who?" Brittany's voice was almost a scream. "Answer me. Who? Who?"

They stopped talking as eight pair of eyes skewered her. Then as if talking to an errant child, a bearded man dressed in tweed answered. "Who? Why, Adam Kingsley."

Chapter Thirteen

It was all just a dream. A nightmare. But though he waited with an expectancy close to mania, frantically wanting to escape this bleak, empty nothingness, Adam seemed trapped. BiGod, if only he weren't so disoriented, so weak. He wanted to get out of here, wherever here was. But then what? Where would he go?

It was as if he were in a long, dark tunnel, groping about, fighting to come into the light. He reached out to consciousness, but it was like trying to walk a treadmill through a dense fog. Darkness was upon him, and though he struggled to open his eyes, he couldn't see. Shadows. Only shadows.

His body was tired. Weary. He heard faint sounds, muted as if coming through deep, murky water. Gurgling. His voice? Yes. The sound of his own breathing became louder and louder until it was a roar in his ears.

He was lying in an awkward position, but he couldn't seem to shift to a more comfortable one. Dull reverberations shot through his body each time he tried to move. Pain!

"Please . . ."

Lifting his hand slowly, he looked toward a glittering gold object but couldn't quite see it. It was like looking through a haze. Even so, he knew it to be something precious and held on tight. It seemed to be his only link with sanity, with reality.

"Brittany . . ." Her name was the only thing that brought him calm.

His head throbbed. His arm ached. He felt as though he'd been through hell. Something had happened, but what? He tried to remember, but his mind was blank, and that was frightening.

A nightmare? His hand moved slowly up his face, pressing against the skin. The intense pressure of his fingers convinced him that he was not asleep. He could feel. *No nightmare then, no dream, but real.* Why then couldn't he quite move back into the world of reality?

"Brittany . . ."

He forced his eyes open again but could only see colors this time. A swirl of bright. But nothing familiar. Where was he? How had he gotten here? He tried to recollect, but his mind was like an empty well. Nothing. He tried to reach further back into his mind for any hint of familiarity but found only a deep, bottomless void.

In desperation he pushed against the mattress in an effort to sit up, only to fall back down again. He willed himself to awaken but it was useless. Something was holding him back. He tried again but the futile exercise only fatigued him. His mind hovered on the brink of consciousness, between sleeping and wakefulness, at last succumbing to his weakened state.

"How is he, Willy?" The doctor was more concerned now that he knew his patient's identity.

"Fighting like the devil to wake up, poor bloke." Willy clucked his tongue. "No wonder he's in such a fog. Cracked his head like a melon they did. Evil brutes. Looks as though they wanted to kill him."

"A fractured skull can be very dangerous. It joggles the brain."

"I've seen some wot never come out of it." Willy's expression showed that he was beginning to think this man might be one of them.

"There's not much we can really do for Mr. Adam Kingsley. Unfortunately, where some things are concerned I'm afraid we're not much better than those witch doctor friends of his."

"He's still calling out for her. Brittany." Willy's eyes strayed to the locket. "Do you suppose that necklace might give us any clue?"

"It might, if we could get it away from him. His hand seems frozen in a clenched position." Kneeling down, the doctor tried to get the locket away from Adam, but had no better luck than Willy. "Wonder why he treasures it so."

"Wonder whose it is . . ." It was obvious that Willy was waiting to claim it.

"It belongs to me."

The doctor's head whirled around to see a woman standing in the doorway. A lovely woman with red-gold hair.

Chapter Fourteen

The flickering flames of the lamp illuminated the face of the man lying on the rumpled cot. Her locket was clutched in his hand.

Dear God, it really is Adam! He looked so crushed and broken. Her world was shattered to see a man once so virile and strong now reduced to such torturous pain. Bending down, Brittany gently wiped the caked-on blood from his face with her handkerchief, cursing the villainy that had brought him down.

"Are you Brittany?"

She nodded.

"He's been whispering your name. I'd hoped we might somehow find you."

The doctor was extremely polite to her, but she confronted him angrily nonetheless. "I want him moved at once! This place is a disgrace."

Brittany looked around with a shudder. It was filthy. The plaster walls were stained with blood and dirt, and there was dust everywhere. The wooden floors looked as though they had never been mopped despite the large pail of water and mop that stood in the corner. The sheets on Adam's bed looked as if they hadn't been changed in weeks, if ever.

"Move him?" Willy took a step back.

"At once! Or if anything happens to him, I will hold you responsible."

Brittany didn't know if it was the dangerous gleam in her eye or her threatening tone, but her orders were instantly obeyed. While she supervised, Adam was moved to a small room down the hall and placed on a bed with clean sheets. It was the doctor's room, or so he said.

"Oh, Adam!" He just had to recover. "Adam!"

Brittany's eyes ran over his half-naked body. His arms and chest were well muscled, and she remembered their strength when he had held her. A tuft of black hair covered his broad chest and trailed in a line down to his navel. He was virility personified even in his unconsciousness.

"You're strong, Adam. You've faced greater foes than a pack of cowardly thugs. Hear me and know that you are safe." Gently Brittany's hands followed the path of her gaze.

Warmth. Warmth and light. Everything was soft and safe. He could sense that someone was with him but he hadn't the strength to open his eyes. Instead he gave himself up to the sensations. Bit by bit an encompassing warmth was stealing the cold from his body.

"Adam. Adam . . ."

A voice was whispering in the darkness. A comforting voice, like an angel's. Fingers as gentle as a soft spring breeze were touching him. Up. Down. Along his arms, across his chest, down his side, across his hips and back again. The icy core inside him began to thaw at the stroking of those hands. It was almost as if he could feel the blood coursing through his veins.

"Come back to me, Adam." He had to get well. The alternative was just too devastating even to contemplate. The world without him would be much too lonely.

He passed in and out of sleep, at last awaking to total darkness, an alien world of unknown place and time. *Where was he and how had he gotten here?* Adam pressed his mind into a semblance of coherency, remembering bits and pieces. He had been attacked. Set upon from behind.

"Oh, Adam. I was going to give you an ultimatum. I was going to tell you that with or without you I was going to Africa." Now she realized that she didn't want to go anywhere without him. "Open your eyes, Adam. Adam!"

A voice calling to him, pleading with him.

I must. It was as if he were clawing his way back to sanity. Once again he opened his eyes,

319

and the vision he saw was a walk in the sunshine.
She was looking down on him, her face haloed
by lamp light.

"Brittany . . ." She was the answer to his
prayers. He reached out. For once he was at
peace.

Epilogue

The sun looked like a golden coin, igniting the sky with fire, balancing on the dark glow of the silken waters. Standing at the railing of the ship, Brittany looked out across the land mass, focusing on the river. It was not blue and shimmering like the ocean but more a muted shade of green, mirroring the foliage that grew so heavily on the banks.

The Nile River, she thought, remembering Adam's description. It was just as he had depicted it. She was overcome by a sense of déjà vu and excitement. She had traveled here so many times by reading his books that somehow, despite the fact that she had never seen it before, it seemed familiar.

"Like nowhere else on earth," Brittany whispered, echoing Adam's words. Surely it was a landscape that reflected the strength and vibrancy of the area. The essence of the continent. The colors were vibrant. The tall solitary trees had delicate foliage, growing in horizontal layers, much different from the trees in England.

Who would have ever thought that someday she'd be standing on the deck of a boat sailing up the Nile? Yet here she was. Africa. The Dark Continent. An unknown land. Its enigmatic presence was exciting to behold.

"So far away. The other side of the world."

Brittany was wearing a tailored jacket of gray, a waistcoat of emerald green cotton, and a flared skirt of gray tweed with two narrow bands of black braid near the hem. Beneath her skirt peeked her laced walking shoes of black leather. Sensible shoes she called them. Her gray felt hat was placed at just the right angle, her light gray gloves matching the shade as if they had been made to be worn together.

"All hands to quarters. Stand by to go ashore!" The captain's gruff tone was as loud as thunder.

Brittany watched as the crew scattered to their duties. Effortlessly the cargo ship sailed to the shore. The anchor was dropped, the boat secured, the gangplank put in place.

She was here! In some ways it was unbelievable. Certainly the voyage had been fraught with moments when she had feared she would never reach land. First she was stricken with seasickness. Then there had been a spectacular tropical storm that had nearly upended the ship. Lightning, booming thunder, and huge waves had made even the bravest on board wail in fear. The ocean had tossed the ship back and forth, yet somehow the steamer had stayed afloat. Now as Brittany looked down at the peaceful waters, it seemed as if it had been little more than a nightmare.

"Is this your luggage, miss?"

"What?"

"Are these your bags?"

"Yes. Yes, all of them," Brittany answered.

"Looks as if you need some help."

With a loving smile Brittany shook her head as her eyes settled on Adam, standing beside her at the rail. Her eyes appraised him from the corner of her eye. His shirt molded to his arms and upper body emphasized his physique. His virile power deeply stirred her as he reached out to hold her in his arms. It was hard to believe the agonizing weeks it had taken him to fully regain his strength. Weeks in which she had never left his side. But her love had worked magic.

"Are you ready to begin your exploration, Mrs. Kingsley?" he asked, gently brushing her hair from her eyes.

"Very ready," she answered, nestling against his chest.

Brittany had been careful in assessing all the things she needed to bring with her. For protection against malaria she had brought a lamp in which a chemical was to be burnt.

She had an emergency medical bag, a pouch containing preparations of quinine, mustard leaves, hot water bottles, and her portmanteau holding all her personal items. And her books and journals. And most importantly she had brought her locket. Reaching up to touch her throat, she thought how very precious it was. A symbol of Adam's love for her and of her love for him.

"I just wouldn't let it go, you know," Adam whispered, noticing her hand. "Somewhere in my brain, despite what had happened, I must have thought that if I lost the locket I'd lose you too."

"But you didn't."

"And I did survive the trip into hell, thanks to you." He would never forget the strength she had shown, fighting for his welfare like a lioness, terrorizing all the doctors, or so he had teased. "If you can handle yourself that well against those butchers, then I am fully confident you can do the same with the natives here, who are in truth less dangerous. You are a remarkable woman."

"And you a most remarkable man."

They stood together at the railing just taking pleasure in their togetherness, calmly and unhurried as the rest of the crew and passengers scurried about.

"Look, Brittany, how the land mass looks like an animal. Dark. Fierce. Untamed."

"Like you," she said with a laugh.

"Like I was before I met you," he countered, nuzzling her throat.

He thought how complete his life was now with someone to share his adventures. Before he had met Brittany he had been so lonely. His travels had been undertaken not so much out of a need for excitement as perhaps in an attempt to run away from that loneliness. But he had no need to run away now. He had someone to run to.

"Aren't you glad you agreed to let me come?" Playfully she kissed him on the end of the nose, reminding him of what a stubborn man he could be. He had argued that he didn't want to put her in danger until she had reminded him of the danger he had put himself in, not in Africa but in London.

"I must admit that I am." It was an argument he was grateful that he had lost. Brittany had proven that she could handle herself in difficult situations. She was strong and brave. More than his match in many things. He had faith that she could handle the dangers of this journey just as well as he. Or at least nearly well, he thought with manly pride. "We really belong to each other now," he said.

His hands moved along her back, sending shivers of pleasure up her spine. For an endless time he held her to him. Then his mouth covered hers, his lips tracing the outline of hers with feathery kisses, his tongue stroking the edge of her teeth. His lips played seductively on hers.

Yes, they belonged together, for now and all time, Brittany thought, wrapping her arms around his neck. The captain of the ship had married them this morning. Tonight, their first night together in Africa was to be their honeymoon. But there was another reason for saying their wedding vows on this day. It was February fourteenth. Valentine's Day. This one, however, was going to be much happier than the one a year before. His kisses showed her how much happier. She belonged to him now and for all their tomorrows.

EUGENIA RILEY
"Two Hearts in Time"

With love and gratitude to Sharon Lloyd—
writer and friend par excellence.

Chapter One

Amid the revelry, a heart was breaking.

On this Valentine's Day, Mardi Gras was in full swing in Galveston, Texas. The midwinter night was crisply cold as gaudy, colorful floats swept down the historic Strand during the Momus Grand Parade. On the decks of the floats, costumed and masked figures stood tossing out beads and doubloons to the cheering crowd. In keeping with the Gay Nineties theme, the floats represented everything from a late-nineteenth-century billiard parlor, to a lacy gazebo complete with eye-gazing lovers, to a miniature circus, to a lawn game of croquet.

329

In the street, jovial spectators mingled with carnival clowns and jugglers. The numerous turn-of-the century three- and four-story red-brick buildings lining the famous old Strand greatly enhanced the historical ambiance.

Pushing a cart laden with Victorian Valentine's Day jewelry, twenty-year-old Amanda Brewster wended her way down the crowded sidewalk, passing gentlemen attired in striped sack coats and straw hats, and ladies wearing flowing, frilly, Victorian-style dresses. Amanda assumed that most of the revelers were headed for a costume ball at a nearby hotel. A fleeting smile curved her lips as she watched a barber shop quartet drift past her, singing "Let Me Call You Sweetheart" in rich harmony. She wished she could share the heartfelt gaiety of the crowd; normally she adored all things quaint and old-fashioned. But Amanda had known too much tragedy during her brief life to feel light-hearted tonight. Even the drab, old-fashioned dress she wore was a constant, painful reminder of her own devastated life.

A laughing young couple in Gay Nineties attire paused before Amanda's cart, the woman crying out in delight as she spotted the old-fashioned gold, ceramic, and silver Valentine's Day pins, lockets, and bracelets. She caught the man's sleeve, saying, "Oh, David, look—how lovely! We must buy one of these!"

As the man glanced at Amanda, she explained, "These items have been donated by local craftsmen to benefit the Strand Preservation Society."

The man nodded, then smiled at his companion. "Which one do you like, Amy?"

The woman picked up a gold pin of a cupid ready to release his arrow. "This one is so charming."

"It's my favorite, too," Amanda put in.

"Then we'll take it," her companion said.

The man paid for the pin and proudly attached it to the lady's dress. "Thanks, miss," he said to Amanda. "Enjoy Mardi Gras."

The two dashed off, laughing. The man's last words, however well-intentioned, seemed to taunt Amanda. *Enjoy Mardi Gras*. How could she possibly enjoy anything right now?

Amanda caught her reflection in a shop window. She saw a tall, pretty woman with her blonde hair in a bun and an air of tragedy in her dark blue eyes. The dress she wore fit her badly, its hem dangling several inches above the tops of her old-fashioned button-down, granny-type shoes. The black cashmere shawl draped about her shoulders would have been more appropriate for a woman much older.

Indeed, everything Amanda wore had been meant for someone else. For Amanda had taken her grandmother's place at the parade tonight. Two weeks ago, mere hours after she had finished sewing her old-fashioned costume for the carnival, Gran had died peacefully in her sleep. The memory brought a tear to Amanda's eye. Gran had so looked forward to doing her part for the Preservation Society.

Despite her grief at losing her grandmother, Amanda had felt duty-bound to take her place tonight. But she hardly felt up to the challenge right now. The merrymaking surrounding her seemed to mock her own pain.

Amanda had been impelled to be so strong for so long—throughout Gran's funeral and the reading of her will. Thankfully, Virginia Brewster had died with her affairs in order, and the settlement of her modest estate would present no undue complications. Amanda had inherited Gran's Victorian cottage in the East End Historical District, and the money in her bank account. The account held sufficient funds to ensure Amanda's graduation from college in two years.

While to the world Amanda might appear a young woman with much to live for, in her own eyes she felt she'd reached a dead end. She had no family left now. Her parents had been accidentally killed during a tragic flood in the Texas Hill Country when she was a small child. Her mom and dad had been at a barbecue at a neighboring ranch when the violent storm began; they had tried frantically to get back to their only child. Ironically, Amanda had remained safe back at the ranch house with a babysitter, while her parents' vehicle had been swept away into the raging Guadalupe River. At six, Amanda had gone to live with Gran. She'd been a sober, quiet child who had preferred to spend her time reading craft and decorating books to being with other children.

She was much the same way today . . .

An elderly couple stopped by her cart, the man picking up and thoughtfully examining a beautiful heart-shaped locket with a watch inside. He winked at Amanda and said, "Time and love. Two of my favorite sentiments. I think I must buy this for my wife here."

The lady clapped her hands and beamed with happiness. "Oh, Bill—it's so lovely!"

"Not nearly as lovely as the years you've given me," the man said gallantly to his wife as he took out his wallet.

After the transaction had been completed and the chain fastened about the lady's neck, she smiled kindly at Amanda and said, "Aren't you cold, dear? That shawl looks so flimsy."

Amanda flashed a frozen smile. "I'm fine, really. Have a great evening."

"Take care, dear," the man added.

As the couple moved on, Amanda watched them. What a sweet little couple. The woman's smile had reminded her of Gran.

She wiped another tear and observed a float moving past in the street—this one bearing a re-creation of H. G. Wells' famous time machine, with a man in old-fashioned garb waving from his seat inside the fantastical device. The enchanting float swept past, to the cheers of the crowd. On its side beneath the platform, Amanda spotted a strange coat of arms—a Roman chariot whose sides resembled ancient armorial shields, and inside the vehicle, a warrior driving a winged Pegasus. How charming and fanciful, she thought.

Oh, how Amanda wished Gran could be here to share the beauty, the whimsy, especially on Valentine's Day. How she would have loved it! Gran had been gregarious, outgoing—the exact opposite of her reserved granddaughter. Yet the two had shared a love of old-fashioned things; in fact, they had planned to vacation this spring in London and Manchester, to experience firsthand Gran's British heritage. Amanda had so looked forward to their trip; as a student of interior design, she loved English architecture and especially anything having to do with the Victorian age. Gran had even taught her how to do Victorian-style embroidery and petit point.

A trio of rowdy teenage boys streaked by Amanda, sideswiping her cart and almost overturning it. "Hey, lady, look where you're going!" one of them called back impudently as they tore past her.

Amanda righted her cart and glowered after the boys; their brash rudeness seemed as cruel as a slap in the face. Suddenly she could be strong no longer. What was she doing here, anyway? She'd been a fool to try to wear a mask of false gaiety tonight, even as grief was tearing her apart. She didn't belong here . . . simply didn't belong.

Was there anyplace left for her now? she wondered dejectedly. Any haven where she wouldn't feel this wrenching heartache?

Amanda turned the corner of a three-story brick building to have a moment alone. Strangely, the noises of celebration around her seemed to recede.

That was when she saw him. Stepping toward her, almost like a vision materializing out of the shadows, was a tall, dark, masterfully handsome gentleman in a black frock coat and a silk top hat. A chill washed over her at the sight of him. In his British, Prince Albert-type attire, the man appeared out of place here.

He stepped closer, his dark gaze seeming to impale her. She noticed that he carried in one hand a nosegay of violets, in the other an old-fashioned Valentine's Day card, a heart-shaped masterpiece of pearls, lace, and cupids.

He spoke with a heavy British accent. "Good evening, miss."

"Good evening, sir," she replied.

He frowned. "What brings you out on this godforsaken night, and what demon has possessed you to stand on this dark, dangerous corner alone?"

His deep, mesmerizing voice and quaint manner of speech unsettled Amanda, until she realized that he must be taking the carnival mood to heart and mimicking the formal speech of the 1890s.

"I had to take my grandmother's place tonight, to sell this jewelry," she explained, gesturing toward her cart.

His expression was bemused as he glanced from the jewelry to her face. "Your grandmother sent you out, unprotected and unchaperoned, to sell these cheap trinkets in the Strand?"

What strange questions he asked. Amanda's chin came up, yet her voice faltered. "She wasn't able to be here herself . . ." Her words faded into misery.

He stepped closer, staring at her intently. "You have the saddest eyes I've ever seen," he murmured. "Why are you so unhappy, miss?"

Scalding tears flooded Amanda's vision, along with astonishment that this utter stranger could make her feel so vulnerable with just a few kind words. "Because I've lost everything that matters to me," she answered brokenly.

"I'm sorry. You're far too young to have known such anguish." He edged even closer, his eyes filled with keen compassion. "For you, m'lady," he added gallantly, handing her the valentine and the violets.

Taking them, Amanda glanced up at him, amazed and moved, losing herself in the sculpted beauty of his face, the mesmerizing depths of his eyes. "Thank you, sir, but you really shouldn't—"

Amanda wasn't allowed to finish, for the stranger's head dipped down and his lips claimed hers.

Normally, Amanda would have felt terrified at this unsolicited advance of a stranger—yet she felt enraptured, transported, even strangely at home. The stranger's kiss was everything she had ever dreamed a kiss could be—magic, tenderness, exhilaration, mystery. Indeed, the heat of his mouth so captivated and excited her that the night seemed to whirl around her and the ground no longer felt steady beneath her feet. The violets and the valentine slipped through her fingers, landing on her cart, and the stranger's arms came up tightly around her, melding her softness to his hard frame. She moaned and poured herself into the dazzling moment.

When the stranger released her, Amanda was trembling, dizzy, deeply shaken. A sense of unreality swamped her, even as she noticed the sudden fog that curled about them, along with an unnerving quiet, a bone-piercing chill.

Disoriented, Amanda stumbled toward the corner, vaguely thinking that she must continue with her duties. Bracing her hand against an unfamiliar street lamp which cast its odd, yellowish glow through the mists, she gazed up and down an expanse of ancient, alien, four- and five-story brick buildings and storefronts.

Good God, what had happened to her? The Galveston Carnival was gone, and now she stared, open-mouthed, at horse-drawn carriages and omnibuses that rattled past in a cobbled street. The quaint conveyances sported lamps attached to their sides or fronts, and were driven by cloaked and hatted coachmen. In the distance beyond the looming buildings, Amanda even seemed to spot the silvery glow of a river.

Panic flooded her, making her reel both mentally and physically. She glanced wildly at the street sign that read "Strand," and then at the words "The Strand Magazine" etched on a nearby storefront.

She trembled violently. She was on the Strand, all right—but what Strand was it?

"Miss—are you all right?"

The stranger who had kissed her had rounded the corner to join her. He gazed at her with grave concern. She stared back, electrified.

"Where am I?" she cried.

"You are where I presume you have been all night, miss," the stranger replied with a bemused frown. "You are in the Strand, in London."

A cry of horror and confusion escaped Amanda, and once again the night began to spin around her. As she crumpled toward the ground, the stranger made a dive for her, catching her in his arms just before she fainted dead away.

Chapter Two

London, England
The Past

"Burgess! A hand here!"

Lord Justin Cartwright, the Earl of Lockridge, barked a command to his coachman, who had just left the nearby carriage upon spotting his master with a woman out in the Strand.

Arriving at Justin's side, Burgess, heavily attired in a wool greatcoat and top hat, glanced askance at the scene. His lordship stood on the corner with the female in his arms—'twas a shop girl by the looks of her, or one of the wretches who sold flowers in nearby Covent Garden. She appeared to be in a swoon, and wore only a dark broadcloth dress, with no wrap on this beastly cold night.

"Bless my soul, your lordship, what goes here?" Burgess asked, his breath forming white puffs on the frigid air.

"The young lady has fainted," Lord Justin explained in a clipped voice. "We must fetch her to the carriage."

Burgess was aghast. "Begging your pardon, m'lord, but where did you come by the likes of her?"

"She was selling jewelry in the Strand."

Burgess snorted contemptuously. "Didn't I warn you that a body should not be out and about on a heathenish cold night like this, with riffraff such as her out to pluck your pockets? I told you this was no time to be takin' yer constitutional into Covent Garden, m'lord."

Standing there holding the girl in the bitter chill, Lord Justin had reached the limits of his patience. Burgess had always been a meddlesome sort, but, unfortunately, he was also a family institution. "Damn it, man," he snapped, "will you cease your infernal lecturing and give me a hand here? The wench may be frail, but I'll swear she's growing heavier by the instant."

"Aye, yer lordship," the mollified coachman said. Spotting a heap on the walkway just around the corner, he dashed off, returning momentarily with a black shawl, a nosegay of violets, and a Valentine's Day card. Extending the items toward Justin, he queried perplexedly,

"Would these objects belong to the lady?"

"Aye, and her jewelry cart is somewhere hereabouts as well," Justin replied. "Why don't you find it, while I fetch her to the brougham?"

As his employer strode off with the woman, Burgess searched the area but was unable to spot the cart. "I see nothing else, yer lordship," he bellowed with hand cupped about his mouth. "Mayhap an urchin from St. Giles' rookery already absconded with the lady's trinkets. Didn't I warn you that a body should not be out and about—"

"Yes, yes. Very well, man, let's be about our business," Justin called back irritably.

Burgess bounded off after his employer. "Where shall we be takin' the miss?"

"Home—to Portman Square," Justin replied firmly.

"Ye gads!" Burgess retorted, half running to keep up with his master's long-legged stride. "Ye can't be takin' the likes of her, dead away in a swoon and no doubt diseased as a rats' nest, home to the stay with the Dowager! Why, the gal is likely eaten up by the pox, or burning up with the fever—"

"Enough, Burgess!" Justin roared. "We're taking her to Cartwright Hall, and cease your carping!"

"But, yer lordship, there must a more suitable place for her—at a church, or at the Society for the Protection of Young Females—"

"The door, Burgess!" Justin snapped as they arrived at his stylish brougham.

Before Burgess could react, one of the liveried footmen sprang off his perch and opened the door for his master. Justin climbed inside the two-seater cab with the still-unconscious woman in his arms.

Seconds later, as the brougham rattled off down the cobbled street, Justin stared down at the creature he held. He still only half believed he had rescued this lowly girl in the Strand. But, as an honorable gentleman, he'd really had no choice, for he very much feared that his own untoward behavior, his brash kiss, had caused her the terrible fright that had resulted in her swoon.

But why had he spoken with her in the first place, then given her the nosegay and valentine intended for Lady Cynthia? Why had he kissed her? Why had he followed her to the corner and then caught her in his arms when she fainted? Burgess was surely right: the girl was most likely a menial who lived in the nearby tenements, and he had no business fetching her home to Cartwright Hall.

Yet there they were bound, through some gut-level decision on his part that he only half understood. He did know that something about this young woman had compelled him, captivated him, from the instant he laid eyes on her rounding the corner with her cart. Indeed, there had been something strange and mystical about their entire meeting—almost as if it had occurred on another plane.

A passing street lamp cast its wavering glow over her pale features, and he thought of how lovely she was, this young street hawker, of how mesmerized he had felt when he first gazed into her lost blue eyes. She had spoken with the strangest accent—American, by the sound of it.

He recalled the pain in those lovely orbs, and her words: "I've lost everything that matters to me." Was it that very statement that had compelled him to kiss her—and afterwards, to bear her to his carriage? It had been an almost earth-shattering encounter—indeed, at the moment of their kiss, the ground beneath his feet had hardly felt stable.

As the carriage turned north on St. James toward Mayfair, Justin thought of the door in Belgravia that he would not darken tonight. Cynthia would be disappointed in him. He had been bound for her Valentine's Day gathering when the impulse had come upon him to stop by Covent Garden to buy her a nosegay. Upon leaving the market, he had selected a valentine in a shop about to close its doors. He had then headed back for his carriage, the perfect gentleman, bound for an evening of courtship.

He had told himself it was time. His wife, Genevieve, had been killed two years past in a tragic accident. Once the requisite year of mourning had expired, Lady Cynthia, Genevieve's cousin, had made it clear to all of London society that she aimed to pursue the eligible widower. While Justin had hardly been an eager party to Cynthia's machinations, the city's elite had long ago assumed that a match between them was inevitable. Indeed, Justin had bowed to the inevitable tonight, by purchasing the flowers and valentine.

But his courtship of Cynthia had never begun, for Justin had given the items intended for her to a comely wench he'd met in the Strand. And at that very moment, he had lost himself in the loveliest blue eyes he had ever seen, and had then feasted on the sweetest lips he had ever tasted.

He glanced down at the girl again, tenderly brushing a wisp of hair from her brow. He wondered idly who *truly* had been rescued tonight.

Moments later, the brougham came to a halt before a sedate-looking town house off Portman Square. Burgess swung open the carriage door, and Justin bore out the young woman.

As one of the liveried footmen sprinted up the path and opened the heavy door for Justin, he bore his charge past the Palladian façade and into a home of lavish proportions. The small foyer led directly into the grand salon with its towering dome—a Robert Adam triumph of gilded plaster fretwork, pale yellow and blue paint, and roundels of original Italian art.

He was barely inside the salon when the butler, Carter, glided up in his black cutaway and starched shirt. "My lord," he murmured, bowing, and glancing confusedly at the woman in his employer's arms. "We hadn't expected you home so early. Has there been—" he inclined his head meaningfully toward the woman "—some mishap?"

"I simply came across an old friend in need," Justin replied curtly. Heading past the bemused butler toward the staircase, he added, "Please have Lady Bess's maid inform her that I'd be much obliged if she'd meet me in the guest room on the third floor."

"Yes, my lord. As you wish."

Justin bore the woman up the magnificent circular staircase with its wrought-iron railings and banister, its marble-wainscoted stairwell, and walls decorated with elegant, softly lit sconces, classical carvings, and magnificent oil paintings. On the third floor, he turned into the guest room and laid the woman down on the Sheraton daybed just inside the door. In the darkness, he approached the bulk of the dresser and fumbled for a moment while lighting the oil lamp. Wavering light spilled over the room.

Justin turned to stare at the woman, who lay, still blissfully unconscious, on the bed. He caught a sharp breath. He had thought her pretty in the shadows of the Strand, but here in the light of the room, he saw at last how truly exceptional she was. Her face was beautifully sculpted, her brow smooth, her cheekbones high, her chin strong, her mouth wide and full-lipped. Her wealth of silky blonde hair was pinned in a chignon, with numerous, enticing tendrils pulling free.

Justin shook his head in disbelief. Despite her modest attire, the girl was quite tall and beautifully proportioned, and she clearly had the face of an aristocrat.

Why had she been selling cheap trinkets in the Strand?

"Justin? My dear, what goes on here?"

He turned to see his mother enter the room in her satin robe and lacy nightcap. Lady Bess Cartwright, the Dowager Countess of Lockridge, was a small, gray-haired woman with a pleasant, rounded face. Justin knew her to be a genteel lady accustomed to commanding respect, but also a fine human being who never lacked compassion or warmth. Bess had single-handedly raised her son after a fever had claimed the lives of both Justin's father and his younger twin sisters, back when he was only four.

Justin turned to peck the little woman's cheek and fondly hugged her. "Good evening, Mother. As it happens, I've brought home a bit of a surprise."

The Dowager turned to peer at the stranger laid out on the Sheraton bed. "My kingdom, Justin!"

"Indeed," he concurred ruefully.

"Who is the girl?" Bess demanded.

He sighed. "She's a street vendor. I found her selling trinkets in the Strand near Covent Garden."

346

"Forevermore!" The Dowager's expression was flabbergasted. "But why would you bring such a creature here?"

Justin sighed. "She fainted, Mother. I think she is in need of our help."

"Oh, my! You were always such a thoughtful lad—but this!" The Dowager leaned over and felt the girl's forehead. "Mayhap the girl is ill? But, then, she doesn't feel feverish. What brought her to the Strand this night?"

"She told me that she was compelled to sell jewelry in her grandmother's place."

The Dowager gasped. "Blessed saints! What sort of person would send her grandchild out alone to earn her livelihood on the cruel, dangerous streets?"

"She said her grandmother was unable to perform her duties tonight," Justin explained. "I took that to mean there was some indisposition—or worse."

Bess stared at the girl sympathetically. "Oh, the poor dear. But why is she unconscious?"

Justin restrained himself to keep from blurting out his guilty secret—that he feared his bold kiss may have totally overwhelmed the girl. "I'm not sure. But I do know she's an American, and obviously just off the ship from the colonies. Perhaps she became disoriented—"

Bess held up a beringed finger and nodded vigorously. "Indeed. Why, London would seem a veritable maze to an American. And that skimpy dress she's wearing would not keep a flea warm on a bitter night like this."

"Aye," Justin concurred.

"But the fact remains—what are we to do with her?"

Justin removed his hat and drew his fingers threw his shiny black hair. "I don't know, Mother. Perhaps you might have some use of her here?"

"Perhaps." Bess gazed at the girl again. "She is quite a striking thing."

"Indeed, she is."

Bess frowned as she peered more closely. "Why, she has the face of an aristocrat!"

"So you noticed that, as well."

"How odd." Bess laid a finger alongside her cheek. "Of course, if she were to stay here, we would need some pretext . . . Perhaps we could help her get on her feet and secure a post."

"A fine idea."

Lady Bess nodded. "We can give the matter additional thought tomorrow. In the meantime, perhaps we should summon a physician."

"I agree."

"Why don't you dispatch a footman for the surgeon, while I summon the maid to get her undressed?" Bess suggested.

"Certainly, Mother. You are most kind."

As he turned to leave, she added, "By the way, did you get by Cynthia's?"

He smiled sheepishly. "No. You see, I had stopped by Covent Garden to buy Lady Cynthia a bouquet, and then I came across the girl—"

"It's just as well," Bess said, waving him off. "As I've mentioned before, I do feel that you and Cynthia would never suit. She's too highstrung—too much like Genevieve—" Abruptly Bess stopped talking.

But a mask had already closed over Justin's features. "I think I am quite capable of judging just who may or may not be right for me, Mother," he said coldly.

She patted his arm and slanted him an apologetic glance. "I'm sorry, son. I know that the subject still pains you."

Justin cleared his throat. "Yes. Well, I'd best see to the fetching of the surgeon, then."

He turned to leave, only to halt at his mother's sudden gasp of surprise. Pivoting toward the daybed, he asked, "What is it?"

A reply wasn't necessary as mother and son gazed down in fascination at the young woman who now regarded both with wide, alert blue eyes.

Chapter Three

Amanda opened her eyes, gazing past the faces of two strangers at a magnificent ceiling adorned with plaster medallions and gilded etchings of leaf and vine.

With a gasp, she sat up, staring at her surroundings in astonishment and disbelief. She was in a large Victorian bedroom, complete with richly detailed Brussels carpet, carved rosewood chairs with tufted silk damask upholstery, a four-poster tester bed with a magnificent counterpane of wine-colored jacquard silk, and windows adorned with hand-painted roller shades topped by embroidered portieres of iridescent green.

Had she somehow been spirited away to one

of Galveston's old Victorian mansions?

She gazed back at the strangers again, recognizing the handsome gentleman who had kissed her on the Strand. Unbidden, a feeling of excitement swept over her as she drank in his beautifully chiseled face and the deep-set brown eyes focused on her so intently. He appeared to be about thirty years old. Next to him stood a gray-haired lady whom she assumed was a relative.

Amanda tried to analyze what had happened to her. One minute, she had been selling jewelry on the Strand; the next minute, the man had given her the valentine and had kissed her. Afterward, she had stumbled toward the corner, and had spotted—good Lord, was it horse-drawn carriages? And, in the distance, a river?

But that was impossible!

"Where am I?" she asked the man.

He flashed her a kindly smile. "Are you feeling all right, miss?"

"I'm fine, thank you. Now, please, tell me where I am."

"Don't you remember?" he asked patiently. "You fainted in the Strand. And I've brought you here to my home off Portman Square, where you will be cared for under the chaperonage of my mother."

Amanda stared at the little woman. "Your mother?"

"Yes," the man replied. "May I present Lady Bess Cartwright?"

"How do you do?" Amanda murmured. Glancing at the man, she added, "And you are?"

351

"Lord Justin Cartwright."

"Pleased to meet you both," Amanda muttered, stunned by the English titles and once again taken aback by the man's formal speech. "I had not realized that we have British nobility living here in Galveston."

The man and woman exchanged perplexed glances.

"Galveston?" the man queried with a dark frown. "But you are not in America, young woman."

"I'm not?"

As Amanda stared at him, flabbergasted, the woman murmured, "The young lady is obviously quite confused and disoriented, Justin." She smiled at Amanda. "Is Galveston the place you hail from in the colonies?"

"Yes." Glancing from mother to son, Amanda was certain she had fallen into the clutches of two lunatics. "Look, I appreciate your kindness in rescuing me, but now I really must go—"

"Leave?" the mother queried. "But where would you be bound, on such a bitter night?"

"To my home in the East End," Amanda replied firmly.

"The East End!" Lord Justin repeated incredulously. "But we cannot allow you to travel back to those nefarious slums alone!"

Amanda's face heated with anger. She rose to her feet and faced down the man who had just insulted her. "Look, you may live in a grand Victorian mansion, sir, but I assure you that I do not live in a slum! Now if you'll excuse me—"

The man caught her arm gently but firmly. "Young lady, we do not even know who you are—or if you are physically well."

Amanda raised her chin. "My name is Amanda Brewster. I am just fine, and furthermore, I'll thank you to let go of me—now!"

He did so at once, muttering an apology, while the little woman cried, "Brewster! Tell me, dear, are you one of the Manchester Brewsters?"

Amanda considered that a moment. "My forebears did come from Manchester, England."

"Why, she must indeed be one of them," the little woman said excitedly, turning to her son. "As you know, Teddy Brewster was the Marquess of Sutton and quite wealthy in his own right. Teddy and my father were classmates at Eton, and our families were always close. But a devilish eccentric the man was. About thirty years past, Teddy gathered up his entire family—eight children and the wife, as I recall—and spirited everyone off to live in America." She peered intently at Amanda. "Are any of your people with you now, dear?"

Amanda shook her head. "My parents were swept away by a flood when I was six. Afterward, I went to live with my grandmother—"

"Ah, your grandmother," Lord Justin put in. "Is she the one who brought you back here to England?"

Amanda stared at him, stunned by his question, especially as she recalled the planned trip to England that she and Gran had never gotten to take. "Sir, I do not live in England," she said coldly.

"We realize that you consider America your home," the Dowager deftly smoothed over. "Does your gran reside with you in the East End?"

Amanda sighed. "She did—until her death two weeks ago."

"Oh, you poor dear," the Dowager cried. "There's so much cholera and fever near the docks. Now you're all alone in the world?"

"Yes, I am."

The Dowager turned to her son. "Justin, we cannot allow this young lady to return to those dangerous tenements tonight."

He sighed. "I agree." He glanced sheepishly at Amanda. "However, neither can we force Miss Brewster to stay here against her will."

Amanda felt relieved to hear the man acknowledge that they had no intention of coercing her. Meanwhile, the Dowager smiled at her guest. "My dear, as a friend of your family's, I consider it my bounden duty to offer you the hospitality of our home until a suitable situation can be found for you."

Amanda shook her head. "Thank you for your kindness, but I wouldn't dream of imposing—"

"It's no imposition at all," the woman argued. "You must at least spend one night. Tomorrow we can discuss finding better lodgings for you, and if you wish, we can gather your things from whatever rookery you abide in near the Thames—"

"Near the Thames?" Amanda echoed. "You speak as if we actually are in London—"

"But we are," Lord Justin put in vehemently. "And if you have somehow convinced yourself that you are elsewhere, young lady, then this is only additional proof that you should not be gadding about anywhere in your present, confused state—"

"Wait a minute!" Amanda cried. "You're saying we're actually in London, England?"

"Indeed," the man replied.

Amanda shook her head in disbelief. "What year is it?"

"Why, it's the year of our Lord 1851."

Amanda staggered on her feet and the man caught her arm.

"Are you all right?" he asked with grave concern, eying her pale face.

Her voice was barely audible. "Would you both just leave me alone for a moment—please?"

"Certainly, dear," Lady Bess said with a smile. "You've had a most trying experience, and you do need your rest. Why don't we straighten out all of this in the morning? I'm sure you'll find a suitable bed garment in the armoire—and I'll have the maid bring in your tea and help you dress for bed."

The two slipped from the room, leaving Amanda to stare down at her own trembling hands. What had happened to her? Had she truly landed in the clutches of a couple of crackpots? But then, how could she explain what she had seen, and what had happened to her, back on the Strand?

Amanda glanced again at the room. As a student of interior design, she was astounded by the priceless Victorian antiques surrounding her—the ornate Staffordshire urn in the corner, the Sheraton chair next to the carved mahogany desk, the Wedgwood vases on the fireplace mantel of white Carrara marble.

She moved over to the window and raised the painted shade, gasping as she gazed out from the third-story window. In front of her stretched rows of Georgian and Palladian town houses, as well as open expanses and squares dotted with trees. In the distance, she spotted numerous huge, looming Baroque or classical buildings and assorted Gothic church spires. The entire urban expanse was banked by sooty black clouds.

She turned from the scene, electrified. Twentieth-century America this clearly wasn't!

Pausing by the dresser, she spotted the nosegay of violets and the old-fashioned card that Lord Justin had given her earlier. She picked up the valentine, and an eerie feeling crept over her as she stared at an angelic, adorable cupid with his bow, surrounded by a froth of lace, pearls, and satin ribbons, and the message in flowery script: "Two hearts beating in time."

Amanda gasped. Cupid had obviously released his arrow—more likely, an entire quiverful!—and then had sent her hurtling off . . . where? She set the card down, still only half believing that Justin Cartwright had given her this out on the Strand.

Most critical of all, which Strand had it been? The Strand in Galveston, Texas, or the Strand in London, England?

Numbly she went to sit on the bed, her eyes widening in shock as she sank deeply into the feather tick. She stared at the potpourri in the pink lusterware dish on the bed table, glanced from the delicate taper in its pewter holder to the oil lamp gleaming softly on the dresser.

Oh, God, what had happened to her? One minute, she had been in Galveston. Then a handsome, mesmerizing stranger had kissed her, the earth had moved beneath her feet, and the next minute—

She had turned a corner in time.

While Amanda struggled to gain her bearings, Justin and his mother sat in the drawing room of Cartwright Hall, their figures outlined in the gaslight spilling down from the chandelier. The Dowager reclined on a blue velvet Grecian couch, while her son sat across from her in a Chippendale wing chair. A fire blazed in the hearth, its roaring flames heating the lavish room with its high, plasterwork ceiling, floral Aubusson rug, gilded harp, and black mahogany pianoforte.

"What shall we do about the young lady?" Justin asked as he sipped his tea in a Paris china cup.

Bess's expression was thoughtful. "This may sound odd, but—"

"Please be candid."

"I feel quite drawn to the girl," she confessed.

He smiled ruefully. "To be frank, so do I."

"There's something so gentle, so lost and compelling about her."

"Aye," he murmured.

"Besides which, the girl obviously needs our supervision," Bess continued. "She's young and impressionable, as well as a foreigner who is totally ill-equipped to deal with the perils of our society. Indeed, I shudder to think of her fate should we allow her to return to the streets as she desires."

"I agree," Justin said gravely.

Bess nodded firmly. "I've a mind to take the girl under wing."

"You do?"

Her expression turned poignant. "You know how I always mourned the loss of your twin sisters. Only three when the fever took them—and your beloved father, as well."

"I know, Mother," Justin murmured sympathetically. With a cautious frown, he added, "You see this girl as a substitute, then?"

She gestured expansively. "The girl is obviously of aristocratic lineage. Why, come to think of it, she even resembles Eleanor Brewster, Teddy's wife. Who is to criticize us if we take in this orphan from an old friend's family?"

Justin had to smile at his mother's less-than-scientific logic. Bess Cartwright, while an upstanding, take-charge sort, also possessed a streak of whimsy that had always amused and intrigued her son. She was also well known throughout London society for her benevolent pursuits and generous heart.

"How far do you plan to take this?" he asked.

"I'd like to see the girl in a suitable post—or even better, in a proper marriage."

He raised an eyebrow. "You aim to launch her, then?"

Bess sighed. "We'll have to see how it goes and what her feelings are. But, with the season nearly upon us, it does seem a prime opportunity. I see no reason why Amanda should not fit in. Of course, as an American, she would need some instruction in the ways of our society—"

"Indeed she would." He scowled. "What do you think of her mad claim that she is living in America even now? Do you think it's possible that she may be a trifle touched?"

Bess shook her head. "Think of what the girl has been through—traveling to England, losing her beloved gran and only living relative, then being forced to take to the dangerous streets alone, compelled to sell cheap trinkets to keep body and soul alive—"

"Aye, it is a tragic story," he concurred with a sigh. "The young lady could definitely use our assistance."

Bess was thoughtfully silent a moment. "Son, I know you don't like the subject brought up—"

"Speak your mind, Mother," he said wearily.

"I realize that you feel compelled to marry and

beget an heir now that your mourning period for Genevieve is over, but I must say that for you to marry Cynthia would be a grave mistake."

While Justin was silent, a muscle working in his jaw betrayed his emotion.

"As you know, I am quite a believe in providence—"

"What are you saying?"

She smiled wistfully. "I'm saying that, isn't it odd that you went out tonight, intent on courting Cynthia, and instead brought home this lovely, gentle girl?"

His brow was deeply furrowed. "Are you implying that the encounter was more than happenstance?"

"Am I?" Bess replied with an enigmatic smile. "Why do *you* think you brought her here?"

An ironic laugh escaped him. "A very good question."

"Son, I'm merely asking you to consider the girl," Bess said primly. "That is all."

Lord Justin was silent, a bemused smile pulling at his lips.

As Justin prepared for bed, he was still mulling over his mother's words. *Consider the girl*, she had implored. If only she knew that he was considering pretty Amanda Brewster even now. Indeed, he had thought of little else besides this lovely, destitute young woman ever since he had spotted her in the Strand.

Had it been providence that had brought this mysterious, charming girl to him tonight, and

had prevented him from beginning his courtship of Lady Cynthia? Had his mother spoken
the truth when she'd told him that his marrying
his dead wife's cousin would be a disastrous
mistake?

He sighed. His first marriage to Genevieve,
Cynthia's cousin, had certainly ended in ruin.
Justin had always blamed himself for her death.
If only he hadn't been arguing with her on that
fateful day when the accident had occurred.
But unfortunately, their entire marriage had
been fraught with conflict. Genevieve had been
impetuous, high-strung, altogether too loose
with her tongue—and with his money.

He again considered his mother's warning.
To be brutally honest with himself, Cynthia *was*
perhaps too much like her deceased cousin.

And yet the possibility of courting Cynthia
Spalding had offered Justin the perfect opportunity to assuage his terrible guilt over
Genevieve's death. He knew that Cynthia was
determined not only to become his countess,
but also to gain control of the fabulous Spalding
jewels that had become Justin's property on
Genevieve's marriage to him. Moreover, a marriage to Lady Cynthia would be quite proper, no
doubt begetting him an heir.

But couldn't the very passions that had
destroyed his first marriage spell disaster for
his second?

Now there was this girl, this Amanda
Brewster. Lovely, sweet, and fair. *Consider
her*, his mother had said. With gentle Amanda,

would he—would *she*—be safe from his own·
destructive passions?

Recalling the raw splendor of their kiss, he
wasn't at all certain.

Nevertheless, for the first time in two hellish
years, Lord Justin Cartwright slipped the silver mourning ring, with its oppressive band of
black, from his finger.

Chapter Four

Amanda had a dream.

Gran was smiling at her as she handed her a gift—a beautiful Victorian hatbox. Amanda gasped as she opened the lid and gazed at the wondrous lacy valentine inside, inscribed with the words "Two hearts beating in time."

Amanda awakened with a smile, finding herself in the same splendid Victorian bedroom where she had fallen asleep last night. She glanced about in surprise and delight. So she hadn't merely dreamed of traveling to Victorian England—she truly was living in the past! With awe, she watched sunlight dance across the Brussels rug and shimmer in the wine-colored, silken bed hangings.

Someone had raised the shades and drawn back the draperies; radiant light spilled in. Amanda spotted a maid at the dresser—a rosy-cheeked woman dressed in black, her uniform embellished by a white, lacy apron and matching housecap.

"Good morning, my lady," the woman said, approaching the bed. "I've placed yer tea on the dresser, and her ladyship the Dowager said to tell you she'll be pleased to meet you directly for breakfast downstairs in the dining room."

"Thank you," Amanda murmured, sitting up.

"May I help you with your toilette, my lady?" the woman added.

"No, thank you. I prefer to take care of that myself."

"Very well, my lady." Curtsying, the maid slipped from the room.

Amanda got up and quickly donned her clothing from last night. Somehow, the dream of Gran had eased her mind. Was this amazing excursion into the past really a gift from beyond? Was there something her grandmother had sent her here to learn? What was the significance of the gift in her dream? Was her time-travel experience truly the journey to England that she and Gran had never gotten to take?

Amanda found it amazing that only yesterday she had been living in Galveston, Texas, in the 1990s, cruising down Broadway in her small car and listening to Foreigner on the radio. Was she missed back on the island? Was her car still parked on the same street off the Strand?

What would happen if she did not reappear? Would her neighbors notify the police? Would she eventually end up in the files of "Unsolved Mysteries"?

Amanda smiled sadly. Who was to miss her, really, now that Gran was gone? Her few casual friends back in Galveston? The half dozen or so boyfriends who had cynically dumped her when they learned she wasn't prepared to put out on the first or second date?

She thought about the dark, dashing Englishman who had rescued her last night, and his dear little mother. Lord Justin's good looks fascinated her; Lady Bess's kindness reminded her poignantly of Gran.

Of course, if she were to stay here, she would need to find a way to support herself, she added to herself firmly. While she wanted to get to know Lord Justin and his mother better, she could not depend on the charity of these strangers, however kind they might be. She had her pride and her independence, after all.

Still, why not play out the role some fanciful Cupid had assigned her on Valentine's Day? Why not put the question of the future—her future back in Galveston—on the back burner for now and simply enjoy this fascinating sojourn in the past?

Who was to say she wouldn't be better off here?

Moments later, Amanda joined Bess Cartwright downstairs in the dining room. Bess, attired in a regal gown of burgundy silk, was already seated and nibbling on toast when Amanda appeared in the archway of the sunny room.

"Good morning, my dear," Bess called brightly, gesturing toward the place set out for her guest. "Did you sleep well?"

"Yes, thank you." Amanda slipped into her chair, gazing in wonder at the gorgeous china, gleaming silver, and impeccable linens laid out on the fine Hepplewhite table. "I hope you rested well, too, Mrs. Cartwright."

"Please, call me Lady Bess," the Dowager replied, pouring Amanda a cup of tea.

Amanda murmured a thank you as she took her china cup. "I'd be most honored to call you Lady Bess. Actually, I must be making all kinds of blunders in addressing you and your son—"

The Dowager waved her off. "Oh, do not fret yourself, my dear. I've always found the manner of addressing the British peerage a ridiculously pompous, convoluted bore. But I do suppose we're stuck with it. And the protocol can be learned—if one is interested."

"You are very kind." Amanda took a sip of her tea. "This is excellent tea."

"We brew it from spring water specially piped in from Hertford," Bess replied. "The springs far surpass the noxious water of the Thames, which produces an unhealthful libation, if you ask me."

Amanda nodded, taking a roll from the basket in front of her. "Where is Lord Justin?"

Lady Bess sighed. "He's at an emergency

meeting Lord Russell called at Downing Street. As an American, you're probably unaware of our politics here, but Parliament is in a terrible muddle at the moment, between the debates over free trade, papal encroachment, and the various reform movements. Indeed, Lord John's administration is tottering even now, and may not survive the week. Justin, as a staunch supporter of the prime minister, is most concerned."

"I'm sorry to hear this."

Bess waved her off. "British politics—always some tempest in a teapot. Let's talk about you, my dear."

Amanda slanted Bess a warm smile. "You were most kind to let me stay here last night, but now—"

"Now, we wouldn't dream of having you go off anywhere else."

Amanda sighed exasperatedly. "Mrs. Cartwright—that is, Lady Bess—I cannot possibly continue to impose here—"

"But you're not imposing at all!" Bess cut in stoutly. "I've so enjoyed your company, my dear, and I'd be bereft without you. Furthermore, as a friend of your family's, it would be unforgivably remiss of me not to extend to you our continuing hospitality. Besides, how would you support yourself out on your own? Selling trinkets in the Strand would never do."

Amanda thought quickly. "Gran taught me to do sewing and needlepoint."

Lady Bess beamed. "Splendid, then. As it happens, I have an entire chestful of new linens in need of monogramming and embroidering before they can be set out. Indeed, I cannot possibly complete our spring airing out without your assistance."

"Lady Bess—" Amanda protested.

Bess shook a finger at her guest. "Now, not another word, you stubborn girl! It's been ages since we've had a delightful guest such as yourself, and I simply refuse to hear any more of this treason about your gadding off. As it happens, Justin has mentioned wanting to take you for a drive later, so in the meantime, we'll be off to Oxford Street to select a suitable frock for you."

Amanda's eyes grew huge. "Lady Bess, I cannot possibly allow . . ."

Amanda continued to protest, but in the end, her arguments were futile and she grudgingly consented to meet Lady Bess in the grand salon at eleven, after the Dowager had completed her morning letter writing.

Lady Bess felt quite pleased with her triumph over Amanda as she went off upstairs. Being with the girl again had only confirmed for Bess her intuition that this young American was a true jewel. Besides, Bess had a feeling that Justin was already quite taken with the girl. Indeed, she hoped that the girl's bright presence would divest Justin of his unhealthy desire to court the high-strung Cynthia—an interest which Bess knew was motivated entirely out of guilt over Genevieve's death.

Yes, having the girl here was a true stroke

of fortune, Bess decided. Today she actually looked forward to answering the normally tedious letters and invitations that poured in daily. She would mention Amanda Brewster to all her friends, and see that this young lady was immediately received in all the proper circles.

When Amanda descended to the grand salon an hour later, Lady Bess had not yet appeared. She sat down on a tufted velvet ottoman and amused herself by studying the ornate statuary and lush ferns and by gazing up at the magnificent dome with its gilt-edged plaster fretwork.

She heard a commotion out in the foyer, and a tall, red-headed woman charged in with the butler at her heels. The lady, sharp-featured, sallow-complexioned, and looking to be in her early twenties, was obviously of the aristocracy as her elegant carriage dress, fringed mantle, and plumed hat attested.

She stared at Amanda rudely. "Who are you?"

Amanda stood. "I'm Amanda Brewster."

The woman sniffed disdainfully as she took in Amanda's modest attire. "Well, Miss Brewster, aren't you aware that menials curtsy in the presence of a lady?"

"I beg your pardon?" Amanda was stunned.

"But, Cynthia," interjected a cold, firm voice, "let me assure you that my guest is very much a lady herself."

Both women turned to watch Lady Bess Cartwright glide down the staircase, her bearing regal.

"Good morning, Lady Bess," the newcomer said stiffly to her hostess.

"Good morning, Lady Cynthia," Lady Bess replied. "May I present our houseguest, Lady Amanda Brewster, the granddaughter of my old friend, Lord Teddy Brewster of Manchester?" Turning to Amanda, she added, "My dear, may I present Lady Cynthia Spalding?"

Amanda glanced uncertainly at Cynthia.

"How do you do?" Lady Cynthia said archly, barely nodding to acknowledge the other woman and contemptuously not offering her hand.

"Pleased to meet you," Amanda said, her voice equally frigid.

"So, Lady Cynthia, how can we be of assistance?" Bess inquired.

"I was hoping to catch Justin in," Cynthia responded, nervously plucking at her gloves. "After he failed to appear at my party last night, I grew concerned that he might be indisposed."

"I see," Bess murmured. "Did my son promise you he would attend?"

Cynthia colored. "Well, no—it was quite an informal affair, but Justin gave me the impression . . . At any rate, is he well?"

"He's perfectly fit, and meeting with Lord Russell at this very moment," Bess assured. "And I'm sure you'll forgive him for not attending your little soirée—" she paused to smile brilliantly at Amanda "—since we did have our lovely houseguest from America to entertain."

Cynthia's complexion darkened to an unbecoming shade of green; she slanted a malevolent glance toward Amanda. "I had not realized that Lord Lockridge was interested in such— American upstarts."

"Oh, Justin has always found the ladies of the colonies to be enchanting," Bess replied smoothly. Her voice took on a menacing frigidity. "And furthermore, I'm sure you were jesting just now when you referred to my guest as an upstart, since, as I've already informed you, Amanda is eminently a lady in her own right." Before Cynthia could comment, Bess rushed on, "Now, you'll have to forgive us, dear Cynthia. Amanda and I are on our way out shopping, or we would invite you to join us for luncheon."

Cynthia's scornful gaze flicked over Amanda's plain frock. "Ah, yes, it does appear that your guest is in dire need of a proper wardrobe."

"Oh, that," Bess put in, laughing. "Dear Amanda's trunk was lost at the docks when she arrived yesterday, and we've had a devil of a time trying to find her a suitable garment. We finally had to prevail upon one of the maids to lend us something. You see, Amanda is so tall, slender, and lovely, isn't she? At any rate, what fun to go shopping for a brand-new wardrobe for such a splendid creature! I can't remember when I've had so much fun. I'll swear, having dear Amanda here makes me feel twenty years younger—and I've noted a new spring in my son's step, as well."

While Cynthia glared at her hostess with chest heaving, Amanda could only shake her head in total admiration of the Dowager.

Bess, too, was feeling quite self-satisfied as Lady Cynthia hissed a curt farewell, turned on her heel and haughtily stormed out. Bess realized that her referring to her guest as "Lady Amanda"—as one would normally do only with the daughter of a high-born peer—was perhaps a bit of a stretch. However, once again, the Dowager remained determined to take no chances while launching her young protégée.

They shopped on Oxford Street, amid charming Mayfair. Lady Bess insisted on buying Amanda a stylish braid-trimmed Worth dress with matching jacket, a derby hat with feathers, a pair of gloves, and fine leather slippers. She also bought Amanda some dresses and lingerie for immediate wear, and then proceeded to flabbergast her guest by ordering an entire new wardrobe for her. Amanda's numerous protests were stoutly ignored. By the time they returned to the town house off Portman Square, Amanda had all but given up on trying to circumvent the strong-willed Dowager. She did promise herself that somehow she would find a way to repay Lady Bess.

As the two women entered the salon, with the footman at their heels juggling numerous boxes, Justin came forward to greet them, looking dashing in his single-breasted morning coat, dark trousers, ruffled linen shirt, and satin-edged waistcoat.

"Amanda, how lovely you look," he said, admiring her in the elegant Worth ensemble, which Bess had insisted she wear home.

"Isn't she ravishing, son?" Bess put in, beaming. "Now you must take her out and show her off."

"Indeed, that's precisely why I've stopped by," Justin said with a grin. "I thought Amanda might enjoy a drive about town—and perhaps an early supper at Simpson's." He glanced at her. "What do you say?"

"I'd be delighted," she replied. "Just let me put these things away and freshen up."

Amanda went upstairs, with the footman trailing behind her with the boxes.

Bess whispered behind her hand to Justin. "We'd best have a chat, son. I'm afraid Lady Cynthia came round earlier and created a bit of a scene."

"Bloody hell," he muttered.

Half an hour later, Justin escorted Amanda into his brougham, and she was stunned to spot on its door the same enchanting coat of arms that she had seen on the time-machine float back in Galveston—a Roman chariot/shield, with a handsome warrior driving his winged Pegasus. Amanda's sense that she was meant to be here, in the London of 1851, was growing stronger by the moment.

As they rattled away from Portman Square, the two smiled shyly at each other, the cozy intimacy of the coach adding to the romantic mood. Amanda marveled at the sense of breathless excitement she felt whenever she was with Justin.

"My, that is a splendid frock," he murmured, again eying her appreciatively.

"I tried to keep your mother from spending all that money on me," she replied morosely, "but I got nowhere fast."

He chuckled. "You must know that Mother is totally taken with you, Amanda. She'd be devastated if you left us now." He patted her hand. "Please don't."

Would you be devastated if I left, Lord Justin? she thought, her heart beating madly at the very thought.

Aloud, she said, "I just don't like feeling . . . well, beholden to anyone."

"But you're not," he protested. "Indeed, we are most beholden to you. I can't remember when I've seen my mother so happy."

Amanda fell silent. How could she argue with that?

They were now moving through a gorgeous tree-lined park, and she spotted a massive, soaring glass structure being constructed in the distance. "Justin, what is that?"

"The Crystal Palace," he explained. "The craftsmen are working furiously on it even now. It will be the grand hall of the Great Exhibition in May."

"Why, it's fabulous!" she cried.

"I'll take you there on opening day," he said with sudden eagerness. "Indeed, I'd be proud to show you off at Queen Victoria's ball to celebrate the opening."

"You would?" she asked, surprised and thrilled.

"The theme will be Scottish." His dark gaze roved over her, gleaming with pleasure. "I should think you would look quite fetching as a Highland miss."

Amanda turned away, blushing and feeling somewhat confused. Was Lord Justin teasing her? Or did he actually intend to court her, when she was a mere stranger about whom he knew next to nothing?

"It does sound like fun," she murmured.

Abruptly Justin caught Amanda's chin, forcing her to meet his solemn gaze. Her heart thudded as his gloved fingers and dark eyes seemed to burn into her.

"Amanda, I do hope you don't still think you're in America?" he asked with concern.

Pulling away from his unsettling touch and gaze, she turned to stare out at the park, at a parade of riders strutting about on blooded horses, and other members of the gentry gliding by in handsome carriages. "No, I do very much realize I'm in London," she replied ruefully.

He cleared his throat. "Amanda . . . I've been meaning to apologize for my ungentlemanly conduct last night. I've even wondered if my untoward attentions were not precisely what caused your confusion—"

"But they were not!" she protested, turning to look at him.

He held up a hand. "Please, hear me out. Truth to tell, I don't know what came over me. It is quite unlike me to try to force myself on a young lady in such a brash manner. There was just—something about your eyes."

She reached out to touch his hand. "Justin, you needn't apologize. I really found it quite sweet."

"You did?" He appeared amazed. "What an odd, fascinating creature you are."

Again feeling self-conscious, Amanda turned away, gazing out at a row of stylish Mayfair shops, watching two ladies disembark from their fine carriage and enter a millinery shop. "How was your meeting with the prime minister?" she murmured.

Justin sighed. "Parliament is under siege at the moment—indeed, I'm due at the House of Lords even now." He flashed Amanda a quick grin. "However, let's not concern ourselves with such tiresome matters now—I've been looking forward all day to this outing with you."

"Have you?" She blushed in pleasure. "You are most kind."

He gazed at her intently then, and reached out to stroke her cheek, again setting off a firestorm of emotion and excitement within her.

"I'm not kind, Amanda," he stated flatly. "You'll do well to remember that."

Amanda was stunned and unnerved, feeling almost as if he had slapped her rather than caressed her. "Why would you talk that way about yourself?" she asked in an incredulous whisper.

He was silent for a long moment. At last he said stiffly, "My mother informed me of your encounter today with Lady Cynthia."

Amanda nodded dismally. "Yes. Your finding me last night kept you from attending her party, didn't it? I'm so sorry."

"Don't be sorry," he quickly said. "I really didn't care to attend that stuffy affair."

Suddenly she snapped her fingers. "The valentine and the nosegay you gave me were intended for Lady Cynthia, weren't they? No wonder she was so angry this morning. Justin, you shouldn't have—"

"I chose to give them to you, Amanda," he cut in vehemently.

"You chose?" she repeated.

His dark gaze impaled her. "I wanted to give them to you."

She stared at him, and he stared back. All at once, the tension and electricity hanging in the air between them was so thick Amanda could not bear it. Her heart seemed to skid and skip a beat, then lurch into an even more frantic rhythm.

"Amanda . . ." he murmured, leaning toward her.

"What?" she cried.

She felt Justin's arm curl possessively about her waist, watched his dark, mesmerizing face descend toward hers, and thought her heart would burst with anticipation and longing.

"My God, you are so lovely," he murmured huskily. Then his head ducked down further and he kissed her.

Desire and exhilaration soared in Amanda. Justin's kiss was intoxicating, so warm and thrilling. His tongue slipped between her lips to tease and titillate unbearably. When she gasped, he seemed to suck her very breath into his body, and the eroticism twisted inexorably deep in her belly. Amanda feared she would die of the delightful, dangerously potent sensations streaming through her body.

"Oh, Amanda," she heard him murmur when at last he pulled away. "I'm going to be so very bad for you."

She was silent, feeling bemused by his comments and still half dizzy from his masterful kiss. Her eyes sought his face to gauge his feelings, but he had already turned away to stare at a passing trio of street vendors, his expression abstracted.

"You know, you may have saved me from a catastrophe—or so my mother thinks," he murmured after a moment.

"How is that?" she asked.

He sighed, then said tightly, "Cynthia was the cousin and closest friend of my first wife, Lady Genevieve, who was killed in an accident two years past."

"Oh, Justin, I'm so sorry," she murmured, her own confusion forgotten in her concern over him.

His shrug seemed to belie his pain. "Over the

past year, I've become aware that Cynthia has, shall we say, set her cap for me—and not discreetly so. Although my mother is convinced that we will never suit, the rest of London society already has Lady Cynthia and me joined at the hip, even though I hadn't planned to start courting her—"

"Until last night?" Amanda supplied.

"Aye."

"And I stopped you?"

He stared directly into her eyes. "I would say you arrested me—thoroughly."

Amanda could barely hear him over her own pulse pounding in her ears. And still he stared at her with such riveting intensity.

"Justin, why did you kiss me a moment ago?" she finally managed.

His arm curled about her again, and his lips hovered so close to hers that she could feel his warm breath, arousing her like the most powerful aphrodisiac. "Because you have the saddest eyes I've ever seen—and because you looked so lost."

Tears flooded Amanda's sad eyes. "And you say you're not kind—"

"Not at all, darling," he murmured as his skilled mouth claimed hers once again.

Justin showed her the sights of London. She was amazed and captivated by the sedate majesty of Buckingham Palace, the Gothic wonder of Parliament, which Justin explained was still finishing reconstruction after the old Palace of

Westminster had burned down in 1834. They circled verdant St. James's Park, passing the pageantry of the Horse Guards inspection near their barracks. Heading toward the center of town, they moved through Trafalgar Square with its fine view of the National Gallery. They watched the quaint trains leaving Euston Station. Amanda loved glimpsing the stately splendor of the many churches and listening to the mellow toll of their bells.

Yet she quickly discovered that there was much misery amid the splendor. Some of the stateliest courts and streets were bounded by appalling slums and workhouses. In the East End in particular, the oppression of the masses was apparent in the sobering façade of Newgate Prison, the sordidness of the mazelike rookeries, and the seaminess of the docks. When Amanda remarked on some of the wretched conditions to Justin, he replied that, along with Lord Russell, he was working in Parliament to effect reform by enfranchising the poor, further restricting or eliminating child labor, and establishing public education. She listened with glowing respect, and again wondered why Justin would call himself "unkind." Was she simply another charity he felt duty-bound to support?

They passed the forbidding Tower of London, Lord Christopher Wren's soaring Monument to the Great Fire, and London Bridge, eventually making their way back to the center of town and the Strand. Traffic was much thicker this late in the day, with numerous carriages, omnibuses, and high-wheeler bicycles competing for passing room. They glided past pillared Somerset House on the Thames and past the very corner where Justin had found Amanda last night. Staring at the very spot where he had first kissed her, Amanda felt an eerie feeling slide over her.

Eventually they stopped at the popular Simpson's-in-the-Strand and shared a hearty supper of mutton with vegetables, sweetbreads, and toffee pudding. Amanda noted that the staff at the restaurant treated "Lord Lockridge" with almost cloying deference and respect.

During the meal, she asked him why she had heard several people today refer to him as Lord Lockridge when his name was actually Cartwright, and he explained to her about his various titles. When pressed, he delivered a head-spinning lecture on the protocol of addressing the British peerage. By the time they left the eatery together, with Justin planning to attend an evening Parliament session after dropping Amanda off, she was happy, sated, and drooping. In the brougham, she nodded off to the soothing clip-clop of the horses' hooves. Her head rested against Justin's shoulder.

In the fading light, he stared down at her. She looked so lovely and so trusting beside him. How he had enjoyed being with her today, and how sweet had been her kisses! His male pride basked in having this destitute girl dependent on him—indeed, the darker side of his nature relished having her under his complete control. He adored her gentle manner—especially as compared to his high-strung first wife and her self-appointed successor, the Lady Cynthia, who was in such a snit at the moment. He smiled ruefully, realizing that his mother had been right. Lady Cynthia would have made an ungovernable wife.

But this girl . . . ! He glanced again at Amanda. This lovely creature would be so biddable. Unlike Lady Cynthia and her predecessor, Lady Genevieve, this girl would never provoke him to passions he would later regret.

If only he could keep his baser desires for her curbed.

He tenderly stroked Amanda's cheek, leaning over and kissing her in her sleep. How warm and delicious she tasted, how tempting.

Lord Justin groaned. He was not going to be good for this girl. Not at all.

Chapter Five

During the next few days, Justin was immersed in the turmoil at Parliament, with Lord John Russell's administration increasingly under siege and then defeated on February 20. Amanda saw him only at a few meals, where he would appear tense and preoccupied. Still, she basked in the occasional smile he cast her way, the glint of admiration in his dark eyes when he regarded her.

Amanda realized that Justin had awakened something romantic in her the day they had gone sightseeing together, and she continually hoped that, when his life became less chaotic, he would want to pursue a relationship with her. She basked in memories of their shared kisses, and her longing for him increased with each passing day.

Lady Bess helped fill the void created by her son's absence; Amanda was becoming most fond of the Dowager. Bess took her guest on daily rounds of social calls amongst her friends. Amanda was introduced to the grand dames of London society, and shared tea and crumpets in their lavish drawing rooms. There, listening to gossip about the coming season, the new crop of debutantes and what matches would likely be made with the most eligible bachelors, Amanda picked up many of the social nuances of Victorian society. She learned how to hold her teacup, how members of the peerage and gentry were addressed, and what subjects were and were not appropriate for a lady to discuss.

As Amanda quickly became a subject of great curiosity among the fashionable, ladies began to call at Cartwright Hall to meet this dazzling young American whom Bess Cartwright had taken under wing. While Bess invariably introduced her guest as "Lady Amanda," at first there seemed some confusion as to Amanda's exact place in the household. One middle-aged caller, the pretty and vivacious Lady Millicent Ogden, upon eying the petit-point dresser scarf that Amanda was working on, exclaimed to Lady Bess, "My stars, I've never seen such fabulous Berlin work! If your guest is ever in need of a post, Lady Bess, I know of a shop on Bond Street that would welcome her with open arms."

Lady Bess ended the caller's enthusiasm with a frosty glare. "Lady Ogden, I must inform you that Lady Amanda is neither a paid companion nor a poor relation here. We consider her a cherished member of our family, and as such, it would be totally beneath her station to seek employment of any kind."

The chastened Lady Millicent at once apologized. "Lady Bess, I'm deeply sorry. I did not mean to insult your guest. I was merely—so overwhelmed by her talent—"

"Ah, yes, Lady Amanda will be the catch of the season, don't you agree?" Bess smoothed over skillfully. "What a lucky man her future husband will be."

"Indeed," Lady Millicent concurred, flashing Amanda a brilliant smile. "And I do hope both of you—as well as Lord Justin—will be attending my ball Thursday next—sort of a pre-season soirée, now that most everyone is back in town."

"Amanda and I shall be looking for our invitations in the post," Lady Bess responded wisely.

"You'll receive them at once," Lady Millicent assured.

And thus, Amanda's place in society was secured.

After Lady Millicent left, Amanda said tactfully, "Lady Bess, perhaps I should seek employment on Bond Street. That way, I could be responsible for myself, and could also repay—"

"Merciful saints!" Lady Bess cried, flinging a hand to her breast.

Amanda became alarmed, as Lady Bess had grown deathly pale. "What is it?"

Lady Bess's voice came weak and fluttery. "I feel faint. Summon Dexter at once."

Amanda bolted from her chair. What followed on Lady Bess's part were histrionics of the first order, worthy of the campiest Shakespearean troupe. The footman dashed in with Lady Bess's smelling salts, and two additional servants had to be summoned to bear the prostrate Dowager up to her suite. Amanda spent the entire afternoon alternately holding Bess's hand and wiping her brow, amid the Dowager's lamentations over her abject helplessness if Amanda should "desert" her.

While Amanda knew Lady Bess to be about as helpless as the steam locomotives she'd seen leaving Euston Station, nevertheless, she did not again dare to bring up the subject of leaving Cartwright Hall.

On the eve of Lord and Lady Ogden's ball, a mood of great excitement gripped Cartwright Hall. Justin, who had joined the ladies for an early supper, was in a jubilant frame of mind as Lord Russell's administration had just been restored, following days of upheaval at Parliament which culminated in the failure of the Tories to establish their own regime.

After the evening meal, all three retired to dress for the ball. A maid styled Amanda's hair in a smooth chignon interlaced with delicate flowers, and then helped her into her fabulous red ball gown—a full-skirted Worth master-piece with low, lace-trimmed décolletage, tight waist, and exquisite lace overskirt. Amanda left the room carrying the silk and ivory fan that Lady Millicent had sent her along with her invitation—ostensibly in apology for the matron's presumptuous remarks the other day.

Amanda lifted her skirts and carefully maneuvered her way down the several flights of stairs to the drawing room. There she found Justin alone, sipping brandy and looking devastatingly handsome in his black velvet cutaway jacket, ruffled linen shirt, white silk cravat, and black trousers. His thick, jet-black hair gleamed in the soft light.

He looked her over with great admiration. "Amanda, how beautiful you look!" He set down his snifter, stepped forward, and took her hand, kissing her fingers through her lacy glove.

Amanda blushed with pleasure at his attention, even as the scent of his bay rum thrilled her senses. "You look quite handsome yourself, my lord."

He chuckled at her manner of addressing him. "You're becoming accustomed to our ways here, aren't you?" A shadow crossed his eyes. "Do you miss America?"

She considered that a moment, then shook her head. "Actually, I'm really enjoying getting to know the country of my forebears. I feel strangely at home here."

"I want you to consider England—and Cartwright Hall—your home," he murmured. He reached out, gently caressing her cheek. "I've missed you, you know."

His words and warm touch ignited a blaze of longing within her. All at once, she could barely breathe as he stared at her so intently.

"You've been busy, haven't you?" she asked.

"Ah, yes, the trials and tribulations of Parliamentary politics." He pivoted to pick up a velvet box off the pedestal table, then turned and extended it to her. "A peace offering."

Taking the box, Amanda was mystified. "But Justin, you have no reason to make peace with me."

"Don't I?" He winked at her. "Any other young lady your age would throw hysterics to have been neglected so shamelessly, and would milk the situation for all it was worth."

She stared at him, electrified by his words, her heart aflutter at the teasing laughter in his eyes. Lord Justin was definitely flirting with her—indeed, his words implied that they were to have a continuing relationship! She was thrilled beyond belief.

"Open the box, Amanda," he directed.

She did, gasping as she spotted the priceless ruby pendant inside, dangling from a sumptuous gold chain. She glanced up at him and found he appeared eminently pleased with himself.

"I cannot accept this," she cried. Remembering an idiom used by one of the matrons who had called, she added, "It's too dear."

Justin didn't reply at once, taking the necklace from the box and opening the clasp. "You're too dear," he whispered intensely, leaning over and kissing her.

Oh, he was so skilled! His mouth claimed hers expertly, his tongue teasing between her lips, then plunging into her mouth with bold intimacy. The deep, dizzying strokes of his passion mesmerized her as he clasped the ruby drop around her neck. With a groan, he clutched her closer, his hand firmly cupping her breast. Amanda arched into his delicious touch and thrust her tongue enticingly against his.

Abruptly he pulled back, his expression dark and brooding.

She stared at him confusedly. "Justin, what is it? Didn't you enjoy kissing me?"

He laughed ruefully. "I enjoyed it far too much. Indeed, perhaps I should have Mother give you a stout lecture."

Her chin came up. "And why is that?"

His dark gaze raked over her. "If you are this readily distracted, darling, think of how easily you might be seduced."

Amanda's face flamed and her hand moved to take off the necklace. "You must think I'm some fast woman, trying to compromise your sense of high morality—"

He caught her hand. "Darling, don't," he implored. "I'm being a cad, I know. I'm not displeased with you, I'm disappointed in myself. All I can think of is how much you tempt me, and how jealous I'll be of every man who looks at you tonight."

At his passionate words, Amanda was surprised that her wobbly legs supported her. Still, she managed to assert, "Those feelings are good, Justin. Why should they make you annoyed with yourself?"

He spoke sternly. "You would not be particularly pleased, young lady, had I brought our encounter to its natural conclusion."

"Are you so sure?" she asked recklessly.

She heard his stunned intake of breath. "You, miss, are a tease," he scolded, shaking a finger a her. "I'd say that you are in dire need of a strong husband."

"Whatever you say," she retorted.

His voice was far from steady as he extended his arm to her. "I say that it's high time for us to leave."

She fought a giggle and placed her hand on his sleeve.

As they headed for the door, he cleared his throat. "Amanda?"

"Yes?"

"Save the first dance for me?"

Delight shone in her eyes. "Of course."

In the corridor, he added, "On second thought, save *every* dance for me."

Despite his chivalrous words, Amanda felt bemused afterward. Why did Justin blow hot one minute, cold the next? Was it just a matter of strict morality on his part? Or was he truly fighting his feelings for her?

* * *

The Ogdens' ball was held in a lavish, well-lit Roman villa, one of the few stately homes gracing lovely Regent's Park.

Justin, Amanda, and Bess were received by the Ogdens in their stunning gold-paneled and frescoed ballroom. Amanda was enthralled by the costumes of the ladies—brilliant ball gowns complemented by pearl necklaces and glittering tiaras. She was equally impressed by the impeccable attire of the men—formal black cutaways and ruffled white linen shirts buttoned with diamond studs. So captivated was she by the ambiance of the event that it was all she could do to remember the various social protocols—how to address the Baroness of Sheffield, and to curtsy for the Duke and Duchess of Rochester.

Justin introduced her to Lords Russell and Palmerston, as well as to several others of the cabinet ministers who were there with their wives. She also met the elderly Duke of Wellington, who had just successfully rallied Parliament to return Russell to power.

An awkward moment came when Lady Cynthia Spalding arrived with her parents. When she spotted Amanda sipping punch with Justin and a couple of his friends, she shot the girl a look of pure venom.

Justin squeezed Amanda's hand and said, "Don't mind her, dear."

But Lady Cynthia hardly took her defeat gracefully. As the ballroom began to fill up, she went off to huddle with a half dozen of her debutante friends, and soon several of the young ladies were turning to stare rudely at Amanda as they tittered among themselves.

In the hour that followed, gossip seemed to spread like wildfire through the ballroom, and soon Justin became aware that he and Amanda were being snubbed. Conversations he initiated became strained and brief, and several of his acquaintances conspicuously avoided him and Amanda. Indeed, even as Justin was attempting to introduce her to a prominent grand dame, the woman had the gall to mutter a lame excuse and stalk off.

By now, the increasingly chilly atmosphere was apparent to Amanda, as well. Their first few minutes at the affair had been wonderful, but now they were being met with pointed stares and cold snubs.

"Justin, what is happening?" she whispered to him.

"I suspect Cynthia is at work," he replied disgustedly. "My dear, would you please go sit with my mother and Lady Ellsworth for a moment?"

Amanda dutifully went off to sit with Lady Bess and her best friend. Justin strode off to interrogate one of his cronies, Darby Middlesex.

"Tell me what treachery is making the rounds tonight, Darby," Justin demanded without preamble.

Darby, something of a dandy, toyed nervously with his cravat. "Well, hello, Justin, old man. I'm afraid there has been some dreadful gossip drifting through the ballroom."

"Damn," Justin muttered. "Tell me what is being said!"

Darby hesitated. "I really don't want to be the bearer of bad tidings—"

"Out with it!" Justin commanded.

Darby sighed. "What I'm hearing is that you truly have the nerve to show up here tonight with your mistress." Spotting the rage glittering in Justin's eyes, he hastily held up a hand. "Ye gads, old man, don't shoot the messenger! You can be assured that I'm not spreading the treason."

"You're right," Justin said, sighing. "If you'll excuse me?"

Justin headed back toward Amanda, his heart sinking. He was eminently aware that, given the high moral tone set by Queen Victoria, the slightest hint of scandal often meant social ostracism in London society.

That damn bitch Cynthia! Due to just a few words of cruel gossip, Amanda could well be ruined. Already, Cynthia's malicious lies had spread through the ballroom like an insidious wave. Now, none of the ladies would speak with Amanda tonight—none of the men would ask her to dance. Invitations for the fêtes and soirées of the coming season would never be forthcoming.

Damn it, how could he quell the escalating disaster?

Staring at the many who regarded him with snickers and snide glances, he made a decision. He would show the gossips what he thought of their idle treachery. He strode over to the dais and spoke with the musicians. Then he strode directly to Amanda, bowing before her.

"May I have this dance?" he asked.

She smiled radiantly and gave him her hand.

Justin led Amanda out onto the dance floor and whirled her about to a Chopin waltz. No other couples dared to join them, but Justin did not care. He clutched Amanda close and gazed into her eyes the entire time. Let the world see that they had nothing to hide! he thought fiercely. Let the world know that nothing else mattered to him but this lovely young lady he held in his arms.

Amanda was gliding on air. She had been appalled and hurt by their reception earlier, but now none of that seemed to matter. Justin was holding her close, staring at her as if she were the only woman on earth who existed for him. She could hardly bear the rapture—she felt so special and cherished. She realized that she was living every woman's fantasy, even by twentieth-century standards—to go back to enchanting Victorian times, to be courted by a dashing gentleman. She loved this man, she realized achingly. Loved him so much . . .

When the waltz ended, stunned silence reigned in the room. And then a wondrous thing happened. The elderly Duke of Wellington stepped forward in his splendid dress uniform with its many gleaming medals. As Amanda curtsied deeply, he asked her to dance.

This time, no other couple dared *not* to join them on the floor.

Amanda was in heaven as she swirled about with the dashing duke, amid the other couples. First she had danced with the man she loved with all her heart. Now she was waltzing with the hero of Waterloo. She was living a moment of history—her very own moment!

On the sidelines, Justin watched Amanda glide about with Wellington. What a lady she was! His heart burned with pride for her.

Justin realized that the evening could not possibly end on a higher note. When the duke released Amanda, Justin gathered her and his mother, and the three of them left the ballroom with heads held high.

Chapter Six

The following morning, the Earl of Lockridge paid a call on Lady Cynthia Spalding.

Cynthia, elegantly attired in a frock of green silk with a lace bodice and sleeves, received Justin in the sumptuous drawing room of her Belgravia mansion. He stood as she entered the room, regarding her coldly.

"Why, Justin, what a pleasant surprise," she preened with a bright smile. "Do sit down and I'll ring for tea."

"I prefer to stand," he replied in a chilly tone. "And don't bother with tea. This is not a social call, and I think our business can be conducted forthwith."

"Business?" she repeated innocently. "Perhaps this subject would best be taken up with my father?"

He laughed ironically at her oblique reference to a marriage proposal. "Cynthia, I must admire your gall. How dare you insinuate that I would be the least bit interested in proposing matrimony, following your reprehensible conduct last evening."

She feigned a look of shock and outrage. "*My* reprehensible conduct? I assure you, I have no idea what you are talking about—"

"Oh, don't bother to deny it," he cut in. "The entire town is aware that you wish to take my late wife's place as the next Countess of Lockridge."

Her face heated. "Justin, simply because I hold you in high esteem—"

"Do you? Did you seek to elevate yourself in my eyes by ruining the prospects of the young American lady who is currently the guest of my mother and myself?"

"That American upstart is perfectly capable of ruining her own prospects," Cynthia retorted spitefully. In a more placating tone, she added, "Justin, please, let's sit down and make our peace—"

"I have no intention of making peace with you, Cynthia," he stated flatly. "Actually, you have engineered your own defeat."

She paled. "What do you mean?"

"You have subjected a guest in my home to possible social disgrace through your cowardly lies regarding Amanda and myself. Consequently, as a gentleman of honor, I have no choice but to marry the young lady to silence the gossips."

Cynthia was aghast. "You would marry that—"

Again he interrupted, lifting a hand in warning. "Take care how you refer to the future Countess of Lockridge."

"Justin, you must have lost your mind!" she cried, wild-eyed. "This—this young woman— will never be accepted here—"

"Indeed, she will," Justin asserted, "and you are going to see to it that Amanda's place in society is secured."

Cynthia laughed incredulously. "You're mad."

"Not at all. After I leave, you are going to go calling, Cynthia. You will go see every gossip in town with whom you committed your perfidy last night. You will inform one and all that a ghastly mistake has been made—that you know for a certainty now that Lady Amanda is as pure as the driven snow, and that all of the lies were started by a vindictive servant who was dismissed from Cartwright Hall after being caught stealing the family silver."

Cynthia was shaking her head. "Now I'm certain you've lost your mind. Why would I do this, Justin?"

He smiled bitterly and called over his shoulder. "Dexter!" Catching Cynthia's bemused expression, he added, "You see, my dear, I've been aware all along that it is not my name you want so much as the Spalding family jewels."

Both stood silently glaring at each other as the footman, resplendent in his livery, strode in and placed a small wooden chest on the inlaid mahogany tea table. Justin nodded curtly to the servant; Dexter bowed and slipped from the room.

Justin flipped the chest open, revealing a glittering heap of gorgeous tiaras, rings, necklaces—ruby, diamond, and emerald jewelry of every description. Cynthia's gaze became riveted on the dazzling jewels, her expression one of avid greed.

Running his fingers over the fabulous array, Justin smiled mockingly at Cynthia; she stared at him with avarice and hatred blazing in her eyes.

"It isn't fair!" she cried at last, with fists clenched. "Those jewels should have been mine! Grandmother gave them to Genevieve instead of to me because Genevieve was her favorite. And now you have them!"

"But you will have them, Cynthia," Justin drawled cynically, "in due course, if you behave yourself."

Cynthia was so stunned she could only stare at him.

"Do I have your attention now?" he asked mildly.

"Totally," she spat back. "Speak your mind, Justin."

"These jewels will be sent to you on the first anniversary of my marriage to Lady Amanda

Brewster—providing you undo the malicious lies you have already spread and do no further harm to my bride's reputation following our nuptials."

Cynthia was silent, her chest heaving, her features clenched with fury. "You bastard," she said at last.

A vein jumped in his temple. "I don't give a damn what your opinion is of me," he said in a menacing tone, "but I swear, Cynthia, if there is the slightest hint of scandal, the slightest sullying of Amanda's name, during my first year of marriage to her, I will blame you and no one else, and you may consider this arrangement null and void. Do I make myself clear?"

"Eminently!" she snapped.

"Do you agree to my terms?"

"Yes." She raised her chin. "But how do you know I won't try to ruin Amanda after the year has ended?"

His smile was frightening. "I won't be transferring a formal deed of ownership, my dear. If you ever again try to harm Amanda in any way, I'll reclaim the jewels as my own."

She laughed contemptuously. "But that is absurd! How could I possibly trust you?"

His voice was lethally soft as he snapped shut the lid of the chest. "You will, Cynthia, because, unlike you, I am a person of honor."

Taking with him the chest of jewels, Justin turned on his heel and strode from the room.

* * *

Late that afternoon, Amanda was summoned to Justin's study.

She rapped softly on the door and heard him call, "Enter."

She slipped in quietly, admiring the paneled room with its many leather-bound books and gleaming cherrywood desk. Most of all, she admired the handsome man sitting behind the desk.

Justin smiled and stood. "Amanda. Come right in."

He came forward, took her hands, and led her to the Jacobean chair in front of his desk. She felt giddy in his presence, especially as his warm, strong hands gripped hers. She noted that he had removed his jacket, and he looked so appealing in his flowing white shirtsleeves and brocaded waistcoat. A curl had pulled loose from his normally impeccably groomed hair and now dangled sexily over his forehead, only increasing his attraction.

She sat down and smoothed her skirts of lightweight blue wool. Instead of resuming his own seat, he leaned his hip on the edge of the desk and stared down at her intently, exciting and unnerving her, especially as she noted how his trousers pulled at his strong thigh muscles.

"Have you been enjoying your time here?" he began.

She smiled. "Oh, yes, very much. I find all the rounds of shopping and calls with your mother fascinating. Yesterday she took me to visit the National Gallery. The oil paintings were divine—Constable and Turner and Reynolds. The entire gallery was magnificent—I could spend a week there." She sighed. "I just wish there were some way I could repay you and your mother for all you've done."

"And when will you get it through that lovely head of yours that it is we who are indebted to you for gracing our lives so splendidly?"

"You are most kind," she murmured. Then, realizing what she had said, and watching him raise an eyebrow, she held up a hand and added vehemently, "I don't care what you say. You are kind, Justin."

He chuckled. "How old are you, Amanda?"

Taken aback slightly, she replied, "Why, I'm twenty."

He nodded, his expression relieved. "That is good. You look so fresh and fair you could be sixteen, but I'm relieved to hear that you're old enough."

She paled. "Old enough for what?"

He stroked his jaw thoughtfully. "Ordinarily, I would take up this matter with your father, or even your grandmother. But since there's no one . . ."

"No one for what?"

He took her hands and stared down at her solemnly. "Amanda, would you do me the honor of becoming my wife?"

Stunned, she shot to her feet. "What?"

He grinned. "Don't look so flabbergasted. I'm asking you to marry me."

"But—but why?" she cried.

He shook his head ruefully. "My, you are direct."

"And I would appreciate a direct answer, Justin," she said seriously.

"Very well, then. I am in need of a wife—and of an heir."

"Oh." Her spirits sank. "Then you're proposing a marriage of convenience?"

"A rather cold way to put it."

"But accurate?"

He did not respond.

She snapped her fingers. "Does this have anything to do with last night?"

His expression grew extremely cautious. "What do you mean?"

She laughed dryly. "Justin, don't try to humor me. I was hardly accepted by your exalted society here."

He sighed. "Amanda, I didn't want to have to bring this up—"

"Bring what up?"

"What happened last night—for which I humbly apologize—really had nothing to do with you."

She spoke through gritted teeth. "Oh, come on! You can't think I'm that näive and gullible!"

"But it's true!"

"Then you'd better tell me what last night meant—right now."

He nodded morosely. "I'm afraid there's been some malicious gossip—started by Lady Cynthia."

Amanda paled. "What did she tell people—"

"Please, dear, there's no sense repeating—"

"Tell me what she said—now!"

Miserably, he confessed, "I'm afraid she spread it about the ballroom that you are . . ."

"Yes?"

He sighed heavily. "My mistress."

"Oh, God!" Amanda cried. "Why would she say that?"

He shrugged. "She had hoped that she and I would become a couple. And you know what they say about a woman scorned."

"Now you feel you must rescue me?" Amanda asked bitterly. "Make an honest woman of me, so to speak?"

His expression was crestfallen. "No, dear, that's not my motive at all."

Tears filled her eyes. "Isn't it? I don't hear you saying that you love me, Justin. Tell me, do you love me?"

He was silent, his expression dark and brooding.

She had her answer. Blinded by emotion, she fled for the door.

But Justin caught her, pulling her roughly into his arms, holding her there against her will.

"No! No!" she cried, trying to wrench herself free from him. "I don't need your help! I don't need your pity—"

"But darling," he whispered intensely, "I need you."

Justin kissed her, smothering her cries. As always, the heat of his wonderful lips snapped her control. The fingers that had clawed at his

404

chest uncurled, and then she slipped her arms around his neck and kissed him back with all the emotion welling in her heart.

At her sweet surrender, a tremor of emotion shook Justin to the roots of his being. He pulled her to the nearby settee and settled her in his lap, cradling her against him. She continued to moan softly; he continued to kiss her tenderly.

"Amanda, I really do want to marry you," he whispered against her hair.

"What of Lady Cynthia?" she asked breathlessly. "She'll still do her best to ruin us both."

"No, she won't," he assured. "All she really wanted was Genevieve's jewels—and I've promised her those in a year, if she behaves herself."

Amanda pulled back, aghast. "I can't allow you to give in to blackmail like that!"

"It's not blackmail. It was all my idea. You see, I've never wanted to keep Genevieve's jewels. I've always intended to give them to Cynthia. That is, unless you should want them—"

"Heavens, no."

He smiled and brushed a tear from her cheek. "Didn't you say you wanted to repay me?"

Amanda could barely speak over the emotion constricting her throat. "But that wouldn't be repaying you."

Tender amusement shone in his gaze. "It wouldn't?"

She stared at him with her heart in her eyes. "No. It would be giving me what I most want in the world."

She heard him groan, then he crushed her

close, his arms trembling about her. "Oh, God, Amanda. I wish you wouldn't say things like that. I could well lose my head."

She lovingly kissed the strong line of his jaw. "But isn't that what marriage is supposed to be all about? Falling in love—losing one's head—and one's heart?"

His arms tightened about her. "You're so young, so idealistic. I wish I could live up to your expectations."

She drew back. "Won't you?"

He smiled sadly. "It's a risk, darling. Well, what do you say? Will you marry me, and make my mother a very happy woman?"

Disappointment lanced her. "What about you, Justin? Will I make you a very happy man?"

"Indeed, you will, darling," he murmured, and kissed her again.

Lady Bess was beside herself over their announcement, weeping with joy and hugging them both. She had the footman fetch their best brandy for an impromptu celebration at dinner.

There followed weeks of whirlwind activity as the banns were read, the wedding costumes prepared. Several of Lady Bess's prominent friends threw fêtes or soirées to honor the betrothed couple. While Lady Cynthia was present at several of these affairs, and treated the couple with chilly courtesy, there was no more unpleasant gossip to spoil the days prior to the wedding.

They married at St. Margaret's, Parliament,

and Lord Russell himself was present, as well as several of his ministers and other members of the House of Lords—and, of course, all of Justin's and Bess's friends. Amanda felt as if living a dream as she stood next to Justin in her beautiful satin wedding gown in the wonderful old Gothic church. She gloried in every second of the marriage ceremony, lovingly repeating her vows, tears filling her eyes at the moment when Justin placed the gold band on her finger—and later, at the end, when his lips briefly, tenderly claimed hers. She didn't know if this man loved her, but at this moment she had enough love in her heart for them both.

The wedding breakfast was a festive affair at Cartwright Hall. Justin seemed in a jovial mood as he sat next to Amanda, both of them joining in the many toasts.

Once the guests had departed, Amanda excused herself and went to her room to change. After the maid had helped her out of her wedding dress, corset, and petticoats, Amanda dismissed her. Then she heard a knock at her door.

"Who is it?" she called.

"Justin."

She smiled. "Come in."

Justin entered the room and closed the door, only to stop in his tracks as he spotted his bride standing across from him, wearing only her sexy camisole and bloomers. His gaze raked over her hungrily, pausing on the lush breasts that strained against the fine lawn of her camisole, the nipples tautening even as he stared at them. Riveting lust shot through his loins, and he was stunned at the raw intensity of his response to her.

"I'm sorry," he muttered tightly. "You're not dressed."

She licked her lush lips in invitation. "And you're my husband."

Justin's meager control snapped. He crossed the room in brisk strides and hauled the lush vision of femininity into his arms. Her sweet scent further inflamed his raging senses as he kissed her with near-violent hunger. His fingers dug into her soft bottom, tilting her into his hard, aroused length.

"You have no idea what you're doing," he said roughly, nipping at her ear. "I could devour you alive, pretty girl, right here and now."

She pulled back to stare up at him in hurt and confusion. "Justin, why does it make you angry that you want me?"

He stepped back, drawing a ragged breath. Spotting her wrapper laid across a nearby chair, he picked it up and awkwardly draped it about her shoulders. "I'm sorry. Actually, I've come to beg your pardon. I must leave for an important session of Parliament. I'm sponsoring a bill on worker reform, and the vote tonight could be critical."

"But it's our wedding night," she whispered, unable to hide her disappointment.

"I know," he murmured, stroking her cheek. "I'll make it up to you. And perhaps while I'm gone, you might have the maids move your things into the suite next to mine?"

It was on the tip of Amanda's tongue to ask why she wouldn't be sharing his bedroom—then she remembered that this was Victorian England. He might well be scandalized if she suggested such a rash move—and surely he would come to her later.

"Of course, Justin," she said.

He kissed her cheek and turned for the door. Her hopes sank when he pivoted to look at her one last time, his expression that of a cold, remote stranger.

"I'll be late. Perhaps 'twould be best that you not wait up for me."

Amanda proudly lifted her chin. "I don't care how late you come home. I'm your wife and I'll be waiting for you."

At her words, a muscle worked in his jaw and he blinked rapidly. But he made no comment as he turned and left her.

The encounter troubled Amanda as she and the maids moved her things to the suite adjoining Justin's. Obviously, her husband wanted her—she had hardly imagined the stark lust in his eyes, the searing ravishment of his kiss, or the hot hardness of his loins pressing into her. Still, he did seem to be fighting his own desire for her. Perhaps as a proper English gentleman, he considered it vulgar and wicked to lose control that way.

Well, if he did, his bride was determined to change his mind!

Late that night, Amanda dressed in the lacy

nightgown Lady Bess had given her as a wedding gift. She waited for Justin to appear, slightly nervous and yet giddy with anticipation over the night to come.

Amanda felt particularly happy that she was a virgin. While she was no prude, back in her own time she had never found the right man to whom she wanted to give herself. Now, she felt so grateful that her gift would be given to Justin alone.

The hour grew late and her husband did not appear. At last she heard him moving about in the next room. She waited for what seemed an eternity, but still he did not come to her. She paced, agonizing endlessly. Did Justin truly not want her in his bed?

Finally she swallowed her pride and entered his room without knocking. He whirled to face her, wearing a brocade dressing gown and smoking a cigar.

He snatched the cigar out of his mouth; his gaze seemed to consume her flesh. "Amanda, is something wrong?" he asked tightly.

She stepped forward. "Yes, something is wrong. It is our wedding night, and you still haven't come to me."

He swallowed hard. "The hour was very late— I thought you would be sleeping."

She stepped closer. "I'm not. I'm wide awake—and here I am."

He stared at her again. "My God, you're ravishing."

But as she moved closer, he held up a trembling hand.

"Justin—what is it?" she cried.

"The gossips," he said in a tortured voice. "It will not do for us to have a child too soon, Amanda."

She felt as if he had just thrown ice water in her face, and her voice reflected her wounded feelings. "Is that all you care about, Justin Cartwright—the gossips? Is that why you married me—strictly for the sake of propriety, and to save my sacred reputation? And now you can't even bear to touch me?"

His eyes were crazed. "No, Amanda, that's not true at all!"

Tears were blinding her. "You're not unkind, Justin Cartwright," she said in a breaking voice. "You're cruel!"

She fled his room.

After Amanda left, Justin damned himself a fool. He'd been a fool to let Amanda go just now—and even more of a fool to think that he could marry this young girl and still keep his feelings safely shut away.

His young wife had looked so delectable just now—just as she had earlier today, when he had all but thrown her down on the bed and devoured her alive. He knew his rejection of her had cut her to the quick, and yet he had felt compelled to send her away for her own good.

Over the past weeks, Justin had hoped to learn to curb his runaway feelings, to keep his raging thirst for this lovely young woman within acceptable limits. But he had failed dismally; if anything, his lust for Amanda had only intensified. It was the prospect of losing control that frightened him the most; if Amanda could make him lose control of his passions, then it followed that she could also make him lose control of his temper. This he could not abide. He had destroyed one woman with his anger, and he could not risk ruining Amanda's life, as well. He loved her too much now. He loved her enough to live with the hell of not having her.

Amanda felt devastated over Justin's rejection. Why had he married her? Strictly to silence the gossips? Did he still love his first wife? Did he still miss her? Had he made Amanda his bride because she was young, impressionable, malleable? Because he could control her, hold her at arm's length while he remained physically and emotionally faithful to a dead woman?

Oh, yes, he must have wanted her for just those reasons—he had certainly manipulated her quite successfully so far! What a fool she had been to fall into his trap, to consign herself to a loveless marriage that would satisfy outward appearances only.

Chapter Seven

Amanda was a bride without a husband.

The next few days brought no change in the pattern. Justin was gone much of the time, at Parliament sessions or at his club on St. James Street. When he was at home, his attitude toward his bride was polite and aloof. He never visited her bed.

Amanda tried to keep herself busy, joining Lady Bess on social calls and helping her take baskets to the poor. When she saw firsthand some of the misery of the London slums, she tried to take comfort in the fact that Justin was working to change the appalling conditions. Yet, as she began increasingly to realize how magnanimous both Justin and his mother were, she had to wonder again if she were little more than a charity case to them both.

While she tried to keep her days full, her nights were pure torture. Emotionally, she felt devastated. She loved Justin with all her heart and could not figure out the reason for his perplexing withdrawal, or even the true reason he had married her. He couldn't love her as she loved him—if so, he would never spend another night without her.

She began increasingly to fear that the roots of his problem could indeed lie in his first marriage. One afternoon at tea, Amanda questioned Lady Bess about this.

"I've been wondering about Justin's marriage to Genevieve," she remarked. "Did he take it very hard when he lost his wife?"

Lady Bess glanced at Amanda in astonishment. "It was a difficult period for us all."

Amanda restrained her private irritation at Lady Bess's smooth dodge. She tried a more direct approach. "How did Justin's first wife die?"

Lady Bess sighed and set down her teacup. "I think it best that you ask Justin about that."

"But he doesn't talk to me about anything!" Amanda cried with frustration. "Please, I'm only trying to understand him."

Yet Bess was unrelenting. "I think that when the time is right, Justin will speak to you of Genevieve."

Amanda was growing desperate. "Lady Bess, at the risk of embarrassing you, I must be frank.

Justin never visits my bedroom."

Lady Bess emitted a small, shrill laugh. "Oh, my dear. You can be assured that when the time is right, Justin will do his duty to provide an heir."

Amanda was crestfallen. "Is that all the English think a marriage is about? Performing one's duty and producing heirs?"

Bess reached over to pat the girl's hand. "Of course not. I know Justin is quite devoted to you."

"I wish I could know this," Amanda muttered bitterly.

Another week passed, with no change. Amanda's spirits grew increasingly depressed.

Then Amanda ran across Lady Cynthia at a tea given by Lady Stanton of Belgrave Square. The drawing room of the lavish town house was crowded with stylishly dressed ladies; Amanda tried her best to mingle, while avoiding her nemesis. But while she was in the dining room helping herself to a scone, Cynthia strolled in.

"Well, is married life agreeing with you, Lady Amanda?" she began snidely.

"I'm doing just fine, thank you," came Amanda's stiff reply.

"I feel so sorry for Justin," Cynthia went on with an air of tragedy.

Amanda's blue eyes shot sparks at this jibe. "Let me assure you, Lady Cynthia, that Justin is in no need of your pity!"

"But isn't he?" she went on with a poisonous smile. "Due to some idle gossip—which I must tell you, I had no part of—Justin has been forced to marry beneath his station."

Amanda's patience was wearing thin. "Justin would never marry simply to silence the gossips," she asserted with bravado.

Cynthia only laughed scornfully. "Then, my dear, you have no idea of the high moral standards of our gentlemen here—not surprising, since you are from the colonies. Let me assure you that Justin had no choice after the talk got around regarding his—" she sniffed disdainfully "—American houseguest."

Amanda's tone was icy. "*If* you'll excuse me, Cynthia?"

But as she started off, Cynthia caught her arm. "You must know you will never take Genevieve's place," she hissed.

Amanda shook herself free of her grasp. "What do you mean?"

Cynthia continued with vindictive relish, "Justin loved her desperately. Unlike you, she was a lady in every way—polished in all the social graces, and an expert rider. Why, they rode together in Hyde Park every day, and Genevieve was always the toast of the town." She laughed cruelly. "What a fool you are to think that Justin could love a gauche little commoner like you."

Amanda stormed out of the room without a word.

* * *

Cynthia's cruel words haunted Amanda. While she knew that the woman was motivated by spite, she couldn't help but feel that the comments might have contained a grain of truth. She very much feared that Justin *had* married her solely out of his Victorian sense of high morality, to silence the gossips. She continued to suspect that he still loved his first wife. Jealousy ate at her every time she remembered Cynthia's saying that Justin and Genevieve rode together each day at Hyde Park.

Well, she would learn to ride, too! She would become even more skilled and polished in all the social graces than Genevieve had been. She would become a genteel lady whom Justin was bound to love.

Amanda decided that her first step should be to take riding lessons. She would keep the lessons a secret, and later surprise Justin. Amanda consulted the groom at the Cartwright Hall stable, and he recommended a riding master who could give her equestrian lessons at Hyde Park. Each day, she took out a sleek black Arabian from the Cartwright Hall stable and met the riding master in the park. She paid for her lessons and for her riding habit with the pin money Justin and Lady Bess kept insisting that she accept.

In the days that followed, Amanda learned how to sit properly on a side saddle, how to walk, trot, and canter her horse, how to make turns. She noted that, each afternoon, tree-shaded "Rotten Row" at Hyde Park became a haven for the fashionable—dandies cantering their magnificent blooded horses, ladies gliding by in their elegant carriages or riding their own splendid mounts. Even prostitutes were present in their gaudy gigs and tawdry clothing, taking outings along the row and trying to catch the attention of the passing gentlemen.

As Amanda became more expert at riding, she too caught the stares of society—particularly of the gentlemen present in the park each afternoon—and she knew it would be only a matter of time before someone mentioned to Justin seeing her there. Thus, only two weeks after she began her lessons, she sent her husband a note at his club late one morning: "Please meet me at Hyde Park, Rotten Row, today at five thirty. Love, Amanda."

When the appointed hour came, Amanda was atwitter with excitement, not certain whether Justin would appear or not. Wearing her blue serge riding habit and feathered hat, she trotted her Arabian up and down the lane, searching for any sign of her husband. Then, even as she was cantering down the row—past men who stared and women who grudgingly admired her prowess—Justin suddenly leaped out in front of her horse. He appeared enraged.

The frightened horse reared, and Amanda almost came unseated before she managed to bring him under rein.

Justin grabbed the horse's reins. His features were white with fury. "Get off that horse!"

Amanda was stunned. Never before had she

seen her husband like this. She felt as if he had struck her. Not a word of greeting, or of admiration—only a deadly cold "Get off that horse."

"Justin? What is it?" she cried.

"Damn it, madam, I said get off that horse!" And he reached up and roughly hauled her out of the saddle.

As her boots hit the hard ground, Amanda felt humiliated, mortified. Justin was creating a dreadful scene. Everyone in the lane was staring at them, and several bystanders were snickering among themselves. But her husband seemed oblivious as he wordlessly dragged her off to his brougham.

"Please!" she cried desperately. "My horse!"

Justin barked a command to the footman. Dexter sprang off his perch and sprinted over to grab the horse, leading him back and tethering him to the rear of the carriage. In the meantime, Justin had propelled his wife inside the cab.

The trip home passed in stony silence. Amanda couldn't believe that the granite-faced, implacable stranger sitting next to her was actually her husband. This man—cold-blooded, near-violent—bore no resemblance at all to the kindly, soft-spoken Justin she knew.

At Cartwright Hall, he caught her hand in a steely grip and pulled her up the three flights of stairs to his bedroom. He did not speak until they were safely behind closed doors.

He snatched her note from his pocket and held it up in a trembling hand. "What is the meaning of this, Amanda?"

"I—I wanted you to see me ride!" she declared.

He blinked rapidly. "*Meet me at Hyde Park*," he quoted with a sneer. "Do you delight in being cruel?"

"I don't know what you're talking about!" she cried exasperatedly.

He shook a fist at her. "Don't you ever, *ever* again let me see you on a horse!"

"Never? But why?" she demanded.

"Because I command it, that is why!"

"Because you command it?" Amanda's vision flooded with red at his arrogance. "Or is it because Genevieve was an expert rider, and you'll never let another woman presume to take her place?"

"How dare you say such a thing!" he shouted, wild-eyed. "Furthermore, you are my wife and you will obey me!"

The passion and frustration of weeks burst in Amanda. "I will not!" she asserted, defying him recklessly. "Furthermore, I do not consider this a binding marriage since it has never been consummated. Therefore, I'm not your wife and I don't have to obey you!"

Naked rage now blazed in his eyes. "That," he snapped, "is about to be remedied."

Too late, she realized his intent. He lunged for her; she lunged for the door. He caught her easily, heaving her up into his strong arms and bearing her, kicking and screaming, to his bed.

He tossed her down on the feather tick and threw himself on top of her, his body hard and very aroused. She caught a frightening glimpse of his fierce, determined features, then his mouth descended brutally on hers. He pried her lips apart with a punishing kiss and savaged her mouth with his tongue.

Amanda sobbed beneath him, tortured by heartache and confusion. Then a curious thing happened—rage turned to tenderness, anger to tears.

He pulled back and caught her face in his hands, his own expression stunned and contrite. "Amanda. Oh, darling, I'm so sorry."

She held out her arms to him, unable to bear another second of the agonizing rift between them. "Love me, Justin," she beseeched. "Please love me."

"Oh, God," he cried. "Why must I want you so?"

With these anguished words, he crushed her close, kissing her with raw passion and urgency. She kissed him back hungrily, no longer afraid but breathlessly aroused.

Justin's warm lips trailed down her throat. He opened the jacket of her riding habit, pushed aside her corset and camisole, and took her tautened nipple in his mouth. Amanda cried out; she had never felt anything so wrenchingly pleasurable. She thrust her fingers into his thick, soft hair and clutched him tightly to her breast, moaning words of encouragement, glorying as his tongue stroked and tormented her.

Abruptly he pulled back, staring at her with desire-blackened eyes as he hastily removed his jacket, waistcoat, shirt, and cravat. She feasted her eyes on his muscular chest with its thick tufts of black hair as he reached down and undid her corset and camisole.

When she was naked from the waist up, he stared at her avidly and caught a sharp breath. "Damn, you're so incredibly beautiful."

Her heart pounded in joy and sweet tears filled her eyes.

Justin covered her with his muscled body again, and his rough, bare chest felt glorious against her tender, aroused breasts. His mouth took hers ravenously, his tongue teasing and thrusting as his hand slipped beneath her skirts. With the barest probing of his fingers against her drawers, Amanda was on fire, her fingernails digging into his strong, smooth shoulders. Passion twisted deep in her gut, a painful aching demanding his hard heat; she wanted him so badly now, she couldn't breath or think.

In the haze of desperate want, everything happened so quickly: within seconds, it seemed, he was pulling down her pantalets, pressing at the portal of her womanhood with his large, rigid length. She arched against him eagerly. She heard his rough groan, felt his mouth grind into hers as he pressed his hot, steely shaft into her virginal tightness. Pain lanced her, and she wrenched her mouth away, crying out. His lips followed to claim hers fiercely, his mouth quelling her soft sobs as he made her his utterly. In the wake of the discomfort, pleasure swept her, along with a feeling of sublime bliss at being joined with her husband at last.

Amanda clung to him, reveling in the intimacy, the melding. He pressed more deeply and boldly with each riveting stroke, and she began to move with him. Together, they rode the crest of mindless passion toward a sweet riot of feeling, until Justin spiraled downward with convulsive, hammering thrusts that made them both cry out at the shattering pinnacle . . .

When it was over, when their hearts, their breathing, at last quieted, neither seemed to know how to react. Justin moved off his wife, staring at her with awe and uncertainty. When she made a tentative move away from him, Justin's mouth descended on hers ardently, and then his hand possessively kneaded her bare, aching breast.

"Don't go," he whispered intensely, and pulled her back into his embrace.

Chapter Eight

The next morning, the Earl and the Countess of Lockridge shared an early breakfast in the dining room.

The atmosphere was so strained that Amanda reflected that it was almost as if the electrifying night of passion between them had never occurred.

But it *had* occurred, and she would never forget it. Justin had loved her almost to insensibility. He had awakened her repeatedly, claiming her passionately in the shadows of the night. While she might still doubt his love for her, she would never again doubt that he desired her.

Even though now, he was again an implacable stranger seated across from her, his shirt linen perfectly pressed, his jet-black hair gleaming, his jaw smoothly shaved, his expression cool, remote, the lips that had roved intimately all over her body tightly pressed as he sipped his tea.

Why was he acting this way toward her, when she knew of the passion raging just beneath the surface?

He caught her perusal and smiled at her briefly. "Are you all right, Amanda?" he asked awkwardly. "I mean, I hope that I didn't—"

"Hurt me?" she supplied, staring at him in anguish and defiance. "You're hurting me now."

At last she witnessed his façade cracking; a muscle worked in his jaw, then he lifted a hand to his brow and hung his head. "Amanda, please don't do this."

"Why are you acting this way?" she cried. "Last night you were like a different person—and now you're shutting me out of your life again!"

He clenched his fist on the tabletop. "That different person you saw last night, Amanda—it's the part of my nature that might well harm you."

"What? You must be joking!"

He stared at her with pain-filled eyes. "Last night was a mistake."

"How can you say that?"

"It wouldn't have happened at all," he continued tightly, "except that, when I saw you riding in the park—"

"Why did that enrage you so?" she demanded.

He stared at her incredulously. "You actually don't know."

"Know what?"

"I had assumed that by now, my mother—someone—would have told you—"

"Told me what? Quit talking in riddles, Justin."

He sighed heavily. "Watching you ride in the park yesterday frightened me."

"But why?"

He swallowed hard, then whispered, "My first wife was killed in a riding accident in Hyde Park."

"Oh, God!" Amanda cried, her hands flying to her face.

"We were arguing when it happened." Justin slammed his fist on the table and spoke with raw emotion. "God, if only I hadn't distracted her at the very moment her horse stumbled. Then she was thrown—a massive injury to her brain. She never regained consciousness."

"Oh, Justin, I'm so sorry!" Amanda cried abjectly. "If I had known, I never would have taken riding lessons." Then, as realization dawned, she gasped, "Oh, no! I've been such a fool!"

"What do you mean?"

She laughed cynically. "I've played right into Lady Cynthia's hands. She was the one who told me you could never love me because I wasn't a polished lady like Genevieve, because I couldn't ride like she did—"

"Damn her!" Justin cursed.

Tears were now spilling out of Amanda's eyes. "Oh, Cynthia was so subtle, so clever, to drop that sentence about you and Genevieve riding in Hyde Park. She knew I would snatch up every word, so desperate was I to make you love me."

Justin rounded the table and touched her shoulder, staring at her with tortured eyes. "Amanda—darling, don't."

"And now I have hurt you more than I could ever imagine," she continued, heartbroken.

He reached down and brushed a tear from her cheek. "Darling, please don't do this to yourself. When you think about it, Cynthia has only hurt herself."

"What do you mean?"

"First she started the gossip that brought about our marriage. Then she tried to drive a wedge between us again through her recent remarks to you. Instead, she brought us together last night."

Amanda was silent, staring at him.

He cupped her chin in his hand and gazed at her tenderly. "Darling, in time, when I learn to control my own nature, we'll be together. I promise you."

Yet Justin's attempt to reassure Amanda had only shattered her hopes, especially when he had reminded her that gossip alone had precipitated their marriage. "You still love her, don't you?" she asked with a terrible fatalism. "You won't let anyone take her place. You won't allow yourself to feel anything for me, will you Justin?"

"You don't understand," he said in a broken voice.

"You're bad for me?" she supplied bitterly.

This time it was Justin who could not speak as Amanda got up and went to the door. "So last night was a mistake?" she asked bitterly. "How can you say Cynthia brought us together? We're apart now, aren't we, Justin? I'd say Cynthia has won."

After Amanda left, Justin felt bedeviled by conflicted emotions. That bitch Cynthia! He was tempted to go strangle her for her latest perfidy—and then he groaned at the very thought of such violent, reprehensible conduct.

Still, due to Cynthia's manipulations, he'd learned something about his bride, yesterday and last night. Amanda was not just a tractable young girl he could bend to his will; she was a strong-willed, passionate woman determined to demand her due in this marriage. Far from being disappointed in her, Justin loved her for her pride and spirit. Making love with her last night had been paradise, and so addictive that he burned for her even now.

And that was the scariest part of all. Why couldn't she understand that he wanted their marriage to work, but that he must somehow exorcise his own inner demons first?

When he'd seen Amanda riding in the park yesterday, he'd become scared to death—and more enraged than he'd ever been in his life. Given his explosive burst of temper, it was a miracle that he hadn't hurt her badly. And the way he'd lost control afterward, rapaciously devouring her sweet, innocent body in his bed . . . Justin was well aware that his passions, when properly provoked, could become as destructive as they were potent.

He mustn't risk losing control again. He couldn't hurt his wife. He simply couldn't.

That afternoon, with heavy heart Amanda went calling on Lady Ogden in Regent's Park. From her she secured the name of the shop on Bond Street that could use a talented seamstress, and then went to the couturier and got a post for herself. She let a room at a nearby hotel and then went back to Justin's town house, secretly packing her bags. Before she departed, she left a note for Lady Bess, saying that she was all right, not to worry, but that the marriage had not worked out. She promised to come calling in a few days.

She left her wedding ring on Justin's dresser. She did not leave her new address.

She went back to the hotel by hansom cab, unpacked, and had supper in her room. Later, she cried herself to sleep.

In the middle of the night, her door crashed open. Amanda clung to the bedcovers, terrified, as she glimpsed the dark form of a man looming in the doorway.

"What in God's name do you think you're doing?" her husband shouted at her.

"I can't bear this sham of a marriage any longer!" she cried.

"Do you have any idea of the hell I've been through trying to find you?" he demanded.

"I don't care!" she flung at him heedlessly.

In his rage, Justin kicked over a chair. "You are my wife, Amanda Cartwright, and you belong in my home! You will never again run off this way, do you hear me?"

"Well, if I'm your wife, then you'd better make me come back to you!" she yelled.

He did, but not in the way she would have liked. He crossed the room, forced his wedding ring back onto her finger, wrapped her in his cloak, and bore her resisting body down to his carriage.

During the long drive home, he uttered not a single word.

Half an hour later, Amanda found herself back in her own room, lying in her cold bed, heartbroken, bereft, and weeping into her pillow.

Chapter Nine

Loving Justin was tearing Amanda apart.

She thought of this on May 1, while the two of them were in his brougham en route to the opening of the Great Exhibition in Hyde Park. Justin persisted in treating her with cold remoteness. She was dying by inches each day she remained with him.

Perhaps, being from the late twentieth century, she simply expected too much intimacy from a marriage. Perhaps this empty pretense was all one could truly expect from a Victorian marriage. She didn't know how much longer she could bear to stay with him—and yet she knew of no way to escape.

The Crystal Palace in Hyde Park was a marvel of nineteenth-century technology. Joseph Paxton's design resembled a mammoth greenhouse, fashioned of millions of panes of glass, with a huge, soaring dome.

Justin and Amanda followed the crowds inside. The atmosphere in the enormous exhibition hall was bustling and dazzling. Thousands of elegantly dressed ladies, gentleman, and entire families strolled through the verdant courts, past fabulous indoor fountains and stately statues. The exhibits ranged from the fascinating and loud Machinery Court to the dark gloom of Pugin's Medieval Court, with its somber crypt and ancient armor. Justin and Amanda marveled over the exhibits of art, china, and lace, and were intrigued by the new machines—one that sewed clothes, another that reaped crops, and a third that cooked food with gas jets. Amanda mused ironically that, while Justin must be enthralled to find machines so innovative and modern, she was equally charmed to view contraptions so quaint and old-fashioned.

Justin and Amanda had little time to study the exhibits before Victoria and her entourage arrived to officially open the exhibition. Amanda had heard many times that the prince had taken a very active role in the planning of the international fair, to the queen's immense pride.

The crowd parted, a hush falling over all in homage to the queen. In the front rows, the men bowed and the ladies curtsied as Victoria passed with Prince Albert, the young Prince of Wales, and the Princess Royal. The royal family was followed by the Bishop of Canterbury and the rest of the royal party.

Amanda curtsied deeply as the queen glided by, passing close enough to touch her and Justin. Amanda couldn't resist glancing up to more closely study the royal couple. Victoria wore a fashionable gown with train, and a white headpiece topped by her crown; Prince Albert wore his dashing dress uniform.

As they passed, Victoria turned slightly to stare at Amanda, her gaze direct and cool. Amanda hastily lowered her eyes.

The group paused on the center dais, and the crowd remained hushed as the Archbishop of Canterbury blessed the opening. A more informal atmosphere prevailed afterward, as the queen and her party toured the various exhibits.

Later, Justin and Amanda were in the Machinery Court, admiring a new electric telegraph machine, when a colleague from Parliament took him aside.

Lady Cynthia strolled over to join Amanda, flashing her usual poisonous smile. "Why, hello, Lady Amanda. You poor dear—to be snubbed by the queen that way."

Amanda tossed Cynthia a frosty glare. Her enemy's tendency to pop up this way becoming most annoying. "What are you talking about?"

Cynthia feigned a look of horror. "You mean you didn't even notice the way Victoria stared at you—the contempt in her eyes? The queen cannot abide Americans, you know. You can ask anyone about that."

"I certainly wouldn't ask you!" Amanda retorted.

"And Justin had such a promising political future, too," Cynthia lamented. "I've heard whispers about his becoming a cabinet minister in time. But if his wife is never received in the queen's court, given the fact that Queen Victoria and her prince take such an active role in the affairs of state . . ." She made a clucking sound. "Too bad. I'm afraid that once it gets around that Justin has fallen into disfavor through his marriage, his political future will be doomed."

Amanda was seething. "I made the mistake of believing you once, Cynthia. I won't do it again."

She stormed off to find Justin.

Despite her bravado to Cynthia, the words of Amanda's rival tormented her later that day as she rode home with Justin. That night, with hundreds of other members of the peerage and gentry, they were due at Buckingham Palace for the Scottish ball that Victoria and Albert were hosting to celebrate the opening of the fair. As a member of the peerage, Justin had been invited, but Amanda knew that this was not the same as an invitation to court for his wife. Was it true that, as an American, she would never be received by Victoria, and that, consequently, Justin's political future would be impaired? The very thought brought a wave of dejection crashing over her. Justin stood to accomplish so much—Amanda knew that he might well help shape British history through his support of the various reform movements. Now, would she ultimately be responsible for sabotaging his goals and undermining his political promise?

She shivered slightly as she again remembered the queen's cold scrutiny. She had heard of other brides receiving invitations to Victoria's court, but so far she had not received one. Had she been a fool to think she could truly fit in here?

Amanda could not remember ever feeling this low. Not only did Justin's future appear threatened; her entire marriage seemed doomed. Why keep up this pretense, when Justin would likely never love her, and she could only hurt him?

Unable to bear the uncertainty any longer, she turned to him. "Justin, are we ever going to have a true marriage?"

He appeared taken aback. "My, dear, but you are frank."

"I have to know where I stand."

He reached out to stroke her cheek. "I thought that this summer, when we go to my estate in Kent, we might try for our heir."

"Try for our heir," she repeated ironically. "Will we ever again make love?"

He turned away in torment. "My God, Amanda—the things you say!"

Tears filled her eyes. "Do you think that by then, Justin, you'll be able to touch me without feeling anything?"

He turned to stare at her. His eyes were crazed, his voice agonized. "I'm afraid that day may never come."

"Then why are you trying to kill everything we have together?" she demanded distraughtly.

He clenched a fist; a muscle jumped in his jaw. "You don't understand," he said hoarsely. "I lost control and caused a woman's death."

"Justin, just because you were arguing with your wife when she had her accident doesn't make it your fault—"

"I was responsible," he insisted.

She sighed, then lifted her chin. "I'm not afraid of you. I'll risk it."

"I won't," he uttered tightly.

Tears spilled over as she asked brokenly, "You do still love her, don't you?"

He caught her hand and spoke vehemently. "Amanda, I swear, I don't love her. I don't think I ever did."

Her laugh was anguished and bitter. "If you didn't love your wife, then I'm sure that only makes you feel all the more guilty over her death. You're still bound to her, aren't you? You're going to lock yourself up in your guilt over her death for the rest of your life. You won't ever allow yourself to love me. Can you deny it?"

He was silent; she had her answer.

Amanda's heart was broken.

That evening, when she should have been dressing for the Scottish ball, she was pacing her room. She would never fit in here, she realized dismally. Just as Cynthia had said, she was an outsider, an American upstart. Worse yet, her husband would never love her.

Yet, if she fled, she knew with a terrible certainty that Justin would come charging after her again. After all, his commitment was to propriety, to preserving the illusion of a happy marriage.

Amanda could not bear living this lie any longer. And she knew that the only way she could truly escape Justin would be to go back to her own time.

But how? How could she make her way back to America and the late twentieth century when she had no idea how she had gotten to nineteenth-century England in the first place?

She had to try.

Perhaps if she went back to the Strand, she might find the answers there.

An hour later, Lady Bess burst into her son's room without knocking.

"Amanda is missing!"

Clad in his dressing gown, Justin whirled to face his mother. "What do you mean?"

"I went to her room to see her in her costume and she is gone!" Bess cried.

"Are you certain she isn't somewhere else in the house—"

"No. I've already had the servants search."

"Damn," Justin muttered, his eyes wild with anxiety.

"Justin, I demand to know the nature of the trouble between the two of you," Bess went on. "Ever since you married Amanda, I've seen nothing but sadness in her eyes. And then there was the incident last week—when she disappeared and you brought her back in the middle of the night."

He sighed. "Mother, I can't allow myself to possibly destroy Amanda as I did Genevieve."

"So you neglect her shamelessly?" Bess demanded irately. "I can't blame her for leaving you."

"You don't understand," Justin said passionately. "I could hurt her—ruin her—like Genevieve!"

"Balderdash!" Bess asserted. "It is you, son, who does not understand that Amanda is nothing like Genevieve. Furthermore, you cannot throw away every chance of happiness out of fear that you'll repeat the mistakes of the past."

He raked a hand through his hair. "Go on to the ball, Mother. I'd best get dressed and go find Amanda."

"A word of advice, son," Bess added firmly.

"Yes?"

"If you can't give Amanda what she needs, don't go after her."

Chapter Ten

If you can't give Amanda what she needs, don't go after her.

The infinitely wise words of his mother reverberated through Justin's mind as he ventured out in his brougham in search of her. He'd ordered his coachman to take him to the Strand—instinct told him that she might have returned there. Would she be there, and safe? Had she already been accosted by some thief or ruffian from a nearby rookery?

Oh, God, if only he could be given another chance.

He realized that his mother had been right. Thanks to him, his marriage had been an empty shell. He might have brought Amanda home forcibly last week, but she had still been lost to him. This time, he couldn't bring her home unless he was willing to change. He might have destroyed one marriage through passion, but now he was destroying a second one through fear. How ironic that, through the best of intentions, he had brought about the very disaster he had most dreaded. He had hurt terribly the young wife who had wanted nothing more than to love him with all her heart.

If he found her, he would give her exactly what she needed—what both of them needed—for the rest of their lives.

Half a block from the corner where he'd first met Amanda, Justin spotted an elderly flower lady with her cart. He barked out a command to Burgess to halt the carriage, then leaped out and purchased a nosegay of violets. The poor woman almost fainted over the gold sovereign Justin insisted that she accept.

With the flowers in hand, Justin sprinted off toward the corner. *Let her be there*, he desperately prayed. *Please, God, let her be there*.

Amanda stood just around the corner, weeping in sheer frustration. "I want to go back!" she cried helplessly, unsure just what force she was attempting to summon. "Please, I must go back!"

She had been trying for the better part of an hour to leave her corner in time. She had tried prayer, pleading, threats—nothing had worked. She seemed to be stuck here, caught forever in the unendurable agony of loving a man who could never love her. Tears were streaming down her cheeks.

And then she saw him, approaching her through the fog in his Prince Albert frock coat and top hat, the nosegay of violets in his hands.

"You have the saddest eyes I've ever seen," he whispered, and caught her to him fiercely and kissed her.

For a split second, Amanda was in heaven, sobbing and clinging to him. Then she remembered, and shoved him away angrily. "No! No, I won't let you do this to me again!"

"Amanda, please, come home," he begged hoarsely. "Please forgive me. I promise you, it will be different this time."

"No!" she cried desperately. "It's too late. You don't care about me. All you care about is appearances."

"That's not true!"

"It is! I'll never fit in here."

"You will," he insisted. "Not that it matters. What matters is our being together."

"No!" she cried. "I won't believe your lies again. You don't even know how I got here."

He pulled her close. "Yes, I do," he whispered intensely. "I know I came for you, Amanda. I know I needed you in my life desperately. I know we met on some other, mystical plane. I know that the entire experience was so unreal, so jolting, that I haven't even been able to talk about it as yet. I know that love brought you here to me—and that love is going to hold you.

I won't let you go, do you hear me? I won't!"

His fervent words were tearing a hole in the wall she'd erected around her heart, but still she protested, "You don't love me. You can barely abide to touch me."

He stared into her eyes, his own gaze haunted. "Oh, pretty girl, you're so wrong. I've loved you desperately from the moment I laid eyes on you, but I feared my passions would destroy you, just as I destroyed Genevieve. You see, with her, we fought constantly, until the anger and the passion became so caught up together that I could not tell one from the other. And then she died, all because of me."

At his obvious pain, she had to reach out to him. She gently touched his arm. "Justin, Genevieve's death was an accident. You must stop punishing yourself. I want that much for you. Promise me you'll quit blaming yourself."

His hand clutched hers tightly. "Stay and make me do it," he commanded.

She stared at him, electrified.

He caught her face in his hands and spoke vehemently. "You see, I want it all, Amanda. I love you too much to be afraid anymore, to let my fear destroy you as I now know my passion never could."

Her restraint broken at last, she fell into his arms. "Oh, Justin, do you truly love me and want me?"

"Yes, darling. Now, come home with me and let me prove it."

*   *   *

He held her in his lap all the way home, kissing and caressing her. She clung to him, her happiness so profound that her throat ached.

Back in his bedroom at Cartwright Hall, he undressed her and kissed every inch of her.

She undressed him and kissed every inch of him.

They fell across the bed together, naked and deliriously aroused. Amanda rubbed her tender breasts against his rough chest. Justin ran his tongue lovingly over her face and ears. He lingered for long moments over her aroused nipples, kissing, nipping and sucking, even as his fingers slipped boldly between her thighs, preparing her. Desire knotted and built in her innermost recesses until she was left panting with her need for him. She hungrily kissed Justin's chest, and then her lips moved lower until she heard his moan of agonized pleasure.

He caught her to him for a ravenous kiss, then pulled her astride him and entered her so deeply that she cried out in wonder. They clutched hands tightly and rocked together, gazing into each other's eyes, letting the tension build until it was unendurable, then surrendering to an ecstasy so complete that it left both of them gasping and crying out their love.

Much later, she kissed his neck. "Will we talk about that night when you first found me?"

"Darling, we will talk about everything," he promised, "except the possibility of you ever again leaving me. You, Countess, are going to

443

grace my life—and my bed—from this moment on, and forever."

"Will you stay and make me do it?" she asked achingly.

Abruptly she was rolled beneath him. His deep thrust and devouring kiss were all the answers she needed.

Epilogue

The following morning, the Countess of Lockridge received her invitation to appear at Victoria's court. When a pleasantly surprised Amanda showed the invitation to Justin and told him of her previous fear that she would never be accepted by Victoria, due to the queen's chilly perusal of her the previous day, he only laughed and replied that many others had previously mistaken Victoria's natural reserve for cold disdain.

Amanda wore her wedding dress and the prescribed feathered headdress to her brief court appearance. She managed to bow before Victoria and—following the brief, pleasant words they exchanged—to back away gracefully, without stumbling. Afterward, Victoria remarked to one of her ladies-in-waiting, who then remarked to Lady Stanton, who then remarked to Lady Bess, that the queen felt the occasion had gone off "quite splendidly," and that she'd found the young American to be "so fresh and lovely."

Not long thereafter, Justin was elected to the Privy Council, and whispers were heard about a future cabinet post for him.

Lady Cynthia Spalding received the Spalding jewels several weeks ahead of schedule, on February 14, 1852. Included with the chest was a hand-written announcement of the birth of Justin's son and heir, Justin Cartwright III, the 5th Viscount of Leeds, born on that very day.

Lady Cynthia went into a goblet-smashing fit and shattered all of the Baccarat.

After she spent her rage, Cynthia passed the balance of the day gloating over her fabulous treasure and planning the ball she would throw to show off the jewels.

Amanda was in bed, Justin by her side, as she nursed their tiny son who so resembled her handsome husband. On the night table was the valentine Justin had just given her—a delicious froth of lace, ribbons, and pearls, inscribed with the words "Two hearts in time."

Lady Bess had just stopped in to visit the small family, seeing her grandson for the first time. Overcome with joy, the Dowager had gone off to finish writing the birth announcements so that Amanda could rest.

Amanda stroked the baby's soft cheek. "He doesn't look like a viscount at all," she murmured wonderingly.

Justin chuckled. "He looks like a baby—the most perfect baby I've ever seen." He kissed Amanda tenderly. "Thank you, my love. He's the best Valentine's Day present ever—as are you."

"Thank you." With tears of happiness shining in her eyes, she whispered, "I feel equally blessed by both of you."

A bemused smile pulled at Justin's mouth. "I still say we shouldn't have sent Cynthia the jewels."

"I'd say Cynthia got precisely what she deserved," Amanda responded wisely.

Justin chuckled. "You know, I think you may be right, darling," he murmured, kissing her again.

As the three snuggled together contentedly, Amanda felt almost as if she could see Gran looking down from the heavens, smiling over her granddaughter's happy family. During the past year, the bond between Amanda and Justin had only deepened and strengthened. The two lovers had shared so much—everything, just as her husband had promised that second night he'd rescued her in the Strand. She'd told him all about her world. He'd shown her more of his. They'd found their time together— forever.

Amanda smiled at Justin and he smiled back.

She realized she had gotten to take her trip to England after all—and that she had found her home.

On Valentine's Day, she had been given a gift—the gift of love.